My Highland Fling

Middlemarch Gathering 2

Shelley Munro

My Highland Fling

Print ISBN: 978-1-99-115875-8
Digital ISBN: 978-1-99-115874-1

Editor: Evil Eye Editing

Cover: Kim Killion

Munro Press, New Zealand.

First Munro Press electronic publication September 2022

First Munro Press print publication September 2022

For Robyn, who always encourages me with my writing.
Thank you!

Introduction

Royal good girl has a fling with a leopard shifter...

Read all about it! Our secret source confirms she spotted Princess Gabrielle leaving a boutique hotel early in the morning after spending the night with a mystery man.

Princess Gabrielle has always done the right thing, worn the proper clothes, and behaved like a perfect lady. Her reward: an unwanted engagement to a playboy prince she has never met and won't see until the wedding. This good girl can't take this "royal organization" anymore—not a minute longer.

Feline shifter Ramsay is attending a gathering of shifters at Castle Glenkirk. During an outing to the pub, the crowd parts to reveal a beautiful curvy woman. It's love at first sight. His fated mate is a human.

1

Drinks and conversation lead to privacy and sweet loving. It's magical. Ramsay is ready to woo his mate, but Gabrielle does a runner, and Ramsay is abandoned like Prince Charming with not even a shoe to help him find his Cinderella.

A leopard shapeshifter and a royal princess hiding her identity face insurmountable problems, betrayal, and danger before their forbidden one-night fling turns into small town happy-ever-after.

Author's Note: Please see the author's website for tropes and CWs.

Chapter 1

Rebellion

Gabrielle Herbert, royal princess of Konstavia, strolled to the window and stared down at the village lights. Resentment crept through her. Her hotel room was the most luxurious in Glenkirk, the Scottish town where she'd undertaken a speaking engagement for a children's charity. A vase of bright pink roses, baby's breath, and greenery sat on a wooden pedestal table at the room's entrance. A bottle of the best French champagne nestled in an ice bucket, beaded with moisture.

Earlier, a maid had delivered a meal of chicken and salad, ordered as per her mother's instructions. Gabrielle's scowl deepened, and she glared at the offending and untouched plate. Tilly, her chaperone and a distant relation, snored in one of the two bedrooms in the hotel suite.

Gabrielle sighed, paced a quick circle past the comfortable furnishings and high-end fixtures, and halted at the window again. This view was the closest she ever got to seeing the countries she visited on behalf of her chosen charities. Her mother preplanned every step of her stays, from what she wore to her hotel and her inevitable speech. She glowered at the healthy, uneaten food again. *Even her meals. Her mother didn't permit Gabrielle to choose her dinner.*

Where was the freedom? The reward for doing an excellent job and bringing wealthy sponsors to support her charities?

Why did she bother trying to please her mother, who continually nitpicked at everything she did? Neither of her older brothers faced the restrictions imposed on her, and this lack of autonomy chafed like an ill-fitting pair of trousers.

Her parents considered her a commodity to bring wealth and power to their kingdom. An example was her upcoming marriage to Gregor, a Swedish prince. She'd never met the man, and her research hadn't impressed her much. He was a playboy with a penchant for fast cars and fast women.

She hated even to imagine a life trapped with a philandering husband.

4

Had she tried to change the status quo? Yes, and her mother or Harold, her mother's secretary, quashed every one of Gabrielle's suggestions. Her life was a well-trodden path with no excitement or adventure on the horizon.

A knock on the door interrupted her agitated thoughts. When Tilly's snores continued unabated, Gabrielle stalked to the door, the skirts of her floral silk dress brushing her calves. She opened the door to a maid.

The girl offered a polite smile and indicated her trolley. "I've come to collect your dinner dishes. Oh! You haven't started eating. I've almost finished my shift, but I could wait for ten minutes."

Gabrielle stood aside for her to enter, the tightness in her chest easing at the distraction. "Please, take them."

The girl parked her trolley outside and headed for the uneaten dinner, her crisp black uniform dress rustling with each step.

Gabrielle studied her. "Is Glenkirk a pleasant town to live in? What do you do for excitement?" The words burst from her in an eagerness to speak off-script. "Is there a place you'd recommend to buy casual clothes?" Dozens more questions trembled at her lips, but she bit them back and waited.

Around Gabrielle's age, the girl stared at her through questioning blue eyes. "We're not meant to speak with guests."

Gabrielle's brows rose. "I'm going nuts here, and talking to myself is no fun."

"All right," she said slowly, weighing Gabrielle's intentions. "Glenkirk is mostly quiet unless they're holding a conference at Castle Glenkirk or here at the hotel like today."

"And your time off? What do you do?"

The girl picked up the tray with Gabrielle's uneaten meal. "Since I'm saving to purchase a house, I don't go out much. I might have a drink at a local pub. I do a lot of walking and cycling with friends. During winter, we cheer on the local rugby team. This year, I've taken up knitting. My granny is teaching me."

A kernel of an idea popped into Gabrielle's head. Could she? Gabrielle's stomach hardened as she considered the ramifications, then she mentally shrugged. Bottom line: she was past caring. Arranging a marriage, despite her objections, went beyond the bounds of decency and respect.

Gabrielle jumped in with both feet. "I have a crazy plan." She glanced toward Tilly's bedroom. The rhythmic snoring continued. "My family expects me to stay in my hotel room for my entire visit without seeing any of the town. I wondered if you'd be willing to give me your clothes so I could sneak out and have a few hours of fun before I return home to Konstavia. I can pay you." She had cash because, governed by instinct, she'd squirreled it away for emergencies. This situation constituted a crisis.

The girl backed up, her gaze darting to the door as if she was considering making a run for safety.

"Please," Gabrielle said. "Can you imagine visiting places and getting confined to hotel rooms?"

"Why can't you just leave?"

"My security team will be downstairs, watching the entrance."

The girl relaxed a fraction. "You want to wear my clothes?"

"What is your name?"

"Linda."

"Yes, Linda. If you'd lend me your clothes, I'll give you five hundred pounds." Gabrielle crossed her fingers. "One night of fun. I don't want to cause trouble. Just have a drink and hit the shops."

Linda still hesitated. "How would this work? What about your security team?"

"My security detail watches the lobby. Is there a staff entrance? The paparazzi swarming the hotel worries my security team more than me escaping. I never have before, but I'm slowly going crazy."

My parents have arranged a wedding for me, and I'm terrified I'm stepping from one prison to another.

Gabrielle held her breath and silently willed Linda to decide in her favor.

"But won't they notice you're missing? I'd hate to lose my job."

"If you're finishing soon, we could walk out together. My security team and the press would never expect me to leave in this manner." *Hopefully, Tilly would sleep until Gabrielle's return.*

"You haven't complained?" Linda grimaced. "I would've."

"My mother tells me to suck it up. Not in those words, but that's what she means." Gabrielle hesitated over what to tell Linda. "The thing is, I believe in my charities and want to do my best. My mother threatened to confine me to the castle until my marriage if I caused trouble. Once I'm married, I'll be my husband's problem."

"Sounds like a fairy tale." Linda narrowed her gaze, suspicion in her blue eyes. "Are you making this up to gain my sympathy?"

Gabrielle sighed. "I wish I were, but it's true. My father and mother let my brothers do what they wish, but I am kept on a short leash because I'm a girl."

"What if someone else notices you?"

"What if I rode on the trolley? Would I fit?"

"Yes." Linda bit her lip, then nodded. "All right. I'll do it. Do you have any casual clothes? Jeans?"

Gabrielle grimaced. "This is as casual as it gets."

Linda frowned and gave her up-and-down scrutiny. "We're a similar size. You should fit into my jeans and T-shirt. I have spare clothes in my locker. You can use them, and I'll wear my uniform home. I only have one pair of shoes, though."

"I have shoes." Gabrielle scooted off to get them before Linda changed her mind. She grabbed her wallet and pulled a wad of cash from a secret compartment in her laptop bag. Although she'd been saving this money, she figured a night of freedom was worth every penny.

She didn't care what she did tonight as long as she received a smidge of autonomy.

It took ten minutes for Linda to wheel her trolley along the passage to the employee lift. In the staff changing room, Gabrielle scrambled into the clothes Linda gave her and slapped a cap on her head before they wandered out of the staff entrance together.

"Thank you so much," Gabrielle said once they were clear.

Linda frowned. "Do me a favor and text me when you're back in the hotel. I'd hate it if something happened to you. Where's your phone?"

Gabrielle scowled. "I don't have one."

"Really?"

"Mother disapproves of phones. My chaperone has one, but not me."

"You know how to use a phone?"

Gabrielle nodded. "Tilly has difficulty with technology. She always asks me to help her. It's our secret."

"Right. Here's my number. Keep it in a safe place and borrow someone's phone to text me. Let me know you're safe; otherwise, I won't sleep tonight."

Gabrielle grinned, a flash of excitement bursting in her as she stuffed the slip of paper into her pocket. "I promise I'll text you. What about your clothes? Do you want them back?"

"No," Linda said. "You've paid for them. Keep them. This is the main street. It's late-night shopping, so most stores are still open."

"Thank you, Linda. I appreciate your help."

"Don't forget to text me."

"I doubt anyone will miss me since. As far as they're concerned, I've retired and will be in the hotel until tomorrow morning."

"I'll leave you here." Linda hesitated, then gave her a quick hug. "Have fun." Then, with a wave, she strode away, leaving Gabrielle alone.

Gabrielle bounced on her toes before getting a grip on her excitement. She inhaled and strolled along the street. While she'd slowed her speed, she couldn't restrain the smile on her lips and the lightness in her chest. Despite the hour, pedestrians wandered the sidewalk, some with an obvious purpose, while others lingered and stared at the contents of the shop windows. Several stores had signs bearing welcome messages for the conference attendees in their windows.

"Oh." Her steps slowed. This one had a sign welcoming Princess Gabrielle to town. It was a clothing store, and Gabrielle entered. She loved clothes and design, but her mother never allowed her a say in what she wore. If she visited a pub or club, a T-shirt wouldn't work. Perhaps she could keep the jeans and buy a smarter top. She always wore her long blonde hair up, so this once, she'd leave it loose and ditch the hat. In casual clothes, she'd escape the notice of the newspaper journalists and any of her security detail should they search for her. *Plan.*

Gabrielle skipped out of the shop twenty minutes later, wearing a pale blue shirt with decorative thistle buttons and tartan detailing on the breast pocket and hem. She carried her T-shirt and cap in the store's bag, along with a second shirt in tartan plaid. Thanks to the friendly salesgirl, her blonde hair swung in curls after a quick finger scrunch and the judicious application of hair styling cream. Even better, not one person in the store had recognized her. Of course, she wasn't as important as her distant British cousins, so that wasn't surprising.

Farther along the street, she spotted a pub sign. A brawny, kilt-wearing man stood outside, his beefy arms folded across his chest. Music spilled from the pub, along with good-humored laughter and shouts.

A pub. Perfect. The handsome Scottish man in a kilt was a sign.

Gabrielle grinned at the man, and he winked in return as she strode into the confusion of noise and bodies. It was like an alien world, and she loved it. When no one tried to stop her, Gabrielle slipped into a space near the bar and watched. Okay, no table service. It looked as if the customers purchased their drinks from the bar. She wanted to try a beer since her parents only allowed a small glass of wine on special occasions.

The men and women didn't pay her any attention, which suited her fine. Then came the weight of a stare. Slowly, she turned her head and spotted a tall man with black hair studying her. He wore a black shirt that emphasized his broad shoulders and muscular biceps. She couldn't see much of his lower half, but he had gorgeous green eyes.

"Hey, want to buy a drink?" he called. "You can squeeze in beside me."

Gabrielle didn't hesitate. She scooted over to him and stepped into the gap he protected with his larger body. "Thank you." She peered at the drinks in front of him. "Can you recommend a beer for me?"

"Do you like lager or bitter?" His black hair was longer than the men she associated with and had a slight wave.

Gabrielle shrugged. "I don't know." Was his hair as soft as it looked?

"Try this one," he said, shunting a full glass toward her. "This is lager. It's cold and has a crisp finish."

Gabrielle took a small sip and nodded. "I like it."

"My name is Ramsay," he said and held out his hand.

Gabrielle hesitated before accepting a handshake. She breathed through the frisson of attraction that struck her unexpectedly and focused on his face. Not a hint of recognition reflected back to her. "Gabrielle." She'd use the truth where possible.

Another dark-haired man with green eyes tapped Ramsay on the shoulder. "Ramsay, where are our drinks?"

"Here," Ramsay said, handing him two large beers. He passed three smaller beers to a second dark-haired man.

They all had green eyes of various shades. "Are you related?"

"No, but we live in the same town. A lot of the residents have black hair and green eyes. No idea why," he said. "Let's get you a beer. Are you a visitor here, or do you live in Glenkirk?"

"No, I'm here for two days. Just passing through." Gabrielle couldn't take her eyes off him. Gorgeous. Those green eyes of his mesmerized her. Her mind went *tick, tick, tick*, and a smile stretched her mouth. An answering grin bloomed on Ramsay, and her heart beat even faster. One night for an adventure—with Ramsay if she pursued him.

An easy decision.

She dared.

Chapter 2

My Sexy Human Mate

Ramsay caught a whiff of her scent first, and it took him seconds to realize the delectable fragrance was human rather than shifter. It had to be a woman because his muscles tensed, and the blood drained to his cock. From his position at the bar, he let his gaze wander to those standing nearby. He finally located the blonde, but when he did, his breathing stalled. The tight sensation in his chest was his reminder to suck in air. His next inhalation of sweet honeysuckle left him weak at the knees.

Do something. Say something! Whatever you do, don't let her go.

A tall biker dude walking toward the bar spotted her, and the man's appreciative gaze shook Ramsay from his stupor. *His.* This blonde woman with lush curves belonged to him. He didn't care he'd traveled to Scotland to meet a fellow shifter at the Glenkirk gathering. He didn't care his mate was a human. All he and his feline wanted was to claim her.

She was his one.

"Did you want a drink?" he asked, offering a friendly smile.

His female friends told him a grin took him into handsome territory, so he did his best work.

She nodded, her gaze direct and full of interest, and Ramsay wanted to cheer. He squeezed over, creating space for her at the bar. "Here you go."

The corners of her brown eyes crinkled, and dimples formed both sides of her mouth as she grinned at Ramsay. "Thanks."

She squeezed past the now scowling biker and pressed close to him. Ramsay felt the heat from her body through the tight jeans and her blue shirt. She was of medium height and came up to his shoulders. Her golden blonde hair fell in tousled curls, and she bore healthy curves that told him she enjoyed food. His favorite sort of woman, given he was a trainee chef.

"What are you having to drink?"

"Do they have beer here?"

"They do." Ramsay couldn't tell where she was from, but she didn't have a Scottish accent. It sounded more continental, but what did he know?

She frowned and stepped from foot to foot. Her behavior was a combination of excitement and nerves, and Ramsay wasn't sure what to do with the info.

"Would you like to try my beer?"

She nodded, and he handed her his pint glass. She took a cautious sip before swallowing the amber liquid.

"That's refreshing. This is perfect."

Ramsay signaled the bartender and asked for another pint of the local lager.

Scott, one of the Middlemarch contingent, wandered over. "Should I take these beers?"

"Please." Ramsay handed Scott two pints. Scott disappeared, and Liam collected the remaining drinks.

Liam glanced at the woman. "I'll tell them you're busy at the moment."

Ramsay nodded his thanks and focused on the blonde again.

"My name is Ramsay. What is yours?"

"Gabrielle," she said after a brief hesitation. She stared at him as much as he studied her, then she smiled, a slow curve of her luscious lips.

Ramsay's thoughts dived straight to sex, and he experienced difficulty controlling his wayward dick. A first for him.

"You don't sound Scottish," she said.

"No, I'm from New Zealand," Ramsay replied. "You're not a local either."

"Just a quick visit," she said. "Could we find a quieter corner? I'd love to learn more about New Zealand."

Hell, yes! Using his height to his advantage, he spied a vacant table right in the back. A fantastic notion.

"Come on. There's a table back there. Let's move before someone else has the same idea." He grasped her free hand and used his bulk to clear a path toward the table.

Excitement roared through Ramsay, a sense of rightness and determination. This woman was his mate. He had a mate. *Him*. After a crummy childhood with deadbeat parents, he and his younger sister had gone out on their own. Terry had fallen in with a dangerous crowd, dragging him with her until he'd found a home in Middlemarch. An adopted family. That was part of the reason he'd attended the gathering. Saber Mitchell, chairman of the Feline Council, had asked him to represent their town, so he'd agreed and come to the Glenkirk gathering.

He hadn't expected to find a mate. Not really, and this blew his mind. That she was a human was more problematic, but he could deal.

"Tell me about New Zealand," she repeated. "You're a long way from home."

"I'm here with six friends. We come from Middlemarch, a small country town in the South Island of New Zealand. We're representing our community at a gathering at the castle."

"A gathering?" She crinkled her nose in an appealing manner.

"It's a Scottish thing. All the attendees have Scottish ancestry. It's a fantastic way to meet others and have fun. Why are you here?"

"I live in Konstavia in Europe. I'm here to help with a local children's charity. Just one night before I head home."

Ramsay closed his eyes, briefly cursing fate. He'd hoped he'd have longer than that, so he'd need to move fast.

"What do you do in New Zealand?" she asked, and the gleam in her eyes indicated her sincere interest. It was a heady thing to have her entire focus.

He inhaled slowly, savoring her honey scent with an underpinning of the Orient. Beneath that, he caught a faint hint of feminine musk, and the three fragrances combined to make an intoxicating snare for a single feline male.

She clicked her fingers in front of his nose, and he blinked. Her bubbly laughter had him grinning back at her.

"It's not flattering when your mind drifts," she said with a charming wrinkling of her nose.

"Ah, but my mind was full of you." Ramsay decided game-playing was a waste of time. He'd cut straight to the point and let her know his interest. "You're pretty with your golden blonde hair and your curves. And even better, your delectable scent..." He leaned closer and gave an audible sniff.

"My mother is always telling me to eat less. I live on skinless chicken and salad."

"Let me tell you—from a male point of view, you're stunning. No, let me rephrase. I find you attractive and can't take my eyes off you." He let his gaze drift to her mouth. "I'm wondering what it'd be like to kiss you."

Her brows rose.

"That's not a line. You don't know me well, but I don't play games." His sister had been a talented game player and loved a challenge, legal or not. Yeah, he was done with those days. He'd gone straight from the moment the Mitchell family had folded him into their care, and honesty was his middle name. That meant he was a man of action, and he never lied or played with people's emotions. Having been on the receiving end of that pain, he hated to inflict it on others.

"You really want to kiss me," she said, leaning nearer as if she was frightened someone was eavesdropping on their conversation.

"Why wouldn't I?"

She gave a faint nod but settled on her barstool and sipped her lager. "And I repeat. What is your job in New Zealand?"

"I'm training to be a chef. I work in Dunedin, which is the nearest large city to Middlemarch. When I'm not there, I work at Storm in a Teacup, a Middlemarch café. Emily, the owner, got me interested in food and cooking." He paused, then decided his mate should hear some of his background. "I come from a troubled family. My parents stole and cheated to get money to survive, so my younger sister and I didn't have great examples. Emily and the Mitchell family gave me an opportunity for a fresh start."

"What about your sister?"

"I haven't seen Terry for several years. Last I heard, she'd hooked up with a small-time thief."

"I'm sorry."

"I miss Terry, but the people in Middlemarch are like family. Tomasine and Felix gave me a second chance. I stayed with them until I went to an apprenticeship in Dunedin. I love Middlemarch and purchased a home there. It's an old farmhouse I'm fixing up in my spare time."

"That's wonderful," Gabrielle said. "Are you focusing on a particular type of cuisine?"

"The restaurant where I work specializes in seafood, venison, and lamb. It's a kind of fusion of fresh produce with Asian influences. We like to use local ingredients. When I work in the café, I do more baking. Lots of cookies and cakes. Our local community is active, and we hold fairs and social functions. Sometimes, I make ice cream or festive fare like gingerbread. The café menu is simple. Hearty sandwiches and soups. Savory pies plus the sweet stuff."

"What is your favorite cake?"

Ramsay didn't hesitate. "Carrot cake."

"Really? That's mine too. What kind of frosting do you use?"

"It's got to be a cream cheese frosting with a sprinkle of nuts for texture."

Gabrielle nodded. "I can't remember the last time I ate a piece of carrot cake."

"If I were at home, I'd make one for you."

"Thank you." She reached over and squeezed his hand, the touch riveting Ramsay.

He stared into her eyes, not bothering to hide the surge of lust that frisked his body. Oh, he craved her badly.

A cover band started playing. Perfect.

He smiled at her. "Would you like to dance?"

"What if someone takes our table?"

"Don't worry. We'll find somewhere else to sit. You can leave your bag with my friends. They'll keep it and our drinks safe."

When they stopped by Scott and Liam's table, the girls had left to return to the castle.

"This is Gabrielle. Can you watch Gabrielle's bag and our drinks while we dance?"

Scott nodded. "I'm Scott."

"Liam," Liam said with a wave. "No problem."

Ramsay clasped Gabrielle's hand and drew her into the middle of the dance floor. It was a slow, dreamy ballad playing, and he wrapped his arms around her, pulling her against his body. They fit perfectly, and Ramsay had never felt so happy. So right.

Gabrielle was definitely his mate, and he needed to fashion a plan to make her come around to his way of thinking.

Chapter 3

Clandestine Arrangements

G abrielle melted against Ramsay. His body was solid and bore no surplus fat. Not like Gregor, her betrothed. She recalled his oily smile during the video call and shuddered inwardly. While she was aware—because her mother kept telling her—she was overweight, at least she maintained some control.

Somehow, she had to wriggle out of the marriage contract.

Three months wasn't long. It wasn't as if he loved her. Prince Gregor was more interested in skiing and the ski bunnies who frequented the bars and trendy hotels. From what she'd read in the gossip papers, he preferred skinny bean poles for his lovers. Thin, she was not.

On the plus side, Ramsay didn't mind her rounded curves. In fact, she'd caught him sneaking a peek at her cleavage, and that hadn't been disgust on his handsome face. His rugged features, tanned, despite his indoor job, had held interest. This awareness reflected in his heavily lashed green eyes. Those beautiful eyes and his glorious muscles did it for her. Now that she'd touched him—they were dancing close together—she could attest to his splendid shape. His black hair needed a trim and perhaps product to tame his curls, but she adored the dark stubble on his cheeks. So sexy. Her fingers itched to touch, but no...

Heck, why not? She could touch if she wanted to. He had the right to say no, and she'd respect his decision.

She lifted her hand and felt a faint tremor but continued anyway, her pulse fluttering at her daring—the crown princess touching a man in a public place. Perhaps the sky would fall. Her hand quaked harder. Finally, her fingers contacted his jaw. His stubble abraded the tips as she dragged them the length of his jawline. He turned his face a fraction and dropped a kiss on her palm. His lips were warm and soft, and something precious twisted inside her. She'd never had such an instant reaction to a man. Not that her parents allowed her anywhere near strange men. This was a first.

Ramsay groaned and drew her closer. While she was a highly guarded princess—a virgin—she wasn't clueless. He wanted her, evidenced by the hard spike of his erection. A ripple of pleasure swept her breasts and sank to the achy spot between her thighs. Intrigue about making love with a man of her choice assailed her, not for the first time. While she'd self-pleasured and experienced a climax, she was curious. Would sex overwhelm her, or was the entire process an exaggeration?

Gabrielle realized she wanted the answer to this question.

"Can I kiss you?" he asked.

The band had started another slow song, and couples swayed together. Ramsay had directed them to the back of the dancefloor, and the dim lighting lent an intimacy to their embrace.

"I'd like that."

Ramsay bent his head an instant later and pressed his lips against hers. Experience had not prepared her for Ramsay's kiss. He went slowly, teasing a reaction from her. Her hands settled on his shoulders, and she opened her mouth, allowing him to twirl their tongues together. She tasted the crisp hoppy beer and a sweetness that could easily become habit-forming. She had an addictive personality, which was why she had trouble losing weight. A poor trait of hers, according to her parents.

If she informed her mother she'd happily live on Ramsay's kisses, that wouldn't go down well. Probably cause a gigantic scene.

Ramsay backed off a fraction, and his eyes glowed weirdly in the dark. She blinked, and when she focused on him again, the otherworldly gleam had disappeared.

"You are such a temptation. I'm desperate to touch you, lick and nibble every inch of your delectable body."

A coil of anticipation tightened between her thighs, and she'd never been so self-aware before. Her breasts felt heavier than usual, the friction of her nipples against the silk of her bra a big distraction. The borrowed jeans constricted her muscles, and a sly craving slid into prominence. She'd love nothing more than to fling off every item of apparel and offer her body to him.

"Yes." She stared deep into those pretty green eyes of his.

"Do you have a hotel room?" he asked.

"We can't go there."

"My place isn't ideal either, but no problem. Why don't I book something in town before we leave here?"

"We can do that?"

He smiled, a dazzling smile that echoed in his eyes and features. A genuine one that made Gabrielle realize how phony smiles abounded at the palace. He had a delightful laugh too and a friendly personality. She'd heard him speaking with the staff when she'd approached the bar.

"Let me check with the bartender. She might recommend a place for the night. Are you certain?"

"Yes." Gabrielle didn't hesitate. And in a fit of bravery, she stretched on tiptoe and pressed her lips to his. A soft groan escaped him—a sound of need.

He pulled back, his gaze on hers. "Tease."

Gabrielle beamed. Her weight had always been a sore point, but Ramsay didn't appear to have problems with her size. She was always on her best behavior at home, but her parents still chided her for not conforming to their high standards.

Ramsay was also efficient, a quality she decided she loved. They left the dancefloor hand in hand. Five minutes later, Ramsay had booked a boutique hotel room for the night.

"Are you ready to go?" he asked.

"Yes." Gabrielle didn't hesitate, instinct telling her she'd be a fool to let him walk away. While she was no match for her parents, and she'd end up married to the arrogant Swedish prince, she wasn't about to miss this unexpected treat. This was a reward for herself—a memory to hold close on trying days.

"Let's collect your bag and leave." Ramsay kept hold of her hand.

When they arrived at his friends' table, they stood.

"We were about to hunt you down," Liam said. "Scott and I are walking back to the castle."

"I'll see you there," Ramsay said, taking possession of Gabrielle's bag of clothes. He tugged Gabrielle to a seat and shunted her drink toward her.

They waved goodbye, and Ramsay grinned.

"They made it easy. We don't have to give explanations. Do you need to call anyone to let them know where you'll be?"

Considerate too. The more Gabrielle learned about this man, the more she liked him. "I'm fine," she said, making a mental note to contact the maid who'd helped her.

This was the craziest thing she'd ever done—leaving with a stranger—but everything about Ramsay thrilled her. She didn't have a single worry. She trusted him.

"Let's go then." He leaned closer and whispered in her ear. "You're so pretty. I can't wait to remove your clothes and run my lips over your silky skin.

Gabrielle huffed out a breath, every part of her tingling. *Wow!* "Is that a promise?"

"Count on it." His gaze grew darker, his eyes a weird stormy green.

29

Gabrielle's heart beat faster. She waited for fear, for common sense, for sanity, and when none of the three showed up, she ran her fingers over his cheek. "Let's party."

Chapter 4

Seclusion

Her hand fitted his grasp perfectly. Ramsay's pulse beat faster, and he wanted to urge her to haste. He hated to fall on her like an animal and scare her because she bore an innocent air. While they hadn't discussed sexual history, as was sensible in these times, he didn't care. From today, she belonged with him, which was all he and his feline needed.

"Here's the hotel."

"It's lovely."

"Yeah, the bartender's auntie owns it. It's recently opened and is still quiet." Ramsay slid a sideways glance at Gabrielle. She was nibbling on her bottom lip. "Second thoughts?"

He didn't know what he'd do if she changed her mind. This sucked big time. The woman attracted him on every level. His mate. And she was only here for a night. Perhaps he could grab her phone number. Her email. Maybe they could sex it up via a private internet meeting.

"I haven't changed my mind. Have you?"

Her quiet words pierced his panic, and he shook his head. "Not a chance. Let me check-in." He left her sitting in the cozy foyer. A door leading to a tiny courtyard garden was open, the curtains fluttering in the evening breeze. The sun set late at this time of the year, and it was barely dark as he spoke with the desk clerk.

"One night?" the man asked.

"Yes, just the one. Unfortunately, we have to leave tomorrow." Ramsay murmured this with a straight face and was proud of himself. Besides, it was kind of the truth and depressing. He shoved aside the morose thoughts and focused on the positive. His beautiful Gabrielle.

"Can I take an imprint of your credit card, please?"

Ramsay pulled out his wallet and handed over his card.

"The room key, Mr. Walton, and the key for the street level door. If you leave again for any reason, you'll require it to enter. Your room is on the second floor—the Buchanan Room. Turn right after exiting the lift.

Ramsay nodded. "Is there a minibar?"

"There is, and you can order room service food and drinks if you'd like. Enjoy your stay."

"Thank you." Ramsay strode over to Gabrielle and reached for her hand. "Come on."

She grinned at him and squeezed his hand hard. "Can't wait. I'm impatient."

"You aren't the only one." His words emerged with a faint growl, his feline exerting his say. He'd settle once they were reclining on a bed without a stitch of clothing. The elevator doors opened, and Ramsay ushered her inside.

It seemed ages before he pushed the room door ajar and stood back for Gabrielle to enter first.

"Oh, it's beautiful," she murmured.

A bed dominated the room, and the designer had arranged a comfy seating area to take in the view. Another door led to an en suite while a small counter against the wall held coffee-making facilities, a mini-fridge, and a selection of glasses and snacks.

"Let me find the light." Ramsay had no difficulty since his feline eyesight was excellent, but it grew darker with each passing minute. "Are you hungry? Would you like a drink?"

"No," she said, turning to him. "I want you."

Ramsay's stomach hollowed out, and his hand trembled before he balled it into a fist and hid it behind his back.

Gabrielle dropped her bag beside the bed. "Do I make you nervous?"

He smiled even as he nodded. "You're beautiful, and I can't believe my luck."

She pressed a kiss to the corner of his mouth. "I'm the lucky one. Can I take off your shirt?"

"Yes." Ramsay stood still while she unfastened his shirt buttons. When she'd finished, he toed off his shoes.

"How does your kilt work? Have I told you how sexy you look in your kilt?"

"It's not my normal attire, but it's part of our Middlemarch uniform. The girls have tartan dresses, and our local seamstress designed the Middlemarch tartan, especially for our gathering. Most attendees are of Scottish ancestry."

"We don't have a national dress where I come from in Europe. Most women wear designer clothes, and the men don suits."

Ramsay smoothed a lock of blonde hair off her face. "At home, I'm normally in a chef's jacket and checked trousers. When I'm relaxing, it's either jeans or shorts and a T-shirt."

"That sounds nice. We don't do casual at our house and have to dress for dinner. My parents are very formal."

"Later for the getting-to-know-you stuff." Ramsay pressed his palm over her mouth. "No more talk of home for either of us. I know enough, and we have way more important things in our future."

"We do," she said, grinning at him after she'd licked his palm. The innocent touch shot through him like a rocket, the flash of sensation lengthening his dick.

"You're dangerous."

"You stole my line," she said with a musical giggle. Not an annoying one but plain charming. He could listen to her all night, watch her expressive face, and memorize every nuance.

"Let me get your buttons. I'm tempted to rip off your shirt, but you look so pretty in it." He took his time, pausing to caress or nuzzle the silken skin he revealed. She enticed him on every level. It wasn't her subtle fragrance but the deeper underlying scent that was her. He and his feline reveled in it. Catnip for sure. He drew the cotton fabric down her arms and tossed the garment on the back of an easy chair. Her breasts were magnificent. Rounded globes filled her lacy bra. "Can I remove this?"

"Take off everything." Her imperious tone lost something because of her broad grin and the sparkle of her brown eyes.

"Your word is my command."

Ramsay wasted no time stripping off her remaining clothes. Once done, he took a step back to admire her. She was all pale golden skin and healthy curves. Her blonde hair curled around her shoulders while a thin blonde landing strip guarded her sex. Pink nipples tipped her breasts, and they'd pulled to stiff peaks in the air-conditioned room.

She crossed her hands over her chest. "You're staring."

"Because I find you beautiful."

"You should get naked, too. It'd be much fairer."

"Nothing I'd enjoy more. Pull back the covers."

"You'll see my butt."

His brows rose.

"I'm reliably informed it's not my best feature."

"By night's end, I'll have kissed that round arse of yours, and other people's insults won't matter." Her appearance pleased him, and he couldn't see a thing wrong with her. It was apparent from their conversation so far that she enjoyed food and could cook. As a chef, he liked to see people enthusiastic about the food he'd prepared. He had little time for customers who poked at their meals or cross-questioned the wait staff about the ingredients. "Go on, pull back the covers."

He waited while her gaze challenged him. Finally, she huffed out an impatient breath and turned away. She stomped the short distance to the bed and tugged at the duvet. It resisted her efforts since the room attendant had done a fine job of making the bed. A cute grumble escaped her, and her backside jiggled with her exertion.

"A little help?" she muttered, her tone coming close to cross. While she'd struggled with the linens, he'd shucked his clothes.

He stalked toward her, drawn like a magnet seeking metal. Ramsay drew near and nuzzled her neck.

"You smell good."

"My perfume," she said. "My aunt—my mother's sister—had it specially blended for me on my twenty-first birthday earlier this year."

He inhaled again and separated the distinct notes of the fragrance. Yes, Gabrielle's bouquet with its flowers and a hint of sandalwood, if he wasn't mistaken, but her personal scent of wildness and musk drew him and his feline most. In a little self-punishment, he nibbled at her mating site—the fleshy pad where neck and shoulder met. The delightful aroma intensified, and he couldn't prevent a groan of pure need from escaping.

She turned in his arms and pressed her front to his. They fit perfectly, and Ramsay allowed himself to kiss her without restraint this time. Too early to voice the words now, but he could show her the truth of them. Passion screamed through him. Yearning. *Need.*

Ramsay scooped her off her feet without breaking their kiss and settled her on the bed. He followed her down and continued kissing her, feasting on her mouth. He battled the primal hunger that filled him and failed. His desire was too great. She was too much temptation. Somehow, he had to slow down and make sure he satisfied her. Yeah, he intended to please her, touch her, make love to her again and again.

She ran her hands down his back and cupped his buttocks. A low, delighted chuckle came from her seconds before she squeezed. Lust roared through Ramsay so fast he'd swear he blacked out for a second.

"Let me taste you," he said.

Her pink lips curved in a seductive smile. "Anything."

Ramsay sighed, taking pleasure in her calm acceptance, her trust because he sensed this wasn't her typical behavior. She wore her innocence like a cloak. He snatched a quick kiss and pinched one taut nipple simultaneously. She jumped at his sudden move, but her gasp was more groan.

"Like that?"

"Surprisingly," she said. "I never knew pain could feel magnificent."

Ramsay growled, the sound more catlike than he'd intended.

She was perfect for him. *Perfect.*

Pleased with her, he licked and caressed his way down her body. She parted her legs before he could ask, and her feminine scent rose to greet him. His first taste had him purring, and he teased her until she moaned her enjoyment. Her fingers tangled in his hair, and he fleetingly thought he was glad he hadn't listened to Emily and Tomasine to get his hair cut. They'd told him women liked their men tidy.

"Your hair is soft. I didn't think I liked long hair, but I've changed my mind," she murmured.

Ramsay laughed aloud. "The ladies who work in Storm in a Teacup informed me women prefer trimmed, tidy hair." He didn't wait for an answer but dived in to savor her. He made an appreciative noise as her musky scent and sweetness swirled around him, inside him. Delicious. Ramsay slid his tongue over her clit, and she gripped his hair and tugged.

"Yes," she ordered.

He lifted his head to glance askance at her.

"I like this. I like it a lot. Do more."

"Has no one gone down on you before?"

"Haven't done this before," she said. "Not with anyone else."

Delight suffused him, and a possessive growl emerged. Her brown eyes rounded, but thankfully, he hadn't scared

39

her. He licked her slit and gathered her honey with his tongue.

"Your tongue is rough. The friction is so good."

His feline, he wanted to tell her, but a human wouldn't understand. Even though every instinct cried she was his mate, he needed to practice restraint. Meanwhile, he'd gift her with pleasure and make her scream. He'd love her so well, she'd think of him whenever they were apart. Yeah, sounded like a plan.

Ramsay gripped her thighs and settled in to tease her into pleasurable screams.

Chapter 5

Lovemaking. Oh, My!

Gabrielle gripped his hair and tugged, her back bowing as pleasure tore through her. He pushed one thick finger inside her, and exquisite sensations shot across her nerve endings. This was superior to touching herself in the middle of the night. Gabrielle squeezed her eyes shut and let herself wallow in the delight, the bliss, the decadence of this handsome man whose attention focused on her. Heady stuff, since most people in her life ignored her or treated her as a nuisance.

Not Ramsay.

He made her feel essential. Worthy.

Enticing and sensual.

Beautiful.

Ramsay stroked her clit before settling his mouth on her.

"Yes," she cried out, grinding against the silken pressure. He wiggled his tongue, and everything inside her yanked tight. Ramsay flexed his thick fingers into her again. Seconds later, pleasure rushed through her, streaking to her toes and up her torso. Her channel clenched around his fingers, the spasms gradually tapering off. She issued a loud, satisfied sigh. Her eyes opened, and she discovered Ramsay watching her, a tiny smile on his lips. Heat collected in her cheeks, but she didn't move or try to hide. She grinned back.

"You look like an angel." His sincere expression told her his words were genuine.

"Thank you." She paused and cocked her head. "Can we do that again?"

"Maybe."

Something in his tone had her stiffening. Would he call a halt? She wanted to cry. He couldn't stop, couldn't tell her he didn't want to have sex with her.

A trace of bitterness slid through her mind, spoiling her feel-good mood. She wanted this so badly. Ramsay had made a significant impression on her and seemed decent. Thoughtful. And weirdly, she trusted him.

The Swedish prince didn't value her, and Gabrielle wasn't stupid. The arranged engagement was a mere blip on his social calendar. She read the tabloids, and Prince Gregor featured each week with a different woman on his arm. Each was gorgeous and sexy. Secure in their beauty. Experienced actresses and entertainers. Common sense told her he didn't shake hands with these smiling, pouting women at night's end. As husband material, the prince was a poor bet.

No, Gabrielle wanted what instinctively she understood Ramsay could give her. Tenderness and sweetness.

He must've sensed some of her thoughts because he rose and moved up the bed to sit by her. "I desperately want to make love to you." He glanced down at his cock, his mouth twisting with what she thought might be irony. "I guess it's easy for you to tell I'm not lying, but your first time is special. If you want more time, I'll wait."

With her marriage to Gregor fast approaching, she'd never have another chance to have normal. Panic beat at her, a burst of adrenaline leaving her almost light-headed. The closer to her wedding, the more fear and doubt rushed her, leaving her heart heavy and dissatisfaction preying on her mind.

When her parents had laid out her future, she'd understood their point of view. She'd had their approval for once—from the moment she'd listened to their plan.

Now it felt as if they were steamrollers, flattening her every protest.

"Gabrielle?" Ramsay's soft voice dragged her from her unpalatable future.

"I wish to make love with you more than anything," she said fiercely. "Please. Let me return the same pleasure you gave me."

His gaze drilled into her, then his broad shoulders relaxed. Those green eyes glittered, and a shadow flickered in them for one moment. No, pure imagination. When she'd been a child, her parents had always chided her for letting her mind run wild. However, her tutor had thought otherwise and introduced her to the world of fantasy and romance in books. Reading had become her secret vice—a sanity savior.

Ramsay shunted her over on the bed and lay beside her, his head on the pillow. He placed his hands behind his head. "Would you like to explore my body? You can touch me wherever you want."

"Really?" She wet her lips, her gaze doing a visual sweep of his many muscles and his chest's mysterious dips and swells. Then there was his cock. She clasped her hand against her breast, hoping to still her racing heart.

Ramsay laughed, but Gabrielle didn't quail at his deep rumble because he wasn't belittling her. His laughter felt more a shared joke, and the fluttering in her belly grew more vigorous. He winked at her, another encouraging sign. "Which spot are you going to pick first?"

"Oh, that's easy." Gabrielle rolled over before pushing up on her elbows. She kissed the tip of his nose and giggled when he wrinkled it.

His eyes glowed. "I'd hoped you were more adventurous. There's one part of me that's aching for you."

"You're more than a collection of parts, Ramsay," she purred. "You're gorgeous, and I want to touch you everywhere." An understatement. She flattened her hands against his lean cheeks, the heat from his skin searing her palms. Her fingers tap-danced down his shoulder and tested the hardness of his pectoral muscles, the warmth of his flesh.

"You have lots of muscles for a chef. Don't you have to sample your food? I'd grow to the size of a double-decker bus if I tested every dish. You must exercise." She walked her fingers down his abs, counting in her mind. One. Two. Eight. "You have an eight pack. Don't guys exercise all day to grow this many muscles?"

"I like to exercise in my spare time at the community gym, and I take self-defense classes. I run and play rugby with my friends. My hours might be anti-social, but I don't spend my down-time sleeping."

"Maybe I'd feel stronger if I worked out more. My mother disapproves of women frequenting gyms." Her hand rested on his hipbone now. He didn't have tattoos—not like Gregor. It was well-known the prince had one on his backside. She'd spotted it in a tabloid photo when the paparazzi had caught him skinny-dipping with three young women. Her mother had confiscated the paper before Gabrielle had scrutinized the tattoo.

"Do you do everything your mother tells you?" His gaze was watchful. Thoughtful.

"Mostly. Not today," Gabrielle amended, going with honesty.

"Do repercussions worry you?"

"No." Gabrielle mulled that over for long seconds, finally grinning. "Do you sunbathe in the nude?" Daringly, she dipped down to press a kiss to the paler skin of his hip.

"That would be telling. You spend little time in the sun. Your skin is a beautiful shade. It reminds me of fresh cream with a hint of peaches."

His sincerity rang out, and the longer he stared at her, the more self-conscious she became.

"It's just me. I'm not judging you. What I am is dying because you're not touching me enough. I want lips and fingers. Your tongue. I want everything with you. For an intrigued person, you're not moving at speed."

His gentle goading prodded her into action. Gabrielle wrapped her fingers around his erection. "You're warm," she said in surprise.

"What did you expect?"

Gabrielle shrugged and leaned over him. Her hair fell forward, screening her face, which suited her because embarrassment heated her cheeks. But curiosity filled her, too. She moved closer and dipped her head, gathering the bead of moisture at his tip with her tongue.

Ramsay's deep groan encouraged her to explore further, but she wanted to please him, and she lifted her head. "Show me what you like. Please. I want to make you feel good."

His hands wrapped around hers, and he guided her in what he wanted. "Use your mouth to explore, too. The heat of your mouth around my dick..." He trailed off. "It's a happy place for any man. Explore my balls. Not too hard there, but you don't have to be so gentle with my shaft."

Soon, she managed a rhythm that pleased her and had him shuddering and groaning, his low words of encouragement making her hot.

"Enough," he said suddenly.

She jerked her head up to study his features. "Did I do something wrong?"

"No." He reached over to grab his wallet and pulled out a condom.

"Ah," Gabrielle said. "That might come in handy."

He rolled her body beneath him, and she stared up at him in wonder. Moisture had gathered between her legs—more as she'd touched him. After analyzing the sensations coursing her body, she said, "I feel... I feel needy."

Smiling, he kissed her with enthusiasm. He played with her breasts, sucking her nipples deep into his mouth. A corresponding tug pulsed in her pussy, and she twisted beneath him, the urge to beg tickling the tip of her tongue.

"Ramsay," she whispered.

"Soon," he promised, and he nipped at her hipbone. The jolt of pain created an exciting contrast to his fingers stroking her clit. Gabrielle lifted her hips, desperate for more of the blissful enjoyment he'd shown her earlier. She tried to follow his touch, but he laughed and backed off, giving her the lightest caress.

Restless heat built inside her until a deep well of need had her almost sobbing for relief. It had never been like this when she'd experimented by herself. *Never.* It was as if Ramsay was perfect for her and knew exactly where to touch to give her maximum pleasure.

Finally, *finally,* he ceased his teasing and reached for the condom. His gaze tangled with hers as he opened the foil packet and rolled on the rubber.

"Are you ready? You might feel a pinch of pain since this is your first time."

"Yes." Apprehension replaced some of her yearning, but discomfort didn't scare her. She wanted to feel and delight in their joining and remember every detail later. This man she'd only met tonight gave her a sense of safety. Even better, he made her feel worthy. She was beautiful Gabrielle with him. Gabrielle, the siren, and he made no secret he wanted her as much as she craved him.

Ramsay positioned and pushed inside. As he'd warned, pain flashed through her, fading into mere discomfort when he paused. Then, his lips were on hers, and he was kissing her and letting her adjust to his size. His fingers played with a lock of her hair, and with his focus totally on her, she bloomed.

He pinched a nipple and nibbled with surprisingly sharp teeth at the spot where her shoulder and neck met. The tiny burst of pain tugged at her sex, and pleasure slid through her. It was amazing and more wonderful than she'd ever imagined. Then Ramsay moved, his thrusts slow yet steady. Gabrielle kissed his biceps and sucked marks on his shoulder. She rose to meet each of his strokes, the initial pain no longer an issue.

"How is that?" he asked.

"Wonderful. Better than anything my imagination conjured."

He sucked hard on one nipple while pinching the other. The sensations roared through her, tugging at her until she was quaking with need. A moan rolled up her throat and out, and he laughed softly. He adjusted her legs so they wrapped around his hips and increased the pace of his thrusts. He invaded her body, withdrawing slowly before surging into her again, planting deep. Gabrielle gulped in air and clung, savoring every kiss, every touch, every wondrous ripple through her body. Their mouths fused in another kiss, his tongue pushing against hers and penetrating her in the same way as his cock. Everything in Gabrielle tightened until she balanced on a magical tightwire. Everything stilled, then she was flying, toppling over into pleasure so great she sobbed.

Throughout, Ramsay held her and continued his strokes. Her channel clenched around his shaft, tiny spasms still running through her. Ramsay groaned, deepening his drives and increasing his speed until he stopped balls deep in her. Strangled words she couldn't understand tore from his throat. He nuzzled her neck and kissed the spot he'd bitten earlier.

Gabrielle sighed, boneless with contentment. Her eyes closed, and her breathing grew slower. Amazing. She wanted to do it again—just as soon as she had a wee nap.

Chapter 6

A Knot Problem

Ramsay held Gabrielle close, enjoying her in his arms. Lazy and contented, he wanted to stay where he was and wallow in the togetherness. He'd made love with his mate, and it had been incredible. While he hadn't experienced many women—his job and ambition kept him too busy for that—sex had never knocked his equilibrium like this.

Now he needed to persuade Gabrielle to give him a chance. It was a complicated problem when they lived on opposite sides of the world, but they could surely compromise. Ramsay kissed her cheek, her heavy breathing telling him she'd fallen asleep. He should move, but he hated to part their bodies. He twisted his hips and bit back a groan, the heat of her body surrounding his cock doing it for him. An unexpected jolt of pleasure surged the length of his dick, and he froze. He withdrew, every part of him wanting to repeat the move, but the drag on the tip of his cock had him desisting.

What the hell?

He edged back again and cursed under his breath. How could this happen? Yeah, he'd heard about it, but it wasn't common in Middlemarch. At least it wasn't something any of the Mitchell brothers or their wives had discussed. He overheard a lot of discussions while cooking at the café. They forgot he was there and chattered freely.

He eased into a more comfortable position while Gabrielle continued sleeping. Well, he'd been in worse places. Holding his mate in his arms was ten times better than when he and his sister, Terry, had been sleeping on the streets. He hadn't had contact with Terry for years. Each year on her birthday, he wondered how she was and if she was happy. Not hearing was the best thing because it meant Terry was still alive.

Gabrielle stirred but didn't wake. He smiled, his gaze taking in the faint sprinkle of freckles across the bridge of her nose. So cute. She had class. It was in the way she spoke and held herself. Her perfect posture. Her jewelry was expensive and tasteful, and he'd take a bet she came from a family that wasn't hurting financially.

He frowned. That could become a problem, but they were mates. As a human, she wouldn't understand the driving urge to make love and spend time with him. He breathed her in, taking pleasure in the fact she'd taken on his scent.

His mate.

Although there were obstacles in their way, he couldn't stop his smile of excitement because he'd never thought a mate would happen for him.

The faint give of his cock had him breathing out in relief. When he shifted his hips this time, he could withdraw. He parted their bodies and stood to deal with the condom. That's when he noticed the tear. He closed his eyes and silently groaned. Well, that was a first. He glanced over at Gabrielle. Blonde curls obscured most of her face, and she looked so peaceful he hated to disturb her. He'd tell her in the morning.

His mind darted ahead. A baby. He'd never thought of having a child. It hadn't seemed like a remote possibility. Ramsay glanced at Gabrielle again and joy spread through him, tightening his chest. He had a mate, and if a child resulted from this encounter with Gabrielle, he'd love them with everything he had. His parents hadn't offered a great example, but his adopted family was another story.

The Mitchells understood how to raise a child right. They'd taught him a lot.

Ramsay disposed of the condom and returned to the bed. He cuddled close to Gabrielle and went to sleep with a smile on his face.

Voices coming from a distance woke Ramsay. He started, then recalled his location and turned over. The bed beside him was empty, the sheets cool. Ramsay bounded upright and sent out his senses, but it didn't take him long to realize he was alone.

Shock grasped him by the chest, and temper swiftly followed. Why couldn't she have woken him? His fists clenched, and he inhaled and let the air ease out.

Calm down, Ramsay.

Maybe she'd gone for coffee or breakfast? Yes, that made sense. Ramsay stalked to the en suite. By the time he'd showered, it was apparent she wasn't coming back.

What the hell? His mate was out there. Her name was Gabrielle, and she'd walked away from him without a backward glance.

Chapter 7

Cinnamon Buns

Gabrielle strolled along the street and paused when the fragrant scent of fresh-baked bread drew her attention. It was late enough that Tilly, her chaperone, was awake and panicking when she couldn't locate Gabrielle. Maybe if she pretended she'd sneaked from the hotel room to explore, Tilly wouldn't make a huge deal. Her return with a sweet treat—that'd seal the deal. Grinning, she entered the bakery, slipping into the existing line of two.

As the woman in front reached the counter and Gabrielle advanced by one, four men sprinted past the bakery. Reporters. Paparazzi. Gabrielle stared after them with a frown. She couldn't be their target, otherwise they would've charged into the bakery and snapped embarrassing shots of her purchasing food. Her mother had forbidden her to eat in public after the tabloids had published photos of her devouring ice cream at age ten. The image had graced the covers of the gossip magazines and tabloids for two weeks afterward, the European press dubbing her Princess Porky.

Gabrielle turned away from the street to study the cabinet. What would Tilly enjoy most? Ah, a cinnamon bun. They could eat one each with a strong tea for a morning treat.

"Two cinnamon buns, please," she said when it was her turn for service.

Outside, more men ran past the bakery. More reporters. More photographers.

"What's goin' on outside?" the girl behind the counter asked.

Gabrielle shrugged. "Some sort of conference at the castle, and isn't that foreign princess here? Maybe someone important has arrived. Who knows? They're crazy the way they hound celebrities. I wouldn't want to be in their sights for a million pounds."

The girl cocked her head, her manner thoughtful as she thrust the buns into a brown paper bag. "One million pounds. That might tempt me, but you're right. The constant intrusion into privacy would get old fast. That's five pounds, please."

Gabrielle fished in her pocket and produced a ten-pound note. "Thank you. These smell amazing."

"Aye, they're tasty too. The baker is fantastic with yeasted goods."

Gabrielle took her change, waved goodbye, and left the bakery. She glanced in the direction the paparazzi had galloped but could see nothing noteworthy. Oh well. Perhaps this would make entry into her hotel easier, requiring less skullduggery.

She spotted not a single tabloid reporter or the nasty photographers when she approached the corner. Excellent. She scooted up the road and into the rear hotel entrance. Coincidence had her almost running down Linda and another worker.

"Sorry!"

Linda winked at her, and Gabrielle grinned in return before rushing off. Aware she had done scant exercise since her arrival in Scotland, she took the stairs to their room. A royal guard stood outside the door.

Uh-oh. That didn't bode well.

Gabrielle straightened her shoulders and sucked in a quick breath for confidence. She'd tell anyone who questioned her she'd sneaked out earlier this morning. Her face was makeup-free, and she wore casual clothes, so it'd be a breeze to pull off this story. Besides, too bad if they didn't believe her. She had cinnamon buns to back up her story.

Showtime. Gabrielle strode toward her room door and the guard. Her mood hovered at high. Ramsay had been amazing, but she'd required time to think. She no longer wished to marry Gregor. Sex with Ramsay had shown her the incredible magic between a man and woman, and now she refused to settle for less. Prince Gregor would make her miserable, and she deserved better.

Marriage to Gregor would be a mistake. She was aware of his philandering, and she loathed bringing shame to their royal family. It didn't matter if he had the money her parents coveted. This arrangement smacked of a sale to the highest bidder. Gabrielle was an adult with feelings, not a possession.

"Princess," the young guard said, a faint stammer in his voice on recognizing her. He opened the door and stuck his head through. "Princess Gabrielle is here."

Someone tugged the door open, and the head guard stood there, his face scarlet with temper. "Where have you been?"

"I craved fresh air, and I was hungry. Nothing on the room service menu appealed to me."

The redness on the head guard's face intensified. "Did anyone see you?"

"No. I didn't see a single photographer at the hotel's front entrance."

"Not one?" The guard's brow furrowed.

"Not a one," she confirmed. "I guess something or someone more interesting came along."

The guard muttered under his breath, and she'd bet that his words weren't complimentary. "Don't leave your room until the car arrives to take us to the airport. Hopefully, no one noticed you. At least you were smart enough to dress in normal clothes."

Gabrielle bit back a retort. The guards thought of her as stupid, fat, and troublesome, taking their cue from Gabrielle's parents. She turned to Tilly, who she respected since the woman did her best and never belittled her. The woman's long silver hair fluffed around her head, and her pale blue eyes held concern. The loose hair told the story since Tilly always restrained her long locks in a tidy chignon—Gabrielle's disappearance had troubled her chaperone.

"I'm sorry I worried you, but you were asleep, and I hated to wake you. Would you like a nice cup of strong English breakfast tea? I thought of you when I purchased these. They're cinnamon. Your favorite."

The door slammed, and Gabrielle let out her breath. It seemed her plan would work, and a giddy sense of happiness filled her. She had Ramsay's business card. He'd given her one when they'd discussed his career and the restaurant where he was an assistant chef. She'd tucked it safely in her bra, and there it'd stay until she arrived at the palace.

Last night had been fantastic and way beyond the experience she'd imagined. She'd fallen asleep, which she hadn't meant to do, but she'd woken rejuvenated. Gabrielle set about making a pot of tea while Tilly fussed over her clothes.

"Where did you obtain those jeans and shirt?"

"I bought them," Gabrielle said, telling half the truth. "I could hardly go outside in my normal clothes." The clothes her mother had chosen for her to disguise her excess weight. Ramsay hadn't minded her curves. In fact, he'd spent considerable time kissing and caressing said voluptuous flesh. She'd keep these clothes as a memento of the time she'd discovered an ordinary man who'd liked her for herself instead of the crown associated with her princess persona.

"Let's have our tea, then I'll shower and prepare for the homeward flight. I didn't have a shower earlier because I didn't want to wake you. You work hard and need your sleep."

Tilly's face softened. "You're a good girl, Gabrielle. You have a kind heart. Few girls would even think about bringing me a cinnamon bun."

Gabrielle grinned, unable to keep her feel-good mood inside her. "I might've had an ulterior motive since I adore cinnamon buns as much as you."

Tilly's blue eyes twinkled as she flapped her hands. "Oh, away with you, child."

Tilly always brought her own tea, so Gabrielle measured two spoons from Tilly's caddy and topped the teapot with boiling water. By the time the tea brewed, Tilly was more alert. She'd wrapped herself in one of the luxurious hotel robes and tamed her hair.

Tilly settled in an easy chair and stared out at the grassy park and copse of trees. "I can't believe you sneaked out. How did you get past the guard?" She held up a hand. "No, wait. Don't tell me. If I don't know I can answer questions honestly. You're a wicked child for putting me in the position where I have to fib to your parents."

"I haven't lied. I went for a walk and purchased the buns from a bakery." Gabrielle hadn't volunteered more information and didn't intend to either. Ramsay was her guilty secret and one she'd hold close. No, not a guilty secret. A wonderful and exciting one.

Gabrielle shivered on recalling Ramsay's roving fingers, his roving mouth. "Let me pour your tea. Would you like to go shopping before we leave for the airport? We have time. We could stock up on that wonderful buttery shortbread you enjoy so much."

"Huh!" Tilly said. "I'm wise to you. You're the one who adores shortbread."

"True." She grinned. "I'd love to purchase some to take home because I've yet to perfect my shortbread recipe." A stab of regret speared her heart. It was lucky Ramsay hadn't recognized her. He might've, but he hadn't behaved crazed or stuttered. His behavior had remained natural. Perhaps it was because he was a New Zealander, but she'd enjoyed the everyday conversations. He hadn't studied her like a lab rat or behaved as if she should use her clout to help better his life.

She'd had a friend like that and one perspective boyfriend her parents had paid off without her knowledge. She'd been mortified on learning this and angry because she'd missed spotting a man intent on using her.

Ramsay—he'd been different. His genuine affection and the attention he'd paid her had Gabrielle fizzing with happiness. *So happy.* Leaving him had been hard but for the best.

Chapter 8

Ditched

Ramsay stopped at the lobby desk to check out and pay the mini-bar bill since he'd downed two miniature whiskies before coming down.

"It's you," the woman said, her face full of nosy interest. "You're the mystery man."

Ramsay scowled, not even attempting his usual charm. He and chirpiness were not friends, especially after waking to find his mate had done a runner. He was pretty sure Saber hadn't written this into the mating manual.

After a sigh, he tried to muster a smile because this woman didn't deserve his bad mood. Ramsay thrust the form he'd completed at her and tapped his fingers on the counter. "How much do I owe?"

She blinked and continued to stare. "I can see the appeal. You're okay to look at and fill out those jeans in a sexy attention grab."

He straightened from his lean. "What the hell are you babbling about?"

"Princess Gabrielle. She left this morning and must've stayed with you because you're the only guest who arrived last night. That's what I told the gentleman who asked about Princess Gabrielle."

Princess? *His Gabrielle was a fuckin' princess?*

Hell, had he misjudged the situation? Had she merely desired a night of entertainment with a commoner?

When he met the receptionist's gaze, rabid curiosity blazed at him. Dozens of questions filled her big eyes. He clenched his jaw. "My account. I'd like to pay it now."

"But..."

"Don't make me call management," he ground out. Ramsay was positive hotel employees shouldn't behave in this prying manner, nor should she discuss him or Gabrielle with a third party.

Ramsay paid his account and tucked his receipt into his pocket in silence. That done, he strode for the door.

The sight that greeted him had him grinding to a halt. He stared at the men holding cameras and those gripping fluffy microphones. Silence bloomed as he stepped forward, then pandemonium reigned. The men fired questions at him like missiles. Camera flashes dazzled his vision.

Ramsay held up his right hand, and the crowd grew silent. "What the hell? I'm a chef and came here to discuss a job with management."

"Why are you leaving via the front door?" a reporter shouted, brighter and faster than the rest.

"The head chef told me to since a delivery arrived at the rear and blocked the entrance." He grimaced. "Must be the other guy you want." He pushed into the crowd and used his elbows when reporters stood their ground. "Let me through. I hate to be late for my next interview."

"What did this other man look like?" A reporter shoved a microphone in his face.

Ramsay shoved it away. "Don't know, mate. Don't care. Let me through."

By the time Ramsay jostled through the press and photographers and gawking locals, sweat beaded on his forehead. His mind bounced and jittered, and all he wanted was privacy to lick his wounds. His mate had used him.

Ground-eating strides propelled Ramsay to a park. A child played on the slide while the boy's father watched him. A yappy white dog wearing a pink bow approached at a growl, sensing Ramsay's otherness. Ramsay glowered at the barking mutt. It whimpered and darted behind its elderly female owner.

Ramsay diverted to a quiet corner and plonked his butt onto a bench seat. He replayed last evening's events. Gabrielle had approached the bar, obviously out of her element. *Because she's a princess*, his feline snapped.

Our princess.

"Not gonna happen," Ramsay muttered. He was no Cinderella about to win the royal. Storybook plots never happened in real life. His thoughts churned, and nothing shook into normal.

Fact one: he'd hooked up with a royal princess.

Fact two: she was his mate, even though she was human.

Ramsay cursed and wished he were at home with his adopted family and friends. They'd help him make sense of this crazy mess. He sat in the fresh air and sunshine and came to a conclusion.

He might be Gabrielle's mate, but with her human status, she'd have no concept of fate or destiny. Soul mates. He'd need to move on and live alone or seduce her to his way of thinking. Since she was a bloody princess, the chances of getting to see her in person were around nil. Honestly, he hated the idea of facing the hoard of press and photographers who'd wanted a piece of her.

No, he'd head back to the castle. It was time to research the princess. He needed to learn as much about Princess Gabrielle as possible. After he'd completed his investigation, he'd plan.

Decision made, Ramsay took the back roads to Castle Glenkirk. The reporters had spoken with the chatty receptionist. She'd be lucky to keep her job if she couldn't keep guest info confidential.

The castle interior was blessedly silent, with most shifters participating in activities. Hoots and boos drifted from the rear garden. Ramsay stalked along a passage and into the library. As he'd hoped, it was silent and empty. He strode past book-lined walls and straight to the computer in the corner. Ramsay followed the directions taped onto the table and soon typed a search into the internet.

"Holy hell," he muttered on seeing the photos and page links. Hundreds of them.

He clicked on the first one and stared his mouth agape. Gabrielle was engaged to a Swedish prince, their marriage taking place in three months, yet she'd slept with him. Ramsay swallowed loudly, his feline riding him hard. Claws protruded from beneath his nail beds, and the sound that escaped him came close to a feline growl.

They'd knotted.

The condom had broken.

Dammit, Gabrielle couldn't marry this smirking Swedish prince with a poor reputation. Fast cars. Fast women. Fast living.

A sigh escaped him, the man in him sticking closer to reality. His family life would appall Gabrielle and her parents. She was so far above him in social circles, it wasn't even funny. Yeah, he was fooling himself if he thought he might have a future with her.

It didn't matter if they were mates.

Because she'd lied to him—not directly—but by omission. She had a fiancé. Ramsay stared at the photo of the prince in full ceremonial uniform. He supposed he was handsome. The women certainly flocked around him, judging by the other photos. How did Gabrielle cope with that? The images weren't dated, so he wasn't sure if they were recent.

Gabrielle and the prince had never made love. Interesting. At least he had that piece of information in his favor. But the knowledge threw up more questions. Why had Gabrielle made love with him? Hadn't she wanted to wait until her wedding night?

"Damn," Ramsay muttered.

His phone rang, but he let it go to voicemail. He couldn't talk to his friends now, not when his feelings darted around like excited, undisciplined puppies, and he wasn't sure what to do next.

Ramsay followed each link, wanting to ascertain basic facts about Gabrielle. After half an hour, he'd learned she had two older brothers, both married.

As for Gabrielle, she was twenty-one years old and worked hard for several children's charities. She attended fundraiser functions, but he couldn't find images of her nightclubbing, hanging out at the beach, or dining at trendy restaurants. Gabrielle didn't make many public appearances if the gossip pages were to be believed. One of her brothers escorted her to functions, or if her brothers weren't present, her parents were at her side.

Ramsay thought back. She'd told him she was here for a work function. A quick search showed it had been another children's charity, but she'd gone solo since it'd been a lunch. She was staying at the hotel in Glenkirk, and he wondered how she'd left without attracting attention. Now that he thought back, she'd kept her head down when they'd left the pub, and she'd let him place his arm around her shoulders. One princess had become part of a couple.

She'd used him.

Ramsay pushed away from the computer and paced, his mind full of pissed feline and angry man thoughts.

He hated the idea she might've wanted to get rid of her virginity and had used him for the job.

Fuck. Ramsay had so many questions, and it didn't look as if he'd receive answers because how did one contact a princess?

Stupid fool. Gabrielle had blinded him with her beauty and charm, and he hadn't asked the usual questions. She'd diverted him when he'd asked her anything, and instead of getting-to-know-you questions, they'd had incredible, amazing sex. The best he'd ever had.

Okay, no point getting even more pissed. He couldn't call Gabrielle. Perhaps he could contact her through one of her charities. An option. When was she due to leave Glenkirk?

He did another search, and his shoulders slumped. Too late. Gabrielle had already left for Konstavia.

Great. Bloody fantastic. What if she was pregnant? He couldn't confess the condom broke, even though he should. He wanted to offer comfort and promise he was there for her if they'd made a child. Hell, if they had, the child would be half shifter, and since feline genes were dominant, their child would shift.

Another headache for him.

He'd go for a walk through the forest and consider his subsequent actions. Yeah. Walking in nature always soothed him—an activity Tomasine had suggested when he was younger. The combination of exercise and the great outdoors always worked for him.

He glanced at the computer and wondered if the reporters had snapped Gabrielle's photo this morning. Ramsay searched for the local paper and found an online version. A hiss whistled between his teeth, the sound pure agitated feline.

A photo filled the front page—a picture of him as he'd left the hotel.

Mystery man spends the night with Princess Gabrielle.

Bloody hell. It was easy to identify him. He'd have to lie low and pray the press didn't discover his name. No more visits to town, not if he wanted his identity to remain anonymous.

Ramsay had never stood a chance with Gabrielle. It was time for him to accept a single life. But somehow, he didn't think he or his feline would forget her in a hurry.

Chapter 9

Prince Gregor Reacts

The journey home to Konstavia wasn't so bad since it was just her, Tilly, and the security team. They flew aboard the family jet without the kerfuffle of a public flight.

When their car left the private airfield in Konstavia, photographers jumped from behind bushes. They fired questions, and Tilly immediately pushed the button to close the rear window. One photographer stuck his hand through to halt the closure, then howled and performed until the driver stopped the car.

The man forced down the window. "Princess Gabrielle, is it true you had a one-night stand with a man you met at the Ye Olde Hawk?"

Gabrielle gaped, so shocked it took seconds for her brain to kick-start. Someone had found out. Ramsay had been amazing and so kind. He'd been gentle at first before, showing her how fantastic it was to make love. Ramsay's behavior had been unaffected because he hadn't known her history—her princess position and responsibilities.

"Not gonna comment?" the man asked with a nasty sneer.

Gabrielle leaned forward to speak to the driver. "Please drive. If this man can't remove his person from our vehicle, let him suffer an injury."

The vehicle shot forward, and the man hurriedly drew back with a curse.

"You haven't heard the last of this!" he shouted.

Gabrielle didn't bother replying but sent a silent apology to Ramsay. He hadn't deserved this publicity, and he wouldn't understand—not at first. She scowled at her hands before she risked a glance at Tilly. To her surprise, her chaperone's face held no anger. She seemed pleased, but that couldn't be right.

"I'm sorry, Tilly. I didn't mean to get you into trouble."

Tilly smiled, her blue eyes twinkling in her lined face. "I was wondering if you had a backbone."

Gabrielle gasped. "What are you talking about?"

"We'll talk later after you've spoken with your parents."

"I don't want to marry Gregor."

"Tell them. It isn't too late to call off the wedding."

Gabrielle nibbled her bottom lip, unconvinced. Her parents had listed the benefits of this marriage, and one of them was Gregor would bring money. He was a wealthy playboy, and her brothers had emptied the palace coffers. Her parents expected her to right this problem. Father had been definite on this point and shouted down her objections. The vein in his temple had throbbed, so she'd hurriedly agreed.

She didn't tell Tilly this but suspected her sleepy-eyed chaperone saw more than she pretended.

Her parents sent for her the instant she arrived at the palace, or rather their man of affairs summoned Gabrielle to her father's office.

"The king and queen wish to see you on your arrival," Harold said with a perfunctory bow.

Gabrielle nodded. "I won't be long. The traveling has tired Tilly, and I'd like to see her settled first."

"Your parents wish to see you now."

"I'll be there shortly." Usually, Gabrielle would obey, but she and orders were currently estranged. She snapped out her reply in a crisp, precise tone, and before Harold mustered an argument, she took Tilly's arm and headed for the stairs.

"I'm fine, dear. It's a short flight from the UK," Tilly whispered.

"I don't care. My parents need to learn I'm not their slave. Neither are you. We're people with feelings, and I'm famished. We should have a pot of tea and a piece of shortbread before visiting my parents."

"I don't think my presence is required, dear."

"Oh, Tilly. I'm positive my parents will wish to scold you for failing to keep me in line."

Tilly released an unladylike snort. "I'm certain shouting will take precedence. I've never known your mother to reproach in a refined manner. Does she understand the word's meaning?"

It was Gabrielle's turn to snort.

"You've changed, dear. This spunk and attitude are attractive, although I doubt it will impress your parents."

"Let's have that cup of tea," Gabrielle said.

An hour later, Gabrielle and Tilly walked to the other side of the palace, where her parents had their suite. It was also the location of her father's office. Gabrielle knocked on the closed door and waited for the summons to enter.

The door flew open.

"I informed Harold we wanted to see you immediately." Her mother's blue eyes snapped with temper, and her cheeks blazed with red circles.

Gabrielle's father sat behind his desk, wearing spectacles perched on his nose and perusing official documents. On seeing Gabrielle, he lifted his head. His expression was stony.

Her parents exchanged glances, and although Gabrielle didn't understand the meaning, her stomach plunged with foreboding. Her father stood.

"Take a seat." He scowled at Tilly. "Both of you."

Gabrielle sank onto one of the uncomfortable, upright guest chairs. Tilly took the other, her groan of complaint making Gabrielle grin.

Her mother stalked across the tiled office floor, her shoes clip-clopping on the hard surface. She stopped beside her husband, and as if they'd planned this moment, both turned to regard Gabrielle and Tilly. Gabrielle's grin died a quick death. *Uh-oh.*

"Gabrielle," her mother fired the opening salvo. "Your father and I believed you understood the importance of your engagement to Prince Gregor. You agreed to the upcoming marriage. Why have you created a public relations tempest by getting caught with another man? A nobody, at that. And you!" Claire turned her anger on Tilly. "You have one job, and that is to protect Gabrielle from impetuous decisions. A night on the town without her security. You should've kept Gabrielle confined in the hotel room. It's what you normally do, so why change your routine this time?"

"I wanted to see the town, Mother." Gabrielle quaked inwardly at her father's pale, rage-filled visage. "What's going on? Stefan and Georges always appear in the tabloid press."

"You are not your brothers," her father said in a cool voice. "The wedding to Gregor must go ahead. Our public relations team will release a statement saying someone assumed your name, and this man believed her story."

Gabrielle opened her mouth to refute this plan, but the sharp elbow to her side had her glaring at Tilly. Tilly's warning scowl had Gabrielle pressing her lips together. Tilly was right. She'd keep her indignation contained and wait until she learned what her parents wanted of her.

"You will tell Gregor you went to bed early, didn't leave the hotel. The person the press is speculating about bears an uncanny resemblance, but it wasn't you," her father repeated. "You will sell this lie, or else you will not enjoy the consequences."

"Are you spying on me?" Gabrielle blurted.

"Surely you're not foolish enough to think my security men didn't learn of your absence?" her father snapped, his eyes flashing. "We know what you did. That you'd lose your virginity for pleasure is idiotic and shortsighted.

Your virginity was a bargaining chip worth great wealth and power. Now, you're useless, and your drive for independence couldn't have happened at a worse time."

Her mother sniffed. "So much potential, and you wasted it on a commoner with no money, no standing, and from a backwater country. I mean, New Zealand, the reporters said. Who would want to live there?"

Gabrielle stared at her parents, disgusted by their narrowmindedness, their crudeness, their lack of support. She'd done everything they'd asked of her—until now. Did they care so little for her wants?

Her mother sniffed. "Prince Gregor's people haven't contacted us yet. If we're lucky, he might miss the entire matter, or a famous politician or film star will cause a more memorable episode and seize the headlines."

Someone knocked on the door, and her father fired visual daggers in that direction. "I'm in a meeting."

The tapping repeated, and the door opened. Harold stuck his head through the gap, his expression impassive. "Your majesty, Prince Gregor is on line two."

The king's lips pulled back, and he bared his teeth as he reached for the handpiece of the antique phone. He jabbed a button, and after a single ring, he spoke. "Gregor, my lad. How are you?" His jolly tone was at odds with the explosive glower he winged in Gabrielle's direction.

Gabrielle opened her mouth to defend herself and subsided at the gentle pressure of Tilly's hand on her knee. Tilly was right. Gabrielle required further information before she spoke.

"What? You saw the English headlines? You know how they exaggerate their stories, Gregor." He paused. "No smoke without fire?" Her father grabbed a stress release ball and squashed it in his left hand, his nostrils flaring even though his voice remained pleasant. "Gregor, my boy. I don't know what you want me to say." A vein ticked in his jaw as his eyes narrowed on Gabrielle. "I see. Are you sure you wish to take that path? Very well. Yes, I'll tell Gabrielle. I'm sorry things ended this way."

Her father disconnected abruptly and his guttural roar resounded through the office. Gabrielle froze, rooted to her chair. She eyed her father, her breath bursting in and out. Audible. At her side, Tilly tensed.

"Prince Gregor has called off the wedding. He wants no gossip attached to his bride, and you have hit the headlines in the UK and Europe." The king slammed his palm onto his desk, the hard hollow sound echoing like a gunshot through the silence. "I don't know what we'll do. We were counting on his funds. Let's hope they don't cancel the trade agreements we've established with Sweden. They're important to our country's survival."

Gabrielle gulped. She'd wanted out of this engagement, but not in this public way. She strove to halt her panic, even though the urge to shout and rail and demand her parents' support whooshed through her, struggling for freedom. They hadn't asked for her side of the story.

Not once.

Chapter 10

Strategic Retreat

The next morning.

"What should I do, Tilly?" Gabrielle scowled at the pile of newspapers strewn atop the gleaming wooden breakfast table in her suite. Several had published photos of her in evening dress, taken during one of the many charity functions she'd attended. The papers had paired these photos with one taken of Ramsay as he'd left the hotel. He wore what he'd had on when they met in the pub, but he hadn't combed his hair or tied it back. The black strands drifted around his face, giving him a mad professor visage.

It was no wonder her parents and the gossip columnists had freaked out—the photos didn't do him justice. Gabrielle ran her finger across the newsprint page, tracing his scowling face. Although she hadn't known him for

82

long, she missed him. She'd liked him a lot, and he'd treated her like a normal person. They'd laughed and talked and kissed...

"If you could do anything, what would you do?" Tilly asked.

"I'd find Ramsay and spend time with him." Gabrielle bounded to her feet and stalked across the expanse of room. She made a return trip, her focus on the papers again. "I liked him a lot. He made me feel ordinary. He let me speak and listened, asked me questions. No one here, apart from you, ever heeds my opinion. Mother and Father talk at me, give me orders, and treat me like an ornamental doll, incapable of rational thought. My parents see me as nothing more than a moneymaker." Gabrielle grimaced at Tilly. "Did you know we were short of money?"

"They haven't paid me for two months," Tilly said.

"What? Why didn't you say something?"

"It didn't matter. I have savings, and I want for nothing. Food and lodging is included, and I have no need to dress as extravagantly as you."

"What about the other staff? Have they received their pay?"

"Your parents consider them more critical to the day-to-day running of the palace."

Gabrielle glanced at the ornate wall clock, barely quelling a sigh. "I should prepare for my speaking engagement. The charity organizers want me to arrive by half eleven and start speaking at five minutes to twelve. The lunch service will begin ten minutes after the hour. I suspect this won't be much fun because it's my first appearance since the papers published this story."

"They don't have facts. All they have is supposition."

"Exactly," Gabrielle said. "But did my parents ask me the specifics? No. They read the story and assumed the worst along with everyone else." Gabrielle paced a circuit of her room before ceasing and turning to Tilly. "If I had the freedom, I'd locate Ramsay and enjoy getting to know him better."

"Seems fair," Tilly said. "I believe your parents will be away for the evening. Your brothers are not at home. There is nothing to stop us from leaving the castle. No one to raise the alarm."

Gabrielle straightened abruptly and squinted at Tilly, trying to read her expression despite the blast of the sun through the immense windows. "You think I should do a moonlit flit to the UK?"

"I'd like to visit my friends in Edinburgh," Tilly said. "I haven't seen them in ages. You can do whatever you wish. You're an adult and don't require a chaperone."

"Then why did you stay?" Gabrielle asked.

Tilly smiled. "That's easy, dear. You're a lovely child. Considerate. You were happy to have me tag along, but unlike your parents and brothers, experience and bitterness haven't dulled your shine. The charity work you undertake is important, and you enjoy helping those in need. You're independent, cheerful, and work hard, which is more than I can say for your brothers and parents."

Gabrielle relaxed her arched brows and wide eyes. "Tilly, let me mull this over. I'll tell you of my decision when we get home. I suppose we should face the press. Let's go." Gabrielle picked up her phone, turned it to silent, and slipped it into the mauve and black clutch that matched her smart purple trouser suit.

The car ride to the hotel where the luncheon was taking place passed in silence, allowing Gabrielle to drift into daydreams of Ramsay. His quiet competence drew her. His confidence. He'd been gentle with her, yet fierce too. If she had to guess, she'd say he was honorable, but he also possessed a playful edge that she'd adored. He'd laughed and joked with his friends. Humor wasn't typical at the palace since everyone tiptoed around her father's temper. She scowled out the window.

Their driver pulled up outside the hotel entrance.

"The press is lurking," Tilly said.

Lurking? To Gabrielle's eye, they bore a bloodlust, much like vampires on the hunt. Or at least the fictional ones she'd seen on telly. Vampires weren't real, but they'd look much like this if they were. She sucked in a fortifying breath. "Let's do this."

Gabrielle waited for the driver to open her door and slid out. Immediately, the noise and shouts battered her ears. She leaned back inside the vehicle. "Tilly, wait in the car until you can exit in safety. I don't want you pushed and shoved or getting hurt."

"Princess Gabrielle, what does the Swedish prince think about your cheating on him?"

"Where is your engagement ring? Is the wedding off?"

"What will you do now? Is there another wedding on the horizon?"

"Who is your mystery man?"

"Is he going to marry you?"

The reporters kept firing questions at her while the flash of cameras had her seeing stars. What was wrong with these people? And of all the times for her parents to economize on security. "Excuse me. Please let me inside."

But the rabid pack ignored her pleas, and the charity organizers had to extract her from the melee. Ruffled, Gabrielle stumbled through her speech and didn't do her best work. When it came time to depart, Gabrielle left via the kitchen, but the press was wise to this strategy and surrounded her, shouting yet more questions, battering her with noise. Thankfully, she'd sent Tilly back to the car earlier. If Tilly or an innocent bystander got hurt, it'd crush Gabrielle.

A policeman helped her reach her vehicle, and he barked orders when the press surrounded her car and banged on doors and windows. Gabrielle's breathing turned choppy, and her hands shook. Maybe they *were* vampires. She was pretty sure their eyes were glowing. What was wrong with them? They hadn't behaved with this fervent interest when her brothers acted stupid. Not that she regretted her actions. If she had the time over, she'd still go to the hotel with Ramsay.

The policeman called for backup and helped her to escape the mass of bodies. Clammy sweat coated her skin, and her silk blouse clung to her torso. Her terror faded once she and Tilly drove through the palace gates.

She refused to face the press again and let them savage her. Her parents had told her she no longer needed security since she wasn't marrying the prince. They'd save the cost and direct the money elsewhere. Tilly's suggestion whispered like a siren lure. Gabrielle decided she'd do it. If her parents wouldn't offer protection, she'd cancel her upcoming engagements and return to the UK.

She'd find Ramsay's business card and ask—beg if she had to—him to spend private time with her. He could only say no.

After a discussion with Tilly, they fashioned a plan. They'd sneak out, get a ride to the airport with one of Tilly's friends, and fly to Edinburgh. They purchased two tickets on the last flight out that night.

Gabrielle dressed in jeans and a T-shirt belonging to a maid. She slapped on a wig while Tilly dressed in her usual clothes and donned a hat. Then, they walked out of the palace with the workers ending their shift. Simple.

"Why didn't I know it was this easy to exit the castle?" she murmured to Tilly.

"You've shown no inclination to buck against authority, dear," Tilly said. "I was here, watching, and if I'd thought you wanted to escape, I would've helped."

Gabrielle digested this, giving the guards a side-eye as she and Tilly strolled through the gates with the rest of the palace employees. The truth was she hadn't wanted to leave the palace badly enough. This made her frown. While she hadn't been unhappy, she had become tired of the predictable nature of her days. "I'll talk to you more in the future."

"I'm here for you, dear."

"Why are you so nice to me?"

"Because you've treated me with respect and caring. You make me cups of tea and speak to me as if I'm an adult. Tell me to rest if you see I'm tired or have overdone things. Your parents treat me like a piece of furniture."

"I'm sorry."

Tilly squeezed Gabrielle's arm. "None of this is your fault. Besides, we're having an adventure now. I'm rather looking forward to seeing my friend. We used to get into all sorts of trouble when we were younger. Maybe we'll manage one or two pranks while I'm in Edinburgh." Tilly's smile was sly, and her wink decidedly naughty.

Gabrielle grinned. "I've never traveled economy before. Do you think anyone will recognize me?"

"None of the workers have noticed you," Tilly murmured, and once they exited the gates, she guided Gabrielle to the right. "That's my friend over there."

"Tilly," the man said with a broad grin of welcome. "Long time no see, chickie."

Chickie? Gabrielle should pay closer attention to Tilly's activities.

The car was an older one but well maintained since it purred down the long drive leading to the town. They followed other vehicles full of staff, and the guards at the end of the road didn't give them a second glance. Gabrielle didn't comment, but she took in the knowledge. Palace security was slack. Why hadn't she noticed the number of guards had reduced? Her parents had mentioned money, and her canceled wedding had cost them.

She made a mental note to quiz Tilly later. Tilly hadn't received her wages. Fewer security guards. What other economies had her parents taken? None that restricted their spending. Her father had purchased a new car last month, and she'd seen him playing with a drone in the palace gardens the previous week, his delight in his toy apparent.

Gabrielle took money for granted, and that was bad. It was time to take personal responsibility. During their flight, she'd talk to Tilly. Tilly was an underused resource.

It was late by the time our flight landed in Edinburgh.

"We'll grab a cab to my friend's home," Tilly said. "He won't mind if you stay the night. I'd feel happier if you did since it's so late."

Gabrielle's brows shot upward. "He?"

Tilly grinned. "I might be old, dear, but I'm not dead."

"Oh?"

"Ewan is wonderful. You'll like him."

"I'm nervous. What if I'm making a mistake?"

Tilly patted her arm. "What if you're not?"

Chapter 11

A Surprise Appearance

A *princess.*

How the hell had this happened? After watching the shifters in Middlemarch—those with mates—he'd seen finding that special someone as something magical and otherworldly. For those long moments when he'd spotted Gabrielle across the pub, he'd wondered if his heart might burst from his chest. Her looks had drawn him, but her scent had told him she was his mate. The floral and honied fragrance drifting from her skin had sent longing skittering through him. After they'd talked, he'd been even more enamored. She hadn't turned up her nose at his cooking profession and his ambitions for the future. She'd seemed interested in his life in Middlemarch.

But she'd held secrets.

A princess.

Bloody hell. With his past, he'd had no right to touch her, let alone kiss her and make love with her. His entire body went rock hard at that thought, and a bone-deep yearning grabbed him by the throat. Hell, what was he going to do? They had no future, and dammit, she'd deceived him. *Used him.* His fingers curled and dug into his palms as anger and excitement warred inside him. It wasn't easy to decide which emotion to express.

"Hey, numb nuts."

Seconds after those words dragged him from his thoughts, he blinked. Before he could react further, one of his Middlemarch friends punched him on his left biceps.

"Leave me alone," Ramsay snapped, his feline coloring his irritated tone. He followed this up with a snarl and allowed his canines to push through his gums.

Liam dropped into the seat opposite Ramsay, unconcerned by his friend's show of temper. "Instead of mooching around like a sulky girl, why don't you do something? All the reporters left once the princess did. You don't need to worry about them hassling you and taking your photo again."

Scott dragged out a chair and handed a beer to each of them. He picked up the third and took a swig. "You're old news, my friend. No one will care if you show your face in town. The girls decided we should purchase a present for Saber and London. They made plans with Liam and me this morning, but now we can't find Suzie. Edwina was shouting at some big, scary bear dude. We didn't want to butt in because the tension between the two was thick enough to slice. You'll have to walk into town with us."

"Why?"

"If we have to suffer through this shopping thing, then so do you. It's only fair," Liam said.

Ramsay scowled. "I thought we were going to shop in Edinburgh. Can't we do it there?"

"We're doing research. That's what the girls informed us," Scott said.

"And we do everything the girls tell us?" Ramsay demanded.

"No, but it helps to look as if we're obedient. We thought we might have a couple of pints at the pub, grab some brochures, and call our research done."

"A pint will work," Ramsay conceded. "I'll go on the condition we eat, too. I missed breakfast and lunch, and I'm starving."

"Deal," Scott said and downed the last of his beer. "Let's move."

Ramsay finished his beer, and Liam did the same. They left the paneled bar and strode into the Great Hall in time to see a large man scoop up Edwina and tote her outside. Edwina was screeching like a banshee and thumping her fists on the man's butt to no effect. Suzie stood nearby, her mouth open wide enough to resemble a fish.

Ramsay strode to her and stared after Edwina and the man. A bear, according to his nose. "Should we do anything?"

Liam clicked his fingers in front of Suzie's face. "Suzie?"

"What happened?" Scott asked.

"Ah, I think they're mates," Suzie said. "At least that's what I think happened. He appeared from nowhere and spoke to Edwina. They hollered, then he snatched her off the ground like she was a feather." Suzie fanned her face. "Why can't I find a man like that?"

"We're walking to town," Liam said. "Researching like you told us."

"And going for a beer," Scott added.

Suzie blinked and shook herself. "I could do with a drink. Let's go."

Ramsay trailed them through the castle grounds and into the town.

"Where do you want to go shopping?" Liam asked Suzie.

"Drink first," Suzie said, her tone brooking no refusal.

Scott nodded and led the way to the pub where Ramsay had met Gabrielle. The memories rushed back in bright color, the images, so real Ramsay imaged she was present. He inhaled, his breath easing in a hiss when Liam elbowed him in the ribs. He'd swear he could smell Gabrielle with her addictive scent. Liam gave him another sharp prod in the gut.

"What?" Ramsay snapped. "Why did you do that?"

"It's her," Suzie murmured. "She's here. I recognize her from the magazine photos Edwina and I checked out. Her photos were all formal. She's prettier in casual clothes with her hair loose."

Ramsay inhaled again, and his nose told him the rest. *Gabrielle was here.*

He scanned the vicinity with his heart hammering, muscles tense, and half-expecting photographers to leap out of the woodwork. The pub remained empty, and his gaze swung across the room and settled on her where she sat at the bar. Lush curves filled out her simple blouse and a pair of black jeans. Her curly blonde hair hung around her shoulders, but her image in the bar's mirror showed brown eyes full of anxiety. A worried expression. If he released a feline growl, he'd bet she'd jump out of her shoes. That she was jam-packed with tension had his shoulders relaxing.

She was here, which was a start.

"Talk to her," Scott said. "We've got your back. No one with a camera will get past us."

"But why is she here? She left without telling me a thing." Irritation flowed through him at this reminder. She'd ditched him.

"If you talk with her, she might explain," Suzie said. "Go."

Ramsay swallowed hard and forced himself to calm down, to breathe. He strolled to the bar, his gaze on Gabrielle the entire time. She didn't notice him since she was peering at the drinks behind the bar.

"Gabrielle."

Gabrielle jolted and almost fell off her bar stool. She swung around, her eyes wide. "Ramsay, you're here. Thank goodness. I couldn't find you."

"I gave you a business card," Ramsay said, his tone flat. She'd kept secrets, and now she was here, all he craved was a kiss instead of demanding answers. Explanations. "Gabrielle." Ramsay placed his hands on her shoulders and stole the kiss he craved. He'd intended something quick, but the kiss turned sweet and tender.

"Beer?" Scott asked in a loud voice.

"Hi, I'm Suzie. We didn't meet the other night," Suzie said as soon as he and Gabrielle broke their lip-lock.

"Gabrielle," Gabrielle said.

"Princess Gabrielle Herbert," Ramsay said. "Something you forgot to mention."

"You would've treated me differently if I'd told you," Gabrielle said with a note of defiance. "You probably wouldn't have believed me if I'd informed you I was a princess."

Ramsay considered this and nodded. "True, but the next morning it would've been nice if you'd left me a note. *Something.* Instead of leaving me confused and walking into that mess of reporters."

Her shoulders slumped, her expression apologetic. "I'm sorry. My life is a jumble. Ever since my parents announced my engagement to Prince Gregor, the press has mobbed me and asked nosy questions."

"That's the other thing." Ramsay didn't bother trying to hide his testiness. "You're engaged. Don't you think that's something you should've mentioned?"

"I read it in the papers," Suzie chirped.

"Helpful, not," Ramsay muttered.

"I'm trying to point out if you read the paper or kept up with current events, you might've known this," Suzie said.

"No one asked you." He glared at Gabrielle. "I don't sleep with married or attached women. You made me into a cheater. To learn about it from the press pissed me off."

He didn't mention the broken chair or the hole in his bedroom wall. She'd made him look stupid, feel small. *Used.* And worse, she was his mate. What the hell did he do with this knowledge? His feline cared nothing for the niceties of modern society. He wanted his mate.

Gabrielle bowed her head, and when she risked a glance at him, tears shimmered in her eyes. "My parents arranged the marriage. I had no say in my prospective groom or any wedding details. My mother is coordinating the wedding details. Was coordinating them. It's okay for Prince Gregor to embarrass me with his boozy retreats and myriad women. When I do something similar, he calls off the wedding."

"The wedding is off?" Ramsay's voice was rough and hoarse and held hope. His feline released an audible purr, and Scott laughed aloud.

"Yes. My parents confined me to my room at the palace, but I spoke with Tilly." She frowned, her brow furrowing. "Tilly, my chaperone, is a rebel and has been patiently waiting for me to reject my mother's strictures. Last night, we left the palace. Tilly is visiting a friend in Edinburgh. I hired a car and drove to Glenkirk, hoping to find you. I don't know what happened to the card you gave me. I couldn't find you. My next move was to visit Castle Glenkirk and ask to see you. I'd hoped you hadn't left yet."

"What will happen when someone misses you?" Ramsay asked. "Will I end up in trouble?"

"No! Of course not," Gabrielle said. "I'm not sure how they'll react."

"That's reassuring," Scott said. "Let's get drinks and grab the table in the corner."

Despite preferring to spend time alone with Gabrielle, this was a better alternative. If people came searching for her, she'd have other people around her. Later... Ramsay had no plan for later because they couldn't take her to the castle. The guards would recognize her human status and refuse her entry.

"Want a beer?" Ramsay asked Gabrielle.

She nodded.

"Suzie, do you want a lager or something else?"

"Some of that alcoholic ginger beer, please," Suzie said.

"Oh, can I try that instead?" Gabrielle asked.

"I'll bring over the drinks," Ramsay said.

"Come on," Suzie said to Gabrielle. "I'm starving. Let's check out the snack menu. We could get potato wedges."

Ramsay watched Gabrielle acquiesce, but it was easy to see she wasn't confident and was out of her element. He wondered if her parents kept her confined all the time.

Ramsay ordered three pints of lager and two bottles of ginger beer. Scott stayed to help him carry the drinks while Liam wandered off with the girls.

"What are you going to do?" Scott murmured in a low voice for Ramsay's ears only.

"She's my mate," Ramsay said.

Scott stared at him, his green gaze full of sympathy. "This is a cluster."

"Yeah. So the answer is, I have no fuckin' clue." His life had never gone smoothly—at least not until he'd arrived in Middlemarch and met the Mitchell family. Why should finding his mate be any different?

Chapter 12

Truth and Privacy

"Where are you staying?" Suzie asked Gabrielle. Ramsay set down the pints while Scott toted the ginger beer and glasses. He listened for Gabrielle's answer, hoping like hell she'd decided to stay in Glenkirk. He didn't know what came next, but having Gabrielle here was a start.

"Tilly—she's a distant relative and my chaperone—she suggested I hire a cottage, so that's what I did. It's within walking distance of the town and backs onto a forest. I didn't stay long, but I left the rental car there and my luggage. It's private, and the owner didn't recognize me."

"Problem solved," Scott said, his voice low enough for Ramsay to hear but not Gabrielle. "Spend time with her, learn more, but don't do anything crazy like binding yourself to her. Saber told me that once you find your mate, it's difficult not to claim her. A human brings obstacles. A royal princess is a quandary magnified."

"Tell me about it," Ramsay muttered.

"What do you do when you're not doing princess stuff?" Suzie asked. "Do you get time for yourself, or is your life one of uninterrupted service?"

Gabrielle pulled a face and picked up her ginger beer bottle. She poured half a glass. "My parents regulate my free time, and I spend hours with Tilly at the palace."

It was easy for Ramsay and his friends to infer what she wasn't saying. Excitement wasn't big in her life, which was a worry. Even though she was his mate, she mightn't reciprocate his feelings. Her reaction to him, her willingness to spend the night with him, might be more about her gaining freedom and enjoying the hell out of this hard-earned liberty. As if he didn't have enough to stress over with Gabrielle.

"How long are you staying?" Liam asked.

Ramsay held his breath. Before flying back to New Zealand via Dubai, he and the others were traveling to Edinburgh. A few days wasn't enough to arrange a future with Gabrielle.

"I booked the cottage for a week," Gabrielle said.

"What will your parents do when they discover you've vanished?"

"Nothing—if they've even missed me," Gabrielle said. "They'll punish me on my return should they learn of my unscheduled absence."

"You're not close to your parents?" Suzie asked, after a moment's silence where they digested Gabrielle's casual recitation of what might happen.

"No." Gabrielle didn't elaborate.

Even though he was no relation to the Mitchell family, they treated him as one of their own. They worried about him. Encouraged him. But he understood Gabrielle's careful words since his true parents should never have borne children and his heart ached with this truth. Money and position didn't bring happiness. This sounded like a vacation break more than a permanent absence, given her words.

"What would you do with freedom?" he asked.

"Live," she said simply. "I want a normal life where I'd shop for groceries. Find a home and a job. I work for three different charities, but it's volunteer work. None of the charities could afford to employ me. It's not as if I have job experience."

"I don't know," Suzie said. "To work with charities, you need excellent people skills. You're used to public speaking, and I'm certain you've acquired skills without realizing it. How are you at party prep?"

Gabrielle's luscious mouth twisted. "My mother deals with the actual planning, but I liaise with her. I'm more like an unpaid assistant who runs hither and thither, but it's easy."

Ramsay gulped a mouthful of beer. "Are you returning home?"

She caught her bottom lip between white teeth and shrugged. "I have limited options."

"It's not as if you need to make immediate decisions," Ramsay said.

"Limited resources as well. If I don't return home, I'll need a job. I can't allow Tilly to foot my expenses."

Pride rose in Ramsay. Despite their brief acquaintance, her strength of character impressed him. Most men and women in her position would expect others to make their lives easy.

"Are you going to run away again?" Ramsay tried not to broadcast his anger. Damn, but that had rankled. They'd had a fantastic night, and he and his feline had gloried in happiness. He'd felt as if his dreams were coming true, then poof! She'd disappeared.

"No, not without telling you. I felt bad, but I thought we were having a fling. Once I walked away, I realized I wanted to spend more time with you."

Ramsay grasped her hand and gave it a gentle squeeze. It wasn't as if he didn't appreciate the confusion she might've experienced. He struggled with the urge to claim her, his feline pushing him to complete this step. But Ramsay understood that might end in disaster. Given Gabrielle's royal rank, he had to proceed with caution. Telling her about his feline status required planning. Worry gnawed at his guts, and he wished he could talk to Tomasine and Felix, to Emily and Saber.

He required a plan of attack. His feline snarled. Thankfully, the cantankerous growl remained inside Ramsay's head, but Ramsay shared the same burning frustration as his cat.

They wanted to claim Gabrielle and hang the consequences.

While he'd zoned out, Suzie spoke with Gabrielle. The conversation had drifted to general topics, with Gabrielle asking countless questions about Middlemarch and New Zealand.

"I've seen the *Lord of the Rings* movies. New Zealand scenery appears spectacular. Was that movie magic?" she asked.

"Our home country is beautiful," Suzie said. "I haven't seen a lot of the North Island, but the two islands are quite different. Stewart Island, the third-largest island, is stunning. We had a family holiday there."

"Your country is tiny and mostly a city with many expensive properties," Ramsay said. "After discovering who you were, I did an internet search."

"True. I much prefer the countryside and mountains. We always went skiing every year when we were children. I enjoy the outdoors. The crisp air and the open spaces. The forests and the mountain peaks."

"You should visit New Zealand," Scott said with a sly glance at Ramsay.

Ramsay didn't bite, content to sit beside Gabrielle and listen.

Suzie glanced at her watch. "We should go soon. We have that speed dating thing at the castle."

"Speed dating?" Gabrielle said with interest.

"You're with me," Ramsay said, aiming for an even tone. "You don't need someone to date."

"Another one bites the dust," Suzie said with a wide grin. "Let's go, boys. We need to make Saber and London proud."

As one, his three friends finished their drinks and rose.

"Text us to tell us what you're doing," Liam said.

"Will do." Ramsay glanced at Gabrielle. "We'll get dinner and play it by ear. Maybe stroll through the forest before dinner."

"Sounds perfect," Gabrielle said.

"It was nice to meet you, Gabrielle," Suzie said.

"Bye. Behave," Scott said.

Minutes later, Ramsay and Gabrielle were alone.

"Can we truly walk?" Gabrielle asked.

"Of course. The forest is beautiful with lots of walking paths. We'll pick one and enjoy the rest of the day until dinner."

She poured the last of her ginger beer into her glass. "Most of the dinners I attend are formal, especially for fundraising. The meals are usually chicken and salad because that's what my mother requests for me. No dessert and I drink sparkling water."

"We can do better," Ramsay said. "Does your cottage have a kitchen?"

"A small one. I can't vouch for the amount of kitchen equipment."

"Maybe we'll eat in tomorrow night. We'll find somewhere quiet to eat tonight."

Gabrielle's eyes widened. "Are...are you staying with me?"

His feline perked up, and a purr rumbled through his mind. "One night wasn't enough."

"I'd like that very much." Her smile was slow and a thing of beauty.

His heart beat faster, and he captured her hand in his. "Let's go."

They ended up eating outdoors in the beer garden of one of the many pubs in Glenkirk.

Gabrielle picked up a fry and swiped it through a puddle of ketchup. "I can't remember enjoying a meal so much. The cod and chips—delicious."

"Mine was tasty," Ramsay said. "How about dessert? I'd like to check out their tasting plate. Interested in sharing?"

"Yes," Gabrielle said, her eyes gleaming with excitement.

He reached for her hand, needing the physical contact. "It's exciting to find someone who loves food as much as me."

"I hate chicken salad," Gabrielle said. "This was such a treat. Do you formulate your recipes or follow someone else's?"

"For my restaurant job, I cook everything as the head chef specifies. Each quarter, we have a change in the menu for seasonal produce. The chef designs the dish right down to the garnishes, and we have special training to learn how to cook everything and how it should taste."

"How is it you don't put on weight if you sample constantly? I spy a sweet or dessert, and the weight stacks on my hips and butt."

"I adore your lush body, but what exercise do you do? Do you play a sport or walk or cycle? Swim?"

Gabrielle wrinkled her nose. "I'd walk if I had someone to accompany me. We have a swimming pool, but my mother doesn't like me using it. She says I look terrible in a swimsuit."

"Your mother has a lot to say for herself."

"Tell me about it. She's naturally thin and lives on fish, chicken, and lettuce leaves. I take after my father's grandmother, who also committed the crime of abundant flesh."

"Ignore your mother. Not all men have the same tastes. It would make the world a boring place if we were identical."

"True, but it's hard to switch off my mother's lectures."

"What about your brothers?"

"They're older and have more freedom." She shrugged. "It's always been this way."

"Is there a reason your mother gives you such a hard time?"

"Recently, it was because my parents hoped I'd marry into the Swedish royal family. My parents feel Prince

Gregor's behavior is acceptable, but mine is not. The double standard drives me crazy, and the fact I got caught. I can't believe the hotel receptionist ratted me out to the press. I hope the reporters paid her well."

"The hotel manager contacted me a few days later and asked what had happened. From what he told me, they reprimanded the girl."

"Did she lose her job?"

"The manager asked for my opinion. She told him a man had entered the hotel and asked for his sister. He showed her a photo of you."

"He tricked her."

"Yes."

"What did you tell the manager?"

"I suggested he talk to her and give her a second chance. She lives with her grandmother, and her job loss would cause the family hardship."

Gabrielle nodded. "I'm happy with that. At least appearing in the press meant Prince Gregor canceled our engagement. I'm sorry the reporters dragged you into the spotlight, though."

"Your disappearance worried me more. It made me feel used when you took off without saying goodbye."

Guilt slashed across her expressive face, and she reached for his hand. "Sorry, I promise not to repeat my flit."

"I'd appreciate that. So the tasting plate. Are you interested?"

"Yes. I'll help you critique the dessert."

Ramsay strode into the pub to place an order.

Gabrielle's phone rang, and she picked it up to study the screen. "Tilly, how is Edinburgh?"

"It'd be better if your mother didn't keep calling to demand we return to the palace."

"Did you tell her where I am?"

"No, dear. I don't react well to shouting and threats. I hung up but thought I should warn you before I turn off my phone."

"Did she say what she wanted?"

"No, she wanted to speak to you."

"No doubt to issue orders," Gabrielle muttered. "I don't want to go home. I'm having fun with Ramsay and his friends. We had fish and chips for dinner, and now we're sharing a dessert tasting plate."

Tilly issued a soft laugh. "You go, dear. Just watch your back. I'll call you tomorrow if I learn anything relevant."

"Thanks, Tilly. I don't know what I'd do without you."

Tilly gave a delighted laugh. "You've given me a purpose, child. I wanted to make certain you lived instead of acting like a passive robot. Your mother shouldn't censor your spirit."

Ramsay returned, raising his brows in askance. He carried a long plate covered with tiny pieces of chocolate brownie, a dainty citrus tart, and what looked like a crème brûlée.

"Tilly, I'll talk to you tomorrow." Gabrielle hung up and smiled at Ramsay. "Tilly says Mother wishes to speak to me. No way I want to listen to her haranguing, but I'll call her tomorrow."

Ramsay plucked the phone from her hand and placed it on the table. "We have more important things to focus on, like dessert."

A laugh escaped her, the chortle full of merriment and happiness. "Somehow, I think your mind is on something else."

"You're by my side, so I don't mind the delay." He leaned closer and kissed her cheek. Her heart beat faster, and arousal frisked every one of her nerve endings.

"Hold that thought."

Chapter 13

Sweet Togetherness

Ramsay watched Gabrielle eat a bite of citrus tart. Her lips closed around the spoon he held, and she drew the morsel into her mouth. Her eyes fluttered shut, and she hummed. Every muscle in his body tightened, and he couldn't look away. With her long golden hair and her pink cheeks, she was adorable. *His mate.*

If only he could claim her and take her home with him.

Ramsay shook himself free of his dreams to focus on the here and now. "What do you think of the tart?"

Gabrielle swallowed and licked her bottom lip with a slow sweep of her tongue. That erotic, suggestive humming started again. "Delicious. Anything citrus is my favorite, but chocolate comes a close second."

Ramsay didn't restrain his groan. His skin sizzled, and every sense worked overtime, flinging smells and sights and sounds at him. He strained to hear every sound she made, and the pads of his fingers transmitted the details of her skin, telling him how silky it was.

"You're not eating. Why don't you try some of the caramel and chocolate slice?"

"I'm having too much fun watching you enjoy the sweet treats," he confessed and cleared his throat. "I'm also imagining getting you in private. My first chore will be to kiss you senseless and run my hands over your body. Then I'll strip off your clothes until you're wearing nothing but a sexy smile." He caressed her cheek and skimmed his palm over the silky strands of her hair. "Last time wasn't enough. I doubt tonight will quench my hunger for you."

"It was difficult leaving you in that hotel bed, and you stayed in my mind. You're still there. I didn't expect to miss you. I thought I'd sleep with you and walk away." Gabrielle crinkled her nose at him. "I guess I'm not capable of a fling without my emotions engaging."

"Nothing wrong with that." Ramsay could've added more and given her the truth, but it was too soon. Gabrielle's royal position might bring danger to his friends and adopted family. It didn't matter they were mates.

He'd forgo the chance of happiness if a relationship meant putting those in the Middlemarch community in danger.

"Have some dessert." Gabrielle spooned up part of the slice along with a little whipped cream. She held it in front of his mouth.

Ramsay accepted the offering without breaking their gaze. He'd dated women he liked, human and shifter, but the strength of his feelings for Gabrielle scared him. God, she was spectacular and tempted him more than any woman in his past. The intensity and simply knowing she was his one and perfect for him had fear and wonder pulsing through him.

"You make my stomach flutter," she whispered.

"Eat more dessert." He smiled, and the pleasure in him must've broadcast on his face because she blushed. He noticed even though the natural light had faded to darkness and artificial lanterns lit the beer garden.

"I thought we were sharing. You need to eat more." She spooned up chocolate mousse with raspberry coulis without waiting for his answer. "This was tasty. What is in the recipe?"

"Raspberries. Dark chocolate—the good stuff. Cream. Eggs. A little sugar. I've made something similar at the restaurant." He accepted the bite and, after tasting it, nodded. "Yep, that's everything."

"The citrus tart is still my favorite, but that one comes close."

They finished the rest, taking turns until nothing remained.

"How far away is your cottage?"

"I walked to the pub, and it took about half an hour because I ambled and stopped and started a lot. The return walk shouldn't take long."

Ramsay didn't care. If he was with Gabrielle, he was happy. He clasped her hand in his, and they strolled along the quiet streets. The streetlamps lit the sidewalk, and two cars drove past. An owl hooted from the nearby forest.

Gabrielle showed Ramsay into the cottage. He locked the door and reached past her to flick on the light when she fumbled to locate the switch.

"You are so beautiful." Ramsay wasn't one for flowery compliments, so he went with his gut. He cupped her face with his hands and kissed her using tenderness. While he couldn't speak the truth now, he could show her with actions. She sighed against his mouth and clutched his shoulders.

Ramsay lifted her into his arms. "Which way is the bedroom?"

"Through that doorway."

With his superior eyesight, he edged past Gabrielle's open suitcase and strode to the bed. He set her on her feet and kissed her again, sipping at her mouth and taking his time. Her lips were soft. Sweet. Addictive.

Ramsay tugged her closer and pressed his face against her neck. Her scent thrilled him, his feline. He licked across her marking site, and a full body shudder swept him. He wanted to bite in the worst possible way. Instead, he swallowed hard and pushed away from her, but the temptation didn't lessen. "Clothes off," he said.

"I can't wait to make love again. Until spending the night with you, I never understood what I was missing." She blew him a kiss and unfastened her blouse. She whipped it off, not making a show but efficiently disrobing. Ramsay stared for long seconds before jerking back to himself.

"Aren't you going to undress?" Gabrielle was down to her underwear.

"Yes," he said and whipped his T-shirt over his head. His jeans were next, but he still watched Gabrielle. By the time he'd removed his boxers, Gabrielle was naked. He took her in his arms and kissed her. *Not enough.* Seconds later, he parted their mouths and scooped her off her feet. He placed her on the bed and followed her down. Taste. Touch. He wanted to wallow in her and ravage her

117

beautiful mouth before reaching the serious stuff. As long as his feline didn't push him, he'd maintain control over his form. His canines ached, shoving into prominence. A quick glance at his fingernails showed shadowed claws and told the truth. His impatient feline craved his mate.

Ramsay pushed the golden hair from her face and offered a faint smile. Displaying his sharp teeth right now wasn't a fantastic idea. "I'm in a hurry." *An understatement.*

"What about condoms? I didn't think to bring any."

Ramsay frowned, recalling the broken condom from last time. His conscience prodded him. *Tell her the truth.* He would, but he'd go crazy—his feline—if he stopped. "I have two condoms in my wallet, so we'll need to get creative until we can buy more tomorrow."

He climbed off the bed, grabbed his wallet from his jeans pocket, and slapped the two condoms on the bedside table.

"Now," he said, his gaze taking in her gorgeous curves. His fingers itched to cup her voluptuous breasts again. Impatience on high simmer. Before she could reply, he claimed her mouth, showing her with actions how much he wanted her. He tugged her legs farther apart and squeezed into the gap between them. Immediately, he inhaled her arousal and closed his eyes. He hoped he didn't look too unhinged, that his feline didn't show in his eyes, but he needed her in the worst way. With trembling hands, he cupped her bottom and lifted her to his mouth, his tongue swiping along her folds. Sweet nectar filled his senses and a longing to witness his woman coming apart at the seams. He tongued her clit, massaging along one edge and back down. He repeated this several times until her moan echoed around them. Her lush curves quaked as he continued, and when she cried out, begging him to make her come, he sealed his mouth over her swollen nub and sucked.

"Yes, Ramsay." He licked her firmly and felt the spasms that rocked her. Her cry of pleasure had his cock filling to the point of pain. No longer. This was plain torture, and he had to be inside her. The other stuff could wait until he gained more control.

"Yes," she repeated, thrashing beneath him. "So good."

Gradually, she relaxed into a satisfied beauty, and Ramsay reached for the first condom.

"Wait," she said and pushed at his shoulders. "Can I explore you first?"

Ramsay flopped over on the bed, his pulse pounding. "Have your wicked way with me, kitten."

Gabrielle pressed a soft kiss to his lips before running her hands over his chest, his abs, and lower to his hips. Her eyes twinkled when she glanced up at him. "You want me."

"Always. Desperately," he said. "Take me in your mouth. Wanna feel the heat around my dick."

Gabrielle moved farther down the bed and curled her fingers around his shaft. Ramsay gulped in air, the touch of her hand even better than his imagination.

"Tell me what to do."

"Grip my cock harder. Firmly. Yeah. Like that. You won't hurt me." Ramsay guided her, showing her what he preferred. She was a quick study.

His belly clenched, and his hips bucked beneath the pleasurable assault of her hands. The thought of her mouth...

She leaned over him, her hair falling forward to cover her face. Not seeing her features bothered him, then her mouth sealed around his tip, and heat suffused him. He quivered like a leaf in a storm. His pulse skittered, his heart beating much faster than earlier. She took him deeper, using her tongue to explore him. His control unraveled, and it didn't take her long to push him into raw, urgent need.

She lifted her head and brushed the hair from her face to grin at him. Her satisfaction in returning pleasure shone in her thickly lashed eyes. She gripped him, squeezing his cock with exquisite pressure. A bead of pre-come formed on his tip, and she dipped her head. An instant later, she licked it away.

Ramsay growled, his feline pushing even closer to the surface. He surged into action, carefully shifting Gabrielle and grabbing a condom. He ripped it open and suited up before turning to the woman he ached to possess.

Gabrielle.

His stunning princess mate.

"I'm too close to the edge. Next time, I promise. I want to thrust into you and feel your warmth surrounding me." Aware of the need for self-preservation, he said, "On your hands and knees. Let me play with your tits and tease your clit." He guided her into position and notched his cock at her sex. One firm push had him sliding into warm, wet flesh. He sighed and shoved forward until he was balls deep.

"Gabrielle," he whispered.

"Yes."

Her snug walls gripped him, her channel clasping him sweetly. She was hot. Tight. Everything that was perfect. He reached beneath her to thumb her nipples and nuzzled her neck. His lips slid across her mating site, and the temptation to bite down slammed through him again. But no, he couldn't claim her like this and rip away her freedom of choice. She clenched around him, the pleasing sensations inducing him to speed. He withdrew and slid deep again.

His balls lifted, and he clenched his butt muscles, trying to stave off his rapidly approaching climax. The enjoyment could be tenfold if his kitten came first. He reached around, sliding his finger over her clit.

"Yes," Gabrielle said. "Oh, man. That feels amazing. I feel you surrounding me with your muscles and strength."

Ramsay pulled back and slammed home. Sensations exploded in him, stealing his breath, but at least he had the presence of mind to stroke her clit and tease her toward her climax.

Gabrielle cried out just as his cock lengthened and dug into her flesh. Ramsay flinched as he felt the pump of his semen, but Gabrielle didn't seem to notice. She convulsed around his dick, coming hard. She collapsed forward onto her belly and didn't move.

Ramsay followed her down, spooning around her body without trying to pull out of her. Did he need to speak with the others and warn them? Drawing attention to this strange occurrence would suck. Hell, he needed to talk to someone about this. Perhaps he could email Saber on the private community part of the website.

"Ramsay?"

"Yes, kitten." He steeled himself for her questions.

"Does good sex always make you tired? I think I need sleep."

Ramsay scowled into her neck. "You go to sleep then, kitten. We don't have to go anywhere in a hurry."

"I enjoy making love with you."

Ramsay pressed a kiss to her marking site. "Right back at you, kitten. Sleep."

Soon her breathing told him she'd fallen asleep. This knotting business wasn't normal. Nor was the fact that Gabrielle kept falling asleep after it happened. As soon as he had a private moment, he'd call Saber. Maybe someone in the Middlemarch clan would understand what this meant because he had no idea.

Chapter 14

Abduction

Gabrielle woke during the night to discover Ramsay kissing her. She enthusiastically joined the program and kissed him back. Soon, he was sliding into her, his cock hitting an angle that had her sighing and her limbs trembling. So good. *So breathtakingly good.*

She clutched his shoulders and cried out when she came, the pleasure almost too much for her body to contain. Ramsay climaxed not long after, and she held him to her, savoring each of his hoarse breaths and how he held her. Possessively—as if she was the most precious thing in the world to him.

Wow, she was falling for him. While the future was hazy, she wanted him in it, standing at her side. It was the craziest thing, but she could imagine spending time with Ramsay. Children. A joyful life.

Togetherness with Prince Gregor had made her break out in a cold sweat. Thank goodness she didn't need to worry about *him* any longer.

Ramsay placed a gentle kiss on her lips. "It's still early. Go to sleep."

Instead of separating their bodies, he tugged her nearer, and it was the nicest, sweetest feeling to have him holding her this way. The last thing she remembered until banging on the door dragged her from a deep sleep.

"Open up! I know you're in there."

Ramsay's arms tightened around her, and he dragged in a deep breath while opening his mouth at the same time. Such a weird expression.

"Why are you pulling faces?"

The explosive thump came again, and he scowled.

"Get dressed, kitten."

"Who is it?"

"Don't know. I don't recognize the voice."

A third blow rattled the door with impatience. Ramsay rose and rapidly pulled on clothes. When the wooden door made a splintering sound, Gabrielle jumped to her feet and scrambled into action. Her underwear had mixed with Ramsay's, but he scooped the apparel off the floor and tossed it at her.

"Hurry," he urged.

She was standing in her bra and panties when the door flew open, and a tall man strode inside—one of the palace guards. Gabrielle pulled a shirt over her head, thankful it was a long one, and covered her to the tops of her thighs. While she aimed for calm, her hands trembled when she picked up a pair of jeans.

After dressing, she straightened and eyed the man as if he were something nasty on the bottom of her shoe. She summoned an imperious princess persona. "What do you mean by bursting into my cabin?"

The man's mouth twisted in disdain, displaying none of the deference she usually received. "We thought you were in danger when you didn't answer the door."

"You didn't give us a chance," Ramsay snapped as three more guards tromped inside. "Normal people sleep at this time of the morning."

"Shut up," the guard snapped. "You're a nobody. Princess Gabrielle, you're coming with us. The plane waits on the tarmac, and your parents are expecting us at the palace."

"Why?" Gabrielle demanded.

"She's not going anywhere," Ramsay said, standing at Gabrielle's side. He curved his arm around her waist, and his solid presence lent her bravery.

"I don't know how you found me, but I'm on holiday."

The guard grabbed her arm and hauled her away from Ramsay. When Ramsay objected, two guards seized him, and the third punched him in the stomach.

"What are you doing?" Gabrielle demanded, aping her aristocratic mother's authoritative tone. "Leave him alone." They'd hurt him, and she couldn't let that happen.

The nearest guard knocked her away, and she went flying. She hit her head on the corner of the bed. For an instant, she saw stars before her vision cleared. Ramsay was fighting back and doing an excellent job when the guards had dismissed him as a nobody. They were taking more care now and approaching with caution. One guard dragged her to her feet.

Gabrielle dug in her heels. "Unhand me, or I'll have you up on assault charges."

"You're getting married." The guard used brute strength to haul her to the door.

"Newsflash—the wedding is off."

"Your parents have arranged a wedding to one of their Russian friends."

A flash of molten heat accompanied the sudden churn of her belly. "What?"

Amusement glittered in the man's dark eyes. "If you hadn't done a flit, you'd be married by now."

"No!" No, her parents weren't that mean. Tilly hadn't known—of that, Gabrielle was confident. "How did you find me?"

"We've known where you were the entire time. Your parents had trackers placed in you and the princes when you were children in case of kidnap attempts."

Gabrielle gaped at the guard. Why hadn't she known this?

A loud grunt from behind had her digging in her heels again. *Ramsay!* "Don't hurt him. Let him go. This situation has nothing to do with him."

"Do you think we didn't recognize him? He took your virginity, and your marketability fell. Your parents had to find someone who didn't care about your lack of pureness."

What? No. None of this made sense. "I don't believe you. My parents would never give you such a detail."

The guard's brown eyes glittered with malice and unconcern for her position. "They did this time to ensure everyone understood the urgency of returning you to Konstavia. If we don't get you back before this evening, we forfeit our special bonus."

The guard yanked her outside, uncaring of the pain he inflicted. She yelped, and behind her, a loud crash, followed by an equally harsh groan, had her wincing.

One by one, the three guards exited the cottage.

"Ramsay. Ramsay!"

He didn't reply.

Gabrielle fought hard, biting one guard on the arm and scratching another. She kicked and screamed, but Ramsay didn't come. A guard snarled when Gabrielle sank her teeth deep and cuffed her over the side of the head. Blackness slipped over her, and she dropped to the ground.

"Why the hell did you strike her?"

"She bit me."

Gabrielle was vaguely aware of someone lifting her. A door opened and shut, and someone lay her on a car seat. She tried to object, but nothing more than a croak emerged. "Ramsay," she whispered, and his name was a weak, nothing sound. *Ramsay*. Surely they hadn't killed him?

Her head throbbed so much she struggled to focus. She didn't want to return to the palace. Was Tilly all right? No, she was in Edinburgh. They'd tracked Gabrielle using a thing her parents had instructed be placed in her body. Their orders had injured Ramsay. This knowledge hurt, smacked of betrayal, and if she'd resented her parents before, she hated them now. She didn't care about herself so much, apart from this marriage business. There was no way in hell she'd marry anyone. Her parents could argue until they turned purple, but they couldn't make her wed.

That they'd sold her, and were still treating her like property rankled even more. Ramsay had shown her more love and affection than her parents had ever offered her. He'd earned her loyalty, and she was halfway in love with him because he treated her with decency and care. He never ordered her around, yet he was no weakling, either.

If her parents thought she'd let them control her, they should rethink their strategy. With Tilly and Ramsay's support, she'd found her backbone, which meant her parents were in for one hell of a fight.

Chapter 15

A New Threat

P ain throbbed through his ribs and head, and he tasted iron-rich blood. Ramsay groaned, shifted position. He forced his eyes open and discovered he was lying on the cottage floor. Memories flooded back. Gabrielle's screams and the bloody humans beating him. He'd got in punches, but he hadn't been able to go full shifter on their arses. Too many, they'd overpowered him. He crawled to his feet and teetered for long seconds until his head stopped swimming.

He patted his pockets but couldn't find his phone. Slowly, he turned and searched the wreck of a room. Pictures hung drunkenly on walls, a wooden desk sagged lopsided, and a pile of books and magazines spilled across the floor. Considering the damage, he was lucky they'd left him alive. Ah, he remembered now. He'd shoved his phone under a pillow to keep it close.

He limped across the bedroom, stepping over broken bric-à-brac and books with busted spines. The cottage owner would have a fit when he spotted the fight debris. Ramsay swiped his hand over his face. He'd have to use his savings to put things right. Meanwhile, he needed advice. Help.

Ramsay dropped onto the edge of the bed and breathed through the pain, daggers stabbing at his side, his back, his kidneys. Someone had kicked him once he'd blacked out. Or, given the way his entire body throbbed, they'd all taken a shot.

He opened his phone and cursed at the low battery notice. Ramsay hit speed dial and waited for Saber to answer. It rang a dozen times before someone picked up. Different time zone. Yeah, that'd slipped his mind.

"Ramsay." Saber sounded only half-awake.

"I have a problem."

"Wait, I want Emily to hear. Okay, the phone's on speaker."

Ramsay inhaled, then winced at the sharp burn in his ribs. His feline always healed him rapidly, and he was bloody lucky his injuries weren't life-threatening. He was alive. Determination stole through him, and he gritted his jaw. Once he grabbed those guards by the scruff, they'd piss their pants. They shouldn't have scared Gabrielle.

"Right," Saber said. "What's happened?"

"Is everyone okay?" Emily asked, her smooth voice holding concern.

Ramsay dived into distraction. "I met my mate, which thrilled me because she's beautiful and makes me smile, but she's a human."

"I'm a human," Emily said indignantly.

"The human part doesn't bother me so much. She's a princess. Princess Gabrielle from Konstavia."

Emily gasped, and there was a long silence before Saber spoke. "Are you certain she's your mate?"

"Yeah, but it gets worse than that." Ramsay told Saber and Emily about meeting Gabrielle, his run-in with the tabloid press. He mentioned knotting and the torn condom, the broken engagement, and how Gabrielle's parents were forcing her to marry a Russian man. Last, he told them about the Konstavia guards breaking into the cottage Gabrielle had rented and abducting her. Her parents had placed a tracker on her, and Gabrielle hadn't known.

"That's despicable." Emily spat outrage. "I'd never do that to my children."

"They hurt you," Saber said, a sharp note in his voice.

"They beat me. I'm sore, but once I take a shower, I'll feel better."

Saber remained silent for a long moment. "Do you want this woman?"

"With all my heart," Ramsay said. "We've met twice, but I knew straightaway we belonged together. Besides, she may be pregnant. If that's the case, I want my child to know his parents, to grow up in a safe environment. I'm worried how she'll react to my otherness, but at the least, I need to rescue her from a marriage to a man she doesn't know or want."

"Why are her parents forcing her into marriage?" Saber asked.

"My best guess is they're suffering money problems, but that's only an assumption. I don't know for sure."

"Where are the others?" Emily asked.

"They're at the castle gathering. They know about Gabrielle, but not what happened tonight. The guards took Gabrielle a few hours ago. I blacked out. Not sure for how long."

"Are you positive you're okay?" Saber asked.

"I'll take a hot shower and chug some painkillers," Ramsay said. "Gabrielle mightn't feel the same way as me, but we have even less chance of getting together if I sit here and do nothing. If we have any chance of a future together, I need to help her."

The tinny sound of a ringing phone rent the air.

"Wait a sec, Saber. Gabrielle must've dropped her phone when the men arrived. It's ringing. Let me answer it."

"Call me back. I'll contact Tomasine and Felix. Maybe Isabella and Leo, too."

The line went dead, and Ramsay searched for the ringing phone. Every muscle in his body ached, and he'd stiffened up while talking with Emily and Saber. He discovered the phone under a pile of bedcovers. It ceased ringing as he plucked it off the floor.

"Fuck," he muttered.

His legs trembled, and he plonked onto the nearest chair. As far as he knew, Gabrielle had purchased her phone here. He doubted her parents had the number. He thumbed the phone to activate the screen and discovered it unlocked. Ramsay checked the recent calls and saw one from Tilly. Immediately, he hit redial and listened to the ring tone.

"Gabrielle," a cheerful voice said. "I wanted to check in with you. Is everything okay?"

"Tilly, this is Ramsay. Gabrielle's parents sent guards to collect Gabrielle and take her back to the palace.

They've arranged another wedding and aren't giving her any choice. I want to find her. Can you help me?"

"They snatched her?" The woman's voice lost its warmth. "Did they hurt you?"

"I have a few bumps. Nothing painkillers won't fix. I wondered if you knew why Gabrielle's parents were so insistent on marriage. Gabrielle and I are happy together. She is an amazing woman, and we have something special together."

"You made her happy. I know that," Tilly said. "Gabrielle's parents have overextended themselves and desperately require money to fund their spending habits. Gabrielle's two older brothers are no better. Why should Gabrielle help them out of this mess? She works so hard for her charities, and her parents won't even let her have new clothes. I makeover the old ones for her. She is a lovely child with a true heart, and I hate her parents using her in this manner."

"What should I do? Do you have any ideas?"

"Most of the guards are loyal to the king, but I'm hearing whispers. They're not paying the staff on a regular schedule. It's possible I could locate employees willing to help Gabrielle escape, but her parents will have her closely watched. I don't know how soon they'll arrange a wedding. It was a big celebration for our country, but now..."

"Do you know the Russian man they're marrying her off to?"

"No, but I'll discover those details for you. I have friends who'll speak with me. I'll call them."

"Don't put yourself or them in danger," Ramsay said.

"You're a decent man, Ramsay. I can tell. Gabrielle is an excellent judge of character, and if you've caught her attention, you're a worthy man."

Ramsay swallowed hard. The Mitchells always treated him with respect and praised him, made him feel respectable and clean after his past mistakes. For a stranger to tell him the same made him feel ten feet tall.

"What will you do?" Tilly asked.

"If you could obtain more info, it would make my decisions easier."

"I'll call you back on this number as soon as I learn something."

"Thanks," Ramsay said. "I'll text you my phone number, so you have that, too."

Tilly hung up, and Ramsay stared at the wreckage in the room. Perhaps Saber could help him here, too, because now he surveyed the damage, he didn't think his bank balance would stretch to cover the cost.

Tilly rang while he was tidying the worst of the mess.

"Gabrielle's parents have arranged for her to marry Adrik Popov. Have you heard of him?"

"No."

"He's a member of the Russian mafia and leads a large territory. A powerful man with contacts in the US." Tilly's voice turned grim. "He's older than her father."

Crap. "When does the marriage take place?" Ramsay's heart beat faster, his feline agitated and pushing into prominence.

"Two days from now. Ramsay, the man has a terrible reputation—he prefers young women, and Gabrielle won't be his first wife. He's married six times as far as I can ascertain. Each of his wives has died under suspicious circumstances. It's no secret he desires a child."

"But what about the stories in the newspapers? The stories of Gabrielle having a fling with a mystery man. The broken engagement? Won't the gossip scare him off?"

"Not from what I hear. Gabrielle's parents would lie, anyhow. To them, Gabrielle is an asset for their use."

"We must be able to stop this marriage. Rumors usually have some basis in truth."

Tilly made a choked sound, and Ramsay thought he heard a sob. It told him everything he needed to know, and the news was terrifying.

Chapter 16

Marriage

Gabrielle opened bleary eyes, her mouth full of cotton wool and her head throbbing. She tried to stir, but her limbs hung like heavy weights. A flash to her right had her head lolling in that direction.

"Ah, you're awake," a female voice said.

The woman's form shifted, the muted colors of her clothes hazy and indistinct as she moved positions. A series of thumps sounded, and the door squeaked open.

"She's awake."

Someone answered, the words too low for Gabrielle to hear above the pounding at her temples. Slowly, she twisted her head, trying to discern her location. The slight change thrust daggers through her skull. She closed her eyes and breathed through the painful waves while attempting to remember how she'd arrived here.

Her thoughts hovered just out of reach.

The woman's clothes rustled as she approached. She picked up Gabrielle's wrist. Gabrielle cried out at the wrenching discomfort through her biceps and shoulder.

"Quiet." The woman pressed her finger to Gabrielle's pulse point. "Fast and thready. I told them not to give you such a large dosage. Men," she spat. "They never listen."

They'd drugged her. That explained the drums in her skull and how her body refused to obey her silent commands.

Gabrielle swallowed. "Thirsty."

The woman stalked to a table and poured a glass of water. Her shoes squeaked against the tiles on her return. She set the water on the bedside table. "Let me help you sit."

Gabrielle didn't make the mistake of nodding this time. She waited and dug through her fuzzy thoughts.

The woman bore easy strength and assisted her to a sitting position. Every muscle in Gabrielle's body tortured her for daring to move, but she bit back her instinctive protest, biting her bottom lip hard to focus her pain elsewhere. This stranger might help, but she showed no softness, nor did she crack a smile. Her hands refused to coordinate enough to hold the glass, and the woman issued an impatient tsk. She touched the glass to Gabrielle's mouth.

"Drink."

Gabrielle drank the cool liquid and swallowed until no water remained. An instant later, the water gushed back, and she vomited over the woman's starched uniform. The woman cursed and cuffed her across the head.

"Stop hitting her," a familiar voice said.

Gabrielle's head rang, and her eyes refused to focus. "Mother?"

"Yes," her mother said. "Clean up this mess. Popov can't see her like this. We'll need to shower her and put her in clean clothes. Call someone to help you."

"Yes, your majesty," the woman said.

"And change your uniform before you return. You reek."

The woman stomped away and slammed the door after her. Her mother muttered under her breath, something curt but unintelligible.

Gabrielle's mind still rang, but she had an answer. The palace. She hadn't been here before, had she? A big blank filled her mind. Gut instinct told her the knowledge was essential, but nothing except emptiness dawned.

"Gabrielle, you've made a colossal mess. Now was *not* the time to discover a backbone. All you needed to do was marry Prince Gregor, but you slept with the stranger."

A handsome face—a man with vivid green eyes and black hair—played through her psyche. *Ramsay.* Had the guards killed him? She glowered at her mother, casting aside the obedient daughter and reaching for bravery. "Why bring me back? You give my brothers freedom yet control my life, constantly giving me orders. I wanted normal for once."

"Your brothers do as instructed," her mother snapped. "Stefan married the wealthy heiress and filled the palace coffers."

"You arranged Stefan's marriage? I thought they met at the Cannes Film Festival." She remembered that, didn't she?

"If you hadn't reacted with stubbornness, your marriage to Gregor would've appeared a love match, too," her mother scoffed. "Your father and I could tell you'd be difficult. You've always asked inconvenient questions and given too much money to the charities."

"What do you mean?" Gabrielle was still having trouble concentrating. It hurt to focus, to converge her hazy thoughts.

"Your good deeds," her mother derided. "We set up those charities to siphon off funds, but you, missy, insisted on declaring the total raised at each function. Made it difficult to explain the missing funds, which meant we had to resort to Plan B to raise finances."

Her parents only cared about their wants and needs. Did they not have enough? She had eyes. The Konstavia citizens needed more help from the palace than they were receiving. One and one suddenly slotted together to make sense. "You're stealing from Konstavia's citizens."

Her mother stiffened, her features turning hard. "We're the king and queen."

Disgust kept Gabrielle from guarding her tongue. "The money I earned for the charities went into your pockets. Funded your expensive tastes. That's despicable."

"Your lack of virginity presents a problem." Her mother shrugged off Gabrielle's contempt. "Now that you're no longer chaste, your worth has gone down considerably. Stupid child. Thank goodness we listened to security and inserted the tracker in you. It made finding you easy."

Gabrielle stared at the woman in front of her. Why had she even bothered having children? Gabrielle wasn't close to her brothers because of the age difference, but had they also suffered through this parental interference?

She'd always thought her brothers led charmed lives. It was apparent she needed to speak with her siblings.

Meantime, what did her parents intend for her?

Gabrielle attempted to get off the bed, and her knees buckled. Her stomach roiled, and she turned her head, nausea rushing up her throat. She vomited again. Her mother made a sound of disgust.

"What did you give me?" Gabrielle craved more water but wasn't confident of keeping it down.

"You were creating such a fuss we had to sedate you. Attracting attention was not optimal."

Gabrielle gritted her teeth. It was evident her parents cared nothing for her. At least Tilly was secure in Edinburgh. As for her personal safety, escape from the palace—impossible. Not with a guard on her door and someone in her room watching her.

"What happens next?" she asked, keeping her tone casual.

"In two days, you'll marry Adrik Popov. The dressmaker will deliver your gown tomorrow."

"I won't do it. I refuse."

Her mother grasped her wrist and twisted. "You will marry and look happy about your wedding."

Her parents couldn't do this when she longed for Ramsay. A cacophony rattled through her head, tinged with panic. "Who is Adrik Popov? Have I met him?"

"No. The man is disgusting and uncouth, but he's willing to pay a princely sum for you. He wants a child," her mother said.

Hellfire. She was to become a broodmare. *Fun times.* It made her fiercely glad the gorgeous, sexy Ramsay had been her first. She'd never believed in love at first sight. She did now. Ramsay. Yes! They'd been together when the guards captured her. She frowned, trying to recall what had happened between the cabin and the castle. Whatever they'd given her had blitzed her memory.

"Nothing to say?" her mother taunted.

"Yes, have you always been a bitch?"

Her mother darted forward and slapped her face. Pain ricocheted through Gabrielle, and her eyes watered. Blood seeped into her mouth, and she carefully prodded her lip with her tongue.

"How do you think I ended up married to your father?" her mother demanded. "This is the way things are done. Your father likes to spend money. It makes him happy and his moods more certain."

Shock doused some of Gabrielle's rage. "What about you?"

"Don't you understand? I have no choice either. I do as your father orders, and I have relative freedom if I do."

Gabrielle stared at her mother. "You didn't think about leaving him?"

"As long as I obey him, I have plenty of money, every luxury I want, and whomever I wish to take as my lover."

Gabrielle took a shaky breath. How had she not known this? Her father had always acted distant, had always shown more interest in her brothers. She tried to recall how her parents behaved when they were together. Neither spent much time with the other. She'd never pondered the reasons because she'd been more interested in her charities and avoiding marriage to Gregor.

In hindsight, her parents had kept her isolated because they'd had plans for her future.

"I have a headache," she said, and she wasn't lying. Her head throbbed in time with the ache of her jaw.

A brief tap sounded. "Yes," her mother called, her tone imperious.

The door opened, and two maids entered with cleaning materials.

"My daughter has a headache and isn't feeling well. Please change the bed linens and help her change into a nightie. Gabrielle, your wedding takes place in two days. Make sure you get plenty of rest. You'll need it."

Her mother stalked from the room. She spoke with the guard visible outside the door. "Keep the door locked unless the maids are taking meals to Gabrielle. Guard her well. If she escapes, you'd better run too because the punishment will be severe."

Chapter 17

No Chance of Escape

Gabrielle's recovery was slow, and it took a day for the aches and pains and the throb in her head to subside. A bruise formed on her face where her mother had whacked her, and she bore numerous others on her limbs and torso. Gabrielle slept a lot, and during her waking hours, she observed, she listened, she plotted.

An escape from this marriage.

She was of age and an adult. Surely they couldn't force her to marry this man, Adrik Popov? What if she refused? Gabrielle pressed her face into her pillow. A maid sat in the corner, her needles clacking as she industriously knitted. The woman never spoke to her, but she chatted with the guard when he made his hourly check to ensure Gabrielle's presence. Mostly, she pretended to sleep since they were chattier this way, and she'd learned a few things.

The wedding would occur in the palace chapel with only the Herbert family and Adrik Popov's connections present. No formal celebrations or announcements. As far as Konstavia residents were aware, Gabrielle would disappear. Her parents would inform anyone who made persistent queries their daughter had quietly wed the man she loved. Tired of the negative publicity and the nosy interest, she was withdrawing from public life.

The guards and servants had heard of Adrik Popov and their opinions varied. Some assumed him to be the mafia head in Russia, while others pooh-poohed the exaggeration. It was true he'd married more than once and suffered extraordinary bad luck with wives. Some whispered he'd murdered them. Others thought they'd killed themselves. Gabrielle wasn't clear what to make of this.

A dart of pain in her belly had her sliding her hand down to cup her abdomen. Cramps. From experience, she knew it was best to take painkillers now before the twinges became worse. Her monthly trial. She grimaced into her pillow. How would her soon-to-be husband react to his bride having her period?

Gabrielle pushed herself off her bed and shuffled toward the en suite. She rifled through the medicine cabinet, popped two painkillers, and followed them with a glass of water.

Her bedroom door flew open, and her parents strode in with Harold. Harold carried a camera.

Her father scowled at her. "You look disgusting. Why haven't you showered and applied makeup to cover that bruise? You," he barked at the servant. "Make her presentable enough for Harold to take photos. One hour." Her father turned to her mother. "Pick an outfit for her that will photograph well. You have one hour to perform a miracle because we can't afford to lose our fish."

Her father dismissed Gabrielle with one of his disdainful glances that had scared her as a child and still sent chills down her spine. That look said *follow my instructions or face the repercussions.*

"I'll choose an outfit. Something to show off your chest but to hide your backside and chunky thighs. You! Put her in the shower and wash her hair. We'll blow dry it and leave it loose. I believe Adrik prefers long hair. We need to package her in the way Adrik favors."

"Yes, your majesty." The servant jumped into action and grasped Gabrielle's arms. "Let's go."

Gabrielle didn't bother arguing. A waste of breath. No, she'd wait and watch and seize the first decent opportunity to escape. Her mind kept straying to Ramsay and her last sight of him lying on the bedroom floor of the cottage. Had he been dead? She didn't know, and they weren't letting her watch television or use her devices. Then there was Tilly. Hopefully, her parents weren't aware of Tilly's location because Gabrielle couldn't live with her conscience if something happened to her.

Perhaps her parents were right, and she was selfish, only thinking of herself. She'd been born into a life of service. It was her responsibility to serve her country. *Yeah, right.* That was complete bullshit. Her parents wanted their luxurious lifestyle, which, for some unknown reason, had come to a standstill. She didn't understand their problems, didn't care. That they expected Gabrielle to fix their troubles for them aggravated her big time.

The servant practically ripped off Gabrielle's robe and nightie and thrust her into the shower in the en suite.

"Hurry," the woman spat. "I don't want a beating because you played precious."

"They punish you?"

"Either that or withhold wages. Why do you think the staff turnover is so high?"

Gabrielle had wondered but hadn't come to conclusions. The threat of physical blows or forfeiting their wages would incentivize servants. The servant's fear communicated itself to Gabrielle, and she hastened to follow instructions. She hated knowing others might suffer for her transgressions. Already, she'd unknowingly dragged Ramsay and Tilly into this mess.

Gabrielle pushed aside her aches to wash and condition her long hair and rapidly cleanse herself with a citrus body gel. Five minutes later, she was out of the shower and drying herself.

"I'll get your lingerie." The servant showed no sympathy. Her chilly expression spoke of disinterest. "Start your makeup and do a good job. I can't afford to lose this position or my wages."

Gabrielle didn't reply but set to work. She covered the multi-colored bruise on one side of her face with concealer, then applied foundation. When the servant returned, her face appeared more normal, and she received a grudging nod of approval.

"Not bad," the servant said.

Gabrielle didn't even know her name. "What's your name?"

"Don't even think about getting buddy-buddy with me and asking me to help you escape," the woman snarled in a fierce undertone. "No way in hell I'd help you. *No way.* Your father has threatened to kill anyone who dares."

"Kill?"

"Bah! Hurry. I don't want to land on the wrong side of the queen, either."

She cast her mind back. Was her father truly that harsh with the staff? Yes, the staff arrived and disappeared with great frequency. But surely her father wouldn't stoop to outright murder?

Her mother appeared in the doorway. "Why are you dawdling? We must dress you for the online meeting with your intended in twenty minutes." She stomped over to Gabrielle and gripped her forearm, her manicured fingernails digging in painfully hard.

"You're hurting me. I can't hide scratches on my forearms."

Her mother released her with a disdainful sniff. Gabrielle had assumed her parents had loved her. It was now obvious they loved no one but themselves.

At five minutes to two, her mother and the guard escorted Gabrielle to the formal sitting room, where her parents greeted visitors on matters of state.

Her father turned from the huddle of staff and stalked over to them. "Let me look at you," he ordered.

Gabrielle hesitated.

"Now," he barked.

At her side, her mother flinched, so Gabrielle hurried to obey. The king nodded after prowling a circle around her. "Not bad. You'll do." An alarm rang, and her father stiffened. "You will speak with politeness when questioned, but let your mother and I do the talking. Is that clear?"

"Yes, Father."

"Mr. Popov is ready for the meeting to begin," Harold said. "Princess Gabrielle, please sit here."

Gabrielle's knees trembled, straining to hold her upright, but she forced herself forward and sat where Harold indicated.

"Smile," her mother hissed in her ear as she slipped into the seat on Gabrielle's right.

Her father sat to Gabrielle's left. He didn't glance her way, yet she was aware of his steely control and determination for this meeting to succeed. Her stomach roiled with nerves. She kept her head bowed and stared at her clasped hands.

"Good morning." The man spoke in an accented voice.

Her mother pinched Gabrielle on the thigh. "Good morning, Mr. Popov." Her ingratiating voice was loud enough to hide Gabrielle's pained gasp.

"Mr. Popov, this is our daughter, Gabrielle," the king said.

Gabrielle lifted her gaze. She had to cooperate and pretend this meeting was typical business. Adrik Popov was a similar age to her parents. He had a thick head of silver hair and piercing blue eyes. They held not a shred of warmth, but he regarded her like a prospective possession. Instinct told Gabrielle he'd behave cruelly should he decide the situation warranted. Heat raced through her body, her clothing suddenly too heavy. Too hot. Her mouth grew dry, and she swallowed to alleviate the problem.

"I'm pleased to meet you. Sir," she added belatedly when her mother pinched her leg again. She couldn't prevent her *eep* of surprise, the croakiness of her voice.

This time, her father spoke to hide Gabrielle's distress. "We have organized the wedding for tomorrow."

"Excellent," Arik said. "I look forward to meeting you in person, Gabrielle. You will make a beautiful bride."

Gabrielle blinked once, but Mr. Popov terminated the meeting before she could reply.

"Well," her mother said. "At least he seems happy enough."

"As long as he keeps his end of the bargain," her father growled. He turned to the nearest guard. "Escort the

155

princess to her room and make certain she doesn't leave."
He rose and strolled away without a backward glance.

Her mother sniffed. "Speak up and take the initiative. Manners, child. No man enjoys a woman who resembles a wooden doll."

"Yes, Mother." Gabrielle rose and stalked toward the guard tasked with escorting her to her room. He opened the door for Gabrielle, and she sailed through. Her jaw clenched, and she held her head high, but inside fear stalked like a slobbering beast. Her last evening of freedom.

That night, she didn't sleep.

Not that it showed the following day when she dressed in the wedding dress chosen by her mother. A makeup artist had applied her cosmetics and covered every bruise and the dark circles under her eyes. Gabrielle appeared dewy fresh and had never looked more beautiful. The groom who waited for her in the chapel should be Ramsay, not this older man.

Tears threatened, but she fought hard to save her war paint. She could do without her mother's displeasure at her for ruining the makeup artist's skilled work.

Her mother entered her bedroom. "Are you ready?"

"Yes." Gabrielle didn't smile. She concentrated fiercely on not crying, but she was sobbing inside. *Ramsay*. She ached for him, and it was useless because she'd never see him again.

"We will leave now," her mother said. "You have the traditional items?"

"Yes." Not that it mattered a whit to her. Given this man's reputation and age, Gabrielle couldn't see happiness in her future.

But there was no escape.

She followed her mother from her bedroom, and the guards outside her door stood to attention. Her mother swept past and clicked her fingers at Gabrielle.

Gabrielle halted in the doorway, panic pelting her mind. A tremor swept the length of her body. "Mother, I don't want this."

"Too bad. You will wed Adrik Popov and pretend ecstatic happiness. My life and your father's depend on this marriage."

"I'm responsible for your safety," Gabrielle said, not bothering to hide her bitterness. "What about my wellbeing? My wants?"

Her mother narrowed her eyes, her lip curling in harsh severity. Not a shred of sympathy or compassion or caring crossed her face. "We're your parents. You owe us your loyalty."

"I don't want this marriage. If you force me to marry him, I will never speak to you again."

Her mother sniffed. "I doubt Adrik will grant permission for you to leave his property, so that won't be an issue for your father or I. I'll give you some advice I wish my parents had given me before my marriage. Don't fight your husband. Let him do whatever he wants with your body. Let him think you enjoy every moment, and once you're pregnant and deliver a healthy child, you'll become more valuable. Gain power. If you fight Adrik or give him lip, he will kill you as he has his other wives."

Gabrielle studied her mother's exquisitely made-up face, listened to her words, and felt nothing but pity. A squeezing sensation around her chest stole her ability to breathe, and she gasped for air. Her mother might think this helpful advice, but she gave away a truth that made Gabrielle uncomfortable.

The bothersome lump in her throat stopped her from commenting, but thoughts dashed through her mind. Her mother had suffered abuse and was now broken and caught in a vicious cycle. All this time, she'd cast herself as a victim and hated her parents for their decisions and power over her.

A single tear rolled down Gabrielle's cheek as the truth pierced her confidence. She and her mother were both casualties with no chance of escape.

Chapter 18

A Plan

Ramsay waited for his friends at a private airfield in Edinburgh. He wasn't sure of the plan, but he had confidence in Saber and Felix. He'd spent the days after Gabrielle's disappearance with Tilly and her friend, and they'd researched Adrik Popov and his southern Russia mansion. Nothing Ramsay learned had reassured him. The rumors regarding his past wives reeked like two-day-old fish. An obvious conclusion was the man had rid himself of the women when they'd failed to produce the requisite child.

The plane landed and taxied toward the hangar.

"Try not to worry," Tilly said, patting Ramsay's hand. "Gabrielle is brave and intelligent. She isn't like her parents or brothers."

Ramsay attempted to smile at the older woman, but he couldn't, not when his gut churned with fear for his mate. He'd tried to talk Tilly out of coming with him, but she'd insisted and he'd found himself no match for her determination.

Tilly clasped his hand and squeezed. He wondered if this was what it was like to have a grandparent—someone who cared and supported and saw you at your worst but loved you, anyway.

The door to the plane opened, and Saber strode down the stairs, followed by Isabella, Leo, Henry, Gerard, and Felix.

Ramsay stared, and when his vision turned blurry, he blinked. They'd come to help him without even knowing Gabrielle. A shudder of fear for his mate almost took him out at the knees. Tilly had discovered through palace friends that Gabrielle's parents had forced her to marry Adrik Popov. Four days ago, her new husband had taken her to his homeland. Four days to terrorize his mate. Another tremor sped down Ramsay's back because he hated to think of Gabrielle in that man's home. His bed.

A growl escaped him, and he forced his thoughts away. *Calm. Use your brain. None of this* is *Gabrielle's fault.* He and the others would find and free her. What she did next was up to her, but he hoped Gabrielle would travel with him to New Zealand. Together, they'd start a new life, but he wouldn't force her. The decision was hers.

"There, there," Tilly murmured. "We'll get Gabrielle back."

Ramsay nodded, not trusting himself to speak. He strode across the tarmac to greet Saber and the others.

"Thanks for coming." Ramsay thrust out his hand.

Saber ignored the gesture to pull Ramsay into a tight hug.

"Is there a place to have coffee?" Isabella asked in her crisp voice.

Ramsay stared at Isabella, who usually worked in the café with him. During working hours, she wore shorts, or jeans when the weather grew cooler, and a Storm in a Teacup tee. But now, she wore unrelieved black, and her attitude reminded him of an assassin.

Tilly stepped forward. "We can have coffee inside the hangar. They have a machine."

"Saber, this is Tilly. She works or used to work as Gabrielle's chaperone and was in Edinburgh with her friend when the guards arrived at Glenkirk to retrieve Gabrielle. She has helped me to learn about Gabrielle's fate. I tried to tell her I had friends to help me, but she insisted on coming to meet you."

"I'm going with you to Russia," Tilly said strongly, determined. "Gabrielle will require a familiar face. You might speak the same language, but if she's injured or drugged or worse, you'll need my help."

"Tilly is correct," Isabella said before Ramsay could argue. "A familiar face will help your girl. We're strangers, so she won't understand that we're trustworthy."

"Tilly, this is Isabella and her husband, Leo. Saber is one of our community leaders and is Leo's older brother. Felix is another Mitchell brother, and this is Gerard, and the blond is Henry. They're friends and ex-military."

Tilly nodded and smiled, not perturbed by the towering men. "I would've picked you were brothers since you're alike. You, young man," she said. "Gerard, you're obviously related too because you have the same beautiful green eyes as Ramsay."

"No, ma'am," Gerard said. "I believe it's a Scottish trait. A lot of Scottish men and women settled in our region."

Ramsay led the way. It was quiet, although several workers tossed insults at each other, audible from the hangar, but they remained out of sight.

"Let's grab our coffee and drink them outside in the sunshine. I'd like to enjoy my first visit to Scotland while I can," Saber said.

"Young man, you're not leaving without me," Tilly spoke with determination.

Saber grinned. "No, ma'am. Would you like me to carry a chair outside for you?"

"Yes, please," Tilly said, mollified by his reply. "I believe I will use the facilities. Ramsay, you know how I prefer my coffee."

"We'll be outside, Tilly," Saber said. "But once our pilot has refueled and done the checks, we're taking off for Russia. We won't dawdle."

"I understand," she said and hustled out of sight.

"I like her," Leo said as Isabella got to work on making coffee.

"Does she know what we are?" Saber asked.

"No, Gabrielle and I were taking things slowly. She's a royal princess, and..." Ramsay shrugged. "I'm not."

"You're a valuable member of our community," Saber said.

"Family," Felix said, speaking almost the same time as his older brother.

Humbled, Ramsay nodded. Felix and his wife, Tomasine, had given Ramsay shelter and a family life when he'd first started living in Middlemarch. He owed them.

Isabella dispensed coffee with quick efficiency. "Do you have plans for what happens after we grab her?"

Yeah. Ramsay had considered that. "It depends on what condition she's in and what Gabrielle wants. I want to take her home, but I won't force her. Every decision has to be her choice. Especially since her parents have foisted outcomes on her. Given everything, it made little sense to spill feline secrets."

"I'm proud of you, Ramsay," Saber said. "Let's walk, and you can share what you've learned so far."

"Tilly takes her coffee with milk. A flat white will be fine for her," Ramsay said.

Gerard and Henry murmured in soft voices, accepted their coffees, and strolled outdoors.

"I might use the facilities too," Isabella said.

"I'll take your coffee. See you outside, sweetheart," Leo said.

Saber picked up a chair for Tilly and wandered into the sunshine.

"Right," Isabella said once they were together again. "Tell us about this man. I've done some research but have gaps. We can't go in blind. I have several contacts we can use, but I've waited until we'd pooled our knowledge."

"Adrik Popov is part of the Russian mafia, as were his father and grandfather before him. He rules a large territory and has ties to the Irish mob in New York. He has married several times to women younger than him, and each wife died—the first in childbirth. The fate of the others is unknown. There are rumors, but none substantiated. His men are well-trained and equipped. His home is a fortress and difficult to penetrate. We don't have an estimate of numbers, but they'll be formidable. We believe Adrik conducts most of his business from home these days. He's in his early sixties. There are rumors about his health, but I didn't find proof, and he traveled to Konstavia to marry Gabrielle."

"Sucks she has to go through this," Gerard said, his gaze intense.

Ramsay only hoped she'd be in her right mind when they'd recovered her. He knew they would find her, but the Russian had taken her to his home days ago. A lot could happen in that time. Ramsay curled his right hand around his paper cup, tension a heavy weight on his shoulders. That man had *his* Gabrielle. The Russian desired a child, so they wouldn't be having tea parties. He hated the idea of the Russian touching Gabrielle, but she wouldn't have much choice.

Do what you need to do to stay alive, Gabrielle. We'll sort out the rest later.

A shrill whistle had them glancing toward the plane.

"Looks like we're ready to go," Saber said.

"Tilly, I'll grab your bag," Ramsay said.

"We'll tuck it under a seat," Henry said. He was a wolf of few words, but Ramsay trusted the man with his life.

They piled onto the plane. Ramsay settled Tilly in a seat next to Saber. Saber would get Tilly talking and pump her for information. It was best if Saber heard everything from the source. Ramsay would report to the others.

"Where are we headed?" Ramsay asked.

"Southern Russia," Isabella said. "I contacted old friends, and they set me up with the guy who owns this private airstrip."

"Is he trustworthy?" Gerard asked.

"I think so. The airstrip is far enough away from Popov's place to avoid nosy interest," Isabella replied.

The seatbelt sign buzzed, and everyone sat and fastened their belts. Minutes later, they were in the air. Once they could move around, they pored over an estate map and the surrounding area. They discussed tactics and potential problems. No one mentioned their shifter forms, but that was the best way to approach the property unseen. Hauling their clothes and weapons was a problem, but Ramsay didn't care if anyone saw him naked. His focus was on getting Gabrielle to safety.

A retreat to the palace wouldn't work, nor would a return to Scotland. Ramsay hoped he and New Zealand might interest her. He doubted Popov would track them.

Everyone would assume Ramsay had gone home. He might need to hang around and fly home as planned, but he trusted Saber to protect Gabrielle. He wondered if Tilly would travel to New Zealand, too. That way, he could ensure her safety.

"Do we have a plan?" Ramsay asked.

"We have the basis of one," Isabella said. "We'll firm up details once we get a schematic of the house. My contact is obtaining one for us."

"How much is this costing?" More than Ramsay could afford. "I'll pay you back. Somehow."

Isabella grasped Ramsay's shoulder. "I'm paying. I have plenty, and this is an excellent way to spend it. You don't owe me anything." She paused, then grinned. "On second thought, this is my fee. Kian has a birthday coming, and I'd like you to bake a cake for him. Also, I'd like a romantic meal for me and my darling husband on our upcoming anniversary. That is my fee. Can you pay?"

"Yes!" Ramsay's eyes burned, and emotion almost bested him. "Thank you." He forced the words past the lump in his throat.

"We'll save your mate," Isabella said.

Ramsay nodded but silently acknowledged a truth. Rescuing Gabrielle from this dangerous situation was possible, but her mental state afterward could sever any chance of happiness for them.

Chapter 19

Monster

G abrielle cautiously turned, the pain in her back and torso bringing tears to her eyes. She bit back a moan and was only partially successful. At her side, her new husband slept, face innocent in slumber.

A lie. Adrik was a monster. Every part of her body ached because he'd tied her up and beat her, striking her with his belt and taking pleasure in her agony. She'd tried to tell him she had her period, but he hadn't cared, hadn't stopped. The information had pleased him, as had the lightness of her bleeding.

"Excellent. No devil spawn. You will bear my child, or I will replace you," the man had growled in her ear as he'd thrust into her screaming flesh and grunted his enjoyment.

Silent tears escaped, and her mind zapped to Ramsay. They'd spent two glorious days together, and she treasured the memories. It might be the only thing to keep her sane because it was apparent her life here would hold nil satisfaction.

Already, the days blurred together. Adrik forced himself on her continuously. Three times, at least. Sometimes more. Gabrielle had learned not to fight him because he'd call for his guards to restrain her. She feigned delight in the entire business. The only blessing was sometimes he couldn't perform. A good thing, in her opinion, since he cared nothing for her. She was a broodmare. If Adrik's pride didn't get in the way, he'd do everything in a lab.

The first night, she'd asked if he might be the problem and not with his previous wives. That had started the beatings, and her agonized screams had stimulated him.

Gabrielle sniffed, trying to remain quiet. She couldn't leave the bed before her husband. One of many rules. Sex or no sex this morning? Time would tell. She kept her eyes closed and lay motionless, waiting for him to wake, waiting for his decision.

Her mother's last words stuck with her. Obviously, Gabrielle had inherited her mother's grit. Play by her husband's rules, and when he relaxed, thinking her broken, she'd carve out his guts with a knife. *She would survive this nightmare.*

She hadn't acquired a knife yet, but she would.

Adrik insisted on a healthy diet, so healthy she'd lose weight since her diet comprised fruit and vegetables, lean meats, and a host of vitamin tablets to prepare her body for pregnancy. She followed each crisp edict to the letter. One day, her guards would grow lax, giving her a chance to save herself.

What happened next was a mystery, but first things first. A weapon, then she'd fashion the rest of an escape plan.

Adrik stirred, and every muscle in her body stiffened. *Please, no.* Her heart beat faster and pounded in her ears so loudly, she wondered if he might hear. She kept her eyes closed when a soft knock came at the door. Adrik muttered under his breath and rose, uncaring about his nakedness. For his age, his body was fit, and he was prideful of this fact.

A murmur floated to her, and Adrik spoke a curt reply before shutting the door with a sharp click. He spat a word in Russian. Gabrielle waited anxiously, her heart still pounding. Goose bumps formed on her arms and legs. *Please, no. Please leave.*

The rustle of clothing hastily donned, and footsteps then the firm click of the door told her he'd gone, but she counted to five hundred before daring to roll to her back. A groan escaped, but she stifled the next. Adrik hated her for displaying discomfort. The weakness poked at his temper.

Slowly, so slowly, she rose from the bed, sweat forming on her skin. Blood filled her mouth. A lip torn from biting. In the shower, she let hot water flow over her bruised backside and aching back. She kept her opinions to herself and faked enjoyment. She ate the food servants gave her. At least she wasn't repeating mistakes. Today, she'd plan the dinner party Adrik had asked her to arrange for several business partners arriving tomorrow.

Yes, she was learning how to be the model wife.

Until the day an opportunity arose when she'd use every weapon at her disposal and take her revenge on her sadistic husband.

She'd do this with a smile.

Chapter 20

To The Rescue

"My contact says they're holding a business meeting at the estate," Isabella said. "That might be our way inside."

"How?" Saber asked.

"We'll intercept one guest before they arrive, and I'll enter in their place," Isabella said. "That's not something they'll expect."

"Popov will have protection, and his guests will bring their security," Felix said.

"Ah, but my contact is a guest," Isabella said with triumph. "He told me each visitor may bring two guards and no more."

"You couldn't have led with that?" Saber asked, his tone plaintive.

Isabella grinned. "Now, where is the fun in that?"

"All right," Saber said once they stopped cackling. "Would he let two of us go as his guards? We'll intercept another visitor, and Isabella can do her thing. She could take in another two of us as guards. Ramsay, you'd have to stay in the background because your girl will recognize you. Not your preference, I know, but that's our best ploy. If we get a chance, we'll let the rest know what's happening. If gunfire starts, come running. Tilly, we'll want you to stay with the plane and do first aid once we recover Gabrielle."

"I can do that," Tilly said. "What about weapons?"

"We won't be able to take firearms," Saber said.

"Yes, they'll get searched on arrival," Isabella confirmed. "We need to use fists. Teeth and claws."

Everyone apart from Tilly understood. She pursed her lips but didn't ask further questions.

"When will we know if your friend will cooperate?" Saber asked.

"I'll call him once we land. I think he'll be fine. He dislikes Popov. My assumption is that's why he's helping us."

Henry shrugged. "As long as we get the job done."

The closer they got to the private airfield, the more nerves jittered in Ramsay's belly. The others ate, but he couldn't. His mind stuck on Gabrielle in the clutches of this monster. He'd stopped reading the information Isabella had amassed because it sickened him. Isabella had discovered proof of the rumors, and that Gabrielle was suffering through this made Ramsay want to strike out. Although he couldn't have done anything more, it didn't lessen his guilt at failing his mate.

"Everyone try to grab sleep," Saber said. "We'll fine-tune our plan when we're half an hour out."

Ramsay reclined his seat and shut his eyes, but everything that could go wrong tormented him. What happened if they failed or one of his friends received an injury during the rescue attempt? And even worse, what if their attempt was successful and Gabrielle rejected him, his feline? What if the fact he and his friends shifted into leopards or wolves scared Gabrielle witless, and she left him?

He must've fallen asleep because his entire body jerked hard when Saber shook him awake. His mind churned and sweat coated his torso, yet chills ran through him. His mind jumped from fear to fear, and his dread morphed to monster proportions.

"Steady, lad." Kindness filled Saber's features. "I get this is hard, but we're gonna rescue your girl, then you can focus on the future."

Ramsay rose to join the others. His hands trembled, but he clenched both into fists and inhaled. He was useless to Gabrielle if he fell apart.

Saber and Isabella ran through the plan again.

"One more thing," Isabella said. "Guards, remember not to speak. Our accents will give us away. Grunts and curt nods for communication."

Once they'd landed. Isabella grabbed a box of clothes and handed out suits, shirts, and shoes, showing her preplanning and commitment to the strategy. "Gerard and Henry, you're used to working together. You're with my friend. This matters to him, so I think he'll come through for us, but watch him anyway. Leo and Felix, you're with me. Saber, you run operations and standby with Ramsay to offer aid where we need it. Questions?"

Those who were playing guards donned the suits.

"Can we keep our footwear? I'm used to my boots," Henry said.

"Sure, that will work," Isabella said. "Stand tall and look scary. Popov will have staff. Grab any opportunity to disarm or lock them in closets, otherwise, we'll improvise."

Tilly frowned. "Surely you need more weapons? What if your plan misfires? This is your one chance to free Gabrielle. Her husband will be on guard if you fail and hire more mercenaries to watch his back."

"We've worked together in dangerous situations," Saber said, his tone reasonable and patient. "Please don't worry. We have an excellent chance of pulling this off."

"But if you don't, Popov will take out his displeasure on Gabrielle. He might kill her," Tilly said.

Ramsay understood her apprehension but couldn't see any other way. "We'll get Gabrielle back," he said.

"Here comes my contact now," Isabella said, her voice calm. Her composure went a long way to settling Ramsay's trepidation. She greeted the man and returned with him at her side. "This is Timur. Four men are attending the meeting, one of whom is Timur's friend."

"How can we be sure you won't betray us?" Ramsay asked, his focus on Timur.

"Popov married my sister. She was dead six months later," Timur growled. "It's time to make him pay. My friend has his reasons, but neither of us will betray you. Isabella, you did me a solid and helped me recover my son after my enemies kidnapped him. I always pay my debts. You have no fears of my loyalty."

Isabella offered a clipped nod. "This is Henry and Gerard. Both are ex-military and work well together."

"Please come with me, and I'll explain how my team operates."

"Have you seen Gabrielle?" Ramsay asked.

"No, but my ex-brother-in-law expects his wife to act as hostess. Popov will ask her to leave once he wishes to discuss business. His first wife, who was pregnant, betrayed him, and he lost his temper and beat her to death."

"Why did you let your sister marry him, then?" Ramsay demanded. "If you understood his predilections."

"I had no choice," Timur snapped. "Popov wished to have a bride, and my sister fell in love with him. He assumed she'd be more biddable if she loved him. The bastard can wield charm if he wishes. We've incapacitated the man you're replacing. His guards fought us and died."

"That works," Isabella said and glanced at her watch. "Time to move."

Ramsay gave Tilly a quick hug and brushed a kiss on her soft cheek. Despite their short-lived acquaintance, he already thought of her as family—a valuable person from his mate's life. "Stay safe. I'll try to let you know when we're returning."

"Can I rely on the pilot?" she asked in an undertone.

"If Isabella trusts him, it'll be all right." Ramsay patted her hand and jogged away to join the others. Henry and Gerard traveled with Timur while the rest of them piled into a white van.

"I don't like this body," Isabella grumbled. "How does one deal with this extra baggage in the front?" She patted her podgy tummy with disdain.

"The trials of being a chameleon shifter." Leo, her husband, bore a broad grin. "I can confidently say I will not be kissing you until you resume your normal shape. It was bad enough when I kissed myself."

The others gawked at Leo before bursting into laughter. A tension release. The apprehension swarming inside Ramsay dialed back a notch, and he realized Isabella and Leo had done this on purpose. The shared merriment had relaxed them all.

Felix, who was driving the van, stopped out of sight of the house. "We'll let Ramsay and Saber off here because they'll search our vehicle at the gate."

Saber and Ramsay slid from the van and melted into the growing darkness.

"Deer," Saber said, cocking his head at the distinctive scent. "I have an idea."

He explained his strategy, and Ramsay nodded. "Let's do it."

Both men stripped and hid their clothes close to the road.

Ramsay shifted, welcoming the burst of discomfort and the rush of his feline senses. As soon as he bore his sleek leopard shape, he trotted after Saber. Once they approached the herd of deer, they parted and cautiously stalked nearer.

These were wild deer and wary. Their heads jerked up as they registered the predators. The does called in distress, gathering their youngsters close. The herd edged away toward the house where he and Saber wanted to drive them. Ramsay scented the roaming guards who stood watch at the property boundaries even from this distance. Fences surrounded the rear of Popov's home, but the view from the front of the house was not enclosed. Yes, guards patrolled the area, but no barrier meant they could drive the deer closer.

Create havoc.

As planned, the herd turned tail and ran, blind in their fear of this unknown threat. Their hooves thundered on the hard-packed road until they reached the manicured grass. They galloped toward the flat land at the front of the house. Ramsay corrected his angle, and he and Saber wheeled the herd to the right. Five minutes later, they tore across the lawn. A guard shouted. Several came running, but not one fired.

Well-trained.

Ramsay watched the herd's progress with satisfaction. No hidden traps or unseen weapons. Popov depended on his guards to protect the property frontage. At his side, Saber called in a low grunt. As one, they melted into the lengthening shadows. Once it was dark, he and Saber would take out the guards, one by one.

Satisfaction filled him.

Hold on, Gabrielle. We're coming for you.

Chapter 21

A Business Dinner

G abrielle checked on the progress in the kitchen.
"Stop harassing my staff," the cook, a stout
elderly woman with steel-gray hair, snapped at her.

"Sorry." Gabrielle understood the woman's quick
retort. Fear drove her. The emotion had about choked
Gabrielle each time she entered the kitchen. She'd created
a tasty yet simple menu with a spectacular dessert as a
centerpiece. The cook could handle this easily.

The cook's lined face softened, but none of the tension
left her shoulders. "Do you think Mr. Popov will approve
of this meal? Are you certain? Usually, he has rich meals
with complicated sauces."

Her accent was English with a tinge of French when she
became animated, and her qualifications were impeccable.
Nothing but the best for Adrik.

"I've observed him eating," Gabrielle said. "His preference is for healthy foods and dishes, not overly fussy with sauces and spices. The joint of beef looks delicious. Your selection of vegetables works, and you have a variation. Some are in cheese sauces, while others require no adornment. You have individual salads while your starter of avocado and prawns is perfect. Please don't worry. Just concentrate on doing the best job you can. If this meal displeases Adrik, I will step forward since I designed the menu."

The cook wrung her hands and cast a disproving stare at an underling paying close attention instead of preparing salads. She lowered her voice. "I've seen and heard what happens to those who fall into disfavor with Mr. Popov."

Gabrielle patted the woman's white, uniform-clad shoulder. "The smells coming from the kitchen are delectable. I foresee a triumph."

"I hope you're right," the cook grumbled. "My gut is jumping." She stomped away to issue orders to an underling.

Gabrielle stared after her, a rash of gooseflesh rippling across her arms and legs. Then, shaking herself, she went to add the final touches to the dining table and check everything lay in readiness.

Adrik arrived as she straightened the silverware. His gaze swept the table and the tasteful centerpiece comprising low squat candles and tiny delicate white flowers. She'd kept the height low to allow the men to talk without craning their necks.

"Very nice, my dear. I approve of the simplicity. It's unpretentious yet radiates class. I am pleased." He took her hand and raised it to his lips. It took everything inside her not to snatch her hand free and wipe it on her red dress. Adrik stepped back a fraction, turning his attention to her appearance. "You look stunning. Red suits you."

"Thank you," she murmured.

Then Adrik frowned. "Do you not have a pretty necklace to wear?"

"My mother kept my jewelry. She removed it from my possessions and informed me the pieces belonged to the family. I couldn't take them from Konstavia."

Adrik's scowl deepened. "I see. Wait there. Our guests should arrive shortly. Please have the guards check their identities before allowing them entrance."

"I will." Gabrielle fervently prayed this task didn't fall to her. She'd prefer Adrik to greet his guests since they were doing business with him, not her. Or was it a test? She frowned, tension sliding through her muscles. Aware she must relax if she was to make it through this evening, she sucked in deep breaths. A Tilly hint.

Immediately, sadness stole into prominence. She couldn't cry—another item on her forbidden list.

Luckily, Adrik reappeared in the dining room before anyone arrived. "Come here, my dear."

Once again, tension slid through her, along with frissons of terror. She forced her legs to propel her forward, to hold her upright. With a racing pulse, she stepped nearer, kept her expression passive. At least, that was her hope.

"Turn around."

Silently, she did as commanded. Adrik came up behind her and pressed cool lips to her nape before slipping the chilly stones around her neck and fastening it deftly.

"Thank you," she murmured.

"You're welcome, my dear. A beautiful necklace for my stunning and lovely wife."

"May I look in the mirror?" she asked because he expected this request.

"You may."

On still shaky limbs, she crossed to the antique mirror hanging on the far wall. Again, she lifted her hand to stroke the dazzling diamonds and sapphires because Adrik expected it of her. "Thank you, Adrik. It's exquisite."

"You deserve the necklace," he said warmly, although the cordiality never reached his eyes. Also unsaid but implied was the idea if Gabrielle behaved, she'd earn more rewards.

Gabrielle forced a smile. "Will your guests arrive soon? We can serve dinner once you're ready. You mentioned you'd like to have drinks first?"

"Yes, I'll greet my guests and take them to the formal lounge. I'd like you to wait there and serve us drinks. Can you do that?"

"Yes," Gabrielle said. Her mother had trained her well, insisting she be capable of hosting a dinner party. Now Gabrielle understood why the instruction had been necessary.

The doorbell chimed—one short peal.

"My first guest has arrived," Adrik said.

"I'll wait for you in the lounge." Gabrielle smiled and glided away, walking not too fast and acting not too reluctant. Let the bastard think he'd cowed her with a few blows and forced sex. Let him grow complacent.

She entered the lounge to find four of Adrik's guards. They stood against the far wall, close to the open terrace doors. A light breeze wafted through the thin curtains and dissipated the late summer heat. Gabrielle ignored the men and checked the contents of the drink cabinet.

Voices sounded in the entrance hall, along with low masculine laughter. All men and her. Such joy. Adrik was taking this opportunity to show her off. She understood that and hated the idea of his friends ogling her.

"Ah, Gabrielle, this is Timur and Constantine. Gentlemen, my wife."

Four men stepped into the room and placed their backs to the wall. They wore identical black suits and white shirts, their apparel from top designers. They glanced briefly at the guards, but their expressions didn't shift.

"You won't mind if one of my men conducts a weapon's search?" Adrik asked in a mild voice.

"We expected it," Timur, a blond with deep brown eyes said with a casual wave. "Go ahead. We have abided by the rules provided in your invitation."

Adrik signaled one of his guards before glancing at Gabrielle. He gave her a curt nod.

She glided forward. "Welcome, gentlemen. Can I get you something to drink?"

"I'll take a Scottish whisky on the rocks," Timur said.

"Same for me," Constantine said. He was an older man, but unlike Adrik, he had a distinct gut.

The bell chimed again.

"Ah, that will be James and Grigory. Right on time."

"Should I serve the canapes now?" Gabrielle asked Adrik.

"Yes, please."

She glided to the intercom. After a few quick words with the cook, she returned to their guests. Her gaze swept the newly arrived guards, her heart beating a little faster on cataloging the two of the men. They looked like brothers, both with black hair and green eyes. She bit back her instinctive cry because they reminded her of Ramsay. One gave an imperceptible shake of his head, and she angled her body to greet the new arrivals even as her mind raced.

Had she imagined his quick warning?

Her pulse galloping, she reached Adrik's side and waited for an introduction. "James, this is my wife, Gabrielle," Adrik said. "Grigory, my wife."

James reached for her hand and placed a kiss on her inner wrist. His avid gaze brought an urge to shudder, but she batted it back and reached for a polite smile.

Grigory nodded a silent greeting.

"I'm pleased to meet you. Can I get you a drink?"

"Straight vodka. No ice. Make it a double," James said.

"Same for me." It appeared Grigory was a man of few words.

"Of course," Gabrielle murmured, her mind busily working as she poured the newcomers' drinks. She handed them over with a faint smile. "Adrik, something to drink?"

"I'll take a vodka. Ice," he said.

Nodding, she prepared the drink while wishing she had poison to tip into it. Something to consider for the future.

One of the young kitchen helpers arrived carrying a plate of hot canapes.

"Maria, please set them on the table," Gabrielle said. "We will serve ourselves." The cook had told her sometimes the visitors molested the female workers. That wouldn't happen while she was here.

James walked up behind the girl and groped her breast. Gabrielle took half a step forward to intervene before Adrik's hand curled around her biceps in a punishing grip.

"Leave," he growled in her ear.

Gabrielle watched James, contempt and disgust holding her stiff. The randy old bastard. The girl was eighteen. Obviously, he didn't intend to cease his harassment, and Adrik would do nothing to stop it.

"James," Timur said, amusement rippling through his accented voice. "Are we going to start our discussions, or would you like us to wait for you?"

Gabrielle didn't think the man's accent was Russian. But she liked the way Timur diffused the situation with humor. James gave the servant a last squeeze and slapped her on the backside. Gabrielle caught the distaste on the third man's face—quickly concealed, but it made her relax a fraction. Her husband wouldn't care what his visitors did because he considered his staff possessions, including her. He might not like them destroyed, but slight damage wouldn't bother him. *Bastard*.

"Gentlemen, I'll check on things in the kitchen. Dinner will be ready when you are." She sent a practiced smile in her husband's direction and waited for his faint nod of agreement. A week with him was enough to make her hate him. She could see how death might be a release from his constant attention.

"Dinner in fifteen minutes, gentlemen? Would that suit you?" Adrik asked.

Gabrielle couldn't tell what her husband was thinking or if he wished to impress these men or kill them. She couldn't read him, and she'd require that skill if she had any chance of escape.

"I need a drink," James snapped, thrusting his empty glass in Gabrielle's direction.

"Of course. Let me get you more vodka." Gabrielle took the glass and barely stopped her shudder when the man's clammy hands squeezed her arm, supposedly in thanks, but she knew better.

He sent her on her way with a furtive grope of her backside. Gabrielle restrained her instinct to slap his face. "I like this one, Adrik. If you tire of her, please send her my way. I've never fucked a princess."

"I have," Adrik said with a chuckle. "This one might be a keeper."

With her back to Adrik and James, Gabrielle poured a generous measure of vodka into the glass and scowled at it. The bastard. A swift kick in the balls would jolt his arrogance free. He was despicable, even worse than Adrik. Gabrielle schooled her expression and turned to the men.

"James, your drink."

When she handed it to him, he thrust his hand between her legs. Gabrielle jumped, then stumbled because she'd landed on his foot. His vodka tipped from her grip and wet his shirt.

"Oh, I'm so sorry," she said.

"Look what you've done," James snapped, swiping at his damp shirt. He reprimanded her with a slap before shoving her from him.

One guard jumped forward and helped her to regain her balance. "Go to the kitchen," he whispered.

"I apologize for my clumsiness," Gabrielle said, trying to ignore her stinging cheek. The guard's accent was the same as Ramsay's. Gabrielle ripped her gaze away to check with her husband. "Would you excuse me while I see to dinner?"

"Of course, my dear," he said, and his voice held a trace of warmth.

Relief had her weak at the knees, but she exited the lounge and made her way swiftly to the bedroom she shared with Adrik. Her dress was wet from the vodka since it had splattered her too. She'd change and go back to the kitchen. If she hurried, she'd have time. She exchanged her gown for another, equally expensive and fussy. In the en suite, she checked her hair. When she reapplied her lipstick, she recalled the items in the medicine cabinet.

She hesitated for a long moment before plucking the jar of laxatives off the shelf.

"Have the guards eaten yet?" she asked the cook in an undertone on reaching the kitchen.

"Not yet. I'm about to plate their stew."

Summoning her courage because this was a crazy risk, she handed the pills to the cook. "Could you add these to the stew?" Was the cook loyal to Adrik? She'd find out soon.

The cook's eyes widened, and she shot a glance at the other staff, thankfully at the far end of the kitchen. For once, they weren't eavesdropping. She turned her attention back to Gabrielle. "Has something happened?"

"Not sure. I know it's a gamble, but my gut tells me now is the time."

They shared a long look, and finally, the cook gave a grudging nod. She slipped the pills into her pocket. "When does the master want his meal?"

"In a quarter of an hour."

The cook checked on her underlings. "Ladies," she called, "we have fifteen minutes before service. Have a quick break, but return in ten minutes."

The staff downed tools and disappeared into the staff room.

"You realize if you've misread this situation, we'll be in danger."

Gabrielle gave her a grim smile. "Yes."

"And you're still willing to risk this move?"

"Yes."

"Very well," the cook said. "Do you have a weapon?"

Gabrielle shook her head.

"Take a fork off the table and slip it into a pocket. Stab anyone who gives you problems, and don't hesitate."

"All right. Can I help with anything?"

"Yes. Pray you've made the right decision, and help me grind these tablets."

Chapter 22

Displeasure

Gabrielle finished in the kitchen and tapped on the lounge door before entering. "Gentlemen, if you'd like to move to the dining room, I'm about to serve dinner."

"No guards," Adrik said. "I wish to eat my meal without distractions."

"Will you have guards?" Timur asked.

"I instructed the kitchen to feed them. We will be alone because I don't wish anyone to eavesdrop on our conversation. Your guards may wait with mine."

Gabrielle heard the words as she left to inform the cook and blanched. No, that wouldn't do. They'd need to feed them. She burst into the kitchen and glanced at the stovetop where the large stew pot had resided. "Is there no stew left?"

"I fed the scraps to the dogs," the cook said.

Relief surged through Gabrielle. "The visiting guards are waiting with Adrik's protection team. Could we make them sandwiches once we've served lunch?"

The cook inclined her head. "Yes, I'll get the girls to make sandwiches. Enough for everyone."

She and the cook completed the appetizers of avocado and prawns for serving. Mindful of the poor maids, Gabrielle carried the four plates to the dining room herself. The guards had disappeared, and only Adrik and the other men remained. "Take a seat, gentlemen."

Gabrielle transported the appetizers to the table.

"Are you not joining us?" Constantine asked.

"Not for the appetizer. I'll give you a chance to speak in private and will return in half an hour to clear the plates."

"Thank you, my dear." Adrik beamed, and she took this as approval.

Once she left the dining room, Gabrielle entered the kitchen to find pandemonium. *Uh-oh.* That stuff must've been strong to act this fast. "What's wrong?"

"She served us poisonous food," a guard said, towering over the cook. He bent without warning and held his bulging belly. Then he fled the kitchen, his heavy, rapid footsteps thundering down the hall.

Gabrielle gasped, affecting shock. "The other guards? Should I check?"

"I suppose one of us should because I deny my food caused this." The cook bristled like a hedgehog. "The girls had a bowl of stew," she told Gabrielle. "Are you well?"

Both kitchen assistants nodded and continued making sandwiches.

"I'll do a quick check before helping you plate the main course. Can you do six meals, please? Adrik expects me to eat with the men."

The laxatives *were* quick-acting, and several guards gripped their stomachs, their faces contorted in pain. The newcomers stood together, out of the way, their gazes watchful.

"What happened?" Gabrielle asked.

An outpouring of Russian, angry in tone, blasted her.

"I'm sorry, I don't understand."

"The cook poisoned us," one guard said.

"Why would she do that? What did you eat?"

"Stew," the man spat.

"The kitchen staff ate stew for lunch. They are perfectly fine."

"Then why are we sick?" the man demanded.

"Did you drink anything?"

"We had beer, as we always do," the man spat.

"Did everyone drink beer?"

"Da."

"And everyone ate stew?"

"Da," he repeated in the affirmative.

"I'm sorry. I don't know what to tell you," Gabrielle said. "It's time to serve dinner for Adrik, but if you're still ill after lunch, I'll ask my husband to call a medical man."

The man paled, slapped his hand over his rumbling gut, and fled.

"Was it something I said?" Gabrielle muttered, keeping her voice low because she'd learned on the first day there were ears everywhere.

Someone chuckled, but not one man looked at her when Gabrielle whirled. Aware of the passing time, she returned to the dining room to clear the plates, making sure she knocked before she entered. Another lesson she'd learned on her first day.

"Ah, there you are, my dear." Displeasure flitted across Adrik's features, and everything inside her pulled taut.

"Did you require something?" she asked in a polite voice.

"James would like another vodka."

"Certainly. Did anyone else require a top-up?"

"Drinks for everyone," Adrik ordered.

A delicate shudder ran the length of her body, and she tried to hide it, but Adrik noticed. Not much escaped him, and he smiled, her fear pleasing him.

"I'll clear the plates and bring back drinks for you." Gabrielle tried not to show her nerves, but the cutlery and crockery jingled together. She delivered the dishes to the kitchen.

She was halfway to the lounge to get fresh drinks when Adrik roared for her. Terror flooded her, and she stood, poised to flee. She swallowed hard, retraced her steps on unsteady feet, and found the headguard with Adrik and the men. Damn it. She'd forgotten the fork.

"Do you know anything about the sick guards?" Adrik demanded.

"No, I've been with you. I checked on them, but I don't know why the guards are sick."

Adrik slapped her across the face so hard she hit the table. Her hand caught the white linen tablecloth as she fell and silverware, glasses, and candle arrangements rained on her head. Oh, this was bad. Adrik would blame her if he didn't kill her for embarrassing him in front of his friends.

"Clumsy bitch," Adrik growled and darted forward to grasp her by the hair. Panic bloomed in Gabrielle—a fear she'd pushed past his patience limits. Instinct had her grabbing the nearest fork and lashing out at him. Adrik released a pained screech and kicked her in the stomach. Agony suffused her. She gasped for breath, and it was like sucking through a straw. He'd winded her. Adrik screeched at her, a string of guttural Russian wasted on her because she didn't understand.

When Adrik kicked her again, she tried to crawl away, to escape. A visitor grasped Adrik and dragged him away, stopping him from striking her again.

Adrik's guard pulled his weapon, but Timur knocked his arm, and the shot went wide. An instant later, Adrik lay unmoving on the floor, and she wasn't sure how.

A crash sounded to her right, and James toppled like a mighty pine. Gabrielle shook, unsure of what was happening.

"You're okay now," a female voice said. "It's safe to put down the fork." A woman with blonde hair crouched beside Gabrielle, her smile friendly despite the trickle of blood from a nick on her chin. "Do you know where our guards are?"

"Down the passage, the door after the kitchen," Gabrielle said, her gaze darting left and right. She edged away. What had happened? Was she safe? Truly? Or was the woman just saying that? And where had she come from? Gabrielle hadn't heard the door.

"I'll go," Timur said.

"Gabrielle, truly, you're safe now or as secure as we can be until we leave here."

"Who are you?"

"I'm Isabella, Ramsay's friend. We came to rescue you if that's what you want. Put the fork down. I promise not to hurt you."

Gabrielle hesitated because she didn't think Ramsay had the resources to create a scheme like this. He was a chef. No. Was this a plot Adrik had hatched to test her loyalty? It was possible with his scheming mind. A laugh burst from her, and even to her ears, it sounded crazed.

"Who the fuck are you?" *Adrik.* He'd woken pissed, and a whimper escaped Gabrielle, but the blonde woman never flinched.

"Bitch," he muttered, spying Gabrielle. "Get out of my sight. And you, Blondie, come here. I might need another wife. You look healthy enough."

"Not an option," a calm male voice said. "Isabella is married to me."

Adrik stood and pulled a gun from the hollow of his back. He gestured with the weapon. "Get over there. I guessed something was up when Timur requested a meeting. Together, where I can see you." Her husband resembled a growling bear with his teeth pulled back in a sneer and his light blue eyes so icy cold.

"Yet you invited him to visit, anyway," the blonde said, not even quailing at the sight of a gun.

Instead of following Adrik's orders, the pair remained on opposite sides of the room. They didn't fear him, and Gabrielle could tell their calmness infuriated her husband.

Adrik gestured wildly with the gun. "Restrain him."

Gabrielle swallowed, her mind overriding her earlier panic. They couldn't let Adrik get the upper hand. Amazingly, she still clutched the fork in her hand. This man had brutalized her, and he'd continue to do so unless she became pregnant. However, pregnancy would only be a temporary reprieve. Once she'd produced a son, he'd no longer need her. She was dispensable.

Gabrielle edged closer to him, unsure of what she intended to do until he fired the gun. Then she acted on instinct. She jabbed Adrik in the thigh with her fork, not holding back in the force of her strike.

Chapter 23

Rescue

Ramsay heard the commotion, the crack of gunfire, and glanced at Saber. He transformed into his human form and waited for Saber to shift. "Should we go in?"

"Not yet, but we'll move closer. The guards haven't changed recently, so let's take out these before they investigate."

"Yeah, I noticed the pair checking their watches and comparing notes. Interesting that the gunfire hasn't shifted them. It's almost as if they expected it."

"Yeah, my thoughts exactly. Isabella's friend doesn't think much of Adrik, which tells me the truth is worse than the rumors," Saber said.

"I'll cover the two on the right."

Saber hand signaled agreement and shifted back to his feline form. Stealthily, he slid into the shadows, and Ramsay did the same. Although Middlemarch had faced danger, he'd never taken part, and he was seeing a new side to his adopted family. They were scary as shit. Ramsay gave a feline smirk.

Ramsay slinked closer to the two guards, who were muttering in undertones. His scant knowledge of Russian was yes and no. He took the first one down by leaping at him. He hesitated to strike a killing blow, then hardened his heart, snapped the man's neck and jumped at the second. These men worked for Adrik Popov and had committed atrocities on his behalf. The second guard thought faster than the first and pulled his weapon. It fired. A bullet burned a furrow along his side, and Ramsay snarled his displeasure. He pounced at the man, anger burning away every scrap of hesitation.

Saber called to him, and Ramsay answered with a sharp growl. He trotted toward Saber, freezing, when a truck slowed at the gate. A man—a soldier—jumped out and cautiously approached the gatehouse. He cut the fence and crawled through when he found no one present. He disappeared, and the gate slowly opened for the vehicle access. It halted again, and a dozen heavily armed men slipped from the rear. They fanned out and approached the house, their weapons at the ready.

Another gun fired indoors, and a man screamed, the sound abruptly cutting off.

Ramsay and Saber shared a glance, each desperate to know what was happening inside—Saber because his brothers were inside and Ramsay because his mate was in danger.

Saber released a roar and fell silent.

A door opened, and Isabella called out. "Saber, we're coming out. We have Gabrielle."

Timur strode outside and whistled. The soldiers they'd watched arrive stepped out of the shadows. "Lock the place down," he ordered. "Most guards are in the room near the kitchen. They're still armed, but they're sick. Gabrielle informs me she and the cook fed them laxatives in their stew, so it's not contagious."

"This wasn't part of the plan," Isabella snapped.

"You didn't think I helped out of the goodness of my heart," her friend mocked. "I've had my eye on Adrik's territory for some time, which will give me kudos with my competitors."

Isabella stared at him, and from where he and Saber stood, Ramsay noted her irritation. "You're going to let us leave with the girl."

"I am," Timur said. "We're square now. Next time you pay."

Isabella offered him a curt nod. "Thanks for your help. Make sure you treat the cook with respect. She is a brave woman to help her mistress."

Timur gave a rueful smile. "I'll help her leave. I'm not sure I'd ever trust a cook who'd doctor the food."

Isabella laughed. "In that, we are of accord. Can we take the vehicle back to the airstrip?"

"Yes," Timur said. "Leave the keys inside, and I'll have one of my men collect it."

"Right guys, we're leaving. Should we take the cook with us?" Isabella asked.

Timur waved a hand and disappeared inside. "If she wishes to leave." His words floated back as Saber and Ramsay moved nearer.

Ramsay strained forward, desperate to see Gabrielle. She emerged behind Isabella. Leo, Felix, Henry, and Gerrard walked protectively behind her, ready to catch her if she fell. And it was apparent she was hanging on by a single thread. Blood covered her frilly pale blue gown, and she shook noticeably.

Ramsay stepped closer, every instinct telling him to go to her, to soothe his mate and tell her everything would be all right.

"Where are you taking me?" Her fear-filled words reached Ramsay. "I won't. I can't return to the palace. My parents will sell me again, and I-I can't..." Tears dampened her cheeks.

Ramsay saw them, and it wrecked him. He hated to see his brave mate crying.

Saber nudged him, and when Ramsay glanced at him, Saber gave a low growl of approval.

Right. Ramsay hesitated, but would there ever be a suitable time to show Gabrielle his feline? He stalked from the faint shadows and stepped into the light.

"Gabrielle," Isabella said. "Ramsay is here."

"Ramsay?"

Ramsay spotted the second she noticed him—his leopard form. He prowled closer, trying to appear unthreatening and failing. She froze, her eyes growing wide. She tried to pull away from Isabella, but Isabella held her ground. Panic slid across Gabrielle's face, and Ramsay sucked in a breath and called up his human form. He needed his words, his arms to hold her and reassure her.

But would she panic when she saw him? Too late to worry about it now.

He morphed further into his shift and winced when he heard her squeak. Isabella reassured her with quiet words.

Ramsay didn't know what they were but discerned the murmur. Then he stood before them, naked.

"Gabrielle," he whispered.

Shock colored her face, and she wobbled. Her eyes rolled back in her head, and Ramsay jumped forward to catch her before she hit the ground.

Saber shifted. "Is she hurt?"

"They're superficial wounds, but we should get her checked out by a doctor once we arrive in Scotland. We'll travel to Edinburgh. Tilly will tend her on the plane, and I can help," Isabella said. "She looks exhausted and has bruises on her arms. We'll find more under her clothing."

Ramsay scooped Gabrielle into his arms. "Where to now?"

"One of us can get the van and drive closer. The rest of us will walk along the road to meet you," Saber said.

"I'll go for the vehicle," Henry said and set off at a jog.

"I'll ask if the cook wants to come with us." Isabella disappeared and reappeared minutes later. "She's staying. Her husband is here, and they'll decide together."

Their departure from the property was down the main driveway and not in the same stealthy manner they'd arrived. Ramsay carried an unconscious Gabrielle, worry nagging him. Had she fainted because of an injury? Or had it been his changing from leopard to human that had done the trick? They reached the van, and she still didn't stir.

"Give her to me," Gerard said. "I'll hand her up to you."

Five minutes later, they were on their way. After a brief stop to retrieve his and Saber's clothes, they continued. They saw no one, but still, relief filled Ramsay once they arrived at the airstrip. Henry parked the van, and everyone piled out. Tilly came running when she saw them.

"Is she all right?" Tilly asked, her lined face full of worry.

"She's breathing. We're not sure what's wrong with her," Ramsay said.

"Why aren't you wearing clothes?"

Ramsay wanted to roll his eyes but resisted. "It's a long story. I'll get Gabrielle settled in the plane, and you can tend her." He didn't wait for Tilly to reply but strode toward the plane.

As he approached, the door opened, and steps settled into position. Ramsay boarded, and Tilly and the others followed him. Ramsay set Gabrielle in a seat and strapped her in. "Tilly, you'll have to sit because we're leaving straightaway."

Ramsay scrambled into his clothes and took a seat. Everyone else hustled too. As soon as they boarded, the plane taxied away from the hangar.

The plane hurtled along the runway and barreled into the sky. Pre-dawn and black, with only the moon and stars for light, they left the confines of the airstrip.

When the plane leveled off, Isabella turned to Tilly. "It's safe to check on Gabrielle. Do you need help?"

Tilly fumbled with her seat belt. "Please. What happened? Shouldn't she have regained consciousness by now? Did someone hit her?"

"Popov whacked her across the jaw and kicked her, but she was awake. She walked from the house under her own steam," Isabella said.

Ramsay unfastened his seatbelt and did the same for Gabrielle. He lifted her out of her seat and laid her on the floor. He and Tilly checked for injuries, but she seemed unharmed apart from the cut cheek and the bruises on her arms.

"Perhaps we should let her sleep," Tilly said. "Her breathing is fine. She's paler than normal, but I can't see any reason for her deep sleep."

Isabella and Ramsay shared a glance. Could shock do this?

"We'll get her to a doctor, I promise. If she takes a turn for the worse, let us know, and we'll divert to somewhere in Europe. Otherwise, we're flying to Edinburgh," Saber said.

They hit a patch of turbulence, and Ramsay placed Gabrielle in her seat. He fastened the seat belt and sat and did his own.

"Try to sleep, Tilly. I'll watch over Gabrielle."

Saber had contacted a doctor, a shifter doctor, and he met them at the private airport. Gabrielle didn't stir until after they'd landed. Ramsay carried Gabrielle into the waiting room and stood back to allow the doctor to examine her.

"Could it be shock, Doctor?" Ramsay asked in a low voice. "She saw me shift. She didn't know."

"Tilly," the doctor said after introductions from Saber. "Does Gabrielle have any health issues I should know about?"

"No, she's healthy and eats a restricted diet. A wholesome diet."

The doctor took her pulse and listened to her heart. He checked the cut on her cheek and leaned closer to sniff. "That distinctive odor. It reminds me of something. It will come to me soon. Will you help me undress her?"

Ramsay stood back but sucked in a harsh breath at seeing Gabrielle's back. Welts covered her skin—the kind made by a belt. Her curved backside also carried the same marks.

"They appear recent," the doctor said.

"They weren't there the last time I saw Gabrielle," Ramsay said.

"She has an infection. Her breathing and heartbeat are normal. I assume she's stressed, and this is her body's way of coping. If she doesn't wake in an hour, I'll start more tests, but truly, I think she's sleeping."

"Doctor," Tilly said. "Her parents placed a tracker at the base of her skull. Would you be able to remove it?"

"Does Gabrielle know of its presence?" the doctor asked.

"She recently learned, and the discovery shocked her," Tilly said.

"Let me see if I can locate it," the doctor said. "Ah, yes. There is a tiny bump. Easy enough to take it out."

"Do it," Ramsay said, his voice hard. "No one should have that sort of control over their adult child. This tracker is an invasion of privacy."

The doctor turned Gabrielle onto her side. "Please hold her in position."

Ramsay held her and watched the quick slice of the doctor's scalpel. "Got it," the doctor said and dropped it into a silver bowl along with his used instruments. "How do you want to destroy it?"

Ramsay shrugged.

The doctor grinned, the curve of his lips taking on an air of cunning. "I have a suggestion. A friend of mine is visiting the Orkney Islands tomorrow. He could take it and drop it in the ocean. The tracker will remain live for longer, but this will confuse anyone who searches for it."

"Done," Ramsay said.

"I'll be off then. If she doesn't wake in the next few hours, call me. I'll come immediately," the doctor said.

"I'll sit with her," Tilly said once the doctor left. "You can watch her later after you've rested. You and your friends will want to sleep."

Saber entered the room. "We're flying home tomorrow. Would you and Gabrielle like to come with us?"

Tilly stared at Saber, her eyes wider than Ramsay had ever seen. "Go to New Zealand? To live?"

"Come for a visit. At the very least, it will keep Gabrielle away from her parents. We can't risk them snatching her again." Saber smiled, but it held an edge Ramsay rarely saw in the community leader. "I can't abide men who abuse women. I want to kill that brute again, and Gabrielle's parents are no better."

"Do you think I frightened her?" Ramsay said.

"You?" Tilly snorted in disbelief. "I doubt it. She has fallen for you in a big way. I've never seen her so happy."

Ramsay swallowed hard and glanced to Saber for guidance.

Saber came to his rescue. "Tilly, we're not ordinary people. All of us are feline shifters, apart from Henry. He's a wolf. Gabrielle saw Ramsay shift before she fainted."

Tilly smiled wide, her eyes as big as her toothy grin. "You're teasing me."

"No," Saber said.

"No," Ramsay reiterated.

Tilly stood and planted her hands on her ample hips. She lifted her head, her gaze full of challenge. "You need to prove it because seeing is believing."

Chapter 24

Ramsay's Secret

G abrielle's head thumped, and her back stung as if it were on fire. She struggled to open her eyes, and a groan escaped despite her attempted silence.

"Gabrielle, kitten."

That voice. She recognized him. This time, she opened her eyes.

"Kitten, how do you feel? Would you like a drink of water?"

Bathroom. "Ramsay," she croaked and struggled from the bed. He seemed to understand and helped her to the en suite. He was waiting when she emerged and led her back to the bed. She sat, not ready to sleep again.

The last thing she remembered was stabbing Adrik with her fork. She vaguely recalled doing it more than once, determined not to let him hurt her ever again. After that, she recollected nothing. No, wait!

"You were there," she said, her brow crinkling. "You were at my h-husband's house. There was shooting and...and..." Her gaze darted to his green one, shock catapulting through her. "I saw a leopard then you were there. Naked. You were naked."

Ramsay's warm hand curled around her cold one. His expression didn't change, and he remained silent, neither denying her words nor telling her a hit on the head had addled her brain.

"Was... Did that happen?" She licked her lips, her heart beating too fast.

"Were you frightened?" Ramsay asked.

"No. At least, I don't think so. My memory is a little hazy. What happened?"

"First, how is your head? Do you have a headache? Feel nauseous?"

Gabrielle tried a cautious stretch and winced. "My back hurts."

"Someone beat you. Your husband?"

She gave a jerky nod.

"You don't have to worry about him ever again. He can no longer hurt you."

Her breath eased out. "Adrik is dead?"

"You stabbed him with your fork. You were so brave. Smart, despite the danger. You helped to incapacitate the soldiers. It gave us a chance to beat Popov."

"He intended to kill me. You...your friends stopped him." She stared at him, puzzlement chased by sheer wonder. "You changed from leopard to man. I didn't imagine that."

"Can you keep a secret, Gabrielle?"

She stared deep into his beautiful green eyes, her stomach swooping and bucking, confusion, apprehension slicing deep. She wasn't sure she wanted to hear what he intended to say. "Maybe," she said and bit into her bottom lip.

"Gabrielle, I care for you. A lot. I want you in my future, but this secret—you need the truth before going further."

"Okay." She drew out the word, still unsure.

"Tilly already knows. She was a hard sell and insisted on proof."

Gabrielle frowned hard enough to crease her brow. "Um, how did Tilly react?"

Ramsay's grin turned broad. "She lined up my friends and me and made us do a reveal. The guys had to call their wives for approval."

"I don't understand."

"You'll have to do with me," Ramsay said drily. "Jealousy will strike if you do a Tilly on me."

"Um, is Tilly okay?" Her mind officially boggled even as it raced for answers. Her thoughts had officially strolled off the highway and onto the back roads.

"Yes. Let me get you a glass of water and a painkiller. The doctor said the welts on your back have become infected. Tilly is sorting out the antibiotic prescription. She should be back soon."

"Where are we?"

"Edinburgh." Ramsay retreated and returned with the water. He handed it and two white tablets to her. "Take these."

Once she'd downed them and the water, Ramsay unbuttoned his shirt and shrugged out of it. He unfastened the button on his jeans.

She blinked. "What are you doing?"

"Showing you my secret," Ramsay said. "You were out of it before. This is the best way." He shrugged out of his clothes until he was fully naked. She stared—starting from his shoulders and working down. His broad chest tapered to slim hips and strong thighs. The wretched man chuckled, dragging her attention back to his face. A faint shimmer formed around his body, and memories stormed back. She'd spotted the leopard, recalled struggling to breathe past her panic, backing up against a wall. The leopard had turned into Ramsay. He'd been naked, and he'd picked her up and carried her to safety. She'd thought... Hadn't that been a dream?

"Ramsay." Her hand flew to her mouth. "Is...is that really you?"

The leopard stalked closer. Every one of her muscles tensed, ready to propel her to safety. The black cat kept coming until his hot breath seared her leg. She gasped, ready to shout, to scream, to do something, but he rubbed his head against her knee and released a rumbly purr.

Her breath whooshed out, and she tentatively placed her hand on his back. She ran her fingers over his silky black fur, and he leaned into her. Footfalls at the door had fear slapping her, but it was Tilly and another man.

"Are you all right, child?" Tilly asked, her eyes twinkling. She gestured at the man beside her. "This is Saber."

Gabrielle managed a nod at him before placing her focus on Tilly. "This is Ramsay's secret?"

Tilly's smile widened. "All of them. They're decent people, Gabrielle. I like them a lot. Saber asked if we'd like to go to New Zealand with them. I think we'd be safe there."

"What about my tracker?"

"It's gone. The doctor who checked on you took it out," Tilly said. "We've disposed of it."

"Thank goodness. I'd hate to put anyone in danger. If my parents have shown me anything, it's that they're unscrupulous and will do anything to save their skins. They care nothing for their children's welfare." Her laugh held dark despair. Bitterness. "I used to think if I was good enough, worked hard enough, gained my parents' respect, it'd be sufficient. Instead, they sold me to that monster."

She shuddered, digging her fingers into Ramsay's fur. His sharp growl dragged her from her memories, but she couldn't rid herself of the fury in Adrik's eyes when she'd stabbed him. He hadn't expected that, and if he'd lived, she would've suffered for the impudence. On the counter side, she'd enjoyed his pain—her revenge and defiance.

"I laughed when I stabbed Adrik and took pleasure in the second time I did it. Am I horrible?"

"No you're smart," Tilly snapped. "Child, if I'd been present, I might've done the same thing. You fought with the weapons you had to hand. That Popov man wouldn't have hesitated to hurt you worse. We've heard the rumors regarding his previous wives, and the chances are the same thing would've happened to you. Push away the guilt. You survived, and that is what you should focus on—your future. Your happiness."

"It's not that easy." Gabrielle stared at her fingers and the contrasting black fur beneath them.

Tilly laid her fingers on her arm, her expression kind. "If you had a choice, what would you want, Gabrielle?"

"To go with Ramsay," Gabrielle said, the words falling from her lips with ease. "But what happens if I'm pregnant?" Tears overflowed, and she lifted her hand from Ramsay's back to swipe at them.

"Even if you're pregnant, you have choices," Tilly said. "Either you wipe your tears, straighten your shoulders, and walk forward with confidence and a can-do attitude, or you slither into guilt and let your parents' actions destroy you. Only you can make this decision. You've craved your freedom for years. Now, you have it, and it's up to you to make what you will of your life."

Gabrielle swallowed hard and focused on the silent Saber. Although he'd remained quiet, he exuded power and confidence. Ramsay respected this man, and she trusted Ramsay.

"What would happen if Tilly and I go to New Zealand with you? Would it be a visit? A holiday or something else? Are all of you like Ramsay?"

Saber smiled. "You remind me of my Emily back when I was trying to persuade her to stay in Middlemarch and become my wife. Like you, Emily is human, although now, because she wears my mark, she's healthier than most humans and ages more like a feline. We live for longer."

"You persuaded her to marry you?" Gabrielle asked, curious.

"I did, and I've never regretted a day of our marriage. Not every day has been a good one. We've suffered through troubles and come out the other side together and stronger. Humans and shifters live in Middlemarch. Several felines have human mates. We support each other and enjoy a good life. You can visit, but you must keep our secret."

"I'd agree to that, anyway. You saved me from Adrik, and I owe your people my life," Gabrielle said. "You have my gratitude."

Saber's expression softened. "Thank you. If you decide to come to Middlemarch, you can stay with Ramsay, or we'll find alternative accommodation for you and Tilly."

"I'll talk to Tilly."

"Sorry to rush you, Gabrielle, but you have a few hours to decide. We fly out this afternoon."

"I'll let you know in an hour."

Saber inclined his head. "Isabella is dragging us off shopping, and we're busting to visit Edinburgh Castle while we're here. Let us know your decision when we return. We'll be wheels-up shortly afterward."

"Thank you," Gabrielle said.

Ramsay followed Saber, but Gabrielle placed a hand on his silky back. "Please stay for a few minutes. I won't keep you long."

Ramsay backed away and shifted to his human form. Gabrielle watched in fascination, although she winced a few times because of the stretching and snapping bones.

"Does that hurt?" she demanded as Ramsay reached for his discarded clothes.

"Can I look now?" Tilly asked, who'd covered her face.

"Keep your eyes closed for a few minutes longer," Gabrielle said. "Tilly, do you think we should go to New Zealand?"

"Yes. The farther we travel from Konstavia, the happier I'll be. Your parents are out of control, and we'd fare better out of their reach."

"I agree," Gabrielle said. "What about your friends? Will you not miss them?"

"New Zealand is a plane ride away. It's not a different planet," Tilly said. "They'll visit me. None of them wanted to go to Konstavia because it was dangerous, but New Zealand is an attractive proposition."

"You don't have to stay if you hate it in Middlemarch," Ramsay said, now fully dressed.

Everything in Gabrielle softened, the decision suddenly simple. "I can't imagine hating Middlemarch when you're there. Ramsay, I'm going with you."

"Gabrielle, just so we're clear, I want you in my life, to marry and mate with you in the feline way. You'll like my friends. My adopted family. You and Tilly will fit in well."

"And if I'm pregnant?"

"If you're pregnant, I'll love your baby, and we'll raise him or her with values and family and support, or if you prefer, there are other options." Ramsay never hesitated, making Gabrielle believe his sincerity.

She stepped closer and kissed him tenderly before stepping back. "Go shopping and sightseeing. Please bring back some Scottish shortbread because Tilly and I are fond of it."

"Done," Ramsay said. "Are you sure you and Tilly don't want to come with us?"

"No, I intend to call my parents. I won't tell them our destination, but I need this closure. I need them to understand I'm done."

Ramsay stole another kiss, and his open approval gave her the extra strength she needed to speak with her parents and draw a line in the sand.

"Just shortbread?" he asked.

"I'd like loose leaf tea and to say goodbye to my friend. Could you drop me off at his place and pick me up when you're done?" Tilly asked.

"Done deal," Ramsay said. "The others are heading out now. Are you ready?"

"Yes."

"Tilly, can I borrow your phone?"

"Yes. I thought it best if we left it here when we leave. The fewer ways your parents have to track us, the better."

"See you soon." Gabrielle waved and sat on the bed. She sucked in a deep breath and dialed her mother's number.

"Tilly, where are you?" Her mother's voice sounded panicked. "Do you know where Gabrielle is? We heard a rival gang took out Adrik."

"Mother, it's Gabrielle."

"Gabrielle, where are you? You must come home."

"So you can marry me off to the next man in the line? I don't think so. I'm calling to tell you goodbye."

"But where are you? Your tracker is behaving weirdly as if it is malfunctioning."

Gabrielle's lips curled, and disgust blasted through the last child/parent bond that had remained. Her parents were still trying to manipulate her into helping them. They cared nothing for her feelings or safety. "If you don't leave me be, I'll take a restraining order against you and

225

anyone from the palace. The Konstavia newspaper will receive anonymous tips featuring the truth. I was lucky to escape Adrik alive, but neither you nor the king cared for my safety. I've had enough, and Tilly and I will not be returning to Konstavia. Not ever."

"That woman is a bad influence on you," her mother snapped. "She should've kept you calm and pliable."

Gabrielle released a snort. "Oh, please. She was my jailor, except she didn't stick with the plan. Let me repeat, I will never return to Konstavia to be your obedient little puppet. I will not help save you from whatever calamity you're mired in. You and Father are dead to me. I've lost what little respect I had for you, and since you're untrustworthy, I'm turning my back on you and walking away. Goodbye, Mother. Have a nice life." Gabrielle hung up and tossed the phone on the bed. Immediately, the ring tone blared again, but Gabrielle ignored it. After a shower, she'd turn off the phone, and she and Tilly would dispose of it. She'd meant every word.

She was turning her back on her family and her previous life and stepping into the future with Ramsay at her side.

Chapter 25

Home Again

*M*iddlemarch, New Zealand.

Emily, Saber's wife, and Tomasine, Felix's wife, were at Dunedin airport to meet them. Exhaustion tugged at Gabrielle, but a lightness in her chest and thoughts had her smiling as they drove from the airport. Gradually, the building clusters gave way to farmland and sheep and cattle. It was a peaceful scene, and her lingering tension faded.

She and Ramsay had talked during the flight home. They had a plan. A future mapped out—something they'd done together, and for the first time in memory, the outlook excited Gabrielle. Because of the time difference, it was mid-morning. It was also much colder than the Scottish summer, and Gabrielle buttoned her jacket against the drop in temperature.

"You and Tomasine have a lot in common, but I'll let her tell you," Ramsay informed Gabrielle.

"Maybe tomorrow," Tomasine said with a smile. "When you're not so tired, but Ramsay is right. Life in Middlemarch is amazing. The locals are friendly, and it's a safe place. Everyone looks after each other, although gossip passes at the speed of lightning. You'll see. Get Ramsay to bring you to the café tomorrow. You too, Tilly."

"I promised Emily I'd work tomorrow," Ramsay said.

"It's arranged then. We'll drop you off first," Tomasine said when she turned off the main road.

"Are you sure you're okay staying with Tomasine and Felix?" Gabrielle asked Tilly.

"I'm positive. You and Ramsay need alone time. I'll see you tomorrow."

Not long after, Tomasine pulled up in front of an old house. The wooden walls needed paint, and the lawn and garden required attention. The roof, however, appeared new.

"It doesn't look like much from the outside, but it's comfortable indoors. I'm doing repairs, as I can afford them."

Ramsay had already told her this, and she saw he was worried about her opinion.

She grasped his hand. "Ramsay, I'm happy to be here. All I care about is being safe and amongst friends. Besides, it will be fun to work at your side and make improvements together. That way, I'll feel as if your house is a minor part of me, too."

"Away with you both," Tilly said, shooing with her hands.

Tomasine grinned. "See you tomorrow. Call if you need anything, but I stocked your fridge. No danger of either of you starving."

"We'll walk to the café later this afternoon, and I'll show Gabrielle around town. We might see you for afternoon tea."

Tomasine raised her hand in farewell and drove off.

Gabrielle shivered at the blast of cold nipping her fingers and nose. "I don't have winter clothes."

"No problem. We'll raid my wardrobe and find you something to wear. Are you hungry?"

Gabrielle squeezed Ramsay's hand in understanding. "Nervous?"

"I want you to like Middlemarch and me." Ramsay unlocked his door and pushed it open. He gestured for her to enter, and she took in her surroundings with interest—the wooden floor and green fern in the shiny red planter.

229

Ramsay led her down a short passage and tugged her into a kitchen with a breakfast bar. The kitchen flowed into a comfortable lounge.

"I love open plan. In my mind, I pictured rooms less lived in and sterile—needing a woman's touch." A row of well-used recipe books filled a shelf. Pots hung from hooks, and a container of colorful pansies sat on the tidy counter. Three barstools lined the breakfast bar. Deep red and navy cushions sat on a three-seater couch, and a large flatscreen telly hung on a wall. "This is comfortable and pleasing to the eye. I love your home. I haven't told you..." she trailed off, wondering if she should state this confession aloud.

"Thanks. Told me what?"

"That you grabbed my attention from the moment I spotted you in the pub. We clicked, and it was so easy to fall for you. Then you helped to save me—you're my hero."

Ramsay stalked toward her, subtly herding her backward until the counter halted further retreat. "You love me?"

"Yes." Gabrielle never hesitated. "You've gifted me with love and caring and more loyalty than anyone apart from Tilly. She has always been my silent support."

"I know that. Saber does, too, so he asked if she wanted to visit with a view to living here."

Gabrielle's heart beat a rapid tattoo. That he'd care enough to notice how important Tilly was in her life blew her mind.

"What about the shifter element? Does it scare you that I can turn into a leopard? That if we have any children, they will shift, but you won't."

"It's a bit to get my head around, but I'll cope." Her serious expression morphed into a wide grin, and Ramsay shook her lightly.

"You're teasing."

"Yeah, I'm teasing you. It's Ramsay I love and admire. Your leopard is part of you, so how could it worry me? Honestly, you and your friends rescued me from hell, and it was my parents who put me there. If it would save their skins, they'd cheerfully do it again. They're supposedly human and civilized, yet I'd never trust them. *Never.* You've given me a dozen reasons to believe you'd always have my back, and for me, that is priceless. I'll cope just fine in Middlemarch." Gabrielle lifted her hands to cup his face. She stared into his green eyes, noting emotion turned them a darker green. "Besides, Middlemarch is your home, and I'll proudly stand at your side for as long as you'll have me."

Ramsay brushed his nose against hers. Seconds later, he settled in to kiss the stuffing out of her. She clung, enjoying his scent, his strength, and his mouth. He pulled away way too soon.

"How does a shower sound? Clean clothes. Once we're done, we can go for a walk. I'll show you where I work for part of the week, and we'll eat at the café. My feline is restless after being cooped up in a plane. It's way too early to go to bed and sleep."

Gabrielle yawned but nodded. "I've heard it's better to acclimatize to local time if you can. Not that I have much experience. All the flights I took were short hops around Europe."

"The shower will refresh you." He tugged on her hand. "We'll share."

The bathroom required updating, but the shower was plenty big enough for two. Gabrielle stripped and trailed Ramsay into the stall.

"You're beautiful," he whispered against her ear as he embraced her.

She winced as a bruise made itself known.

Instantly, Ramsay stepped back, concern shining on his face. "God, Gabrielle. I wasn't thinking. I'll let you shower by yourself. You'll need time."

"No!" she said. "No, Ramsay. You're not him. Please. I'm not frightened of you. I loved our kiss and didn't think of him once. He didn't do kissing. Kissing between you and me—that is our thing, and he will never interfere with that."

Gabrielle sighed. *Better not to lie.*

"Sex might be harder because I'm learning memories can be like scary ghosts. They jump out when you least expect them. If I freak, talk to me until you're sure I recognize you and I'm not caught in the past. I don't want Adrik in my head, but he barged in there, and I haven't shoved him out properly. Not yet."

"I never want to hurt you. Never. You're my kitten princess."

"I always wondered why you called me kitten. It seemed an unusual endearment. At least, no one I knew ever used it."

"Now you know." He ran his fingers over her cheek, the tenderness in his expression making her close the distance between them. "Let me wash your back. I want to see how you're healing."

In answer, she presented her back. "The dressings are wet, anyway."

There was a faint pull as Ramsay tugged off the plasters and peeled them away from different spots on her back.

"They've improved immensely. We'll make an appointment to see Gavin. He's our local vet, but he acts as the doctor for our shifter population. We can sort out contraception, so we don't need to rely on condoms."

A doctor could do a pregnancy test for her, or at least she could ask if it was too early. "That's a fantastic idea."

"Can I ask you something about Popov?"

Gabrielle stilled, her pulse suddenly racing and nerves doing a number on her breathing. "What do you want to know?"

"What positions did he take you in? I'm asking because I don't want to take you by surprise. I understand this is difficult." He swallowed hard.

Gabrielle closed her eyes, hesitating. Ramsay wasn't a cruel man and nothing like her parents or Adrik. He wouldn't use this information to cause her further pain.

"Adrik always took me from behind. I got the idea he hated to watch my face. He kept a picture of his first wife beside his bed. She was blonde, but we didn't look alike." The memories rushed her, and she gulped. "He was rough. Cruel, and it excited him to beat me. It made him hard. Harder."

Ramsay nodded. "Thank you for telling me. The last thing I want is to bring back horrid memories or upset you." He reached down to caress her bottom before giving her a quick pinch. She jumped. "The hot water doesn't last long, kitten. We should hustle."

He gently washed her back before grabbing a washcloth and briskly cleansing his body. Gabrielle washed her hair using Ramsay's shampoo, and by the time the water cooled, she felt refreshed with a second wind.

Ramsay exited the shower first. He dried himself and disappeared, reappearing minutes later with a pile of clothes. "Tomorrow, we'll go shopping in Dunedin. That's the best place for clothes, although Caroline might have a few dresses or trousers to fit you. We'll stop by there today."

Wrapped in warm clothes and barely recognizable, she and Ramsay set off exploring. Middlemarch was bigger than she'd imagined, but it was still a sleepy country town.

"This is the police station. The vet's office is two doors down. Service station and mechanical repairs. On the main street, we have a supermarket—a small one. Caroline's dress shop is next door, and farther down, you'll see Storm in a Teacup, Emily's café. This is where we have a weekly market. The town hall where the community has get-togethers. We also have exercise sessions, self-defense, and other types of classes. I think they teach music. The school is that way. The older students take the bus to a larger town where they have a high school. Local bank. Post office. That's the place to go for plants."

Storm in a Teacup was a quaint café with an empty bike rack out the front. Ramsay led her through an open gate and past a rose garden, the bushes just leafless branches during the southern winter.

"Emily has developed a sheltered outdoor area, which is great for kids. The hedge acts as a barrier to keep rambunctious children inside the café," Ramsay said.

A doorbell tinkled when Ramsay opened the door and stood back to usher her inside. The scent of coffee and a cheesy richness filled her first breath. Several tables held customers, and quiet conversation buzzed around the interior. The noise ceased momentarily as everyone turned their way. Ramsay raised a hand and shouted greetings while ushering her to a counter. Tomasine stood behind, making coffee while Emily served a woman who dithered over a chocolate chip cookie or a blueberry muffin. Gradually the conversation resumed, and she and Ramsay joined the service line.

"The locals are nosy. Saber won't share information about what happened in Europe. None of us will, so the feline locals are wondering why I'm returning from the gathering with a human mate." Ramsay whispered these words against her ear. "Once we have coffee and something to eat, I'll tell you about the gathering and what we were doing there. I couldn't share before."

"Color me curious."

Ramsay laughed. "Come and meet Emily properly. We didn't do intros earlier. She is Saber's wife. Emily, this is Gabrielle."

Emily's welcoming smile grew broader. She was around the same height as Gabrielle but slimmer, and her brown eyes glowed with a warmth that made Gabrielle feel at home. Emily's brown hair held golden highlights, and she wore it in a high ponytail. Her red and white check apron carried splotches of food and a weird purple stain.

"Busy?" Ramsay asked.

"My cabinet is getting empty, and people keep coming in," Emily said. "An outstanding problem to have, but still an issue."

"Gabrielle and I will sort the cabinet for you, Emily."

"You've just arrived home. You'll be tired," Emily protested.

"We're trying to stay awake, but doing something would help," Gabrielle said. "I'm going to live here. I want to contribute."

Emily beamed, and Ramsay's hand tightened on hers.

"Have at it," Emily said with a sweeping gesture of her hands.

Ramsay hustled Gabrielle around the counter and out the back. The first thing he did was kiss her until she was breathless.

"Hey," she said, laughing. "We're working."

"You told Emily you were going to live in Middlemarch. You're staying?"

"I want to be with you."

Ramsay's beam was one of joy and happiness. "Hold that thought."

Chapter 26

Truth and Adjustment

It was after five when Emily sent Ramsay and Gabrielle home, along with a dinner of soup, fresh bread, and meat pie. Ramsay walked briskly since the temperature had dropped. He raised his nose and snuffled.

"What are you doing?" Gabrielle asked.

"Testing the air. It will snow tonight. I can smell it."

"Does it snow in town?"

"Mostly, we see snow on the hills around Middlemarch. If we get a fall in town, we normally have a party and a snowman competition. We have hot tea and coffee and mulled wine for the adults. Hot chocolate for the kids. It's fun."

"Emily is lovely."

"She is. She and Saber have been awesome to me. I told you I lived with Tomasine and Felix for several years, but I became a chef because of Emily. She spotted my flair for flavors and asked if I'd like to help her. My interest developed from there."

"You were lucky to find such a fantastic support network."

"I give thanks most days." He paused and cast a glance at her. "I've had a thought. You've worked with charities, so I'll introduce you to London. She's Gerard's wife and does administration work. She's also human and English. I think you'd have a lot in common. I'll call her tomorrow."

"Are you sure? I'd hate to impose on your friends."

"London will enjoy meeting you. She's on our Feline Council." He'd explained the gathering and its purpose before they turned into his driveway. The temperature had dropped further, and their breaths emerged with puffs of steam.

Ramsay pushed open the door and stood aside for Gabrielle to enter. "It's a lot to take in, but if anything confuses you, ask for clarification. Are you hungry?"

"I shouldn't be after demolishing the scone and the cupcake you decorated for me. Will you give me cooking lessons?"

"I'll teach you," he said, so freakin' happy to have her in his space. He detested her parents for marrying her to Popov. She'd gone through so much, and terrible memories—nightmares—were understandable. He'd exercise patience, but he wanted so badly to mark and claim her. But first, he needed to explain and give her the option.

"Come into the lounge. I'll light the fire, and we'll eat our dinner on trays in the warm."

"I'll help."

"No, rest," he said. "Heating the soup won't take long—five minutes at most. Then, there's something important I should tell you. Actually, two things." He frowned. The barb thing—he should've confessed days ago.

By the time he entered the lounge with a tray of soup and bread, she was sound asleep. Not surprising given the last week. If he wasn't mistaken, she'd lost weight. Ramsay put aside the tray and lifted Gabrielle into his arms. She never roused as he carried her into his bedroom and set her on the bed. He tugged off her shoes and socks and covered her with a warm blanket. Tomorrow was soon enough for weighty conversation.

An out-of-the-ordinary noise dragged Gabrielle from the best sleep she'd had in ages. Warmth suffused her, and the aches and pains she'd suffered for days had decreased. She guessed she was healing. Excellent news. The racket, strident and insistent, continued. She opened her eyes to darkness. Puzzled, she floundered for a location until a male groan sounded from behind her.

"Ramsay," she murmured.

"Shh. Go back to sleep. It's my alarm."

"Why is it so loud?"

"Because I'm terrible at getting out of bed. Would you like a cup of tea before I go to work? I promised Emily I'd give her a few hours this morning."

"I'll come too." Her stomach rumbled, and she pressed a hand to her belly.

"I'm not surprised you're hungry. You went to sleep in front of the fire."

"You should've woken me."

"No, you needed to sleep."

Another memory surfaced. "But you wanted to talk to me."

Ramsay crawled out of bed, and a blast of cold air had her shivering. He stalked across the room, proudly naked, and slapped a hand on the top of an old-fashioned alarm clock. The insistent din ceased. Ramsay pulled on jeans and turned to her. "I was kind of glad to put off our conversation. I'm worried about your reaction."

Gabrielle stared at him. "Ramsay, I'm here. How bad could it be?"

He gave a clipped nod. "I'll make tea. If you want to come with me, I'll make us breakfast at the cafe."

"Will Emily mind if I go with you?"

"She'll put you to work."

Pleasure suffused Gabrielle. "You don't know how nice that would be—to cast off my princess persona and become normal."

"Talk to Tomasine if she's there," Ramsay said. "She has a royal background, too."

Gabrielle's brows rose. "Really?"

Ramsay grinned. "Something about Middlemarch draws royalty." He checked his watch and scowled. "Hustle, woman. We'll need to have our tea there since I'm running late."

Tomasine and Emily were at the café when she and Ramsay arrived.

"Oh, good," Tomasine said with a bright grin. "Slave labor. Gabrielle, come and help me set the tables."

Tomasine issued instructions, and Gabrielle set out salt and pepper shakers, condiments, and placemats on the tables while Tomasine rearranged chairs.

"Officially, I was the queen of our clan, but Isabella helped me to flee an abusive situation. She kept my daughter and me safe, and finally, we arrived in Middlemarch." Tomasine said. "The locals nicknamed me Peeping Tom."

"Really?" Gabrielle's eyes widened.

"Yes, it took me time to win over the locals. As Sylvie, my daughter, would say, I crushed hard on Felix, but it was difficult winning his trust."

"But you did."

Tomasine chuckled. "Coming to Middlemarch was the best thing Isabella and I did. Oops, we'd better hurry. It's almost opening time." She placed the remaining chairs in position and opened the front door. "How do you feel about a cup of tea or coffee?"

"Tea sounds lovely."

"Right, I'll show you how we make it. You can be my helper during the breakfast rush."

They managed a quick tea before the first of the customers arrived. Tomasine had Gabrielle scurrying back and forth and showed her how to take orders. Gabrielle loved every minute and the next three hours flew past. The next thing she knew, Ramsay arrived with two plates of food.

"Emily told me to take a break," Ramsay said. "Let's sit in the back corner."

Gabrielle savored every mouthful of scrambled eggs and crisp bacon, the meal fun and relaxing with Ramsay because he didn't continually scold her for overeating.

He glanced at her, his expression serious. "Each time we've made love, something strange has happened. Well, a few things. First, you always seem to conk out and go straight to sleep. Next is that we've knotted together, and third, each time, the condom has broken."

Gabrielle felt her eyes widen, and she opened her mouth and shut it again.

"Sorry. I should have told you earlier, but I kept putting it off because you left before I woke. The discovery of your royal position threw me, then your parents abducted you. I'm so sorry. My shifter status was another complication, but I still should've found a way to let you learn the truth."

Misery hunched his shoulders, and compassion filled her. Yes, he should've told her, but she understood why he'd hesitated. She might've done the same if she were in his shoes.

"The knotting thing—it has only ever happened with you. I figure we'll check with Gavin since we're visiting him later today. He's the doctor."

She froze. "I'm not pregnant, or at least, I had my period at the palace after my parents snatched me." She swallowed hard. "If I am pregnant, it will be Adrik's baby."

Ramsay reached for her hand. "If you're pregnant, the baby will belong to us, no matter their parentage, and we will love that baby and any others who come after it. Do you understand?"

Tears stung the back of her eyes, and she blinked hard to hold them at bay. "You would accept a baby if it wasn't yours?"

"I love you, Gabrielle. The baby is part of you. They are an innocent being, and I have a wealth of love to offer. I want a family with you, and this would be a start, but there are other options too. We'll do whatever you think is best for you."

She smiled through the shimmer of tears. "What did I do to deserve you?"

"God, Gabrielle. I should've told you earlier, but we had so little time together. You have every right to be angry with me."

"True. I might've panicked, but now that I know you better, it doesn't matter. As I said, I had my period, so any baby will—"

"*Will* be ours," Ramsay said.

"Yeah." Despite his words, doubts scurried around her brain like foraging mice. Could he truly accept Adrik's child as his own? Could she cope with having that monster's child?

The café had emptied, and only two couples remained from the breakfast rush. Both sat by the window, reading the newspaper and drinking coffee.

"There is one more thing related to my feline nature."

"You're a decent man, Ramsay. I can't think of anything that will put me off you."

He grinned, a boyish smile that made him appear younger. "Okay, when a feline finds their mate, it's love at first sight. They instinctively understand this person they've met is their other half, the one to bring joy to their lives."

Warmth grew in Gabrielle's chest. She loved the way he spoke to her, giving her sweetness and truth and making her feel worthy—deserving of his presence in her life.

"Once they're ready, the feline part of the couple—or both, if they're feline—mark each other. I'd bite you here until I drew blood." He placed his fingers at the juncture of her neck and shoulder. "This allows the enzymes in my saliva to enter your body. This will give you stronger immunity, and you should live longer and age more slowly.

You'd match me in aging. The bite will leave a small scar, which, from what I hear, is sensitive to the touch."

"Do the other woman have the scar?" Gabrielle asked.

"Yes. Emily and Tomasine will tell you about it and answer your questions if you have any I can't answer. One more thing," Ramsay said, his eyes glowing a vibrant green.

"What?" Her breath caught as she stared at him, entranced. He was patient, and it was clear he wasn't intending to rush her into having sex again. She appreciated his caring, but she'd held Ramsay tight to her heart since they'd been forcibly parted. Making love with him would make her feel clean and new again.

"The bite can occur at any time, but mostly it's given during lovemaking. I've heard this adds a little something to the pleasure."

"All right," Gabrielle said. "Thank you for explaining this to me and telling me about the condoms."

An indecipherable something flashed over his face before his expression smoothed. She'd disappointed him with her answer. That couldn't be helped because she wanted to speak with the doctor first. If she was pregnant, best she learned this before she committed to Ramsay. Despite him telling her he'd welcome a baby—any baby—she couldn't be so sure.

The last thing she wanted was for Ramsay to resent her.

Chapter 27

Mental Torture

S omething was wrong.

Ramsay sensed the tension in Gabrielle. She'd grown pale and looked as if she might barf when they entered Gavin's surgery, which was in the house where he'd lived before he mated with Leticia and Charlie, one of Middlemarch's cops.

"Take a seat," Ramsay said because she wavered on her feet as if her knees might buckle.

Gavin entered what used to be the lounge. He was tall—over six feet with straight black hair in need of a cut and green eyes. The second his gaze landed on Gabrielle, he hurried over to her, his concern evident.

Gavin squatted in front of her. "Hello, you must be Gabrielle. I'm Gavin, the local doctor. Why don't you come to my surgery, and we'll give you a checkup? Can you stand on your own?"

In reply, she stood, but she wobbled as if she might fall.

Gavin slipped an arm around her waist. "Let me help you."

Ramsay hung back, watching the pair disappear into Gavin's surgery.

"I want Ramsay," Gabrielle said, an edge of panic to her tone.

Relief fluttered through Ramsay, and ground-eating steps took him to the surgery. He grasped Gabrielle's hand, concern filling him. She'd been fine until it came time for this appointment.

Gavin took the lead, and Ramsay was glad he'd briefed their doctor. The knotting phenomenon had intrigued Gavin, and he intended to research this since, as far as he knew, this hadn't happened to others apart from Rory and Anita. "Gabrielle, let's do a full physical. First, I'll listen to your heart, take your blood pressure."

"Can you check to see if I'm pregnant?" Gabrielle asked, the words exploding from her.

"We'll do a urine test," Gavin said.

Gavin's calm manner seemed to soothe Gabrielle, and when they left an hour later, she was noticeably stronger.

"Ramsay, what if I am pregnant? Having his child would be torture."

Ramsay ached for her, her distress, which continued even though he'd tried to reassure her. "He went through a lot of wives. The odds are high Adrik was the problem, not his wives. Gavin told us he could do most of the tests, and we'll get the results tomorrow. If you're pregnant, we'll deal with it. Gavin will give us the options, and we'll choose the best for you."

"I don't want reminders of him!"

"Kitten, no one here—not one of our friends—will think less of you if you have a baby. There are other alternatives, but let's not worry until we hear the test results. I thought I might take you to visit London. You remember Gerard and Henry? London is Gerard's mate, and Emily told me she needs an assistant. You could be that person."

Gabrielle scowled. "I don't think—"

"Henry breeds puppies. I've been thinking about getting one." He hadn't, but Gabrielle might enjoy having a pet. At the least, it would claim her attention and perhaps divert her a little.

As he'd hoped, London and Gabrielle got on well, and London offered her the position. They ended up staying for dinner, and Gabrielle was wilting by the time they arrived home.

"I don't know why I'm so tired," Gabrielle said. "It's not even eight o'clock."

"It doesn't matter. Go to bed. I'll be there shortly and expecting a cuddle," he added.

His phone rang, and Gabrielle went statue-still, barely breathing. Her eyes held terror.

"It's okay," he whispered, although his gut bucked with alarm on seeing Gavin was the caller. "Hi, Gavin. Yeah, okay. Just let me put the phone on speaker for Gabrielle."

"Am I pregnant?" Gabrielle asked, her cheeks pale again.

Gavin hesitated, the silence telling. "Yes."

Gabrielle swallowed hard, and Ramsay had his arms around her in two steps.

"There's a chance the baby is mine," he whispered, every part of him wishing it were so.

Gabrielle sobbed, and when she pulled back, tears shrouded her gaze. "I had my period."

"How heavy was it?" Gavin asked, reminding Ramsay the shifter doctor was still on speaker. "Ramsay told me he knotted in you twice. There's still an excellent chance the baby is his."

Gabrielle paused, and this time, when his gaze met hers, he spotted hope. "Is...is there a way of telling?"

"Yes, I can do a test to learn if Ramsay is the father."

"It won't hurt the baby?" Ramsay asked.

"No," Gavin said. "We have to wait until the seventh week of your pregnancy, and it's a simple matter of taking blood tests from both you and Ramsay."

"And if it's not Ramsay's baby?"

"Then we'll talk more about your options," Gavin said, his tone non-judgmental. "Abortion or something else."

The next six weeks were hell. Ramsay tried to remain upbeat, but Gabrielle's distress affected him. Saber and Felix, the rest of his adopted family, helped him get through, and they tried to keep Gabrielle busy. London had a ton of work for her, but his kitten wasn't sleeping well. They shared a bed, but the gulf between them yawned wider every day.

Ramsay was cautious with his affection, but she didn't reject him. They didn't make love and hadn't since the day Gabrielle's parents had abducted her. Ramsay missed her teasing and laughter, even as he understood. Now, even in death, Adrik Popov was coming between them.

Finally, the day came when Gavin drew their blood for the test. The lab workers would compare the baby's DNA, which was released in Gabrielle's bloodstream, with his. This was one test that Gavin needed to send away to another feline group in Australia. The next fifteen days worked on Ramsay's last nerve. He and Gabrielle snapped at each other, neither getting much sleep and both losing weight.

"How much longer will it take for the test results?" Gabrielle asked. "I can't take much more."

"You and me both," Ramsay muttered.

A knock came at the door. Ramsay tensed since he recognized Gavin's presence. He stalked to the door and snatched it open. "Please tell me you have good news." He stood aside to let Gavin inside.

"Is Gabrielle here too?"

"Yeah. In the lounge." Ramsay led the way. "Gavin's here."

Gabrielle leaped to her feet, her face losing all color.

A delighted smile spread across Gavin's face, his green eyes sparkling. "Congratulations. You were a match. Gabrielle, the baby is Ramsay's."

"Ramsay's baby? He or she will be a feline shifter?" Gabrielle clapped her hand to her mouth and tears sparkled in those brown eyes of hers.

"They will," Gavin confirmed.

Gabrielle buckled, but Ramsay snatched her up before she hit the floor.

"Put her over here." Gavin checked her pulse. "She hasn't been sleeping."

"Neither of us have."

"Has she been eating properly?"

"I've made her eat. Even if it's soup."

Gavin nodded. "Bring her by the surgery tomorrow, and I'll check her progress. She has been under a great deal of stress, and I want to monitor her."

"Okay."

"Congratulations," Gavin said. "See you tomorrow."

Ramsay walked Gavin out and closed the door behind him before returning to Gabrielle. He plucked her off the couch and carried her to bed. He was going to be a father. A parent. His smile started slowly, but it spread across his mouth until it was so wide, his lips ached. They had a baby coming, and he couldn't wait to meet him or her. He and Gabrielle had had rough childhoods, but they'd landed on their feet with a tremendous support network.

They'd be fine. Ramsay knew it.

Chapter 28

Happiness Abounds

G abrielle roused to warmth surrounding her, and one slow breath against her shoulder and the citrus scent told her it was Ramsay. Ramsay's baby. Their child. Without volition, she cupped her belly.

Tears rolled down her cheeks, along with relief. Such intense relief that the child she carried belonged to them and not that monster. They'd made no plans, but now they could. She could tell their friends and share her excitement. She and Ramsay would love this baby.

Behind her, Ramsay inhaled deeply, the breathing pattern of an exhausted man. Lately, they'd snapped at each other. She'd known it was the stress making her crazy, yet that hadn't halted her fear from leaking free to infect Ramsay.

"Gabrielle, kitten. Are you crying?" His warm breath caressed the back of her neck.

"I don't mean to," she whispered. "I'm so happy the baby is yours."

"Ours."

Gabrielle turned in his arms. She couldn't make out much of his features in the dim light, but she thought he was smiling.

"I love you, Ramsay. Sorry I've been so bitchy. I kept thinking about Adrik and his determination to have a child. The idea that our baby..."

"Shush," he whispered. "I understood. I did. We don't need to mention that man ever again. He's dead and can't hurt anyone now."

"Yes." Gabrielle paused. "You haven't tried to make love to me. Do you not want me anymore?" There was a distinctly plaintive note to her tone, and she winced inwardly.

Ramsay laughed softly. "Gabrielle, kitten. I want you. I've always wanted you. Do you not understand that? But that man beat you, brutalized you. I wanted to give you time. I ache with wanting you." He took her hand and settled it on his groin.

Gabrielle's fingers curled instinctively around his swollen shaft. "Oh."

"Yeah. Even when we're much older with grandchildren, I'll desire you."

Gabrielle wriggled closer and sought his mouth. His kiss was soft. Tender. It wasn't aggressive or overly passionate, but it told her everything, and the burden she'd carried dissipated. Ramsay loved her. He wanted their baby, and he didn't blame her for the marriage forced on her by her parents. She pulled back a fraction.

"Make love to me, Ramsay. Let's celebrate our fresh start. Celebrate our baby."

"Kitten. Let's get rid of this nightie of yours. It's so big it's like armor."

She giggled. "I was cold."

"I'll always keep you warm." It was a promise, and it raised a smile she was certain made her appear a little loopy.

Ramsay lifted her, whipped the nightie over her head, then pulled her close again and started slow and languorous kisses. He didn't hurry, but she understood the difference. This was the touch of a man who adored her, a man intent on making her happy.

The careful stroke of his hands down her spine thrilled her. Her wounds had healed and were no longer tender. Ramsay told her she had scars, but she thought of them as badges of honor. She'd survived, and she wasn't sorry for her part in Adrik's death.

Gabrielle shoved away thoughts of the bastard and focused on Ramsay. She could touch him and give him pleasure in return. She could participate as she had before instead of lying unresponsive.

"You make me so happy," she whispered as she traced his muscular chest with her fingertips.

He lifted her hand and kissed it before grinning at her. "We're having a baby. I can't believe it."

"You're happy?"

"So happy," he said. "Are you certain you're ready?"

"Yes. Thank you for asking instead of taking."

"Know what you've been through," he said simply. "Never want to scare you or make you uncomfortable. Never."

This time, he kissed her with passion and let her feel his urgency. Not fear, but excitement. The pulse at the base of her throat beat a wicked tattoo. He drew back enough to expose her breasts, using the gentle suction of his mouth to tease her while his hands skimmed with purpose. She sighed happily because the man had skills.

"I want you so bad." The words were a ragged half-whisper, but heat flared in his eyes.

She sucked in a breath and let it ease out again. "Mark me in the feline way. Claim me."

Ramsay issued a blunt curse that had her freezing.

"You don't want me."

"Don't misunderstand me, kitten. I want to mark you. I want that more than anything, but we have time. It shouldn't be impulsive. We should make it an extra special moment."

His fingers strummed the fleshy pad at the juncture of neck and shoulder, pushing a shudder of awareness through Gabrielle.

"This is where I'd bite you. It will hurt at first, and I won't let go or leave the marking half done. That wouldn't be fair to either of us. You need to be positive this is what you want because we'd be bound. This is a tie stronger than marriage, and I'd hate to freak you out."

She gave him a lingering look before reaching up to cup his jaw. "One thing I'm very clear of is that letting you walk away would be the biggest mistake I could ever make. Think again if you believe I'll freak out when we make love. You are nothing like that monster. *Nothing*. Since we've arrived home, you've given me love and affection even when I've been bitchy and out of my mind with worry. I'm ready to take control of my life again, and you're a huge part of my future. I want you, Ramsay. Please, never doubt my love for you."

"Kitten," he said, the endearment filled with so much joy and love it made her chest hurt.

He pressed his lips to the wildly beating pulse at her neck. It was a blur of touches and kissing, teasing and sweet words from then on. Gabrielle ran her hands over Ramsay's chest, his shoulders luxuriating in the freedom to caress her man as she willed. When he finally pushed inside her, it was with sweet tenderness, and she rose to meet him, every part of her desperate to ease the tension rising in her belly. She moved with him, loving the stretch and the fullness. Their lips met again and again as Ramsay took her higher. The powerful thrust of his body finally pushed her into pleasure. On the second spasm, Ramsay ran his tongue over the marking site.

"Bite me." She shoved upward to meet his next rock into her.

He kissed the patch of flesh, and as her climax surged to a crescendo, he bit down hard.

Pain slashed through her, and she bit back a scream. He hadn't been kidding when he'd said it'd hurt.

Then his thrusts grew faster, harder, and the sharp throb receded.

He lifted his head and smiled down at her. "I'm told the next bit makes up for the pain."

Before she could ask, his tongue, rough and slightly abrasive, swept over the spot where he'd bitten her. Sensations streaked down her body to the place where they joined, and when Ramsay drove into her again, he hit the spot inside her that lit her up with bright, beautiful, soul-stealing pleasure and a tightening of her channel. When she'd expected soreness, she received sweet, sweet bliss.

She gasped and rocked into his next thrust. He licked again and lifted his head to smile down at her.

"My beautiful kitten." He surged into her and halted balls deep. A groan escaped him, heartfelt and guttural, as he spilled into her warmth. His finger stroked across the spot he'd marked her. It no longer hurt, but it pushed happiness through her, made her feel light and whole. Completed.

"I love you, Ramsay."

"Right back at you, kitten." He placed his lips on her mark and stroked it with his tongue. Everything inside her lit up again.

"Has it left a big mark?"

"It's not huge, but it's slightly raised. Now, every time I touch it, you'll experience a burst of excitement. Sexual pleasure."

"I wish I could bite you in the same way."

Ramsay lifted his head, desire flaring in his gorgeous green eyes. "We'll both receive the benefits of this mark. That's a promise."

"I couldn't believe I'd be this happy. So lucky to meet with you at that Scottish pub."

"I believe in fate," Ramsay said. "Something magical brought us together, and now we have a future to look forward to with our baby."

Gabrielle laughed. "All I wanted at the time was a little Highland fling with a sexy man, but I received so much more. I love living in Middlemarch and working with London. Now that I know our baby's parentage, things will be easier."

He kissed the tip of her nose. "We've reached the sweet beyond the pain."

"Yes." And the beyond held so much charm and appeal. She brimmed full of love and awe at his total acceptance. "Make love to me again. I want to experiment with the power of the mark."

And so they loved long into the night, and it was amazing.

Chapter 29

Epilogue

*S*everal *months later.*

Gabrielle waddled into the café to meet Ramsay for lunch since he was filling in for Emily on his day off from the restaurant. Sun shone from overhead, and after a week of rain, the bright light was a welcome change.

"Hi, Tomasine," Gabrielle said as she pushed through the front door of the café.

Tomasine waved. "Ramsay is doing a last-minute order. He won't be long. I've reserved a table for you. It's over in that far corner."

"Thanks."

"You look as if you need a cold drink."

"A mind reader," Gabrielle said. "Could I have a ginger beer?"

"I'll bring one over."

Gabrielle wove through the tables, stopping to chat with neighbors, friends, and two older women on the Feline Council.

"When is your due date?" Agnes Paisley asked. She'd styled her salt-and-pepper hair in an elegant chignon while an unexpected hint of mint wafted from her person.

"A week ago," Gabrielle said drily. She scanned the surrounding people and went with tact. "The doctor says it's normal with a first baby, but I'm ready to see my feet again."

Agnes cackled. "Even though it has been years, I recall that feeling well. You take care of yourself and make sure your man waits on you hand and foot."

"He does," Gabrielle said, and despite her swollen ankles and enormous belly, a lightness suffused her. These days, she recognized it as happiness. She hadn't heard a word from her parents or older brothers, and most people here had never heard of Konstavia. That suited her perfectly.

While the Middlemarch community didn't have a blood tie to her, they treated her like family. It was eye-opening that a clan of felines would accept her and unstintingly offer their support while her family considered her a possession. Each day, she gave silent thanks for picking the pub with the kilt-wearing doorman—that she'd gone with her gut and hooked up with Ramsay. Her instincts had led her straight to love and happiness.

"Gabrielle, over here," a familiar voice called.

Gabrielle adjusted her direction. "Tilly, you look busy."

Tilly had charge of several under-fives and was conducting a tea party with actual food and drinks. Dolls, teddy bears, and two toy trucks sat beside the girls and boys. The tots were shouting over the top of each other, and if Gabrielle wasn't mistaken, an argument was brewing.

"Now, now. Enough of that," Tilly said.

One girl giggled at Tilly's wagging finger, and soon the risk of disagreements had blown over. Tilly honestly had a knack for people. Gabrielle had watched her maneuver the Middlemarch men when it suited her too, but she did it with humor and kindness.

"Hi, Gabrielle," one little cherub called.

Gabrielle waved.

"You have a fat tummy," a little boy piped up.

Gabrielle laughed. "I do."

"Hey, kitten," a familiar voice whispered in her ear. "I like your big belly."

She leaned into his warmth.

"It's not polite to tell people they're fat, young man," Tilly said sternly. Her eyes twinkled with silent laughter as she instructed him to apologize.

"We'll see you later, Tilly," Ramsay said. "I want Gabrielle to rest."

He guided Gabrielle to their table. "How are you and baby doing?"

"Baby is a rugby player," she said, her tone dry. "He or she is active today."

Ramsay grinned as he placed his big hand on her belly. Immediately, their baby settled as if happy to recognize their father. Gabrielle didn't mention the pains that had started. Although she thought Ramsay would remain calm, she'd wait until they became worse and closer together. She'd talked to Gavin, and he'd told her to drop by if the pain became severe or if she had other concerns. He'd also told her he was reasonably sure she was in the early stages of labor. Once her waters broke, she was to go straight to the birth suite.

"Are you hungry?" Ramsay asked.

"Not really, but Tomasine is bringing me a ginger beer."

"I made cinnamon scones," Ramsay said, well aware of her weakness for anything cinnamon.

"You might persuade me to eat one."

He grinned. "That's what I thought."

A sudden surge of moisture had her glancing at her feet. A puddle formed, and she stared at it for a fraction longer.

But her mate was already standing, moving to help her to her feet. Tomasine appeared beside them, her gaze and sense of smell taking in the situation with one glance.

"Tomasine, can we take that to go?"

"Sure," Tomasine said.

"I've made a mess," Gabrielle said, heat flooding her cheeks since customers were staring.

Tilly appeared at her elbow. She patted Gabrielle's hand. "Let me know the minute something more happens."

"You'll be the first to know," Ramsay promised.

Tomasine returned with a bag of food and an unopened bottle of ginger beer. "Keep us up to date. Felix and I will drop by to see you later."

"Thanks," Gabrielle said, her heart full even as a pain tore through her. "We should go now. This baby wants to meet us." Even though Gavin had warned them labor took time, every instinct told her that this baby wanted out as much as she wanted to see her feet again.

Gabrielle was amazing, and the labor progressed faster than everyone had assumed. Ramsay held her hand and helped where he could, amazed at her strength. Throughout the hours she labored, Gavin was unflappable, and it reinforced how lucky their community was to have a doctor such as Gavin at their disposal.

During the months of her pregnancy, they'd decided on names. It was easy, given that neither of them had parents around. Felix and Tomasine stood as adopted parents for him and Gabrielle, and they'd wanted to honor this support by naming their child after them. While he and Gabrielle didn't know if they were having a boy or a girl, their name choices were simple. They hadn't told Felix or Tomasine, but he thought they'd be excited.

A baby's cry rent the air, and he squeezed Gabrielle's hand. She smiled at him, and although it was obvious she was tired, she'd never appeared more beautiful.

"You have a baby boy," Gavin said with a grin.

"Tomas Felix," Gabrielle whispered.

Gavin did whatever he needed to do with the baby before handing him to Gabrielle.

Gray eyes blinked up at them, and Tomas's tiny face scrunched up in a frown. With his heart so full, his chest ached, Ramsay smoothed his finger across his son's silky cheek.

"Look what we did," Gabrielle said, sounding in awe.

"He's beautiful," Ramsay whispered, confident he was feeling the same stunned amazement his mate was experiencing. It made him determined to live a good life and do right by their child, encouraging Tomas and teaching him right from wrong. "I love you so much, Gabrielle. And I adore our son. You've done good."

"It's been an adventure," she said.

Ramsay understood what his mate meant. "Sometimes, you have to endure before you get to the sweetness."

"We have a lot of that. Love. Good friends. A beautiful child."

"We do." Ramsay cocked his head, hearing visitors arriving. "Tilly is here. Felix and Tomasine, too." Ramsay bent closer and kissed their son on his wrinkled brow. Then, he kissed Gabrielle, and she kissed him back with tenderness. They were a family now, and he'd never, ever experienced such joy.

After one last kiss, he pulled away from Gabrielle to greet their support team. "Just in time," he said. "Come and meet our son, Tomas Felix."

Afterword

Wondering what is up with Edwina?

The last time we saw Edwina, a large man scooped her off her feet and carried her away. If you're curious about what happened to her, check out her story in **My Highland Wedding**—coming soon!

I hope you loved Ramsay and Gabrielle's romance. If you did, please feel free to leave an enthusiastic review for **My Highland Fling** and rave about my brilliance at your favored online bookstore. *grin* Don't want to miss a new book? Sign up for my entertaining newsletter at my website www.shelleymunro.com/newsletter.

Shelley

About Author

USA Today bestselling author Shelley Munro lives in Auckland, the City of Sails, with her husband and a cheeky Jack Russell/mystery breed dog.

Typical New Zealanders, Shelley and her husband left home for their big OE soon after they married (translation of New Zealand speak - big overseas experience). A twelve-month-long adventure lengthened to six years of roaming the world. Enduring memories include being almost sat on by a mountain gorilla in Rwanda, lazing on white sandy beaches in India, whale watching in Alaska, searching for leprechauns in Ireland, and dealing with ghosts in an English pub.

While travel is still a big attraction, these days Shelley is most likely found in front of her computer following another love - that of writing stories of contemporary and paranormal romance and adventure. Other interests include watching rugby (strictly for research purposes), cycling, playing croquet and the ukelele, and curling up with an enjoyable book.

Visit Shelley at her Website
www.shelleymunro.com

Join Shelley's Newsletter
www.shelleymunro.com/newsletter

Visit Shelley's Facebook page
www.facebook.com/ShelleyMunroAuthor

Follow Shelley at Bookbub
www.bookbub.com/authors/shelley-munro

Also By Shelley

Paranormal

Middlemarch Shifters
My Scarlet Woman
My Younger Lover
My Peeping Tom
My Assassin
My Estranged Lover
My Feline Protector
My Determined Suitor
My Cat Burglar
My Stray Cat
My Second Chance
My Plan B
My Cat Nap
My Romantic Tangle

My Blue Lady
My Twin Trouble
My Precious Gift

Middlemarch Gathering

My Highland Mate
My Highland Fling

Middlemarch Capture

Snared by Saber
Favored by Felix
Lost with Leo
Spellbound with Sly
Journey with Joe
Star-Crossed with Scarlett

RUBY

SISTER WITCHES OF STORY COVE SPELLBINDING COZY MYSTERY SERIES, BOOK 3

NYX HALLIWELL

Beach
Path
Publishing

Ruby, Sister Witches of Story Cove Spellbinding Cozy Mystery Series, Book 3

By Nyx Halliwell

© 2020; 2022 All rights reserved

Previously published as Red Hot Wolfie

Re-release date November 8, 2022

Print ISBN: 978-1-948686-71-6

Cover by Fanderclai Design **www.fanderclai.com**

CHAPTER
ONE

The early morning forest greets me with birdsong. A scattering of maple, birch, and oak leaves cover the trail.

I pull my cloak closer against the chill and swing the basket of homemade candies that I've brought for Nonni and Poppi. Their farm is on the other side of these woods and I make a daily run to check on them and collect eggs from their hens.

Lenore, my Raven familiar, chitters and caws as she chases Korbin, my cousin Snow's omen hunter, through the high limbs of the trees. As I catch sight of Korbin's blue-black feathers sweeping through the dappled sun, I pray he hasn't appeared to warn me of brewing trouble. An involuntary shiver skitters down my spine at the thought.

We've had enough trouble this year. A peaceful Thanksgiving next week will be welcome.

The two birds enjoy entertaining each other and

knock more leaves into my path, making me laugh, as they play tag among the branches. I put all thoughts of omens and trouble aside, and breathe the fresh pine scent deep into my lungs.

Squirrels are at work collecting acorns. Songbirds skedaddle out of Lenore and Korbin's way.

A small mouse peeks at me from the trunk of a fallen tree several feet off the path. "Hello, my friend," I call to the tiny creature. The face is familiar, a white patch under an eye. This is one of the mice my sister, Cinder, rescued in the early fall. The litter lost their mother, and we nursed them back to health, then returned them to the forest once they were big enough. "All is well?"

The mouse twitches her whiskers and scurries into the trunk. This late in the fall, many forest creatures are readying themselves for winter. In our area of Georgia, the season is fairly mild, compared to most of the country, but can still pack a punch.

A piece of litter near the trail catches my eye, and I frown. A candy bar wrapper. I pick it up and shove it in a pocket to dispose of later. It saddens me when those who use the woods throw trash in them.

Lenore flies low as she lands on a nearby boulder. Her claws click on the hard rock, her shifting weight and flapping wings attracting my attention. Three short caws signal an alert. I slip from the path, going around several trees to get to her.

The boulder is almost as large as I am. At the base is a track shoe someone left behind.

I wouldn't want to traipse through here without shoes, but perhaps it fell from a backpack. I bet the person is missing it, nonetheless, but there's no lost and found for the forest. "Looks like I need to bring a garbage bag and clean up," I say to Lenore.

The shoe trembles, and I step back, wondering what magick is this? A tiny head with a pointed nose pops out, and I chuckle—another mouse. "I see you found an interesting home. I'll leave it be, then, but if you're responsible for this,"—I show him the wrapper —"I should warn you chocolate is bad for you."

The miniature creature chatters and ducks back inside.

I'm fairly certain it's a man's, certainly large enough for more than a single mouse. I notice stains on the fabric on the side, several spots of rusty red.

Lenore flies down and pecks at the boulder. There are more stains there. Smears, really.

Blood?

"Hello?" I call, hearing my voice echo amongst the evergreens. "Is anyone here? Are you hurt?"

The birdsong dies in response. I note Korbin has disappeared. The forest is eerily quiet.

Cautiously, I retrace my steps to the worn path, feeling my magick humming in my veins. As a witch who uses plants, trees, and herbs for many of my potions, recipes, and healing salves, I've grown up here; I do not fear these woods.

What I do fear are people.

Lenore skims past, her wings taking her up to the

treetops once more. Mottled light hits my face as I step fully onto the trail, avoiding a large pinecone. Birds resume their singing, and I take a deep, reassuring breath.

Scanning the trees, I hesitate another moment, sending magickal feelers into the area. I sense no maleficence.

"Be on your way, Ruby." A spectral body suddenly appears nearby.

I startle and then squint to see better. "Grandmother?"

"What's done is done."

She evaporates into the morning mist.

I've only seen the face of my fourth great-grand-mother, Eunice, in vintage photos from the eighteen hundreds. She is the founder of The Enchanted Candle and Soap Company that my sisters and I now run. Although this spirit came and went so quickly I could barely get a good look at her, I suspect it was indeed her.

While I don't interact with the spirits of deceased often, they do occasionally seek me out. I'm reading her journals we recently discovered, and since she's blood kin, I have an unbreakable bond with her that can foster our link. The old books were hidden in a sealed-off room in the mansion that includes our home as well as our business. My connection with her at this moment is stronger because I've been delving into her life.

I long to speak with her, but it doesn't appear to be

possible this morning. With another glance at the shoe and boulder, Lenore and I continue.

The grandfather oaks arching over the end of the path are draped in low hanging Spanish moss. They're a welcome sight as we emerge from the dense forest.

Korbin rests on a fence post and Lenore settles not far from him. Nonni is coming from the hen house, a basket on her left arm. She's dressed in fuchsia pink yoga pants, a thick woolen barn coat and red rubber boots the same color as my cloak. She waves. "Morning."

I greet her, kissing her wrinkled cheek. "A mighty chilly one, but beautiful all the same."

Poppi jogs down the porch steps, holding a steaming cup of what I assume is his already second dose of coffee. He's dressed in a flannel shirt and jeans, seemingly oblivious to the temperature. "Are there enough for omelets?" he asks her.

Nonni laces her arm through mine. Her white hair is neatly curled, and the blue of her coat matches her snapping, intelligent eyes. "Only if you intend on making them yourself, old man."

She winks at me as Poppi blusters. I can tell by the way she leans into me that her arthritis is bugging her. "You two arguing?" I tease.

Poppi lends a hand to help her up the steps, taking the basket and eyeing the speckled prizes inside. His hair is the same color as hers. "She was out doing a silly moon ceremony last night and aggravated her hip. I warned her this would happen."

"Ahh, the full moon in Taurus on Saturday only happens once in a, somewhat, blue moon," she jokes, patting my arm. "I might not be here for the next. Gotta get in all the dancing and celebrating I can."

Her mischievous gaze switches to her husband. "Besides, it's not silly. The moon is incredibly powerful. Seeing her shining down on me in all her beauty makes me want to sing and frolic like I used to. You should try it. Might do you some good, crabbypants."

Poppi makes a face, then holds the door open for all of us. "I can't decide if that's the witch or the gypsy in you."

She laughs. "Does it matter?"

A lift of her chin in defiance gets her a smile from him. "Not one iota. I love you either way."

I get her settled at the kitchen table. Poppi goes to work on whipping up omelets, and Nonni sneaks chocolate from the basket. "Everything okay?" she asks. "How are your sisters? Haven't seen much of any of them since Halloween."

"Cinder's busy with the remodel." I hang my cloak on a peg near the door. "But she's made huge progress already. She wants to have the fireplace working as soon as possible, and definitely in time for Christmas Eve, and my commercial kitchen is nearly done. If I could keep Zelle from experimenting with the recipes Belle's been feeding her, I might actually get to use it soon."

"Zelle's cooking?" Nonni's astonishment is amusing. "That's dangerous."

"Not food, thank goodness. Her talents definitely don't lend themselves to cuisine. I love her, but she burns toast, for heaven's sake. She and Matilda would starve if it wasn't for me. I can't imagine either of them actually cooking a meal." I straighten Nonni's boots by the door, smiling to myself at my youngest sister's, as well as my godmother's, attempts to master the simple art of preparing food. "No, this is something else. With Belle gone so much, she seems a bit...lost."

The twins are as close as any sisters could be, but Belle is spending a good chunk of time with her boyfriend, Leo, these days. "She's been working on a secret project," I continue, "using one of Eunice's books. More times than not, however, she manages to blow up whatever she's creating."

"Just don't let Matilda help her," Nonni says dryly, "or they'll take out the whole building."

She's not wrong. Both Zelle and Matilda possess some intense magick. Zelle's is mostly contained, but my godmother's is prone to going wonky and creating havoc.

"How did Zelle's date with that Melton fellow work out?" Poppi queries.

Johnny Melton was at least two guys ago. "It didn't."

The eggs pop and sizzle as he adds a sprinkle of herbs. "She's never going to get over what Sawyer did to her, is she?"

Nonni waves a hand, dismissing the idea my sister is still brokenhearted over her childhood love. "Zelle is

strong, like the rest of you," she says to me. "Give her time. Maybe she's trying to concoct a potion to heal her heart."

Could be. For a moment, I watch Lenore and Korbin flirting with each other. Cinder has found true love with Finn Starling; Belle with Leo Kingsley. Zelle found her soulmate at the age of eleven, but he left four years ago, and she's never been the same.

I wonder if I'll ever find mine, and the old saying *it's better to have loved and lost than never to have loved at all* runs through my mind.

Magick could help me find true love, and I've come close a couple times to taking that plunge. But it seems like cheating in a way, and I always end up chickening out of using any kind of divination spell to assist me.

Feeling a bit unsettled about the whole thing, I tug the candy wrapper from my pocket, thinking about the culprit who discarded it so haphazardly. "There was a shoe in the woods near the giant boulder just off the path. Seems odd to find one there."

"Ah." Poppi motions for me to sit then places plates in front of me and Nonni. The scent of warm buttered biscuits and the herb omelet makes my stomach growl. "People have been traipsing through there constantly after what happened during the book fair. Did you know there are paranormal investigators from TV in town? I heard they're searching for the creatures who attacked Leo and the others."

This is news to me. I shove the trash back in my pocket. "That's not good."

One of the books my sisters and I discovered in Eunice's library was a grimoire full of spells to bind wild creatures. An unscrupulous man got hold of the volume, then used them to cause animals to attack folks in town. While he's now in jail, few know that magick was involved, or that the book came from our great-grandmother's private collection.

We'd prefer to keep it that way, and these days, we're careful to store all the editions under lock and key.

"Those poor creatures," Nonni says. "Imagine having all those people harassing you and messing up your home. They're irresponsible and thoughtless. Don't they know the woods are full of wild animals that might harm them?"

The food is delicious and I eat another bite. "What do they hope to discover, Poppi?"

He returns to the stove and plates his own breakfast. "Who knows? Footage for their show, I suppose. They have some kind of web blog and a podcast. I was curious the other day, so I pulled up a few episodes. They wouldn't know a real paranormal case if it punched them in the nose."

"You watch videos and listen to podcasts?"

Nonni rolls her eyes, and Poppi refills her cup and his before he sits. "I might be old, but I'm not dead. I've got to keep up with what's going on in the world, don't I?" He digs into his omelet. "Like Nonni said, those dingbats better be careful, running around out there, though. I heard the wolf pack howling last

9

night. Probably having their own lunar—or looney —ceremony."

Nonni bristles and points her fork at him, as she starts to retort, but he winks at her and places a hand over hers to lower her weapon. "They keep disturbing the woods and the creatures in it,"—he chews and returns to cutting another piece—"they'll get themselves into trouble, you can count on it."

Trouble. My gaze strays to the window, even though I can't see Korbin or Lenore.

Nonni sighs and deliberately changes the conversation. "Do you have a booth at the last farmer's market this Saturday?"

"Of course."

"I heard the new veterinarian has a grand opening that day." She shuffles a newspaper in front of me and points at the photo of a handsome man on the front page. "You should make him a gift basket of your candies. Introduce yourself."

I've been secretly looking forward to having someone new in town who loves animals as much as I do. Story Cove is so small, we don't get new blood too often. It doesn't hurt that he's cute. "That's a great idea. Very neighborly."

Poppi and Nonni share a covert smile. "I hear he's single," Nonni adds.

I ignore the innuendo behind the statement. "That's nice."

Poppi shakes his head. "Good grief, woman. You don't even know the fellow and you're playing match-

maker. He's probably too busy to date, and I'm sure Ruby would appreciate you staying out of her personal business."

"No one's too busy for love," she counters, "and I want to see all our granddaughters happy before I die."

"While I appreciate your concern and I value your wishes, you're not leaving us anytime soon," I insist. "No more talk of dying, okay?"

She pretends to read, ignoring me, as the three of us finish our meal in silence.

"I'll clean up," I tell Poppi when we're done. "I know you have chores."

"Brodin is stopping over in an hour to help with the fence. A section of the north pasture needs repair." He pulls on a coat and reaches inside the pockets for his gloves. "He's a good farmhand. I'm glad Snow hired him. After that, I thought I might mosey over to your place and see if Cinder wants some assistance."

"She'd love to see you," I tell him, filling the sink with warm, sudsy water. "I'll let her know you're coming."

After he walks out, I start washing. Nonni retrieves a dishcloth and wipes off the table. "You're right," she says. "It's not my time yet, but I do want to see you girls settled before I go."

All this talk about death makes my skin crawl. At least Korbin is nowhere in sight. "Don't worry, Nonni. We have each other, and I know my sisters will always be there for me."

After we're done, I accept the rest of the eggs from Nonni and she walks me out. Brodin has arrived and he and Poppi are loading the old pickup with tools and new fencing.

"Morning," Brodin calls.

I wave.

"Be careful going home," Poppi says to me. "Steer clear of those paranormal investigators."

I tap my cape, feeling the magick flowing through it and into me. Lenore appears, cawing to me from an oak. "I'll be fine," I assure him.

The woods are welcoming on my way home. Nothing bothers me, and soon, I'm mentally planning my day. I'm experimenting with a new candle scent I've named Autumn Reading Nook that combines the scents of books, a cracking fireplace, and a faint aroma of spiced cider. I also have an order for Finn's mother to fill.

I'm happy and ready for the day, until I approach the rear entrance to the shop. "Oh no," I mutter as Lenore circles overhead, her call sharp and brittle.

Lying on the bottom step of our back porch is an unmoving form—long gray and black hair, a protruding snout, and a bushy tail.

The beautiful fur is marred with blood. The chest barely rises and falls with the animal's breathing, the eyes closed.

A wolf, at least six feet in length, lies unconscious and bleeding at my feet.

TWO

"You poor thing." I set the basket down, Lenore landing on the railing. "What happened?"

Hurriedly, I remove my cape and throw it over the wolf's massive body. It barely covers him; his hindquarters and head stick out on either end.

As I adjust the material, I whisper a healing charm. Then I take out my phone and search my contacts for the veterinarian's office.

My sisters and I have cared for many injured forest animals through the years. Our mother used to as well, and we learned our skills from her teachings. However, we've never nursed a wild wolf back to health.

As the landline at the clinic rings and rings, I kneel at the head, careful to maintain some distance in case it wakes. An injured animal is always dangerous, and he could eat me in one chomp.

In his sleeping state, he looks quite harmless, and I

risk stroking the beautiful muzzle. "Please don't die," I murmur to him. To the ringing in my ear, I say impatiently, "Come on, come on. Be there. I need help."

The wolf's eyes crack open.

They're rich, dark chocolate with flecks of emerald green. A deep, laborious exhale flutters his lips, revealing the ends of his canines, and I cautiously draw my hand back.

"Don't worry, now," I soothe. "I'm going to take care of you." *If you'll let me.*

I sense the cape trying to heal his wounds. Unfortunately, it doesn't work on animals. I rack my brain for a spell, but I can't seem to remember one for this type of situation. "You're going to be okay."

His eyes stay locked on mine. The pointed ear I can see twitches, as if he's homing in on my voice.

The line continues to ring, and I click off. Where is this new vet? Why doesn't he have an answering machine hooked up? Doctor Frederick always did.

I consider calling the veterinarian Story Cove had for over forty years, but he's now retired, and last I heard, he and his wife are in southern Florida for the winter.

As I hold the wolf's steady gaze, I chew my bottom lip. I could call my cousin, Robyn, at the police station, but she'll contact animal control. They won't be able to help the wolf either, only remove him from this spot. There's a wildlife reserve fifty miles away, but what should I do with him in the meantime, if they'll even come and get him?

The wolf's eyes drift shut.

Heaving a sigh of relief, I stare again at my magickal cloak. Passed down from my mother and hers before her, it's a beautiful deep red. It can heal many human ailments. Not all, but some. We've tried it on animals, and once on a beloved tree hit by lightning in our backyard, to no avail. It only seems to respond to human DNA.

Cinder! Surely she'll know what to do. The four of us should be able to move him if necessary, and Uncle Odin and Matilda might also be able to lend a hand.

It's an hour until the shop opens, but as I fly through the house, it appears almost empty. I hear someone in the shower, the water pipes rattling as I climb the stairs to the second floor. Must be Zelle—I bang on the door. "I need help. Meet me out back!"

I continue down the hall and knock on Uncle Odin's bedroom door, then on our godmother's. There's no response from either. *Where is everyone?*

Belle must be on her way to the bank for the morning deposit. I scan my brain, trying to remember if the van was out back, but I was so distracted by the wolf, I didn't notice. Cinder probably took it and is at the hardware store or lumberyard buying materials.

In desperation, I try the vet clinic again, while grabbing a sweater for myself, along with a blanket for the injured animal. After half a dozen rings, I give up once more and hurry to the porch.

The screen door slams shut behind me as I stand in shock at the sight that greets my eyes.

There's no longer a wolf on the bottom step under my cloak.

But there is a naked man.

THREE

He runs a hand through his black, wavy hair and stands on shaky legs. "Where am I?"

The cloak falls. I can't stop my gasp. He snatches it, attempting to hide his lower half. He manages to do so, but not until I've seen his muscular legs, and...other interesting things.

His feet and legs are covered in grime. Dark traces of blood are mixed in. His arms are also a mess. There's a generous amount of dried leaves tangled in his hair.

Blushing and tearing my gaze away, I try to get my voice under control. His fit body is hard to ignore, despite the dirt and wounds.

The wounds are starting to heal, thanks to my cloak. Human, wolf... My mind turns that over. I unfold the blanket, shaking it out and holding it like a curtain between us as I pretend finding a naked man in my yard is an everyday occurrence. "You're at the

Enchanted Candle and Soap Company, my home. It appears you've had a rough night."

He's well over six feet. When I dare peek up, his intense gaze is on my face over the top of the blanket. "And where is this place? What town?"

This isn't good if he can't remember that. "Story Cove."

He looks blank.

"In Georgia."

I sense him trying to reorient himself. "I'm Ruby," I tell him, my mouth dry thanks to his intense stare. "Ruby Sherwood."

"Ruby."

My name sounds like a purr on his tongue. I know my cheeks must be as red as my cloak.

The garment falls to the ground at his feet, and he accepts the blanket, his fingers brushing mine as he takes it from me. I linger a heartbeat too long, staring into those beautiful eyes flecked with bright green like the wolf's.

"You're a..." my mind can't wrap itself around the word. I've heard of them, of course, in fairytales and through popular media, but to come face to face with one?

My sisters and I are witches. Some folks believe we're not real either.

"I'm..." Two creases form between his bushy brows. "Huh. I can't seem to remember who I am." A shake of his head, the dark waves brushing his shoulders. "For the life of me, I can't recall my name."

His voice is husky, raw. I think of Poppi mentioning the howling last night in the woods.

A shiver runs through me. I hear Korbin's call.

Trouble.

"Perhaps you hit your head." I force myself to release the material and step back, averting my eyes as he wraps it around himself. "A case of amnesia. Your memory will return soon. You just need a rest. How about we go inside and clean you up? I have salve for your injuries, and I'm betting a cup of warm, spiced cider will help your mental state."

"Injuries?"

I point to an obvious gash on his shoulder. It's no longer seeping, but it's still an angry red. "You had a rough night in the woods."

He echoes me again, seeming not to understand any of this either. "The what?"

I gesture, and his gaze follows. "You have birch leaves in your hair." I motion to one. Now that he's secured the cover at his waist, I step in to retrieve the yellow serrated piece of foliage. "There are quite a few near the stream."

His frown deepens. "I've never been in the forest."

At my raised eyebrows and pointed look, he concedes. His gaze goes to his muddy feet, a few crumpled leaves stuck to them as well. "Right. If I can't remember my own name, how do I know if I've been in it or not?"

"What is the last thing you do remember?"

The screen door slaps, startling both of us. "What in the world?"

Zelle is wide-eyed as she stops on the landing and takes in the sight of him.

His eyes also go wide, seeing my sister and her spiked, bright orange hair. She's wearing a cute jumper in a turquoise shade that normally clashes with such a shocking orange, but on her, it looks stylish. She may not be able to cook, but she's definitely the sister I go to for fashion advice. She's also an amazing hairstylist and makeup pro.

One corner of her mouth quirks, and she leans a hip on the railing, causing Lenore to dance backward. Her familiar, Rumpelstiltskin, races down the steps to stop at the man's feet.

The ferret sniffs then sits on his hind legs and cocks his head as if perplexed by the stranger.

Join the rest of us. "We have a visitor," I tell her in my most gracious voice. The sun glints over the treetops and Lenore's beautiful wings glisten. "He's had a slight mishap and requires a bit of assistance."

Matilda, in an elaborate multi-tiered skirt and patchwork tunic sweeps through the door and stands next to Zelle. "Well, hello," she says, looking the man up and down.

Uncle Odin, in his usual trousers and smart vest, emerges behind her and nods at him. "Are you joining us for breakfast, young man? I'll set another plate."

Zelle chuckles. "Ruby, you're a constant source of surprise. I didn't know you had it in you."

My cheeks fire up again, the heat coming up the back of my neck this time. I narrow my eyes at her. "I'm sure I have no idea what you're talking about."

"I'm Zelle," she says to the stranger, then points at the others. "This is Matilda and Odin."

"Who are you?" my godmother asks.

"We haven't gotten that far," I tell them, smiling at the man.

His lips twitch, but he doesn't return it. He shifts from foot to foot, embarrassed.

Gently taking his arm, I guide him up the steps and past my family. "Make some food, Zelle. Don't burn the toast. Matilda, there are eggs in the basket. You can help her."

As I push him through the door, I give them all a look. "Best behavior, please. We have a guest to feed."

CHAPTER
FOUR

Upstairs, I settle the man on the closed toilet seat in the bathroom, shifting Zelle's hair products to the side. The mirror is still steamed, but I see the high color in my cheeks. Whether it's from the chilly air, or the fact I've just seen this man naked, is up for debate.

"This place smells amazing." His nostrils flare as he breathes deeply. He studied the house as I walked him up the stairs to our living quarters. "Great architecture, too. Sort of Gothic with a little Victorian thrown in, huh?"

I snag a clean washcloth from the tiny linen closet and start the hot water tap running. "It's been in the family for centuries."

"And you make candles and soap?" At my nod, he takes this in. "Those sell well here in... What town did you say this was?"

"Story Cove, Georgia. Sound familiar?"

A shake of his head. "That's your family?" He points downward. We can hear the others talking as they climb the steps to our kitchen, although their hushed voices are not distinct enough to tell exactly what they're saying.

Small miracles.

"Yes. A few." I gather first aid supplies from the medicine cabinet and arrange them on the cleared counter space. "I have two more sisters, plus my cousin, Snow, who lives on the other side of the forest next to our grandparents. Then there's Robyn, another cousin. She's a detective with the Story Cove Police Department."

"And your parents?"

My heart gives a twinge. "They passed several years ago. Cinder was eighteen, and became our legal guardian. Along with Nonni and Poppi, Matilda and Uncle Odin helped raise us."

"I'm sorry for your loss."

I soak the cloth and ring it out. "Do you think you have family around here?"

He squints as if searching his memory. "I'm not sure, but my gut says yes." He chuckles without humor. "Like that's an accurate indicator."

Actually it is. "You don't believe in instinct?"

The creases appear and he stares at the floor. "Funny, but now that you ask, I think I do."

"My dad always claimed that your gut was more

accurate than your mind because it's never learned to doubt itself."

"Sounds like your father was a wise man."

"Extremely." I search for cotton balls, thinking about what Poppi told me earlier. "I know most everyone who lives here, but I don't know you. Perhaps you're a visitor?"

He shrugs, his shoulders muscular and strong. "It's possible."

"What about TV shows?" I'm reaching now. "What do you like to watch? Paranormal Investigators ring any bells?"

The look that crosses his face suggests I've lost him. "None."

Good. From what I've seen, he's more likely *what* they're hunting than one of them.

He frowns as I move in with the supplies and a blue glass bottle containing tea tree oil mixed with witch hazel. "I'm sorry to be a bother."

I use the wet washcloth to clean his forehead and temples. Quite a bit of dirt comes off. Soaking the cotton ball, I bend forward and touch it to a jagged scratch near his hairline. "It's no bother."

He doesn't flinch, just screws up his nose at the odor. "Do you know what you're doing?"

I halt my ministrations and realize we're practically nose to nose. "Would you prefer I take you to the hospital?"

"No, no." He takes a deep breath. For the first time,

his face relaxes, and a faint smile touches his lips. "It seems I'd rather stay here and try to figure out what happened. I mean, if that's okay with you."

Wrapped in the blanket, he still has plenty of skin exposed. None of his injuries seem life-threatening, mostly scratches and a few puncture wounds.

As witches, my sisters and I are all well-schooled in healing teas, tinctures, and potions. I dab at the scratches and cuts, cleaning away the blood, dirt, and grunge. "I know a good deal of healing applications. You can trust me when it comes to this."

"I believe I can." His eyes meet mine and hold.

My cheeks heat again and I break eye contact. What is wrong with me? "However, if you have a concussion, that's out of my league."

"Are my pupils uneven?"

Forcing my gaze back to his, I check. "No."

"I'm not dizzy or sick to my stomach. Vision is normal." He runs a hand through his hair, disturbing the hubris stuck there. "Pretty sure there's no concussion."

"Have you had one before?"

He stares off in space for a moment. "Can't say."

"Could you be a doctor? Or an emergency technician? Seems you know a bit about concussions, if nothing else."

He considers this, then shakes his head. "My gut says no, but its...odd."

"Odd how?"

"I'm not sure how to explain it. I got a little tug when you asked, like I might have experience with medical stuff, but...I don't know. Everything is so fuzzy. Like my memories are right there, yet out of reach."

I toss the dirty cotton balls, then gently remove the leaves from his long strands. As I run a comb through the tresses, it's hard not to drool over his large biceps, muscular chest, and flat abs. He has an intricate tribal tattoo on one defined pec.

Teasing the knots from his hair, I watch as he closes his eyes. This gives me the chance to openly stare at his long black eyelashes, his smooth skin, now clean.

Cleaner, anyway.

His torso and legs are still a mess. He'll have to take care of that himself. I use a special cream of Cinder's on his open shoulder wound that's made from a mixture of herbs and more tea tree oil. He sucks in a breath from the sting, but is otherwise stoic.

As I examine the cut, I tsk. It's bleeding again from my tinkering. I dab at it with a cotton ball. "On second thought, you may need stitches for this gash."

He glances at the cut and fingers the skin around it. "Nah, it's not that deep. It should heal fine on its own."

"How do you know?"

He shrugs. "Um... I just do?"

I clean off the fresh blood gently and bandage a

cotton ball to it. "Let's hope it stops on its own. Press your fingers to it."

He does as I set the container on the counter and study him. With the worst of the grime gone, he looks slightly familiar. His hair is longer, his skin more tanned, but...

The picture in the newspaper flashes across my mind. Everything clicks into place. "Wait! I know who you are."

He rises and his eyes light. "You do?"

"Yes." But the real question is *what* he is. "You should take a shower and clean up the rest of the way. I'll gather clothes and leave them outside the door. We'll get you home after that."

"You're not going to tell me my name?"

"As I said, I'm no expert on concussions, but amnesia? I know a few facts about that. It would help your brain if you remember that on your own."

"But maybe if you tell me, or at least give me a hint, it would spark the rest of my memory."

He towers over me, the blanket shifting and nearly falling before he clutches it. We both laugh.

Maybe he's right. "Renfroe. Sound familiar?"

The creases that I find endearing appear between his brows again. He knots the material. "Can't say that it— Wait!"

He paces, a hand going to the back of his neck. "That's it." He returns and grabs my upper arms, his face splitting in a grin. "My name is Renfroe Woolsey. Renfroe Redfern Woolsey, to be exact."

Relieved, I return his smile. "Nice to meet you, Renfroe Redfern Woolsey."

"You're amazing, Ruby." He releases me, still grinning from ear to ear. Holding out his hand, he gives me a nod. "My friends call me Ren."

CHAPTER
FIVE

The kitchen is filled with the smells of coffee, eggs, and unfortunately, burnt toast. Entering, I see Zelle at the toaster, and I shoo her away.

"So, who's the naked guy in our shower?" She feeds a portion of the nearly blackened bread to Rumpelstiltskin.

"His name is Ren Woolsey. He's the new vet. Don't embarrass him when he comes down, okay? He's definitely had a bad night."

She winks. "Sure, sis. Whatever you say."

Cinder flips an egg onto a plate as I push slices of bread in, adjusting the timer. "I'm sorry I missed the fun. Why exactly is he here?"

Grabbing the butter from the fridge, I spill the details I know so far, including that Poppi heard wolves howling in the forest last night. "Are werewolves and shifters...real?"

"They sure are," Matilda says. There's a quirky smile on her face. "I knew a werewolf back in the day. He was *hot*. We fought like cats and dogs...well, just dogs, I guess, but man, he was something else when it came to—"

"Thank you." I raise a hand to stop her. "We don't need details."

Zelle laughs and passes a carafe of orange juice to her. "I had no idea you dated a werewolf."

The smile grows wicked. "*Dated* isn't exactly the term I'd use."

"Can we get back to our guest?" Flustered, I concentrate on the toast. "I can't say for sure, since I didn't witness him shift, but there's a strong possibility he's one or the other. Crazy, right?"

Uncle Odin sips his coffee slowly as he accepts a plate from Cinder. "Woolsey, did you say? I believe that's from the old English name, Wulfsige."

We all look at him, waiting for him to continue, or add why this is important. Our beloved uncle is full of facts and somewhat useless information, but we love him dearly. He salts his egg, offering nothing further.

The toaster pops and I place the slices on a plate and drop four more into the slots. The butter is still cold and doesn't want to spread evenly.

Matilda prompts him. "Wulfsige refers to what, a wolf?"

"Yes, yes." He nods and accepts a piece from me. "Quite so. W-U-L-F equals wolf. Sige stands for victory."

"What do you believe is most likely?" I ask. "Were or shifter?"

He considers this. "We'd need to know if it runs in his family."

Cinder gives Matilda an egg. "Shifters pass the gene to their kids, right?"

He swallows a bite and nods. "Weres are, in general, created by the bite of another of their kind. Regardless if it's wolves, bears, or cats, the saliva transfers the virus, but there have been cases where it was passed from a parent to a child, I believe. I can research it in more detail."

"Is it possible he doesn't know?" I ask, bringing the rest of the toast to the table.

"Are you sure he doesn't?" Matilda reaches for a jar of apricot jam. "You said his memory is spotty, so maybe his ancestral wolf-y lineage will come back like his name."

"Sorry—ancestral what lineage?"

Ren stands in the doorway. His dark hair is now wet from the shower. The sweatpants I gave him are far too small, his ankles clearly on display.

"Come in. Have a seat." I hustle up food for him, setting the plate at my place around the large farmhouse table. "How's your shoulder?"

"Fine," he states, nodding at the others.

"Would you like cider, too, or do you prefer coffee? We also have juice."

Cinder gives me a small grin that makes me realize I'm rambling.

All eyes turn to Ren, and he looks uncomfortable being in the spotlight. "Can I have some of each? I'm famished and dehydrated."

There's an assortment of grins and chuckles. "That a boy," Uncle Odin says, sneaking jam for his toast. "You may be a shifter, son. Did no one tell you?"

Silence falls, and I halt mid-pour with the juice.

"Shifter?" Ren's gaze flicks to me. "I'm afraid I don't understand."

Belle enters at that moment, her porcelain cheeks pink and her blond hair in a beautiful braid decorated with ribbons. "I didn't know we were having company." She shrugs off her coat, while Jayne Eyre, her Pekingese, sniffs Ren's feet. "Hi, I'm Belle. You're a shifter? What kind? I didn't realize we had any in the area."

Ren's face contorts as he glances between me and the others. I see some form of understanding starting to take hold in the depths of his eyes. "You mean, like a supernatural creature?"

We all remain quiet, as we wait for him to process this.

He scans the kitchen, then snickers. "Ah, I get it. Funny. You guys are messing with me."

Cinder clears her throat and offers Belle an egg. "The poor guy has had a rough night. Let him eat."

The clang of silverware and normal family conversation returns, Matilda telling us about her latest workshop with a group of women embracing their

inner goddess. She's holding another of her full moon rituals later in the week near the edge of the forest, since Cinder has banned her from holding them inside. Last month, her candles nearly set the place on fire.

Only Ren doesn't immediately dig back in.

"Did you invite Nonni?" I ask offhandedly, careful to avoid staring at Ren.

"Of course." Matilda doesn't know the meaning of rude, and openly watches him. "She'll be howling at that ol' moon, just like the rest of us, come Saturday night."

I pour myself a cup of cider, give Ren another, then begin cleaning the skillet and spatula.

"You're not eating?" he asks as he shovels down the food. He's definitely hungry.

Like a wolf.

I bring the coffee carafe over and refill cups. "I've already eaten with our grandparents. By the way, Cinder, Nonni could use an extra jar of your medicinal cream. Her hip is acting up in the cooler weather, and she's already begun her celebrations, dancing in the moonlight last night."

Everyone chuckles, except Ren, who stops eating.

"Poppi said he'll be by to help with any work you plan to do today," I continue, and my older sister nods.

"I can use all the help I can get."

Belle and Zelle talk about a book of recipes Belle has discovered in Eunice's library. Zelle tells her she'll

look at it tonight. She has a large wedding this weekend to prepare for. The bride and her bridesmaids all want Zelle to do their hair and makeup.

Conversation slows as they finish off their breakfasts. Ren checks under the sweatshirt and glances my way. "That stuff you put on my cut really works." He inhales another forkful of food. "The wound is nearly healed already. How is that possible?"

"Ruby's cape is magickal," Zelle says with no preamble. "It heals people."

Ren freezes mid-breath.

"Hey, my cream is pretty powerful," Cinder argues.

Ren places his fork down. "I'm sorry. A magickal cape?"

Zelle resumes eating as Rumpelstiltskin chitters at her, begging for more toast. She points to the garment in question, hastily thrown over an extra chair in the corner. "It's one of a kind, just like Ruby."

The look he shoots me seems to contain a question of whether or not we're pulling his leg again. "I'll have it cleaned for you. Do *magickal* clothes require special handling?"

His tone holds a note of teasing.

"No need," I assure him, inwardly cringing. To a mundane—someone without magick--we must sound unhinged. "It's self-cleaning."

As he stares, mouth gaping, Zelle laughs and winks at her twin.

Belle giggles. "Hey, Ruby, Zelle and I will open the store so you can take him home."

"I don't know where that is." His expression turns befuddled. "Do you?"

Relieved to change the subject, but sorry he's struggling, I nod. Does he blank out like this after every shift? "You're a few blocks away. Do you remember anything besides your name?"

"I'm good with my hands." He looks at them and flexes his fingers, then his attention switches to Rumpelstiltskin. "And I like animals."

The ferret is now taunting Savannah, our shop cat, and trying to displace her from her favorite perch in the corner.

Lenore caws from her cage—the door is open, but she's nestled on the bar. Her wise, black eyes watch everything. "Time to go," she declares. "Time to go."

Surprise and delight lift Ren's brows. "He talks?"

"She," I correct. "Yes, she can speak when she wants to."

He glances at the wall clock and bolts from his chair. "It's nearly nine. I have to..." He sets his napkin down and pauses, scratching his head. "I have to do something. It's my...first day."

He walks to Savannah and Rumpelstiltskin, then studies Lenore. Jayne sniffs him again, and Cinder's hedgehog, McAllister, scrambles out from behind our antique pie cupboard.

He bends and scratches the ferret's neck, pats Jayne, and laughs as McCallister races under the table to check for crumbs. His face lights up, and he pivots back to me. "I'm a veterinarian."

"Very good." His joy makes me smile. "Yes, you are, and we better get you to the clinic. It's going to be a big day."

CHAPTER

SIX

"I like that soap you had in the shower." Ren sniffs his exposed wrist. "It's refreshing."

Main Street glistens in the sun. Other shops are starting to open. Minerva Montes at the quilt store is sweeping her sidewalk and waves as we go by.

"Frosted Pine," I tell him, returning it and wondering if Sawyer, her grandson, will ever come home for Christmas. She's getting older and could use the help. With his featherbrained mother always off chasing her next husband, Sawyer is all Minerva has left for family.

But boy, would that create havoc with Zelle. "It reminds me of the forest in November," I tell Ren.

That brings forth a sigh from him. "I sure wish I could remember what happened."

"You will." I hope that's true. "Is there anything you can recall about today's appointments?"

He's quiet for a moment, then rattles off several facts about the pets coming in for checkups. His memory is definitely returning, it just has a ways to go yet.

"I think I wanted to move here because of something more than the clinic being for sale," he says after another block. "The town itself appealed to me."

"Do you come from the city?"

"I believe so, but I still can't recall my parents. It's...weird."

"Maybe you should check your phone, or see if you have an address book. I'm sure their contact info will be in there."

He smiles at me and it warms my insides, much like the heat from the vent warms my hands. "Good idea."

"Story Cove is a nice, small, southern town," I tell him. "My sisters and I grew up here, and most folks accept us."

"What's not to like?" He doesn't mention the "witch" label, but I sense it behind his statement. "Your family seems great."

I have the feeling he's using that term instead of odd. "We laid a lot on you at breakfast. I hope you're okay with our frankness."

"I'd rather know the truth than be kept in the dark."

I pull into the clinic parking lot. "Here we are. Do you recognize it?"

"Yeah, I do." His voice is full of wonder. "I know

this place. I moved here last week. There's an apartment upstairs but I haven't unpacked my stuff yet, and I feel...at home here."

My heart tweaks. This is good news—all of it. "The town needs you. Most folks have at least one pet, and the farms around here have livestock. My sisters and I rescue injured forest animals and sometimes they need more care than we can provide."

His gaze swings my direction and he studies my face. "Apparently, you take in strays, too."

Staring into his eyes, I feel like I'm drowning. I understand he's referring to himself. He hasn't quite grasped what he really is yet, but he will. "Happy to help."

"I'd like to buy some soap from you. I'll return your clothes later and get a couple bars then, if that's okay."

"Absolutely."

We simply stare at each for another long moment, and my pulse skips and dances as I feel that rush of connection. I wonder if it's something deeper than simple gratitude for me doctoring and feeding him.

"Would you like me to come in with you?" I ask, reluctant to leave. "I can answer calls, set up appointments, or whatever until you're back to full speed."

He reaches over and pats my hand. His fingers are warm. "You've done more than enough for me. I know you have your own business to run."

I suspect he's going to be fine, but I give him one of our business cards with my personal number on the back. "Don't hesitate to call if you need anything. I

know you have a full schedule, but try to take it easy, if you can. Get some extra rest, and consider seeing Doc. He can run tests and treat the memory loss."

"I will, and thank you." He leans across the divide and kisses my cheek unexpectedly. "You've been incredibly kind and I appreciate it."

The back door to the clinic is locked, and he obviously has no key. I wait until he pries open a window and climbs in. It's no hardship to watch him, his body graceful and strong.

Once he's safely inside, he waves. I have to roll down the window on my way to Enchanted to let in cool air. My fingers rest on the spot his lips touched and I can't keep the silly grin off my face.

Wait 'til I tell Nonni!

The open sign is out when I arrive. We take turns running the place, and Matilda and Uncle Odin often help. I think Eunice would be happy to see what we've accomplished.

From her appearance this morning, she *is* hanging around, so she probably does know.

Belle and Zelle each have outside jobs, along with their duties at our shop. Belle works part-time next door at Beanstalk Books. Zelle is a hairstylist who is known for her unusual and unique styles.

With the holidays around the corner, she's booked. Her own hair grows at an astronomical rate, and although she usually starts the morning with it shaved, or at least cropped close to her scalp, it's down to her ankles by the time evening comes.

Belle is busy at the bookstore this time of year, too, receiving regular daily deliveries for the holiday buying season.

Cinder longs to spend more time on the remodeling project to expand our floor space and create a better flow in the workroom, but this time of year leaves no spare time for anything else. She makes most of the candles, and our in-store and online orders have recently skyrocketed.

I grab a fresh cup of warm cider before getting to work. Matilda has sent Zelle off to her appointments and is at the register. Belle is assisting a customer.

By ten, Cinder is restocking shelves as fast as they empty out, and I've replaced our godmother at the counter. I take payments, bag products, and answer the phone.

Although it's not even Thanksgiving yet, people are already buying for Christmas. Right before noon, the women's auxiliary members stop by and fill the shop with gossip and plenty of good-natured teasing. The thing about the rush is that it keeps my mind off Ren.

When things slow near lunchtime, Matilda returns with tea in her unicorn mug. Cinder brings out the last of the Autumn Walk candles from our inventory, and we restock holiday scents like Mistletoe, Christmas Hearth, and Jingle Belle Berry.

"Katie Beane about wiped us out," Cinder jokes. "Sure hope her family likes soap and candles."

"They're great stocking stuffers." I replenish our

signature gift bags under the counter. "She said she's done with her shopping now."

Which reminds me, I haven't even thought about what to get my sisters.

"Did you get your wolfie friend home safe and sound?" Matilda asks, peering out the front window and petting Savannah.

Another reminder. "Yes, and he remembered more on the way there. I should check on him, though."

Cinder carries in an armload of glass candles. "I wonder why he was drawn here?"

I take two from her. "Family name aside, he could still be a werewolf, right?"

She sets the rest on the center table display. "Does it matter?"

"I think it does. When his memory fully returns, I hope he's aware of his abilities and has control of them. He seemed completely lost when we were discussing the supernatural earlier."

Matilda leaves her perch and sniffs one of the candles. "He sure was beat up and bloody when you found him. He must have had quite a tussle with something."

Cinder arranges them to her liking. "He was probably chasing rabbits. Good thing he left Nonni's layers alone, you do not mess with her chickens. Poppi might have shot him."

She grins, but I don't. Just thinking about it makes me shudder. I retrieve my phone from behind the

counter and dial Robyn. The police department operator informs me she's at lunch.

I call her personal number and she answers on the first ring. "Hey, Ruby. What's up?"

"Have there been any unusual calls or incidents recently?"

She's used to our involvement with occasional activities that lean into the magickal and mysterious. Doesn't mean she's comfortable with them. "It's nearly a full moon. Unusual and strange are plentiful. Can you be more specific?"

"Any attacks?"

A pregnant pause. "Human or animal?"

I hesitate. "Animal."

This pause lasts longer. "Don't tell me there's another witchy book on the loose, resulting in possessed creatures."

"No, no, nothing like that. Poppi heard howling in the woods last night. Not entirely unusual, but he seemed disconcerted. I'm checking to make sure there hasn't been anything peculiar going on."

Her sigh of relief comes through loud and clear. "Nothing's been reported involving wild animals. I do have a bunch of non-locals running around and causing a stir, and Danny Oldestein got drunk and took some frustration out on Mrs. Perlman's magnolia tree. She's pretty upset. The tree has deep ax gouges in it. That thing dies, Danny's going to rue the day he was born."

She asks about the feast Nonni and Poppi are plan-

ning for the holiday before I disconnect. We discuss that for a moment then say our goodbyes.

Matilda is on the sidewalk talking to a friend. Cinder, having overheard parts of the conversation, says, "See, no harm has been done."

"Still, I should keep an eye on him, don't you think?"

Her lips twitch. It's almost a smile. "Of course. At least until you're sure he has his full memory again." She arranges red and white peppermint soaps among the candles. "And you have to make sure he understands he's a wolf."

A man and woman enter, stopping our discussion. They're dressed in odd leather outfits with vests that look like leftovers from Halloween costumes.

"We heard you were witches," the man says when Cinder offers to help them. He's medium height with a pot belly and a funny mustache. He hooks his thumbs in the loops of his jeans. "We're part of the Paranormal Investigation Team. You've probably seen our show."

Both of us school our faces and give him a blank look.

The woman steps forward, eyeing the display. "Smells great in here, and these are so pretty." She lifts a candle and sniffs, her high ponytail swinging forward and brushing a cheek. "We were hoping to talk to you about the coyote attacks that happened in September. We heard you were involved."

Cinder brushes my hand—a warning not to say anything. "This is Georgia." She offers a polite smile

reserved for nosy tourists. "Animal attacks *do* happen. No one was hurt."

The woman sets down the item. "But a man died after being mauled by a bear. We saw reports stating the creatures were possessed. Any chance you can confirm that?"

I scoff. "By what, exactly?"

Her eyes don't smile when her lips do. "That's what we're trying to find out. Do you...cast spells? Sell potions?"

Cinder and I exchange a glance. I can almost hear what she's thinking. *How fast can we get rid of these two?*

"No." Cinder crosses her arms and appears bored. "We sell soaps, candles, and candy. Would you like any?"

The man shrugs and takes out his phone, pulling up notes and reading through them. "Someone mentioned a Belle Sherwood knew about the attacks. They said they saw her boyfriend defend himself from four crazed coyotes and a bear." His gaze rises to glare at us. "Sherwood, that's you, right?"

Matilda saunters in and seems to know what's going down. "Leave your card. We'll call you if we think of anything."

"Is Belle here?" The woman is undeterred. "Are you her?"

"No," Cinder and I answer in unison.

The man pockets his cell, the trace of a smile crossing his lips. He knows we're not being totally truthful, he's just not sure about what. "We're

shooting a live show on the full moon in the woods. Maybe we'll encounter some of those possessed creatures." He offers a wink, but his dark eyes are flat, menacing. "We could use some witchy stuff to add to the setting. You know, smudge sticks, amulets, skulls. That sort of thing. Props."

"We don't carry items like that." I'm glad that's true, since I can't stand the sudden thought of having to help him even a minute longer. "Check two towns over at the Chicks With Gifts Emporium. They carry a full line of...*props*."

And hopefully one of them hexes you.

The woman slides a business card onto the table. "My name is Jenny. Thanks for your time." The overhead bell jingles as her partner exits. "Please tell Belle I'd love to interview her and her boyfriend for our show. We can make them famous."

This time, her smile is real, as if this is enough to lure anyone into talking with her.

Once she exits, Cinder picks up the card in disgust and drops it in the wastebasket.

With Matilda back, I can take a break. I walk out to the back porch and stare at the woods. Another shudder runs through me at the thought of Ren in wolf form encountering those TV show people, or anyone else for that matter. I need to warn Poppi so he doesn't go after him with his shotgun.

I grab my cloak and discover one of Ren's hairs on the collar. In the sunlight, I see a mix of red, brown, and black.

The wolf.

I call Belle at the bookstore. "Be on the lookout for those paranormal investigators Poppi warned me about. They came in looking for you, claiming they want to interview you and Leo regarding September."

"They were already here. I hid and let Daisy handle them. She claimed ignorance and they left."

"Good. Have you come across any spells in Eunice's books pertaining to shifters?"

"Not that I recall." Her voice is perky as she greets a customer before returning to me. "I can check our stash later. Or you could always ask our great-grandmother."

Communicating with spirits can be tricky. "I'll try, but she only seems to appear when I least expect it."

"At least you can see and hear her. That's an amazing gift, Ruby."

She's right, even if it doesn't feel like it at times.

Placing the hair in a container, I tuck it in my pocket, put on my cape, and walk to the woods. Since I saw Eunice there this morning, maybe I can access that connection again.

Lenore comes with me, happy to have another jaunt. I dally a bit off the path once we get to the spot. The shoe is still there, and I call Eunice's name several times as I circle the boulder, but only birds reply. A squirrel catches my eye as he scurries past, his cheeks fat with acorns.

As my gaze follows him, my breath catches. Bloody fingerprints mar a white birch trunk.

Upon closer inspection, I find mashed leaves and broken sticks forming a trail. I follow it, my stomach flipping when I notice more drops on the ground.

I anticipate the body before I see it, and my heart sinks to the soles of my feet.

The man is obviously dead, lying at the base of an ash tree, visible gashes and bite marks evident on his face and hands.

Cinder was wrong. Harm has been done.

CHAPTER
SEVEN

Cinder keeps an arm around me, but even in my cloak and her embrace, my teeth chatter.

Robyn and her team unroll yellow crime scene tape, cordoning off the body. The forest rings with the crackle of police radios and human voices.

She steps underneath a bright yellow strip of tape, lifting it over her head before she stops in front of us. The birds are silent, the poor mouse evicted from his house boot.

"No ID on the vic. I don't recognize him, do you?"

I shake my head. "Hard to tell, though, with all the dirt and..."

Blood. I can't say it.

She draws out a small, blue pocket-sized pad from inside her jacket. "There are bite marks and scratches." Her gaze flicks to me, then over to Cinder, back to me. "You called earlier, asking if there'd been any unusual

activity or animal attacks. Did you suspect something like this?"

The accusation is there. My legs feel soft and shaky. "Not exactly. I found the shoe this morning, and Poppi mentioned hearing the wolves last night, and, well... Because of what happened before, I thought it prudent to check."

She flips pages and glances at her notes. "This is far too similar to September. If you suspected anything, you should have called me right away."

Was the man still alive this morning? Could I have saved him? Is his death my fault?

We all pause a moment, remembering the horrible incidents surrounding the Beastly Book of Spells.

"We haven't let any of Eunice's books out of our possession," Cinder reassures her, her arm tightening around my shoulders. "We had no reason to believe something like this might have happened."

"Look, I know you guys had nothing to do with it, but it is rather coincidental, don't you think?"

We hear a clicking noise, but it's not coming from the investigator shooting crime scene photos.

"Hey." Robyn marches toward two people a few yards away. Jenny holds an expensive camera with an even more costly lens. "Get out of here. This is the scene of an accident."

"It's a free country," the man replies. He's wearing leather, like the PIT members earlier, only his vest is covered by a windbreaker. He wears a bandana around

his head and biker boots. "Was the guy killed by an animal? Who is he? What species?"

Jenny lowers the camera from her face. "We don't want any trouble, officer." She gives Robyn her trademark smile and extends a hand. "I'm Jenny from the Paranormal Investigation Team. We're doing a live show—"

Robyn cuts her off. "I'm well aware of who you are and why you're hanging around. Your fans, too. The permit for filming out here was rejected, as I recall, and now there's a police investigation that you're meddling in. I strongly suggest you clear out, or I'll be forced to confiscate your camera and cite you for trespassing."

Her smile never falters. "I'm sorry, I didn't catch your name."

I give her credit for perseverance.

"Detective Woods."

The man starts to argue about their right to be there, but Jenny tugs on his arm. "No problem, Detective Woods. We're going. We've appealed the permit to gather and film here, by the way. Your Chamber of Commerce actually loves the idea of getting media attention for Story Cove."

Robyn curses under her breath as they leave. When they reach the path, Jenny turns to look at me and makes a "call me" gesture with her hand to her ear.

Once they disappear, Ren comes into view.

"What's he doing here?" I ask.

"I called him." Robyn waves him over. "Dr. Woolsey, thank you for coming."

My pulse skips all over itself when he looks at me and smiles. "Hey."

"Hey back." The grin from earlier breaks across my face. "How are you doing?"

"You two know each other?" Robyn asks.

"We met this morning," Ren answers.

She watches him still smiling at me and raises a brow. I ignore the unspoken questions in her eyes. "Okay, well, the medical examiner is on his way, but I want our new vet's opinion on the bite marks."

Ren nods and glances toward the body. "Glad to help."

Robyn leads him away, careful not to disturb the scene. Unfortunately, evidence may be hard to detect in the forest detritus anyway.

Cinder gives me a jab. "Don't jump to conclusions," she murmurs.

"How can I not?"

We huddle together, watching. My breath feels like it's stuck in my chest.

Ren uses a small magnifying glass and a measuring tape, angling this way and that while signaling Robyn to shine her flashlight on different areas.

After a few tense moments, he leans back on his heels. "The bites could be from a dog."

Robyn flicks off her light. "Not a coyote or a wolf?"

"Possibly coyote, but doubtful it's a wolf."

He points at the dead man's left shoulder, the coat

and shirt torn wide open. "A wolf has considerably more strength in its bite, somewhere in the range of fifteen hundred pounds per square inch. That's about twice the pressure of a German Shepherd, for example. A coyote's is consistent with a medium size dog. I'm no coroner, but I don't believe these killed the man."

"Why not?" Robyn scribbles on her notepad.

"There's not enough blood, for one." He points to the area around the victim. "I know it seems like there's a lot, but this guy didn't die from bleeding out either."

"Any guess as to what did kill him?"

"No, all I can tell you is that the punctures missed major arteries."

Robyn thanks him, the ME arrives, and she tells Cinder to take me home. "I'll be in touch later with any news."

Shaking Ren's hand again, she holds up the tape for him and the examiner to trade places. "A word of caution, though," she says to me. "Stay clear of the woods for now, okay?"

I start to protest, but Cinder drags me toward the path. Ren joins in, the two hustling me along. My emotions are a rollercoaster. If he died because of the attack, is Ren somehow responsible?

None of us say a word until we are inside Enchanted.

"It wasn't me." Ren stares into my eyes. "I don't know what happened last night, but *I* didn't hurt anyone, and..."

I'm not a wolf. I see the words in his gaze.

"You didn't recognize the man?" Cinder asks.

He shakes his head. "I don't think I know anybody here, outside of you all, and definitely not him."

"Any chance you got in touch with your family?"

An odd look crosses his face. "I did like you said and checked my phone and address book. "I don't have any contacts with the same surname."

"I'm sorry."

"It's okay." He touches my arm. "My memory's returning and that's a good thing."

Torn, I show him out and hang up my cloak. Upstairs in the kitchen, I put the kettle on for tea and Cinder retrieves a handful of candies from the pie cabinet. We share them in silence as the water heats.

"You heard what he said—the bites could be from a dog or a coyote, not a wolf."

I try to buy her reassurance, but it doesn't work. "Yes," I say, "seems he's in the clear."

But what if he's lying?

EIGHT

The rest of the afternoon goes by in a rush of customers, and more tea to calm my nerves.

Poppi calls at one point, having heard the news. I end up repeating my story to him, Belle, Zelle, Matilda, Uncle Odin, and Finn Starling, Cinder's boyfriend. She puts him to work on building storage shelves for our redesigned space.

Nonni refuses to let Poppi walk the trail to come see us, and they show up in Poppi's truck, bringing two apple pies fresh from the oven.

Leo arrives as well, and we take turns enjoying slices in the kitchen and discussing the disturbing events.

"I don't like this at all," he says, running a hand through his golden hair. He's already eaten two large pieces, trying each pie, and declared Nonni is the best cook in the county.

She blushed and looked pleased.

"What can we do about it?" Belle says to no one in particular. "First of all, Ren stated he didn't think the victim died from an animal attack, and secondly, if Robyn can't run those PIT members out of town, who can?"

Zelle finishes chewing and points a fork at her twin. "I vote we hex them. Break their cameras, give them a rash, make them wish they'd never come here."

Belle chastises her, but if doing so might prevent them from uncovering Ren's secret or someone else getting hurt, I'm in.

As the others continue to discuss it, I take my tea downstairs, wondering how to prove Ren is innocent of the man's death.

Shortly after closing, I'm pouring pumpkin scented goat's milk soap into silicone forms when Belle's footsteps sound on the turret stairs.

"Ah-ha!" She hurries into the room, Jayne on her heels. "I found something that might help us figure it out."

Cinder and Finn are painting trim around the new display window. Cinder sent Poppi and Nonni home after a few hours of their help. Matilda and Zelle are on the showroom floor, finishing with the last customer.

Leo emerges and goes to talk to Finn.

The bell over the door tinkles as the shopper leaves and Zelle strolls into the room, leaving Matilda to close the register for the day. "Figure out what?"

Belle marches to me at the work table, flopping a large, leather-bound volume on the scarred wood. "A

spell to tell us whether you know who is you know what."

Her twin rubs her hands together. "I love a new spell. Let me see it."

I finish the soaps before the base hardens, casting a glance behind me to make sure no customers are left to overhear. "From the hair I found? Are you sure? We only have one."

Belle runs a finger down the list of ingredients. "That should do it."

Zelle reads it over her shoulder. "I'm game."

Cinder passes us, her paintbrush in hand as she heads for the mop sink to clean it. She gives me a worried glance, sensing trouble. "For what?"

"We need to perform a spell to see if Ruby's boyfriend is a werewolf," Zelle responds. "It involves mixing a potion."

Leo and Finn join us, Finn wiping paint from his fingers. He wanders over to look at the recipe and screws up his face. "Spit from a pregnant toad? Seriously? That's an actual ingredient?"

He and Leo have seen magick in action, but it can still be a lot to process when you didn't grow up with it and it's not part of your everyday world.

"Where are we going to find that?" My hope sinks. "Do toads even get pregnant this time of year?"

Belle taps the book. "Don't worry. It's optional. It gives the potion a boost, but we should be able to still make it work with the other items."

Leo points to the turret door. "Are we done up there?"

Belle nods absentmindedly, studying the directions. "For now."

"I'll shut off the lights." Leo is big and broad like Ren. He squeezes through the door, which was even smaller when we first discovered it beside the fireplace, and the wall switch clicks. "I think I should patrol the woods tonight, just in case," he says.

"I'll go with you," Finn adds.

"The two of you will do no such thing." Cinder dries her brush with a clean rag. "If anything, I want you at Nonni and Poppi's to watch out for them. None of us are going into the woods."

"It's supposed to storm tonight," Zelle tells us. "Maybe that'll keep the paranormal idiots away."

"Ruby?" Matilda is behind me, and I pivot to face her. "There's someone here to see you."

The person waiting on the showroom floor is Ren. "I didn't hear the bell. How are you?"

"Hi there." His eyes light up when he sees me. "I'm fine. The question is, how are you?"

I study his face, those serious eyes. "You've remembered more about yourself?"

A shrug. "A little You okay after this afternoon?"

"I'm..." How can I respond? "I keep wondering if I could've saved that man if I'd looked harder this morning."

He steps closer and takes my hand. "He'd been dead longer than that, Ruby. I'm sure of it. There was

nothing you could have done for him, even if you'd found him earlier."

"I hope that's true."

He hands me a bag with an advertisement for heartworm medication stamped on it. "I brought your clothes back. Sorry I didn't have anything nicer to return them in. I did wash them for you."

They're nicely folded inside and smell of laundry detergent. "Thank you. You didn't have to do that."

"I was hoping to buy some of that pine soap."

"Right, yes." I place the bag on a stool, noticing my family, as well as Leo and Finn, have disappeared. All but Matilda, who's sitting at the worktable watching us with a smile that says she's enjoying the show. I glare at her and motion for her to scoot. She wiggles her fingers, picks up her unicorn mug and heads upstairs.

Facing Ren once more, I leave the counter and head for the soap shelves. "How was your first day at the clinic?"

"Busy. The filing system needs an overhaul, plus the computer...don't even get me started on that."

I lead him to the Frosted Pine section. "I imagine Dr. Frederick was a little antiquated with his paper-work and files."

"I have so many plans for that place." He collects three bars and holds one to his nose, breathing deeply. "I've studied both large animals and exotics. I want to bring those services to the clinic. I also plan to help the

rescues and do free spay/neuter clinics all over the county."

If it weren't for the body, I'd be enjoying this conversation a whole lot more. "That's wonderful." *But about turning into a werewolf at the full moon every month?*

Probably not the best topic at the moment.

He grins from ear to ear. "I'm having a grand opening Saturday from three to seven, so I can get to know the locals and introduce myself. Will you come?"

The night of the full moon. If he *is* one, he'll shift, like it or not.

But what can I say? At least I can keep an eye on him. "That'd be great. Of course, I'll come."

He leans down and stares hard into my eyes. "Are you really okay, Ruby?"

I want to be. Thunder rumbles in the distance, and I swear, I feel it in my bones. There's a storm coming all right, and it's not just bringing rain.

He sees my hesitation. "I'm sorry about this morning. I really am. I must've blacked out, maybe did some sleepwalking. The move has upset my normal rhythms, I think. I promise not to show up on your doorstep naked again."

Well...it wasn't all bad. At the register, I ring him up, and he makes me promise once more that I'll attend.

Upstairs in the kitchen, I find everyone gathered around a large cauldron on the stove. Even our cousin, Snow, has arrived, with her wolf hybrid, Runa.

"Heard you have a wolf problem." There's a teasing glint in her eyes. Her white pet nudges against her leg and she rubs her head. "Thought Runa and I might lend some support. We brought the thistle and wormwood."

"Thanks." I fetch the hair from my cloak. "How will it tell us if he's a were or shifter?" I ask Belle.

She adds a yellow powder and stirs. A bubbling begins. "When you drop the strand in, the liquid will turn gold for shifter and black for a werewolf."

From it, a pungent aroma fills the kitchen and Zelle waves a hand under her nose. "Are you sure you mixed that correctly?"

"Hey, at least I don't blow things up when I make a potion."

Zelle screws up her nose at both the odor and her sister's jab. "I can't help it if Eunice liked to experiment with combos that are volatile."

Matilda laughs; Cinder rolls her eyes.

"Is it ready?" I ask.

Belle gives a final stir then moves aside. "As much as it will ever be."

Taking a deep breath, I hold the strand over the concoction, wondering which I hope for—is it better for Ren to be a werewolf or a shifter? Each has its pros and cons.

Still unsure, I drop it into the bubbling liquid and prepare myself.

CHAPTER
NINE

"Is it supposed to do that?" Finn asks, eyeing the potion over Cinder's shoulder.

Belle checks the ingredient list and directions, as we all watch the brewing liquid pop and fizz.

A fine layer of tiny bubbles appears on the surface. "It looks like that seltzer stuff folks use to neutralize acid in the stomach," Finn says.

"What do you think, Belle?" Cinder asks.

"I don't know." She stares at it, glances back at the book. "It doesn't say anything about fizzing or foaming."

Leaning closer, I watch a single bubble grow larger and larger. When it fills the top of the cauldron, I have to angle away. "Everyone move. This thing could blow."

Belle turns off the burner and we all take several strides backward to a safer distance.

"Now who's blowing things up?" Zelle jokes.

The main bubble continues to expand, rising into the air over the rim of the cauldron. A sheen from the kitchen light reflects on it. Rainbows appear on the surface.

Belle picks up her spoon, pointing, ready to poke it. "Maybe I shouldn't have used burdock root in place of the ginger."

"Wait!" I hear Eunice's voice and see her phantom figure hovering half in and half out of the cabinetry to my right.

"Don't do that." I put out a hand to stop Belle's arm.

Sure enough, the glistening bubble shimmers and flexes, becoming cloudy in the center. The interior mist begins to roll and undulate.

"It's acting like a crystal ball." I nod at our grandmother's spirit. "Thank you."

"Huh?" Zelle frowns at me and glances to the spot I'm staring at.

"Eunice is here," I tell the group.

Before they can assault me with questions, I see the mist thin inside the bubble. A silvery orb emerges. "Look." I point. "Does anyone else think that resembles a moon?"

Murmurs of agreement issue from the others. We wait and watch, the orb growing fuller, brighter.

Zelle is holding her nose and she sounds like she has a cold. "Is the potion turning colors yet?"

Cautiously, Belle draws as near as she dares,

gazing at the edge, trying to see through the globule. "It's still pinkish."

"So, what does that mean?" Leo asks, towering over most of us. "Is he a were or shifter?"

Leo has an inner beast and sometimes it comes out, especially if he's angry or upset. He doesn't shift, per say, but pretty close, and I wonder if he has a personal interest in this.

Uncle Odin opens the refrigerator and takes out a can of ginger ale. "Shifters can change into a wolf or other animal on command. Wolves technically shift just like them, but it's not controllable and is brought on by a full moon."

Cinder and I exchange a look—our uncle is once again blessing us with information that could be helpful but seems odd at the moment.

"Thank you for the clarification, Odin," Matilda says.

The moon in the crystal-like bubble hovers, and the last of the fog clears. If I had any doubt of the meaning, it disappears when I hear a lone howl outside in the woods.

"He's a werewolf." My skin chills. "We're only days away from the full moon."

Uncle Odin pops open the can and enjoys a sip, adjusting his eye patch. "The three nights leading up to it and the three after can trigger a shift as well."

Now that *is* helpful.

"The full moon is Saturday," Snow reminds us. "He shifted last night and that was only Tuesday."

"Five days," Finn states. "That's outside the norm."

Eunice disappears. Another rumble of thunder, this one closer, echoes through the house. My legs grow shaky, like when I found the body, and I crumple in a kitchen chair. "We need to talk to him. He's dangerous."

Matilda pats my shoulder. "Why don't you invite him for dinner? We can break it to him gently."

I'm tempted to take the easy way out and accept her offer, but it'd be better if we don't ambush him. "It's a good idea, but I think I should do it."

I leave them and go to find my phone.

CHAPTER
TEN

Ren doesn't answer the clinic phone, and I don't have his personal number. The storm kicks into high gear, rain pounding the windows.

The electricity flickers and the lights go out. Next the phone and cell towers start having issues, leaving us with no reception.

Cinder's wish list for the remodel includes a generator, but she hasn't found one suitable yet. She grouses about not having it and Finn tries to lighten her spirits by promising they'll head to the nearest home improvement chain store first thing the next day to buy one.

Matilda and Uncle Odin gather us around the fireplace downstairs, and the animals join us. The flue is sticky and the chimney needs a good sweep, Cinder reminds them, but soon a small fire is crackling and sending off warmth. Zelle brings me a blanket and

Lenore perches on the back of my chair. I stare into the flames, but my mind is elsewhere. "I should have insisted he stay earlier."

Everyone knows who I'm talking about.

"Don't beat yourself up," Zelle insists. "Even if he shifts and runs around in the woods tonight, no one will be out there in this storm."

I hope that's true.

"Here." Belle hands me a pack of envelopes, tied with a faded ribbon. "You'll like these."

Dust comes off onto my fingers as I accept the stack. "What are they?"

"I didn't look through all of them, but some are from great-grandpa Ezra. I think they might be love letters."

I have to admit, this does cheer me up. We know quite a bit about Eunice, but not much about her husband.

"Where did you find those?" Matilda asks.

"Hidden in a compartment in Eunice's desk." Belle beams with pride at discovering this treasure. "I think our great-grandmother liked her secrets."

"I want to read them when you're done," Zelle says. "Meantime, I'm going to tackle my project."

She heads for my work kitchen, and I refrain from asking her not to. The power is out, but she can still use the gas stove.

Matilda sees me cringe, and she pats my hand. "I'll keep an eye on her."

After she disappears into the other room, I murmur, "How is that better?"

The group laughs.

They play a board game, and I read by candlelight, becoming totally absorbed in the letters.

Ezra was a man of polite, but passionate, expression. He definitely loved Eunice, and the two kept up a long-distance relationship while he traveled the coast, buying and selling wares for the general store he planned to establish here in town. It later morphed into the Enchanted Candle and Soap Company when Ezra passed and Eunice took over.

"*We are transforming this land forever*," he wrote in bold, flowing script. "*What an amazing time to be alive!*"

Eunice must've encountered some resistance from her family about her plans to marry him. She was Episcopalian and he was Methodist.

I wonder if he knew she was also a closet witch. Did she use religion to hide that fact, or did she view her potions and spells as simply part of her spirituality? It was definitely a different time, and knowing how to use herbs and plants was a more important area of life.

Eventually, the storm relents and the lights return. As soon as they do, I try calling the clinic once more.

No answer.

Belle, Leo, Zelle, and I file into the van and drive there. I told them I'd go alone, but they refused to leave me unsupported.

I pull around to the gravel lot behind the clinic and park. "I should've made him spend the night with me."

"You didn't know for sure, and you're being too hard on yourself," Belle tells me in a chiding voice.

The clinic is dark. Dr. Frederick and his wife lived outside town, but there is an apartment above the clinic. No lights there either.

I cut off the engine. "Maybe he went to bed early. I'll knock and see if I can raise him."

"He lives here?" Leo asks. His bulk takes up the more significant part of the back seat.

"Yes."

Zelle leans over to look up at the second floor. "I haven't heard any gossip about him buying or renting another place, so I'm sure that's true."

She hears all the good stuff from her clients. Some not so good as well. Small towns—everyone knows everything.

I hop out and knock on the back door. Overhead the waxing moon watches me. "Ren?" I call. "It's Ruby. Are you in there?"

There's no response and I put my ear to the door, trying to pick up interior sounds. Hearing nothing that sounds like Ren moving around, I wrangle my way around a set of dense boxwoods to peer in a window. A nightlight illuminates the area behind the receptionist's counter, but the waiting room is dark. I go to the front entrance and knock some more, but he's not here.

Leo gets out and jiggles the doorknob, heaving a shoulder against the wood.

"What are you doing?" Belle calls, and at that moment, it pops open.

Leo grins. "He could be sick or something."

We go inside, seeing the usual clinic furniture and supplies. Upstairs, we barge into the apartment.

He's definitely living here, but he's not home. Only a parrot in a cage in one corner greets us. "Intruder! Intruder!" it trills.

Downstairs, I know we have no choice but to go to the woods and look for him. Leo seems to read my mind. He grabs a large kennel from the back room that's filled with assorted dog and cat food products for people to purchase.

"We may need it," is the only thing he says before he drags it out to put in the van. Eyeing the bags and cans, I take a small sample of dog food, telling myself, I'll pay for it later.

Inside the vehicle, Belle squeezes my shoulder. "We can drive around town," she says. "See if we find him."

I know where he is, and it's not anywhere in town. "We have to go to the woods."

Zelle yawns. "Cinder said—"

"I'll drop you guys at the shop and go myself. I'll be fine."

"Cinder doesn't scare me." Leo winks at me in the rearview mirror. "I'm going with you."

"Me, too." Belle squeezes once more. "We all are."

Zelle grins. "You know I'm in. Do you want to round up Matilda?"

"No," the rest of us say in unison.

I have to take a circuitous route, passing Snow's farm, in order to be out of sight from Nonni and Poppi's place. We're not far from the park on the north end and the path that leads to the stream. From there, it's north all the way to the beautiful National Park that stretches for miles and miles. Robyn loves to ride her bike there on weekends.

"Okay, look." I point to where the kennel is. Cinder has assorted tools and flashlights stored there. "Everybody take a weapon. Not only could Ren be running around in wolf form, but there are actual wolves out here."

"You could freeze them," Zelle says.

"I haven't done that spell in years, and it was weak then."

Leo easily removes the wire kennel and places it on the ground. I open the dog food, putting several handfuls in the pocket of my cape after I whisper an incantation over them. My sisters grab flashlights and Zelle helps herself to a crowbar.

The forest seems slippery with shadows and more daunting than I usually find it, even at night. Everything is muddy and the trees drip from the rain, our moon mostly hidden behind a curtain of thin clouds.

"The paranormal investigators may be here now,

too," I remind them. "They have fans in town as well. Any or all of them could be dangerous, but I'm more worried they might be filming stuff. The last thing we need is to run into them, got it?"

They all nod. I lift a heavy wrench out of its place, holding it close to my leg. "We stay together as much as possible. If you see anything, raise the alarm."

"What are we going to do if we find him?" Leo asks. "In wolf form, I mean? It's one thing to have the kennel, but how do we get him into it?"

I show him the kibble. "I hope this will work, but we can't approach him and scare him away until I'm sure it's him. I'll handle it from there."

We head in, sticking to the path. The kennel is heavy, and although Leo has the strength of two men, it's also awkward to carry and he leaves it near a tree that marks the edge of the park.

My beam lights the trail, sliding over boulders, as well as trunks. As we search, I realize we could spend the whole night here and never find him.

I needn't have worried. As we round a turn that leads to the creek, my flashlight sweeps across the eyes of an animal.

A very large one.

I stumble backward as it growls. The hands of my sisters catch me.

The face and muzzle are familiar, but it's the eyes that clinch it. As I lower my beam, it flashes off emerald specks in the dark pupils.

"Ren?"

The wolf cocks its head, sniffs, and locks gazes with me for a tense moment.

"It's me. Ruby." I carefully reach a solicitous hand toward him. "I'm here to help you."

The night air fogs white from his huff. Then he lifts his muzzle and lets out a hair-raising howl.

CHAPTER
ELEVEN

The eerie sound shoots icy shivers down my spine. It's full of pain and anguish.

I hear Leo behind me, my legs shaking as I stand my ground. The sharp cry echoes through the forest, and a second goes up a reasonable distance away.

"Easy," Leo says to me as Ren lowers his head and makes eye contact again. "No sudden moves."

Believe me, I have no intention of provoking the giant wolf. One leap and he could be on me.

"It's okay," I soothe, the statement for both Ren and Leo. Carefully, I withdraw a handful of kibble. The wolf's ears prick and his nostrils flare.

I toss several to him.

At first, he continues to stand at attention. Preternaturally still, he scrutinizes me. I stay as immobile and, hopefully, as nonthreatening as possible.

"Ruby..." Belle's voice quivers. "This is dangerous.

"Shh..." I toss another piece. "Everything's going to be fine."

I smile, hoping somewhere inside him, Ren sees it. *Remember me.* I start a chant in my head on the off chance he can pick up on it. *I'm your friend. You feel safe with me. It's time to go home.*

The third time I go through the recitation, I see a softening in his stance. Wariness continues to blaze in his eyes, but he seems to understand on a basic, gut level that I mean him no harm.

Doesn't mean he's ready to come with me, however.

"Everyone take a slow, easy step away from us."

"I'm putting up a protective ward around you," Zelle says.

The wolf snarls.

"That's not necessary." I never take my eyes from him. "Just do as I say. Take a step back so he doesn't feel like we're ganging up on him."

"It's a good idea," Leo says. I sense all three reluctantly moving.

I drop a few more bites, leaving them like breadcrumbs, and do the same. "Come on, buddy. I'm not going to hurt you."

He drops his muzzle and sniffs those closest to his massive paws. His gaze stays on me as he eats one, then another.

A rush of satisfaction floods me. "That's right. We're all good here."

After finishing the kibble nearest him, he moves

forward. His head stays lowered, focus never leaving my face.

"Careful," Belle warns when he takes a second step, close enough I can hear his breathing.

Maintaining my slow movements, I lay out more food, retreating as I do so. My heart does a leap of relief each time Ren takes a bite. "Don't worry. He'll be out soon."

I hope, anyway.

Like the Piped Piper, I continue to entice the wolf to follow us.

"Wait, you charmed the food?" Belle's whisper is a mix of astonishment and admiration. "I thought you were just feeding him."

Ren halts and cocks his head, as if understanding the conversation, I stop all movement. *Come on, come on. Eat.*

My lungs release the breath I'm holding when he resumes. Stepping back, I narrowly miss a fallen limb. I toss more morsels to distract him. "It was either that or tranquilize him," I murmur. "Since that wasn't an option, I went with this."

Zelle chuckles. "Resourceful, as always, sister."

It's agony going so slowly. Every snap of a branch or skitter of a nocturnal creature captures Ren's attention. By the time we reach the trail, however, he begins to sway.

"Looks like it's working," Leo comments.

"Get the kennel and bring it here," Belle instructs.

"I'm not leaving the three of you alone with a werewolf, even if he is about to pass out."

Ren growls, and I again sense he understands us. "It's okay," I coax. "Look at what I have for you."

Extending a shaking hand, I display a giant bone, flavored like chicken according to the package I removed it from. His nose wrinkles and he closes in.

The edible chew toy is recommended for large breed dogs and measures at least a foot. He sways again but clamps on the end of it and jerks it from my grasp.

His front paws stumble, the rear ones giving out. Even as his massive jaws bust through the bone, he crumples to the ground in front of us.

Leo tugs Belle behind him. "How long will he be out?"

Zelle's hand is on my lower back. I hadn't noticed it before now, but I feel her fingers gripping my cape and trying to tow me farther away.

Ren manages to snap another section before his eyes roll up in his head. He sags to the side.

My breath whooshes out of me. "Thirty minutes?" I've never spelled a werewolf before, but I read in one of Eunice's books that this works on a variety of supernatural creatures. It's effectiveness ranges from half an hour to a whole day. "Let's get that kennel."

"I'll stay with Ruby." Zelle keeps a close eye on Ren, even as her hand relaxes on my cape.

Leo and Belle take off through the woods, and

Zelle tiptoes around him, sizing up his paws, his ears. "He's so...big."

I crouch and gently stroke his muzzle. He growls softly in his sleep. The parting clouds allow the moon to glint off his canines. "How am I going to explain all of this to him?"

"Not exactly how you want to start a relationship, is it?"

"There won't even be a friendship if he can't accept this, or decides a witch isn't his swipe-right kind of girlfriend."

She scratches her hair, growing out from its ponytail. "You are who you are. Nothing to be ashamed of."

"The same can be said for him. I need to convince him of that."

"You fell pretty quick."

Sometimes you just know when it feels right. "I'm getting ahead of myself, I guess, but from the moment I saw him, I felt..."

"The click?"

Zelle's term for being compatible.

"Yeah, there was definitely a click."

We watch him breathe, the night forest sounds subdued.

She kneels next to me and rubs several strands of his fur between her finger and thumb, testing the texture of it. "The way his eyes light up when he sees you tells me he's definitely interested in being more than friends. Give it a chance. He might surprise you."

"Right." I search for some grounds for hope. "He

didn't run screaming when he heard us discussing werewolves and shifters. That's a positive, right?"

"I'd say you have a good shot at helping him understand what he is and how to cope with it." She puts a hand on my shoulder. "I think you two will make a good couple."

I chuckle nervously. "We barely know each other."

Footsteps approach, along with the sounds of snapping branches. I assume it's Leo and Belle, but my inner sense of danger raises the hair on the back of my neck.

Zelle senses it, too, whirling to shine her flashlight into the nearby trees.

Removing my cloak, I drape it over Ren's body and mutter a quick spell to activate the cloak's invisibility powers.

"Oh, hi, Ruby." Jenny emerges from a copse of trees to our right. "We thought we heard voices out here."

Zelle steps next to me, her shoulder lines up with mine. The moon slides behind the clouds again, as if assisting us in putting Ren in the shadows. "Who is she?"

"Zelle, this is Jenny, one of the paranormal investigators. Jenny, my sister."

"Hey, nice to meet you." Jenny gives her a shy wave. "You must be Belle's twin."

Zelle doesn't answer or return the gesture.

"Are you out here alone?" I query.

"Nah." She grins and points over her shoulder. "Wagner's with me."

The man who accompanied her at the shop catches up to her now, breathing heavily. He's dressed in all black and they have on their matching vests. "You were correct. It's the witches."

"We're shooting footage." Jenny keeps smiling, her enthusiasm obvious. "What are you two doing out here?"

Zelle ignores his question and poses her own. "Where's your camera?"

Jenny raises the phone in her hand. "We do some on these. Gives the show a special flare, sort of a Blair Witch vibe, you know?"

"Never cared for that movie myself."

"We're on our way home from visiting our grand-parents," I tell them, diverting the conversation.

Wagner smirks. "Dangerous to be out here at night, isn't it? We heard howling. You didn't see any wolves or coyotes, did you?"

In the distance, a siren blares. We turn our heads in that direction. "No, but,"—Zelle laces her arm through mine—"this is their home. They howl all the time. We've found the wild animals don't bother us if we don't bother them."

The siren draws closer. Jenny pockets her phone. "Well, we best be going. Good to see you."

Wagner stays planted until she tugs on his arm, and they finally disappear the way they came.

Zelle lowers her voice. "Do you think they saw anything?"

My stomach feels like there's a hundred pound brick in it. "We better hope not."

"They give me the willies."

"Me, too, and we better have Poppi keep an eye on their blog. I fear they may have more than we like on film."

TWELVE

The task of hauling Ren into the cage and then the van takes a bit of doing. Even with magick, he's no easy beast to move.

Leo's size and strength helps, and Zelle and I keep our senses on high alert as Belle assists him, but it's slow going.

To complicate matters, two police cars pull in a few yards from our vehicle before we can load Ren. Red and blue strobes rake the trees.

Officers bail out and discuss their plan to comb the main path. We hide in the shadows and Zelle and Belle use their combined magick to weave a spell around us that has the effect of blurring our images.

I place the cloak over the cage, the chilly air seeping into my bones. We hunker down for long minutes until they divide up to start their search. One walks right past me, and I hold my breath.

The magick holds, and he moves on. I swallow the fear in my throat and silently breathe again.

Once they disappear, we leave our flashlights off as we navigate to the rear doors. When everyone is in and buckled, I place another spell over the engine for it to run whisper quiet.

No one speaks until we're at the shop. I back in as close to the rear entrance as possible, and Leo manages to wrangle the cage out.

In the workroom, we stand in a circle, trying to decide what to do with Ren now that we have him here. The kennel takes up so much space, we can barely move around it.

"If he wakes still in wolf form, he'll be frightened and confused," I say, working over various ideas in my head. "He'll try to break free."

"If he wakes up human, he'll still be confused," Leo states.

"And naked," Zelle adds with a lighthearted wink at me.

Belle gently smacks her sister's arm. "We'll get him a blanket."

I watch his eyes moving under the heavy lids as he dreams. "I can charm the cage to hold him, but it might be better if he wasn't...on display. Plus, I don't want to scare the others when they come down."

"Your room?" Zelle asks, all innocence.

"It's not big enough for this unless I move everything but the bed out."

Zelle quietly claps. "Sounds like a plan."

Belle and I both smack her this time.

"What?" She acts put out, but chuckles. "I'm just trying to help."

Reaching in her pocket, she draws out her phone and points it at Ren. "Say cheese."

I grab the phone. "What are you doing?"

"It's for my scrapbook."

"No pictures."

"The tower," Belle says, pointing. "If we move the couch to the west wall, there will be plenty of space."

Leo gives her a look like she's lost her mind. "You want me to navigate those stairs with this?" He taps the wire bars.

"We'll supervise," she assures him, a bright smile gracing her lips.

It's a good idea. That way, he'll be out of sight and not bothered by anyone when he shifts.

Leo is a sucker for Belle. When she turns on the charm, he can't say no. "Fine. Let's do it."

She hugs him and he peels her arms away, as if she's still on his list, but I see the way he smiles under his beard.

The same spell I used to keep the van engine quiet works equally well to keep our progress up the narrow stairwell from waking the others.

From all the jostling, however, Ren wakes. As we scoot the couch aside and Leo deposits the cage in its place, Ren snarls and whines, then scratches at the bars.

"What now?" Belle asks.

I check the clock on the desk. "Sunrise is in a few hours. He'll shift back soon. I'll stay with him. You guys get some rest."

Ren lunges, snapping his jaws together. I perform a quick spell to reinforce the bars and anchor the kennel to the floor. He lifts his muzzle, and before I can silence him, he howls.

So much for our efforts to remain quiet.

The cry raises the rest of the family. Cinder, Matilda, and Uncle Odin show up, shocked. I listen to half an hour of various chastisements for going into the woods and bringing home a werewolf, combined with utter fascination that I captured one.

The reality of a magickal family.

Eventually, everyone leaves and that alone helps to calm Ren considerably. I make tea and bring water for him. I manage to slide a narrow bowl through the bars to pour it in, his eyes monitoring my every move the whole time.

He continues sniffing and whining. I put fresh non-bewitched kibble in beside the water. He turns, lifting his chin, much like Nonni when Poppi gives her grief about her moon dancing.

"I know I tricked you. Not very nice of me, was it?"

His steely gaze comes back to glare at me. I sip tea and sit nearby, using my cloak for padding. He scratches at his confines, trying to find a way out, and lets loose another howl that sends goosebumps all over my skin.

I snap my fingers, sending a bit of magick toward

him as a warning. "None of that. You'll keep the others awake. How about we talk?"

He paces as best he can, the cage too small for him to do more than turn circles. He whimpers and shakes, flinging hair everywhere.

I ignore the display, telling him what I know about werewolves. "Many cultures have stories about them, what they're associated with, what cures them or kills them. Weres are created from the bite of another and can't control their shifting. A shapeshifter can. Then there's an Animagus, a rare type of witch who can use magick to become an animal. That's an entirely different variety. It appears you're a werewolf, and this month's moon has triggered your shift. Why is the key to figuring it all out."

He listens and then laps at the water but ignores the food. I go to the shelves and scan Eunice's books. A history of the area catches my eye. The aged volume is sticking out as if someone returned it but didn't line it up with the rest.

Back at my seat, I flip through the yellowed pages. An interesting note in her penmanship stops my search.

"Your name. You told me it was Renfroe Redfern Woolsey."

The wolf gnaws at the wire bars.

"As if, buddy. You can't break out of there. Trust me."

I move to the desk and thumb through a local directory from the same time period, which contains

brief accounts of the town, even smaller back then, and a list of inhabitants.

Redfern is listed once, the address is unfamiliar. "Do you have relatives from this area?"

He answers with a growl.

Making a note of the name on a slip of paper, I return to my seat next to him and resume reading the latest diary entry of Eunice's. It's the spring of 1800 and she's listed all the herbs and flowers she plans to grow that summer in her garden. She and Ezra are married now and expecting their first child.

My body becomes stiff and heavy, my eyes tired. What a day it's been. The adrenaline and shocking discoveries have left me completely drained.

I catch myself falling asleep more than once. Ren makes yips and moans, sad and painful sounding. At one point, he lies on his side, legs jammed against the metal bars, and his breathing becomes harsh and quick.

In fascination, I watch as his chest heaves and his cheeks puff from his breathing. His eyes flutter closed, and I realize he's going to shift soon. Daylight is only a few minutes away.

He lets out another groan. It must be arduous— the shifting and breaking of bones, the stretching, and reforming of tendons and muscles.

Realizing he is at the mercy of his body and risking my well-being on the hope he can't attack me now, I quietly slide open the kennel door and lay my cape over him. Perhaps it will make the transition easier.

Closing and locking it once more, I yawn. Stacking pillows near the cage and grabbing an old afghan, I make a bed beside him.

He settles under the cape, and I promptly fall asleep.

CHAPTER

THIRTEEN

"What's going on? Why am I...? Oh no, not this again. How?"

I jerk awake in time to see Ren dragging my cape over him. Forced to crouch, his head smacks the top of the kennel. Muscles ripple, and I get the chance to examine the intricate tribal tattoo in more detail.

Rubbing sleep from my eyes, I try not to stare. His hair seems to have grown two inches overnight. Not as fast as Zelle's but definitely more than a normal person's would.

His voice is husky as he continues to mutter complaints. The cape slips off one thigh as he adjusts it. He hastily fumbles to cover himself when he discovers I'm watching.

I can't help my chuckle as I stand and stretch. "We have to quit meeting like this."

My attempt to lighten the mood fails. His dark eyes glare from behind the bars. "What am I doing here?"

The gash on his shoulder has healed nicely. At least he didn't end up with any new wounds from his latest jaunt. "Do you remember anything from last night?"

His brows furrow and his gaze slides to the floor. "I closed up the clinic, did some paperwork, took a walk—"

"In the woods?"

Silence hangs in the air between us for a heartbeat as he searches his memory. "I was in the park. I thought I saw a man several yards away. He was..."

Again he trails off. At least he has some recall this morning. That's a good sign.

He glances up. "I think he was chasing an injured wolf."

I unlock the door, turning my back to him as he exits. "This man—was he about so high?" I hold a hand a few inches above my head. "Dark hair, wearing a utility type vest with lots of pockets?"

"I barely got a glimpse of him from the back. He wore a windbreaker. The storm was coming up and I thought I'd better head in." His voice comes from directly behind me. "But the wolf, I saw him before he dashed deep into the woods. He was limping."

"You wanted to help him."

"The man cursed at him. It made my gut go on alert."

I spot a neat pile of men's clothes on the desk. Uncle Odin has offered slacks, a shirt, and one of his

green striped vests. He's at least five or six inches shorter than Ren, so that should be interesting to see.

I hand the stack of garments to Ren, keeping my gaze slightly averted out of politeness. "So you followed them into the woods?"

"I think so." He stares at the items, but his gaze is a million miles away. "Everything gets a bit blurry after that. I remember smelling the pine trees and soil."

"That's good. Scent is tied to memory, so focus on those fragrances."

Shaking his head, he takes the proffered clothes. "I believe it started to rain. I heard an owl hoot, and a coyote howl."

This is good. "Do you remember looking at the moon?"

He falls quiet, shakes his head again. "Hey, can you give me a minute?"

He wants to dress. I pivot once more to give him privacy and straighten a stack of journals on the desk. "Your memory is better today. That's promising."

"I came to a clearing," he finally says, "and yes, I remember looking up at the sky. I could just make out a sliver of the moon over the trees."

I hear the snap of material as he shakes out the trousers to put them on. I pick up my teacup. The last few dribbles are long cold. "And then what?"

"I woke up here. What time is it? How did I..." He comes up beside me, shirt in hand. "Ruby, why was I in a wire kennel? Was I drugged? I feel like I have a hangover."

I should probably have something stronger than chamomile before I attempt to explain any of this.

"I'd like to have a closer look at your tattoo."

"What?"

Touching his shoulder, I move so I can fully examine the compass. The center is a paw print, and I'm betting it denotes a wolf's. "Let's go downstairs and get some coffee." I lead the way to the steps. "I have a lot to tell you."

"How about we stay right here, and you explain it?"

Determination sets his features in hard lines. I'm too tired to do this delicately, and the truth has to be revealed. "Look, I'm a witch, and you're a werewolf."

He blusters. "There's no such thing."

No such thing as a witch? Or a were? "I did a spell to prove it. You're a supernatural creature. The stuff of legends."

He blinks and doesn't move. It's like staring down his wolf in the woods.

"I charmed dog food and fed it to you in your wolf form. The hangover is from that—it put you to sleep— and I'm sorry, but I had to capture you before you hurt anyone." I refrain from adding, "else."

"This is nuts. You're joking, right?"

Yep, the odds of him wanting me for a friend are dwindling fast. "You'll have to come back tonight and stay in the cage again. Every full moon, you'll have to restrain yourself."

He continues to stare at me, mute now. The clock

on the desk quietly ticks off the seconds, as he struggles with himself. With me.

I hear Zelle's voice from the forest: *Give it a chance. He might surprise you.*

As though coming to a decision, he shrugs on the shirt and begins buttoning it. "I'll take that coffee now."

FOURTEEN

"Sleep well?" Uncle Odin asks when we enter the kitchen. "Good to see you again."

The smells of melting sugar and warm vanilla greet my nose. Matilda is leaning on the oven with a mitt on one hand while she texts with the other. Cinder is pouring coffee for herself and grabs another cup for me. "You look like you need something stronger than tea this morning."

Ren doesn't seem happy to see any of them, but he's still gracious as he tells Uncle Odin, "Thanks for the clothes."

Uncle Odin smiles. "Any time. Have a seat. Do you like streusel? Matilda made cherry."

"I can't stay."

"Sure you can." Cinder hands him a mug. "I'm sure you have questions."

Matilda pockets her phone when the timer goes off. "Lucky you, we have answers."

Belle breezes in and hugs me before I sit. "How are you doing?"

"Stiff from sleeping on the floor, but otherwise okay."

Zelle enters in a cloud of jasmine and papaya, and heads to the fridge. She grabs the orange juice and starts pouring it into the glasses already on the table. She's shaved her head, but it's already formed a layer of peach fuzz over her skull and her magick has turned it icy blue. "You've got quite the howl, wolf boy."

Ren's face falls. "Sorry?"

"We aren't quite there yet," I tell her. "Still trying to come to terms with...that."

"What's the problem?" She glances at him. "Being a werewolf is pretty cool, if you ask me."

He clears his throat, but accepts the glass she hands him. "Werewolves don't exist."

"Knew I should have got a picture last night."

I pass a glass to our uncle. "Can you call Poppi today and ask him to keep an eye on the PI team's blog? A couple members were in the woods last night. I want to be sure none of us show up on video."

"Done." He pats my hand.

"Nonni called," Cinder says. "She was worried you hadn't shown up for eggs this morning. I explained about Ren."

A muscle jumps in his jaw.

Matilda sprinkles powdered sugar on the streusel before she puts a hot pad on the table and places the dish on it. Cherry juice bubbles from the ends.

"You made this?" Even with the wolf topic taking center stage, I'm in awe of the fact she baked something so delicious and didn't burn it.

"Don't be so shocked." She cuts it into slices and begins dishing it. "All I had to do was put a spell on the oven."

Ren chokes on a swig of juice.

"But you don't bake," I remind her.

"I watch The Food Network. They make things far more complicated than necessary, but they don't possess magick, so I suppose that's forgivable." She leans over to pass a plate to Belle. "Plus, it's reality TV. They've got to have the ticking clock and drama. Mundanes love that."

I accept a serving for me and one for Ren. "Where did you get the recipe?"

"From one of Eunice's books," Cinder explains. "Beware, the streusel is charmed."

"Is *not*." Matilda appears affronted. When we all look dubious, she adds, "I swear. I didn't need to charm the ingredients, only the oven so it wouldn't burn."

"You know, I really should be going." Ren pushes his chair away and stands. "I have, uh, appointments."

He strides out, leaving the rest of us staring after him.

"So that went well," Zelle says, digging into her portion. "That boy needs proof."

I'm not sure even a video of him shifting would convince him right now. My heart hurts for the confu-

sion he must be encountering. "How would you feel if you thought you were purely human, only to move to a new town and discover you're something out of a fairytale?"

"You don't think he ever shifted before he moved here?" Belle asks around a mouthful of her breakfast. "How is that possible?"

"I have no idea." The coffee has turned sour in my stomach and I play with the food on my plate as I hear the door slam downstairs. "All I know is he's shifting now, and the woods are not safe. How do I keep him from encountering those investigators?"

And how can I be sure he didn't kill that man?

Cinder reaches over to touch my arm. "You have to keep trying. He'll come around. Remember what Mom always said about Daddy? How she had to work on him for months to prove she was a witch?"

Our parents' courtship is legendary. Dad was non-magickal and Mom totally fell for him in elementary school. Even though he didn't believe in such things, and called her a weirdo for years, she eventually won him over in tenth grade by fixing his beater car—not with magick, mind you, but with her skills.

"I could kiss you," he'd told her, and that's when she did, in fact, use magick to take him up on the offer. That apparently knocked his socks off. He was putty in her hands after that.

I smile, remembering them. How in love they were. From the letters Belle found, my fourth great-grand-parents were like that, too. Even Nonni and Poppi are

role models for meeting a soulmate and being together for the rest of your lives.

Time. Is there ever enough?

"I'll try again this afternoon. If nothing else, I have to convince him to stay here tonight and not look at the moon."

"I'd rather not repeat our time in the woods," Belle remarks.

"You and me both."

"Eat," Matilda orders. "I want to know what the cook thinks."

Giving in, I taste the confectionary treat. "It's good." It is too. I take another bite. "I may need to hang up my apron strings if you're this talented at feeding us."

She guffaws, but looks pleased. "Don't get used to it. I have no intentions of doing this on a regular basis."

Cinder winks at me, seemingly relieved. "Take Ren some candy," she advises. "That will win him over."

That afternoon, I walk to the clinic, my best selection of chocolates in my basket. The waiting room is empty, and I find him in the back room, putting together a new shelving unit.

"Need any help?"

He glances at me, then away.

"Intruder, intruder!" The parrot sits on a branch screwed into the wall.

"Meet George," Ren says.

The bird flaps his bright wings without flying, tilting his head at me. "Already met. Already met."

I laugh. "Nice to meet you officially, George." Then I explain about the previous night. "I still owe you for the kibble."

"Nah. Hand me that screwdriver, would you?"

I look to the spot he's pointing at and retrieve the tool. "How's the reorganizing going?"

Our fingers brush as he accepts it. "Slow. I keep finding more things to do, and I dread going near the filing cabinet."

"I'm good with computers and paperwork. I can start on the files, if you want."

He meets my gaze and studies me for a moment. "What's in the basket?"

I lift the napkin to show him. "I wasn't sure if you prefer milk or dark chocolate, so I brought a selection of both."

"I'm not picky." He chooses a truffle with raspberry flavoring. Before he's done chewing, he nods vigorously. "That's delicious."

"No magick involved," I promise.

He gives me a side-eye gander, then returns to the shelving unit construction. "What's it like? Magick?"

That subject would take years to delve into. "I can't imagine life without it. It's...magickal, pun intended."

He screws a plank to an upright leg. "But you're a witch. You control it, not the other way around."

I see where he's going. He's been mulling all of this over, which is good. "Being a werewolf isn't all bad."

"In horror movies, they're monsters."

"Hollywood likes to overdo it on the drama."

He attaches the shelf to the wall, the sound of the cordless driver noisy enough to make George flap and fly to the waiting room. "Next, you'll be outlining the ten pros of being a werewolf."

Ten might be stretching it. "Your senses are heightened, and you'll have increased strength. That's pretty awesome."

Considering it, he begins screwing in the next shelf. "I suppose."

This doesn't seem to be winning me any points. "I bet you can use it to tune in to your patients and understand what's wrong with them."

That gets his attention. "Really?"

"Of course."

"How, exactly?"

"Your compassion and ability to understand them on a more primal level. It has to be an advantage."

He stops, grabs another candy, and makes a blissful face. "Man, these are amazing."

"Secret recipe that only a few special people get to sample."

"I'm special, huh?"

I flash my biggest smile.

He puts down the tool and shows me to the receptionist's station. "You sure you want to tackle this?"

The file cabinet is piled high with cream-colored

folders. The computer is nearly as old as I am. Papers cover the desk, and the answering machine is disconnected.

What a disaster. "You should see our office after a big sales day. I'm undaunted. Go work on your shelves. I'll have this cleaned up and organized before you're done."

"Is that a challenge?" I can see the idea fires up something in him.

"Are you a betting man?"

"I'll buy you dinner at your favorite restaurant if you get this mess fixed first."

I hold out a hand. "And if you win, I'll supply another basket of my gourmet candies."

"You're on, Little Red Riding Hood."

We shake, and I hide my grin, knowing magick is going to help me whip this place into shape in no time.

He'll be putty in my hands before the moon rises.

CHAPTER
FIFTEEN

"We've made an interesting discovery," Robyn tells us before closing later that day.

The store is empty for once, but I've had too much mint tea and chocolate, the caffeine putting my nerves on edge, even though my body feels like rubber. At least Ren agreed to come over tonight, and was quite impressed by my reorganization of his office.

Winning him over with candy and my skills seems to be working.

"What is it?" I ask, wondering if she has somehow discovered Ren's secret.

"The man you found in the woods has been identified."

Cinder turns the door sign over and flips the lock. "Who is he?"

My fingers shake, and I clasp my hands together to

hide it. Cinder moves to stand next to me and her steady presence is appreciated. "A local?"

Robyn sniffs a bar of Luscious Lime soap. "His name is Brady Hargraves. From Lancaster, Pennsylvania."

Not from here then. That could be good or bad. "What was he doing in the woods?"

"I believe he was following the Paranormal Investigator Team, trying to prove they're fakes. I'm getting conflicting reports from the fans who accompanied them here. Hargraves definitely had a fixation with them and was, apparently, part of their team at one time. I've spoken to his family, and they have various theories about why he might have been here. I want to interview the members and see where it leads."

I consider telling her Jenny and Wagner were there last night. About Ren seeing Wagner chasing an injured wolf.

Having to explain why *I* was there, however, isn't a good idea.

"Has the medical examiner determined the cause of death?" Cinder asks.

"Dr. Woolsey was right. Hargraves wasn't killed by a wild animal. The ME discovered a blow to the back of the head and believes that's the cause. He hasn't completed the autopsy, so we should know more once it's finished."

The relief I feel is overwhelming, yet the bite wounds are still a concern. "But this fellow *was*

attacked by a large dog or possibly a coyote, like Ren suggested?"

"Not per se." Robyn looks pensive. "The wounds are consistent with the animal using its teeth to drag the body. Weird, but maybe it was trying to take it to a cave or den. There are some of those in the National Park." She shrugs. "Anyway, I don't think magick was involved. This looks like plain old homicide."

Cinder puts the lime soap in a bag and gives it to her. "No charge. Any clues to the identity of the killer?"

"Thanks. I appreciate it." She folds the bag and tucks it in her inside coat pocket. "No solid leads yet. Until I find the culprit, be extra careful and stay out of the woods."

This is directed at me. How many times am I going to hear that this week?

I go to the wastebasket and remove Jenny's business card from it. "One of the investigators, the woman taking pictures, gave us this. She wanted to talk to Belle about what happened in September. She and her partner, a guy who goes by Wagner, are the two that have been the most persistent. I know there are others as well."

"The guy with her yesterday?"

"That was a different one."

"Thanks." She tucks it in her pocket. "I've left messages via their website contact page but haven't heard back from anyone yet. Guess when I told them to scram, they took it to heart. Some of the names they go by aren't legitimate—they're like stage names. I've

looked into the backgrounds on several members, but none have turned up more than a few unpaid parking tickets and misdemeanors."

"Either Hargraves had an enemy," Cinder says, crossing her arms, "or he stumbled onto something he shouldn't have and was silenced."

Robyn nods. "No one knows where the PIT members are staying, and although they filled out an application for the permit to film on city property, the phone number listed goes to a voicemail account that says it's full. If you see any of them, call me, okay?"

We assure her we will and she leaves.

"What do you think?" Cinder asks.

I cash out the register. "Maybe Ren was trying to rescue him from the killer."

"Possibly." She rearranges the display to fill in the spot left by the lime soap. "Or another animal did the damage."

"Ren told me he saw a man near the park last night, chasing a wolf. It appeared injured."

"Could he describe either?

"Not really." I place the cash and credit card receipts in a zippered pouch for Belle. "But I believe it might be Wagner."

"So maybe Hargraves and the wolf both stumbled on something the PIT team didn't want them to see."

We fall quiet, going about our normal end-of-day routine and considering all the possibilities.

"I don't like any of this," I tell her as she turns off the lights and we head to the workroom.

"You definitely have to keep Ren in tonight."

When I have a moment to myself before dinner, I call Snow. "Have you seen Runa's wolf mate lately?"

While Runa lives with her, the hybrid dog's mate —a full-blooded wolf—roams the woods. He's mostly a loner, but occasionally hangs out with a small pack that comes down from the National Park.

"Ferrin is in my barn with an injured left flank," she tells me. "Broden tried to check it, but you know how Ferr doesn't like humans."

I can't say I blame him.

She continues. "I called your vet, and he's swinging by after the clinic closes to see if he can sedate him and take a look. Should be here any minute. Does he know he's a were creature?"

"I've explained it to him, but he's having trouble wrapping his mind around it."

"Magick is like that for the non-magickal. A lot of them love stories referencing it, but when it becomes real, it freaks them out."

"I can't imagine *not* wanting to discover magick exists, although being a werewolf would not be my first pick for supernatural powers."

"Ditto. Have you given any more thought to coming to work for me?"

Snow lost her baker at Halloween and is searching for someone to fill her shoes. It would be an easy job with flexible hours, so I could continue on at the shop. "I'm outlining a plan that I think will benefit both of us."

"I can't wait to hear it. Next week at Thanksgiving?"

I hedge a bit. "Possibly, but I need to talk to Cinder and the twins first. Get their okay."

"I understand." I hear Broden's deep voice in the background. "Dr. Woolsey's here. I better go."

"Don't keep him long. He needs to come here before the moon rises."

"He's staying with you?"

I sure hope so. "I have a space set up for him. It's the only way to keep him"—and everyone else— "safe."

SIXTEEN

T'm biting my nails as the sun sinks. "He's not coming."

Cinder waits with me on the porch, the squeak of the rocking chair grating on my nerves as she calmly moves it forward and back. "He'll show."

I pace. "How can you be so sure?"

"Your chocolates."

I pivot and stop, gaping at her. "You're giving them"—*and me*—"too much credit."

She smiles serenely and keeps moving. "He was charmed by you from the moment you draped your cape over him."

"That may not be enough."

Lenore dances on the railing. Clouds are rolling in from the west. Out in the woods, I sense creatures bedding down for the night as others wake. "He does owe me dinner after I tidied up his office and completely restructured his filing system."

"We'd be lost without you doing the books for us."

I put thoughts of Ren on hold for a moment. "Which reminds me, we're out of coconut oil base again. The liquid, not the solid. Where is it going?"

"I'll give you one guess."

Her tone is a hint. I lower my voice. "Zelle?"

A downward movement of her chin.

"What is she working on?"

Cinder flares her hands out in a *who knows* gesture. "She won't even tell me which of Grandma Eunice's books she's testing recipes from."

I resume pacing. "It must be some kind of new beauty product she wants us to sell."

"Why doesn't she come out and tell us, then?"

Lenore makes a soft chortling noise in her throat to catch my attention. I pet her wings gently. "Zelle is unique. She likes to keep things secret until she perfects them."

"Which is why I haven't bugged her too much about it. She'll tell us when she's ready."

"As long as she doesn't ruin my new kitchen in the meantime."

Cinder stands, stretches, and comes over to the railing. "You like it?"

"I love it. I can't wait to start on Christmas candies for the bakery next week."

The sound of tires on gravel turns our heads. Ren is here, driving into our parking lot behind the shop. The sinking sun glints off the hood.

He waves and I return it. The relief I feel is palpable. "Thank goodness."

"See?" Cinder elbows me. "Told you so."

"You're a wise big sister."

"You're only now figuring this out?"

She's done so much to keep this family together and the shop running. "I've known it all along."

She squeezes my arm. "Everything's going to be okay, Ruby. Enjoy your night."

As she disappears inside, Ren climbs out of the SUV. "I heard you've got a tower room made up and waiting for me."

Joking is good; maybe he's accepted who he is.

"For you? Always. How's Ferrin?"

"Cranky." He goes to the back and lifts the hatch. "But he'll survive."

"That's good to hear." I watch as he takes out a large, folded contraption. It looks heavy, but he carries it with ease. "What's that?"

He climbs the steps and Lenore greets him. He smiles at the bird and then at me. "A bigger cage."

"You didn't tell me much about magick. What's it like being a witch?"

The larger kennel is better fitted to his size. My relief at seeing him was partly because we need to keep his beast contained, but also because, well, I like him.

A lot.

The click is there every time I see him.

I hand him a caramel candy through the bars. We've padded his cage with blankets and pillows, and I've made another temporary mat next to it. While the new one is bigger and heavier, I've still used a spell to anchor it to the floor. "I love it. Magick is simply using energy in different forms to help people."

His fingers touch mine as he reaches for it. "Not everyone uses it for good, though, huh?"

"Hollywood got that part correct."

He swallows the candy. "Is that why your candies are so tasty? You use some kind of magick on them?"

I laugh. "I told you, I don't use it for that."

He motions for me to hand him another. "Good to know, but you don't use it only to disable werewolves, I assume."

No reason to tell him I used it on his office. "I'm sorry for knocking you out last night, but you wouldn't have come peacefully."

"Apology accepted. I should thank you for helping me. It's still going to take me some time to come to grips with this."

Slipping a book through the bars, I'm grateful he's come this far already. "Here, read this."

He examines the title and cracks it open. "Lycanthropy?"

"This explains it as well as I can, and it offers a bit about hereditary genes versus the virus that causes it. I

figured you'd want the scientific and medical information."

"I didn't realize there would be any."

"I wasn't sure either, but according to various sources I've found, werewolves have been around a long, long time. My fourth great-grandmother had at least a passing interest, since I found this on her shelf."

He follows my gaze to the spot. "She was a witch, too?"

I nod. "You're still a bit of a mystery to me. Your name and tattoo suggest you may descend from a shifter family, but the spell says you're the type of were who shifts because of the moon."

"My name and tattoo are clues?"

I relate what Uncle Odin told us about the Woolsey surname. "You haven't remembered any more about your parents?"

"I have actually. I don't have any memories of my dad, never knew him. According to my mother, he was shipped overseas before I was born. Died on a mission in Turkey."

"I'm so sorry."

He toys with the book. "My mom was devastated. She went a little nuts after it happened. Grief can do that. I ended up with my grandparents, then mom disappeared. When my grandmother and grandfather could no longer care for me, I was adopted through the Catholic Children's Services."

"So you may have gotten the genes from your father."

"Makes sense. My adoptive parents were nice folks, if a little reserved. They were traditional Catholics and quite strict."

He's talking about them in the past tense. "Did something happen to them?"

"While I was in vet school, they died within a year of each other. My adopted father had cancer and my mother...well, she had a heart attack after he passed. Seems like I keep losing people I love." He flips open the book. "You're lucky to have those you do."

"I am. Have you met the Redferns who live on the edge of town past Snow's farm? Maybe you're related to them."

"I believe I may be distantly on my mom's side. It's one of the reasons I moved back here. I didn't know anything about my ties to them until a few months ago. A DNA test helped me track them down. We've spoken over the phone a few times, I simply didn't put two and two together the other day when I only saw their first names in my call history."

"I bet they're excited to have you here." I also hope they'll have some idea about his were-heritage. "They didn't mention anything about staying inside during a full moon?"

He chuckles. "Not that I recall. They seem pretty normal, so for now, I'd prefer to keep this between us."

"Understood." I drink some of my tea. "When did you get the tattoo?"

"The day I turned eighteen. It...called to me."

I bet it did. "You felt a connection to it?"

"I designed it, actually, so yeah, I did."

"You're an artist as well as a vet?"

He chuckles. "Not at all. I simply knew what I wanted."

"That's amazing. I wonder if your heritage was sending you a message."

"Like a wakeup call?"

"Yes. Either way, it's a beautiful design. I've never seen one like it."

Pride shows in his smile. "Thank you." He reads in silence for a few minutes as I comb through a book Belle found in Eunice's stash on curative magick.

"I'm so glad you could help Ferrin," I say, using my finger to mark a page.

He nods without looking up. "There was swelling in his left hindquarters, probably from a blow to the flank. Nothing is broken that I could ascertain without an x-ray. He should be good as new once the puffiness goes down."

"Do you think he's the same wolf you saw the man chasing last night?"

Now his head raises. "I'm sure of it. What I'm *not* is if that guy meant to help or hurt Ferrin further."

I use my phone to find the PIT video channel. Poppi texted and said nothing has shown up yet with us in it. "Let's see if you recognize this guy." I scroll through the long list of videos and see one labeled "Werewolves Among Us," then hit the play button and lean close so Ren can watch, too.

Wagner and another man are in woods over-

looking a rapid flowing river. It's night and you can hear the howl of wolves in the background, but they almost sound staged. "Are werewolves real?" Wagner is decked out in his PIT clothing and the lighting is poor, but his features are clear enough. "We're going to prove one way or the other tonight!"

Another howl goes up.

"Yep, that's him," Ren confirms.

We continue to watch, my disgust growing exponentially with each minute. Wagner shows the viewers a camp they've made, and claims something was stalking around it the previous evening. The camera pans to a set of giant paw prints near one of the tents. "They came on silent feet," he stage whispers to the camera. "They could have ripped us to pieces."

After that, there's a lot more drama and scant evidence suggesting they actually saw anything, much less wolves, even though they set out bait and spend the entire night on watch.

I click off. "Wagner and Jenny seem convinced there are possessed animals in our forest. Maybe he was chasing Ferrin to film him?"

"Could be. He might have been following him to see if Ferrin went back to his pack."

"True. Ferrin is mostly a loner, although there have been a couple wolves in the woods on occasion that he sometimes hangs out with. I've never seen them, but Nonni and Poppi have. It's sort of a misfit club, you might say."

"Like me."

His smile is sad. I'm not sure if he's talking about his human self or his wolf.

"You're not a misfit, and now you know you have family. It's good you're here."

"I felt...called, you might say, to move to Story Cove. Sounds crazy, but I remember after speaking to my aunt, it seemed like destiny."

It's definitely in his blood. "Have you ever had any of these types of experiences before? Waking up with no memory? Time lapses? Odd occurrences around the full moon?"

"None."

"Then something has triggered it."

He sits up straighter. "Like what?"

"I'm not sure." I tap the book on my lap, considering an answer. "But it seems to coincide with your move."

A leather volume suddenly falls from one of the shelves. I see a faint outline of Eunice moving toward it. The book opens and pages flip, thanks to her nearly invisible hand.

"What's going on?" Ren grabs a bar and stares at it. "Are you doing that?"

"One of my grandmothers."

"Come again?"

"Along with my magick, I can see spirits sometimes. Eunice, the grandmother who established our family business, just popped in. This was her office."

The pages stop. She looks at me and points.

Ren is still processing all of this. "You see ghosts?"

My chances of landing a date with him are growing slimmer by the minute. "Belle claims it's a gift," I say as cheerily as possible.

"Some gift."

Sighing, I rise and pick up the book. It's one of Eunice's collections containing various local legends.

I scan the page titled *Wood Walkers, Shamans of the Ancient Ones.* "This is it."

"What does it say?"

I read as fast as I can. "It gives us a clue to what triggered your wolf."

"It does?"

I meet his eyes and smile. "And now that I know that, I may be able to make a potion that can help control it."

CHAPTER
SEVENTEEN

Morning arrives and Ren is still human. He has been all night, not even the slightest bit of wolf emerging, unless you consider his very loud snoring.

Hope soars in me that we have finally figured out why he's a werewolf, what triggered his genetic code to unleash it, and how he can control it.

No one is surprised when we enter the kitchen together. An extra place has already been set at the table, as if he's family already.

Unfortunately, we are once again subjected to burnt toast and runny eggs, thanks to Zelle. This is why I took over the cooking when Mom died.

When we're all seated and digging into the food, Uncle Odin asks the question I know is on everyone's mind. "Did you shift, Renfroe?"

Ren swallows a mouthful. "No, sir. Quiet night.

Ruby is helping me to understand all of this. It's quite overwhelming."

I bring them up to speed on the new information Eunice provided, as well as my own deduction on Ren's situation. "Yes, he's a werewolf and it's in his genes, but they were never triggered until he moved here."

"Tribal ground?" Matilda asks.

"How did you know?"

She sips from her unicorn mug, a sly grin on her face. "I had a were friend once. He had a similar reaction when he stepped on sacred ground out west."

"There's a legend about indigenous wood walkers in this area," I tell them. "They're a supernatural line of shamans who only shifted under certain conditions, most especially when any of them, or the tribal holy ground, was threatened."

"Cool," Zelle says, mopping up egg with her toast. "I had no idea."

Ren butters his slice, not seeming to mind the extra crispy edges. "They were a type of shifter-wolf-hybrid, normally able to decide when and where they changed, but unable to control it if they, or their land, were threatened on or around the full moon."

"I believe Ren is a descendant of theirs." I'm excited to finally have a lead. Plus, I love learning something new about the woods. "He must have witnessed a threat the other night."

Before I can tell them what I speculate happened

with Wagner and Ferrin, we hear sirens. The landline on the wall rings.

Cinder gets up to answer it. "Nonni? Whoa, slow down—"

She pauses to listen and Belle whispers, "What is it?"

Cinder motions for her to wait. "Oh, dear. Okay, stay put. We're on our way."

She hangs up, and I jump to my feet, Zelle and Belle following. "What happened?"

Cinder looks pained. "Poppi found another body in the woods."

THIRTY MINUTES LATER, we've calmed Nonni as much as possible, and we're listening as Poppi explains to Robyn what happened.

"The wolves scented something and were on the trail of it." He sets his shotgun, now empty of bullets, aside as Robyn takes notes. "Had to be three, a pack for sure."

"Wolves," Robyn clarifies, "or coyotes?"

"You don't think I know the difference, young lady?"

She smiles at his bluster. "Go on. What'd they do next?"

He points to the tree line. "They skirted the edge, along there, noses to the ground, darting in and out, whining and looking back at me. Then I kept hearing a

weird motor noise. Not sure what it was, but it spooked 'em good. I didn't even need to fire a shot to scare them off. Whatever was making that noise did the job."

"Like an ATV?"

"Nah, nothing that big." He rubs his chin in thought. "It was smaller, whinier. I can't place it."

"I saw something odd," Nonni adds. "Two small lights, in fact. They were up in the trees, like floating headlights."

Ren glances at me and I can read his mind. *Supernatural?*

I shrug.

Several CSI techs come and go from the forest. "But you didn't see anybody?" Robyn asks.

Our grandparents shake their heads.

"Those paranormal investigators have been hanging around. Their fans, too." Poppi's disgust echoes in his tone. He brushes his hands together and eyes his gun. "It's no wonder the wildlife is acting up. Can't say I blame them, neither."

"Can you run them out of town, Robyn?" Nonni pleads.

I put an arm around her shoulders.

Robyn closes her notepad. "I'm trying, Nonni. I really am."

Snow and Broden arrive with their black cat, Jinx. We take Nonni and Poppi inside to the kitchen table, while Ren accompanies Robyn to look at the body.

I fix Nonni a cup of her favorite ginger and honey

tea. Poppi pours himself a coffee and offers Broden one.

"Is it possible Wagner and his team were filming from up in the trees?" I ask Cinder. "Could that have been the lights Nonni saw?"

Everyone ponders this as Nonni sips the steaming brew. "How could they get a camera that far up? They had to have been fifteen feet or more off the ground."

Snow leans on the counter. "Would a camera make the noise that Poppi heard?"

Poppi waves that off. "Nah, it had to be something else."

Broden holds a wiggling Jinx in one arm as he tastes the coffee. The cat stares up at him with big eyes and purrs lovingly. "Was it a continuous noise? Or did it fade in and out?"

Poppi worries his fingers. "Come to think of it, it moved, like something flying around, making laps."

Snow looks at Broden. "A motorized thing flying around in the woods with headlights?"

"A drone."

We all contemplate that as Broden continues. "They might have had a camera secured to it or they were simply using it to rile up the animals. If they're trying to prove the wolves are possessed, they could create anxiety in the pack, make them crazy. That might give them the footage they could pawn off as paranormal activity."

Nonni's hand shakes as she sets down her mug.

"Those poor creatures. How dare they upset them! I hope Ferrin is okay."

Snow reassures her. "He's in my barn. Unhappy to be restrained, but he has an injured leg, so Ren fixed him up. Runa's with him."

"What happened?" Poppi demands.

She tells them she doesn't know for sure, and I explain what Ren saw the other night. "Unfortunately, we don't know if Wagner was trying to help Ferrin or possibly do more harm."

"I'll shoot that idiot if he hurt Ferrin," Poppi says, shaking a fist.

Nonni reaches over and pushes his fist down. "No more violence. The woods have been upset enough."

He glances away with disgust, but relaxes his arm. "The wolves I saw tonight had a lot of black in their hair."

Like Ren's. "They weren't the usual misfits that hang out with Ferr?"

Poppi shakes his head. "These were the biggest wolves I've ever seen. Definitely not part of Ferrin's rag tag group."

"They're werewolves," I tell him.

Broden stops petting the cat. "For real?"

Zelle grins. "We have a pack of weres on the loose."

"Cool," he says.

I relate the legend about the indigenous wood walkers and see Snow and Broden's eyes light with understanding. "The shamans have been triggered," Snow states.

I nod.

"By what?" Broden asks.

"Who are they when they're human?" Snow adds.

"We don't know yet." Matilda stares at a cat statue on the shelf over the sink. "This stretch of forest sounds like it could be holy ground. Ruby was telling us about it at breakfast."

Glancing out the window, I see Ren approaching. "I think one of their own has been threatened."

He enters before I can say more and acknowledges everyone. "No bite marks, cause of death is still up in the air, but the man has blood in his hair. It's possible he was hit in the skull."

"Like our other victim," I murmur.

He shows surprise. "He had a head injury, too?"

"It could be what killed him."

Ren frowns. "Must have been some blow."

The rest of us share a look. "We better tell Robyn about the drone," I say, and head for the door.

"Drone?" Ren queries.

"I'll tell you while we walk." I grab his hand and drag him outside once more. "The PIT group may be using them to gather footage for their show."

He nods, sunlight glancing off his hair. "That makes sense."

"At least we know you had nothing to do with this."

He stares off in the distance. "Yeah, but..."

His pause makes me itch. "But what?"

Those beautiful eyes rise to meet mine. "Who did?"

EIGHTEEN

We catch up to my cousin and I motion her aside from the techs.

"Broden thinks the noise Poppi heard might be a drone," I tell her.

"Hmm."

"They may have mounted a camera on it to video the animals," I add.

"Makes sense." She pockets her notebook. "If I ever get them to return my call, I'll ask them about it. They aren't endearing themselves to me at this point."

A thought crosses my mind. "Have you scanned the woods and river?"

"One of my deputies checked today, but no one was there." She glances around at the dark landscape. "You think they might be camping out here?"

"They've done it before." Ren pulls out his phone. "Ruby and I watched a video where they were chasing..."

Her radio buzzes with a call coming in about an accident outside the city limits. She responds and replaces the unit on her belt. "Great, just what I need on top of this latest body. Look,"—she glances at us—"there's a lot of ground to cover, and I'm already short-handed, but it's a good lead, Ruby. I'll check the woods tomorrow."

"Let us know if there's anything we can do to help you," Ren says.

She calls to the techs, informing them she has to leave. They acknowledge it and she heads for her vehicle. "You've done enough. Talk soon."

While this new victim is terrible, the fact Ren had nothing to do with it lifts my spirits.

"I'm so glad I was at your place last night," he murmurs as we cross the forest to head back to Enchanted.

The fact that he stayed in his human form gives me hope. "The shift only happens in conjunction with the moon when it's waxing or full, which is actually good news. That's manageable."

"Yeah, I guess I need to face facts, don't I?"

He sounds so disappointed, my heart sinks. "I understand you feel like this is a curse, but we can turn it into something positive."

"If you say so."

Just like Belle telling me that seeing ghosts is a gift, I know that's how he feels about being a were-wolf. I take his hand, our footsteps nearly silent on the forest floor. "Combined with the potions in Eunice's

books, we have a good chance of keeping it fully controlled."

Heavy in thought, he leaves without a goodbye. Determined to help him, I open the shop.

ENCHANTED IS busy that afternoon with folks purchasing candles for the Thanksgiving holiday.

Between the steady flow of customers, I collect items to take to the farmer's market. I'm sad it's the last of the year, but it will bring in a huge crowd from neighboring counties for that very reason. I'm hoping to capitalize on it and sell as many products as possible, as well as take orders for my new candy enterprise.

Finn stops in to buy a bottle of men's face tonic. "Cinder couldn't bring you some?" I tease.

He glances toward the area of the shop where she's re-wiring an outlet, utterly oblivious to us. McAllister runs around her, hopping in and out of the large metal toolbox open at her feet.

"She's a bit preoccupied. I've asked for a bottle three times, and she's forgotten every request."

He enquires about the morning commotion at the farm. "Cinder texted and said your grandparents are all right, but if you want Leo and I to keep an eye on them tonight, don't hesitate to ask."

I thank him and offer him his receipt. He strides over and plants a kiss on my older sister's head.

"Ruby?" I look up to see Mrs. Briggs from the bakery smiling as she comes through the door. "We're already wiped out of the chocolate truffles and the tiny white chocolate pumpkins. Can you make more by morning?"

"You sold all of them?" I gave her two dozen of each on Monday. "They went so fast."

She chuckles at the disbelief on my face. "You really should expand your offerings, start your own candy shop."

My witchy friend, Sugar, in a town several miles away, runs an amazing candy store. You'd swear her confections are from a land of fairytales. She's been offering advice on recipes, how to handle my perishable inventory, and which outlets appeal to candy lovers. "I could never leave the family business and go off on my own." I see Cinder glance my way, overhearing my statement. "But I'll make more for you tonight."

"Perfect. Thank you. Did you meet the new veterinarian? Cute as can be. My daughter made an appointment for her cat that she doesn't even need so she could see him." She purchases a few bath bombs before saying goodbye. "You've got your key for the store, right?"

I assure her I do, and she exits the shop.

Cinder walks to the display where I'm putting out fresh Autumn Splendor candles. "Have you considered Snow's offer?"

"Yes, and I'm working on a plan. If I can up

production or hire help, I can supply Snow and the bakery, but my place is here with you and the others. I love our shop."

She throws an arm around my shoulders and gives me her bossy, big sister hug. "I'm not sure we can run it without you."

Matilda saunters in with her unicorn mug. She's wrapped her long hair in a turban with a jewel the size of my hand in the front to hold it. "Go and make candy, Ruby. I'll watch the shop."

I hug Cinder and Matilda, then use my new kitchen to get started.

A FEW HOURS LATER, I stop by the vet clinic to see how Ren is doing, a small plate of sample chocolates in hand.

His excitement at seeing me makes me blush. He hurries through his last patient, to the woman's dismay, to lock up. Then he turns to me, downs three of the candies, and begins showing me around, describing his plan for the space.

George sits in his cage in the waiting area, the door open so he can fly in and out. "Intruder! Intruder!" he screeches.

I wish I could win the bird over with my candy. "He's not going to let me forget that, is he?"

Ren chastises him. "She's our friend."

Friend. The word disappoints me a bit. "Did you get the backroom the way you want it?"

"It's a work in progress." He begins a tour, directing me through the area. "I want to blow out this wall and expand the footprint of the building."

He opens the rear door and we look out at the parking area. "With another fifteen square feet, I can use it for surgeries, then have a room over there for rescue animals to socialize them, upping their chances of getting adopted. I want to hire more staff and take on exotic animals as well."

Listening to him brings a smile to my face. The sun is sinking, and I casually brush a hand down his arm. "You're a good addition to this town. I'm glad you felt the need to move here."

We are jammed in the doorframe. Before I can ease back, he faces me and touches my cheek. "I'm lucky to have met you, Ruby Sherwood."

The fading sun sends a rainbow of peach and blue stripes over us. My pulse skips. He leans in for a kiss.

"Watch it!" Lenore cries as she flies past us.

We both jump and laugh. Ren looks as self-conscious as I feel. "She seems quite vocal around me."

"At times I wish she couldn't speak."

Another chuckle. "I'll get my things so we can go."

He's still standing close. I can smell our fir soap that he used this morning. I have a sudden urge to run my fingers through his hair, see if I can still get that kiss. "Go?"

He grins at my confused look. "To the tower?"

Oh right. How embarrassing. "Of course. We'd better get you safe inside."

While he locks up, I wait outside for him. Lenore lands on a nearby post. I glare at her. She rarely speaks, and I'm more than slightly glad about that. "Your timing needs work."

She dances a little, one beady eye meeting mine, as she tilts her head. "Odin sent me."

"Regardless of his tendency to act like my father, I'm old enough to kiss whoever I choose, and you're my bird."

Ren emerges and secures the door behind him. "Ready?"

"Watch it, wolf," Lenore screeches.

I swear she winks at me as she rises into the air.

NINETEEN

Saturday dawns bright and chilly, everyone abuzz for the farmer's market and pre-Thanksgiving sales.

I wake to find Ren pretending not to watch me. "Will we have to do this every month at the full moon?"

"Probably." The lie tumbles out of my mouth before I can call it back. I only hope I wasn't snoring or drooling. "Breakfast?"

"Yes, please, if it's no trouble." There's a twinkle in his eyes. "But I prefer your cooking over your sister's."

The two of us enjoyed a quiet night getting to know each other and diving more deeply into the local legends. He had lots of questions about magick and shamanism, and asked about the potion I want to make to see if it helps him control his beast.

I don't know exactly what threat has triggered it, other than assuming the murder of the first man in the

woods is to blame. But what if now that it *is awake*, it never goes dormant again?

"The legend claims that after the threat to the holy ground and/or the wood walkers passes, the werewolf shamans once more become normal people," I tell my family at the table. "Even at a full moon, they don't turn into wolves because they're not needed as protectors any longer."

Ren downs a forkful of biscuits and gravy. "We're hoping that's true in my case, too, but Ruby's afraid to experiment."

"The threat isn't past yet," I remind him. "Maybe next month."

"We'll help," Zelle tells me. "All of us. When the full moon comes around, we can free Ren and see what happens. If he does wolf out, we'll corral him again."

"Thanks, I think," he says.

Once the meal is over, I walk him to the front door. "I'll work on that potion today, if I have time, but with the market, I can't promise anything."

He kisses my cheek. "See you at three for the grand opening?"

"I'll be there," I reply, cheek tingling.

Back in the kitchen, I find everyone smiling like goofballs. "You two are so cute together," Belle says with a wink.

"Don't be silly."

"I can't get over how handsome he is." Matilda peeks at me over the edge of her mug. "Every single

woman in town has her eyes on him, a few of the married ones as well."

The teasing continues as I pack the van. Uncle Odin and Lenore accompany me. "Don't let the others get to you," he tells me. "They like seeing you happy, is all."

The park is bustling, the sun warming the cool air and melting a light covering of frost. Uncle Odin sets up the folding table after we get the tent secured. Together, we line up products and put out business cards.

Many of the local crafters and gardeners wave and chat as they walk by. Plenty stop to ask about Ren— new blood in town always gets tongues wagging.

I'm enjoying my conversations with him, learning more about him. The fact I'm getting used to sleeping next to him, even if there are bars separating us, makes me smile. I hope tonight, when the moon is completely full, we'll still have a quiet—as in no wolfing out—time. When he saw me looking over Eunice's letters, he asked about them. Tonight, I plan to read some of them out loud to him. Ezra loved animals and wrote about a few he helped in his travels.

"I heard that new vet is spending a lot of time at your place," Missy Tompkins calls as she carries a basket of gourds past us to her stand. "Did you put a spell on him, Ruby?"

I laugh, but pull my cape tighter, thinking about the potion I need to whip up. I'd really like to give it a

test run tonight, but my time is sucked up with other duties for now. "Just giving him a proper welcome to town."

The police station is a block away and I notice Robyn arriving for the day. She hikes over to check on the booths and greets us. It's five minutes until we officially open and customers are lined up at the entrance to the park.

She lowers her voice and keeps an eye out for eavesdroppers as she speaks to me and Uncle Odin. "The second victim is from a group called Caught on Camera. Ghost hunters. They use various equipment, including night-vision cameras, to prove ghosts exist."

"Ghost hunters?" Normally, I might find this entertaining. Today, it feels creepy, exploiting earthbound spirits to sell a TV show. "Any idea why he was in the woods?"

"He went by a stage name—Rambler Horseman— and I've reached out to the others in the group with little success. No one will pony up his real name, but from what one of the PIT fans told me last night, he used to be part of the investigators, just like Hargraves." She shifts, eyeing the growing crowd. "There's definitely bad blood between the two groups. It makes me suspicious."

I straighten a line of apple cranberry soaps. "You think one of the members killed him?"

She has *that* look as she scans the gathered folks. Everyone's a suspect right now. "No evidence to that, yet. But if someone was using a drone outfitted with a

camera to try to capture activity in the woods, they might have caught the killer on video, as well."

They might also have discovered Ren shifting. "What's your plan?"

"I finally discovered several PIT members are staying at the hotel under false names. I'm waiting on warrants to search their rooms. Hargraves was sleeping in his car, so I'm also searching that once it's impounded. One way or the other, I will find out what happened."

Uncle Odin adjusts his bow tie. "And the live full moon ritual tonight? Do you think they're trying to stir up the forest creatures in order to create something out of nothing?"

"I've asked the mayor to close off the woods up to the national forest, not only the crime scenes."

"Good luck with that," Uncle Odin says, sounding skeptical.

Robyn frowns and sighs, as if she knows it's an uphill battle. "The Chamber is fighting me every step of the way. If it were locals in the morgue, they might be on my side, but as it stands, they want to keep the murders hush-hush and grab the publicity from the shows."

"I'm sorry you're in such a pickle," I tell her.

"Thanks. I'll talk to you later." She says goodbye and makes her way to the station.

The clock in the square bongs, announcing it's time to open. Folks rush the booths.

The morning is filled with customers, questions,

and sales, but I manage to chastise Uncle Odin during a reprieve for sending Lenore to keep an eye on me the previous day. My familiar stays mostly on her perch as customers come and go, thankfully silent, even when young children want to pet her. She's not overly affectionate, but she is tolerant, allowing them to do so.

My uncle smiles and winks at me, then tells the bird, "Good job, Lenore."

Zelle brings us sandwiches from one of the food carts parked on Main Street for the event and gives me a break to grab inventory from our vehicle to restock the table.

As I'm placing cinnamon and vanilla scented soaps into the cart, Jenny appears. "Hey there, need help?"

I don't, but Eunice comes into view and nods. "Sure," I say, handing Jenny a stack of bags. "Could you carry these?"

I close up the van, and Lenore lands on the stacks of candles, soaps, and lotions. "I'm sorry to hear about the man in the woods. He was a friend?" I can't exactly text Robyn without appearing rude and possibly scaring Jenny off. I might as well see if I can get any information from her.

She laughs derisively. "Hardly. He was trying to steal our spotlight. The Caught on Camera crew does that all the time. We've gained national recognition, and it eats them up."

I play dumb. "Is there a lot of competition in your field?"

We start back toward the park. "Rambler—that

was his name—and Wagner used to be best friends. They started PIT together. Rambler disagreed when Wagner wanted to expand and do more than ghost hunt. You know, we saw the bigger picture. We wanted to investigate old wives' tales and local legends about werewolves, vampires, witches. All that fairytale stuff."

I nod, and a passing neighbor says good afternoon. I speak to her, continuing to act like everything is normal. "Have you found evidence that any of that *fairytale stuff* actually exists?"

Jenny tilts her head toward the sun. "Well, sure. It's fascinating, really. I mean, you and your sisters are witches. You believe magick is real."

I decide to leave that alone for now. "What happened with Rambler?"

"He and Wagner fought, and Rambler took two of the other members and broke away from us. Problem is, they turn up every once in a while, attempting to steal our glory."

"So that's why Rambler was in the woods the other night? What about the second victim? Did you know him."

"Sure, that's Luther, his new partner. He and Rambler followed us here to see what we were doing, and find a way to interfere with our live show. They've gotten us banned from various haunted sites, so they could swoop in and get the story for their webcast."

I pretend the cart is heavy and walk slowly, my

mind spinning. "Did you tell Robyn— Detective Wood —this?"

She looks down at the bags in her arms, a bit sheepishly. "I don't want to get Wagner in trouble, and he's already angry with me. I mean, it makes him look sorta bad."

Maybe for good reason. "You really should cancel tonight's event. It's too dangerous with a killer running loose."

She shifts the items to one arm and reaches into her pocket to pull out a candy bar. "Sorry, I haven't had lunch." She peels the end of the wrapper, takes a big bite, and chews. "Gorgeous day, isn't it?"

Everything inside me goes still. The wrapper is like the one I found on Wednesday. It's probably nothing, since I already know she's been in the woods with the others, but there's something about it that feels like a red flag. Especially since she's now trying to change the subject.

I glance around, hoping to spot my great-grand-mother. Her presence would be a definite sign I'm on the right track. Unfortunately, she's nowhere to be seen.

Despite the cool air, I'm sweating. Jenny doesn't notice, but seems a bit flustered. "I know it's not a great idea, but Wagner says the police can't keep us out. He says we'll honor Brady's—I mean, Rambler's —death and dedicate the show to him."

I glance over at her, ignoring the slip up with the

name. Robyn already knows about that. "But you just said they were enemies."

She shrugs and swallows another bite, jamming the trash in her pocket. She won't look at me. "Makes for good TV. Our viewers will love it. Some of them were big fans of Rambler back when we started PIT, plus the suspicious deaths only heighten the live event. People are begging for this tonight."

We arrive at the table, and she still won't glance at me. Anxious? Or is the reality of being in the woods tonight where two men have been killed beginning to freak her out? "It's not worth your life," I say in a voice I've learned from Cinder. "And there are no possessed animals for you to film, anyway."

She hands me the bags and shoves both hands into her pockets. "We do dangerous filming all the time. Say, can I buy some soap?"

If I didn't know she's hiding fear, I'd think she has an attention disorder. Zelle begins unpacking the products and gives me a questioning look. Holding in my frustration, I help Jenny with her purchase.

If I can't stop her, I need to change tactics. "You know, I could go with you. Watch your back, so to speak. I'm quite familiar with the forest and the animals in it."

Uncle Odin clears his throat and Zelle gapes at me.

Robyn will kill me, but maybe I can find out more about Wagner and Rambler's relationship and help her solve this case.

Jenny accepts the bagged soap and hands me cash.

"Oh, I couldn't ask you to do that. We'll be fine." She waves as she starts to walk away. "Keep the change and thanks for the soap."

When she's out of earshot, Zelle shakes her head. "Are you nuts? What was that about?"

"Can you stay for another few minutes?"

"Sure, my next appointment isn't until two-thirty."

"I'll be right back."

I leave her and Uncle Odin once more to race to the station to tell my cousin what I've learned.

TWENTY

Robyn is quite interested to hear about the falling out Wagner had with Rambler/Brady, and as we're discussing it, a call comes in confirming the second victim is Luther Brandon.

She taps her pencil on the desk. "If Brady and Luther were running the Caught on Camera group, then it's now devoid of its leadership."

"Taking out both of them would undoubtedly stop some of the issues the two teams had with each other."

Her eyes scan her notes. "Which makes Wagner my prime suspect."

"Be careful," I say as she walks me out. "If he's the killer, he's not afraid to do whatever it takes to stop anyone who gives him trouble."

She reassures me she'll be safe, but I wrap a bubble of protection around her all the same as I hug her.

The farmer's market is supposed to be done at

three, but plenty of visitors have kept the booths busy. Matilda shows to relieve me and help Uncle Odin clean up.

"I'm holding the full moon ceremony at the shop," she tells me.

I cringe. "But I'll have you-know-who upstairs," I reply.

"Well, it looks like even the park here is off-limits tonight and I have to host the women somewhere."

They're a new thing she's been doing for several months now, gathering ladies who are on the witchy side of life to get together, drink wine, and counsel each other. They're harmless from what I've seen, but I still don't want them downstairs, on the chance Ren shifts and starts howling. "Isn't there anywhere else you could hold it? I thought you preferred being outside."

She waves away my obvious concern. "It'll be fine. The whole thing lasts an hour, then they'll be gone. A few complain about the cold, so they'll be happy we're staying in."

I stew as I walk to the clinic, but there's really nothing I can do. It *will* be fine, I tell myself. As long as Ren isn't threatened and doesn't see the moon, he'll stay in his human form.

The grand opening is off to a great start when I arrive. Local folks stream in and out of the small clinic, some with their pets, others without. I notice a few Story Cove residents who don't even have any animal

companions enjoying the commotion in order to meet the newcomer and see their friends.

Many carry paper cups filled with punch and sample bags with treats for their dogs and cats.

Ren is laughing and smiling, George seeming to relish the attention as well. The parrot greets people, and then talks trash about their outfits or animals. Most are good-natured about it and laugh it off while Ren looks slightly embarrassed as he chastises him.

"You made it." He catches my arm and guides me out of the flow of traffic to the area behind the desk.

"I told you I'd be here."

He playfully tugs on a lock of my hair. "I saw how swamped you were at the farmer's market. I'm glad it was a success, but I worried you wouldn't get a break."

"Can I help with anything?"

"I never expected this many and didn't make up enough goodie bags. Would you mind putting more together and handing them out?"

I shrug off my cape. "You got it."

While I'm stuffing them, I overhear a group of young boys talking about the ghost hunters and the live full moon event.

I warn them to stay out of there, seeing in their eyes they have no intention of following the directive.

One of the chamber members, Mrs. Ollifax, waves off my warning as she approaches the desk. "Your cousin arrested the culprit a few minutes ago. All is well."

"She caught the killer?"

The woman shushes me and nervously glances around to see if anyone heard. "Yes, and the mayor has permitted the event to take place in the area behind the park. That's far enough away from the crime scenes, so as not to disturb them, and it'll be quite safe, plenty of people about. Nothing to worry over now, and we welcome the paranormal investigators." This last bit is said a little louder.

"That is good news," I manage to force out, and then I lower my voice to a whisper. "Who was it? The killer?"

She pulls me farther behind the desk. "Robyn received an anonymous tip right before I came down here. I was at the station, talking to her about tonight. A man showed up with evidence proving a technician with the Caught on Camera team was trying to capitalize on the feud between them and PIT, and he killed both of those poor men. Robyn left to arrest him."

As soon as she moves on, I call Robyn but get her voicemail. I leave a message, asking her to let me know if it's true.

A group of three without pets are talking about getting on camera for the show, especially now that it's right behind the park. They're bringing their children, as well, and acting as though it's a town party.

Over the next half hour, each of my sisters stops by before heading off for their Saturday night fun. Cinder and Finn are going to a live theater performance, and she's dressed up, which I don't see too often.

"You did great today at the market," she tells me.

"We made enough profit to pay for the new counter I want to put in."

"We're ordering it first thing on Monday." Finn puts an arm around her. "Right after we pick up the generator."

"That's wonderful." Our remodel is moving along more swiftly than anticipated. "Have fun at the show."

Cinder adjusts a dangling earring, as if it's bugging her. She rarely wears jewelry, and this piece looks too flamboyant to be one of hers. It must belong to Matilda. "We'll need to double our wax order, too. The new Magical Forest and the Balsam and Cedar scents are huge hits."

I smile, pleased to hear my take on two of Eunice's recipes are adding to our bottom line. "I'll make a note to do so." I motion her to lean closer. "Did you hear that Robyn may have caught the killer?"

"No! What happened?"

I share what Ollifax told me, but I still haven't received a call to confirm it.

"That's a relief," Cinder says, finally removing the earrings and shoving them in a pocket. "The woods are safe again."

Maybe, I think.

Leo and Belle show as they're departing. "We're staying in at the mansion tonight to play board games," she tells me, Jayne in her arms.

Leo towers over most people there. "As long as you don't need us," he adds.

My gaze falls on Ren, across the way, who's talking

and laughing with Belle's boss, Daisy. "We'll be fine. Sounds like Robyn caught the culprit, by the way."

Belle's hand goes to her chest. "What a relief!"

"If I need you, I'll call," I tell them. "Enjoy your evening."

An hour later, Zelle enters, turning heads. She's left her hair down and put relaxed curls in it, inserting a sparkling hairpin or two throughout. The color is a rich copper color and she wears a slinky, blue dress and matching heels, her beauty dazzling.

She stops at the desk, eyeing the remains of the gift bags, and my simple navy skirt and tunic. "Looks like this is going well."

"It is. I take it you're going on a date?"

The Happily Ever After dating app has provided her with several potential guys in the past month, but none have panned out. She gives an offhanded shrug. "He's cute and he likes to cook. I'll give it a try."

I can see in her eyes that she's not interested in this fellow, but she keeps trying to find a relationship that will bring her happiness. The only man she's ever loved left her when they were eighteen. I wonder if she'll ever get over that heartbreak. "I hope you have fun."

"Can you keep an eye on Rumpelstiltskin for me? They're predicting storms again later and he gets so agitated when I'm not home and it thunders."

"No problem."

"Thanks. Have an...uneventful evening."

Once closing time comes, Ren and I clean up the

empty cups, wash out the punch bowl, and straighten the chairs. The night air is nippy as we walk to Enchanted, and I can smell rain in the air. The setting sun reflects off the glass panes of shop windows as we pass, and I feel relaxed, even happy.

I make potato soup and warm homemade bread as he relates stories folks told him about their pets. Rumpelstiltskin and McAllister take turns climbing in his lap for attention.

Uncle Odin has gone to get a spot to watch the live show and Matilda's group won't be here until seven, but she is bustling around in the new section downstairs, preparing for it.

"Your open house was a huge success." I feed Lenore in her cage. "It was a great idea. A bunch made appointments and I wrote them in your calendar. I hope that was okay."

"Of course." He smiles, pleased. "I knew moving here was a good idea."

We keep the conversation light as we eat. The various pets scrounge around looking for crumbs or trying to plead with me to give them sections of the bread.

Ren has a second bowl of soup. "Delicious meal. You're an amazing cook."

"Thank you. My mother was, too. I miss her."

"You and your sisters have a fascinating heritage. I'm envious."

"Family means everything to us. Have you had a chance to speak to the Redferns yet?"

"We're getting together for Thanksgiving. I'm really looking forward to it."

"That's wonderful."

I refill our beverages. "Say, I've been thinking. You really don't need to stay in the cage tonight." Everything feels so normal, so...right.

"Did you make that potion?"

By the look on his face, I'd have a hard time getting him to take it, even if I had. "No, but..."

Ren shakes his head, wiping his hands on his napkin. "I don't want to chance it, especially if you're having the gathering downstairs. We know a lot more than we did, but until I'm positive I have a handle on this, I don't want to risk your health or anyone else's."

We clean the dishes, and I bring a few candies up to the tower with us. Lenore hops the steps and settles on the back of Eunice's chair.

Ren and I freshen our respective beds and I take out the stack of letters. The first I choose is from Ezra a few months before he made it back to Story Cove and Eunice. "Seems like Ezra had a regular menagerie of animals he took care of," I tell Ren.

He leans against the rear bars. "I want that, too. A big house, kids, lots of pets."

Our eyes meet. "That sounds lovely."

An invisible hand ruffles the letters in my hand, making me start. I look down and find the one on top is about Eunice and a pack of wolves she's seen in the woods.

"Listen to this," I tell Ren. "'I saw them again—the

giant wolves—last night at dusk. They are at least as tall as you, I imagine, if they were to stand on their hind paws. Is it possible dire wolves aren't extinct, as long thought? Such dark eyes that are intelligent, and a preternatural stillness as they watched me gather the hens to put inside for the night. They're probably to blame for the recent livestock killings, but I wonder. They seem to wish me no harm, and it's almost as if they're trying to tell me something. How I wish you were here to advise me!"

I scan through a few more and find another entry six months later. "There's been skirmishes in the forest again between the settlers and the natives. I wish this all would stop! This land belonged to them, long before we came and invaded it. I love it here, that is the truth, but I feel terrible for them. They have children and such to care for, they wish for peace and a warm hearth, just as we do. If only we could all live in peace."

"The wood walkers," Ren says. "They were trying to protect the land and their homes."

Before either of us can say anything else, my phone rings. It's Robyn.

"Sorry, I was neck-deep in this investigation. That Wagner fellow is as unlikable as they get. I thought he was going to have a stroke when I refused to let him do his show."

"I thought it was back on?"

"No way. The chamber tried, but I got Judge Mecum to declare the area off-limits. My officers are

keeping an eye out to make sure Wagner doesn't attempt it anyway."

I put her on speaker so Ren can hear, too. "But you caught the killer, right?"

She hesitates for a second too long, alerting me that something is bothering her. "Martin Fusel appears to be our guy, but I don't like it, Ruby. The video evidence Wagner gave me could be doctored. I've asked our tech expert to examine it, but it may take her a day or two. And although I found a drone in Fusel's hotel room, he denies knowing anything about it. I've got that feeling in my gut that says he's telling the truth."

"Is there any way to prove it's the one that hit Hargraves in the head?" Ren asks.

"On initial inspection, it looks like a strong possibility. It even has hair on it. Could belong to our vic or the animal who dragged him. It's the right size, and it makes a noise like Poppi described, but the medical examiner can't rule out other weapons."

Ren and I glance at each other. "What kind?" I query.

"A thick tree branch or a baseball bat. Doc found tiny splinters in Hargraves' hair, possibly from the weapon. He's determined some of the puncture wounds are not from an animal bite. They're too rough, again suggesting our victim was poked, perhaps postmortem. There's more to this story than I've figured out."

"Oh, dear."

Ren's eyes narrow. "He was hit after death? That suggests anger or rage."

"Exactly." Robyn agrees. "His attacker beat him up pretty good, that's for sure. Whether the killer knew the victim was dead or not, I can't say."

"And the other man? Same cause of death?"

"Similar." Someone speaks to her and she responds to them before coming back to me. "Look, I've got to go. As I feared, Wagner and his crew are still trying to cause trouble."

She hangs up before I can even say goodbye. "I'll be glad when tonight is over."

"You and me both."

"What made you shift that night?" I ask myself again.

"I thought it was due to me or the sacred ground being threatened."

"Most likely, yes, but what if you witnessed the first murder?"

His brows rise and then he seems to get my drift. "And I tried to stop it. In my wolf form."

I nod.

"If only I could remember that night."

I toy with a piece of candy. "Well, I hate to bring it up, because I know you didn't like it before, but there are spells I can do to enhance your memory."

He screws up his nose and snags the last candy from the plate. He's about to say something when my phone rings again.

153

"It's Nonni," I answer and put her on speaker. "Everything okay?"

"Oh, Ruby, you have to come." She's out of breath. "The wolves—they showed up again. The big ones. They were acting so strange. I don't know what happened, but Poppi went to chase them off and..."

Her voice cracks, and my grip on the phone tightens. "What, Nonni? What happened?"

I hear her stifle a sob, fear plain in her voice. "He went into the woods with them, and Ruby, he hasn't come back."

TWENTY-ONE

My first call is to Robyn—it goes to voicemail.

I grab my cape.

"What are you doing?" Ren asks from the cage.

I send a group text to my sisters and Snow. Uncle Odin doesn't have a phone.

"I have to find Poppi. He could be in jeopardy."

"But Robyn caught the killer."

I slide the phone into my pocket. "You heard her, her gut says there's something off about it."

He grips the bars and his knuckles go white. "Then let her handle it."

I tie the cape. "She's not answering and may not get my message in time."

"Let me go with you," Ren demands. "I can help."

"Not with the full moon." I stop at the stairs and turn back. "I'm sorry, but you *will* change if you go out. That won't help."

He rattles the bars, making it slide slightly on the floor. "It's too dangerous for you alone. At least take Matilda."

The spell on the cage holds, but I covertly send another tendril to reinforce it. "Don't worry. I can handle this."

With another wave of magick, I cause the lock to become invisible so he can't undo it. Lenore squawks and flies to my arm.

Ren frowns at the now concealed lock. "You don't trust me?"

My heart sinks at the hurt in his voice. "I'm sorry."

I turn once more to the steps.

"Wait! You said one of the pros of being a werewolf is my enhanced senses. I can sniff Poppi out for you. And I have increased strength to protect you."

He's making this terribly hard for me. I don't look back, knowing I can't meet his eyes. "I'll be careful, and my family is on the way. Poppi may be in danger, I can't just sit here."

His voice rings out after me as I hustle down the stairs, "Ruby, no!"

Downstairs, Matilda is welcoming two of her followers into the shop.

"There's a problem," I tell her, pulling her aside.

She sees my fear. "What is it?"

I give her a brief summary of what Nonni shared. "I'm going after him."

"I'll come with you."

"What about your group?"

"I'll cancel. Give me a minute."

I grab her arm. "Then I need you to go to the farm and stay with Nonni. She's not one to sit on her hands, and the last thing we need is for her to go searching for him."

She gives a furtive sigh. "You're right. Okay, go. I'll take care of her."

I hurry outside and run for the path. Lenore takes flight. "Find Poppi," I command.

The night is cloudy, wisps like pale shrouds thread over and under the moon's glow. The predicted rain is close but not falling yet.

Lenore appears and disappears among the tree tops. I wrap my cloak tighter and pull up the hood. "Make me imperceptible to my enemies," I whisper to it.

My flashlight beam seems too small as it scans the trees and path. It catches the glowing eyes of nocturnal creatures—toads, possums, raccoons, and others I'm unsure of, scampering amongst the foliage and debris.

The air is cold on my nose, the damp soil and rotting leaves pungent. I wrestle with the idea of calling for my grandfather—if anyone is out here, they'll know I am, too.

The killer is caught, I reassure myself.

Please let them be caught!

After several minutes of fighting with myself and no humans in sight, I take the chance. "Poppi? Are you out here?"

There's no reply, and I silently pray that Robyn does have the right person in custody.

Lenore caws and I twist to find her.

My beam glances off metal. A shotgun! It's leaning on the boulder where I found the shoe and bloody prints. I swing the light in an arc, knowing instantly, it's Poppi's.

He's nowhere to be seen, however.

The sad hoot of an owl makes the hair on my arms stand up. A twig snaps. Leaves rustle behind me. I pivot in that direction. "Poppi? It's me, Ruby."

What appears in the illumination is not my grandfather.

Dark hair, long snouts, snarling mouths. My heart pounds so hard, it feels as though my rib cage will burst.

Three wolves, as big as Ren, their eyes glowing, stare back. They can see right through my cape's invisibility ward.

And by the look in their gazes, they've decided I'm a threat.

CHAPTER
TWENTY-TWO

"Do not fear." Eunice's ghostly form hovers a few yards away.

I don't take my eyes off the approaching pack. "Easy for you to say."

She floats toward me, and I notice she's surrounded by spirit animals, wolves, who stand nearly as tall as her elbow. They look as menacing in the shadows as their live counterparts. "They're here to assist you, granddaughter."

"You aided another set of wood walkers all those years ago, didn't you?"

"This was their people's land. When their tribe was forced off of it, they still had a strong tie to the spirit of this place. A few wouldn't leave, no matter what the settlers did to them. These woods, and many that no longer exist, were tied to their souls. But because no one understood who and what they were,

they were hunted, injured, some killed and others imprisoned. I did what I could to ease their pain."

I feel such a bond with this woman. "I'm glad you did. I want to help them now, but I don't know how."

One of the living wolves paws the ground. Eunice nods. "Go with them, granddaughter. They'll show you the way."

I reluctantly glance at her then back to the animals in front of me. "I would be more willing to do that," I tell them, "if you would kindly retract those fangs."

Like synchronized swimmers, the three lay their ears back, lift their heads, and howl.

The eerie wail sends shivers through my already chilled body. "Yeah, that's not helpful, nor inviting, if you want me to follow you."

As one, they turn and race off. Eunice and her pack dissolve into the forest after them. "Godspeed, Ruby. You've been entrusted with a great gift."

Another one I'm not sure I want. "So, that's not weird or anything," I say to Lenore, who's on a nearby branch. "Follow the werewolves, Ruby. It's only a creepy night in the woods where two men have been murdered."

I scan the area again, biting my bottom lip. A light mist is falling now, coating my skin . Lenore takes flight, the branch bobbing up and down like a diving board. Her wings hit leaves and they cascade in front of me, laying a trail. "I feel like the heroine in a horror film."

Should I go? Am I too stupid to live, or brave and daring?

At least my fourth great-grandmother put her stamp of approval on it. She wouldn't lead me wrong. "Well, here goes nothing, I guess."

Calling up my courage, I tramp into the shadowed forest.

The trees become more numerous, dense foliage tangling around my ankles. My breath billows white in the frosty air. Hustling to catch up, I twist my ankle on a large pine cone and fall to my knees. The jarring drop sends my flashlight flying.

I calculate we're farther north than I have ever been, close to the national forest. After brushing dirt and leaves from my skirt, and rubbing my injured knees, I scramble to find the light.

But now I've lost the wolves. "Hey, guys? Where are you?"

Above, the moon peaks through the clouds and filters past layers of branches. A fog is rolling in from the river. "Perfect. Adding to the horror movie ambience."

The scents of sugar pine and cypress fill my nose. I continue to shine the beam over the murky landscape, a rise in the terrain leading to a hill with a cave in the distance.

Definitely national park property.

The illumination catches the eyes of an animal. Not one of the wolves—Lenore.

"Did you find him?" I ask the bird.

She caws, opens her wings, and carefully zips through the skeletal branches of the nearby evergreens. I pivot and slide between two, noting multiple boughs are broken in places, as if large creatures have come through here.

When I finally spot the wolves, the relief makes my body sag. Lenore lands on a downed trunk, covered in vines and moss. She dances and flaps her wings, happy.

Against the ancient trunk leans my grandfather.

I wipe rain from my face, as I rush to him. "Poppi!"

A wolf flanks him on each side, the large animals poised like sphinxes. The third paces a few feet away, looking off into a dark copse beyond.

"Ruby." Poppi's voice is weak and he seems groggy. There is blood coming from a jagged cut on his temple.

He reaches for me and I take his hand. His fingers are ice cold.

Mine aren't much better. I bend down and wrap him in my cloak as quickly as I can. "What happened? Are you all right?"

"My head." He touches his temple with his free hand, then wipes blood on his pant leg. He pets a wolf on the neck. "I can't remember exactly."

He tries to push himself up to standing but can't gain his balance, even with the tree at his back for support.

"Take it easy," I tell him, and he once again slumps to the forest floor.

The wolves whine.

He rubs his head. "Something hit me."

Fingers of frosty air seep into my bones without the warmth of my cape. I adjust it around his shoulders, and examine the wound. "This will heal you, but it takes time. Help is on the way. I'm going to get you on your feet in just a minute. For now, rest."

He waves my ministrations off. "Someone's in trouble. You need to find them."

"Who?"

He shakes his head, grimacing as though the act causes him pain. "The wolves... That's why they've been coming to the farm. To warn me and ask for aid. I didn't figure it out before." He grips my arm. "The men who were killed—the animals were trying to save them."

The three beasts growl low. The two beside Poppi stay put, but the third walks away, jogs back, and repeats the action. He wants me to follow him.

"I can't leave my grandfather," I state, hoping he understands.

The wolf returns, bringing himself face-to-face with me. He holds out one massive paw.

I hesitate, not sure I understand, but take it anyway. "What is it?" I ask.

All of a sudden, my hand warms to an unbearable heat. My vision whites out and I'm transported back in time, through a funnel, watching centuries fall away.

I see the inhabitants of this area long before other cultures invaded. The people, the families, and their connection to the land plays out like a movie in my

head. In each generation, one man or woman steps forward—a wood walker.

They are shamans, mysterious and beautiful. Power radiates from each of them. I see them moving, sometimes alone, but mostly in groups, traveling from tribe to tribe, exalted and welcomed. They are healers, storytellers, wisdom keepers.

The forest reveals secrets, too. The trees become more dense, nature teeming with wildlife. Deer, rabbits, coyotes, and raccoons. Birds of all kinds, some of which are unfamiliar. From the meekest mouse to the fierce mountain lions and panthers, I feel as though I'm in a tropical rainforest, rather than southern Georgia.

And then, I see the first wood walker. He is only a child, but he talks to the trees, the water, the animals.

Those around him speak in hushed tones about his gift. He heals the wounded, sings over the dead to transport their souls to the afterlife, blesses the babies born to the tribe. As he grows, his gift becomes stronger. He can go for days without sleeping, without eating. He never gets sick. His youthful body becomes that of a strong, muscular, and powerful man. People travel great distances to see him, asking for healing. Even his touch is regarded as a blessing.

He looks like Ren.

As if he senses me, he meets my eyes at one point. I hold my breath, but the connection is so real, so intense, I can't stay silent. "Can you see me?" I whisper.

Language is a barrier, but he cocks his head. He *can* by the way the emerald slivers in his eyes sparkle. He moves and I see the tattoo on his back. "Ren?"

My voice breaks the connection. He is gone, and the centuries move forward again at lightning speed. My stomach churns as the rapid images fly past me. I close my eyes, but it doesn't help. In fact, I feel like I'm drunk and the world is spinning.

"Ruby. Ruby!"

My grandfather's voice pulls me out of the vision. I drop the wolf's paw and stagger to a spot a few feet away, trying not to toss up my dinner.

"Are you okay?" Poppi asks weakly.

Teeth clenched, I nod but don't trust myself to speak yet. The wolf nudges my side, as if apologetic for the rough ride.

Lenore caws and I glance at her. She's staring toward the hill.

"You must go now." Poppi points at the wolf and then to the distance. "He'll take you. Stick close to him."

"Take me where? Who's up there?"

"Someone in danger." He leans his head back on the rough trunk, his eyes struggling to stay open. "This ground belonged to their ancestors and is still sacred, but the killer has defiled it. We need to make this right."

I push from the tree I'm leaning on and stagger over to him. My vision continues fading in and out, the blinding light seeming to have damaged my eyesight.

"I just need to sleep…" he murmurs.

"Do not pass out." I gently tap his wrinkled cheeks and this revives him a bit. I'm scared he's in shock and I have no herbs to treat him.

Retrieving my phone from the cape pocket, I use an app that sends a beacon to my family with the location. Reception here is spotty, but I place it on Poppi's lap. "Keep this on you. Cinder and the others will be here soon. If you can, try calling Robyn and tell her what happened."

"Be careful," he mutters. "The wolf will protect you, but don't underestimate what this killer will do." He points at the sentries on either side of him. "One of these two will bring Cinder when she arrives."

Reluctant to leave, but knowing I have to, I get to my feet and study the wolf who's ready to go. His— her?—dark eyes entreat me to trust what my grandfather has said. "Nonni's never letting you out of the house again, you know."

Poppi's lips tweak in a fatigued smile. "More likely she'll insist on coming with me next time."

"True. I may have to put her in a cage."

"She's a good woman."

I pat his leg. "I'll tell her you said that."

I follow the leader, seeing Lenore gently landing on his back. The wolf doesn't seem to mind.

With his immense size, long strides, and natural agility, he flows through the trees like water. I'm sure his ability to see in the dark doesn't hurt either.

I'm breathing hard in my attempt to keep up.

Shadowing his path isn't easy. He's in a hurry and doesn't look once to check if I'm falling behind. The fog seems to encircle him, and water drips onto my head, running down my face and the back of my neck.

Teeth chattering, I don't hear the sound of bubbling water in the distance at first. It's only when I stop for a moment to check our surroundings that I pick up on it.

We're a ways from the river, but this may be an offshoot. About fifty yards ahead, I see a clearing and an odd glow.

Running once more, I catch up to the wolf and bird as they slow. I'm so close to my guide, that when he stops dead in his tracks, I nearly topple over him.

Jostled from her perch, Lenore knocks the light from my hand as she takes flight. The beam goes out when the flashlight hits the ground, throwing us into shadows.

I freeze as I hear a woman's voice, one I've come to know over the past few days. I hide behind a massive oak with low hanging branches. Twigs snap underfoot, and she goes quiet for a couple of tense seconds. Only when she starts talking again, do I let out my breath.

The wolf eases in next to me and I put a hand on his scruff. I part the moss that hangs like a curtain in front of my face, and watch as the soft glow of two lanterns illuminate the scene in front of me.

Wagner is tied up, hands and feet bound. He's

woozy, his back to the hard side of the limestone hill. The scent of blood and animal musk fills the air.

There's a black, yawning cave entrance to his left, and a candy wrapper lays on the ground at his feet.

Rain coats everything, soaking through his jacket and vest. His hair is plastered to his face, his boots muddy. Jenny emerges, night vision goggles on top of her head. She carries a camera.

"You won't...get away...with this." Wagner's speech is slurred. He can barely keep his eyes open.

Jenny places the camera on a tripod hidden behind a manufactured pile of stacked branches and rocks. She carefully adjusts a knob, then piles more moss and sticks over the equipment. "Of course I will. I'm about to be the most famous paranormal investigator the world has ever seen."

CHAPTER
TWENTY-THREE

In the moonlight, I notice another grouping of twigs and rocks only two feet from the oak tree. A second camera is hidden there, moss draped across the top.

I step close and look through the lens, realizing she has set the stage for whatever it is she intends to record tonight.

Examining the equipment, I locate the red record button and push. The area is lit only with the lanterns and the video may turn out grainy, but it's worth a shot.

Wagner struggles against his bindings, cursing and muttering. They hold fast.

Jenny disappears once more into the cave. I can see the remnants of an earlier fire, a few other camping items strewn about.

I knew it. They were hiding out here.

She returns with a bucket, and begins tossing pieces of red meat all around him. She's baiting a trap.

"The wolves will come, and I'll document the whole thing," she says with her normal upbeat voice.

She throws several chunks on Wagner's lap and legs. He tilts his body to slide them off, but they stick to his wet clothes. "You won't get away with this."

"Won't I? So far, I've done a bang up job of casting the spotlight you're always so desperate for right on you. You should be thanking me. Your memory will go down in history for the show."

"Jenny... You can't..." His voice fades in and out. "Please..."

She ignores him, continuing to bait the lure. "With some artful cutting on the darkroom floor, I'll have good footage of the *werewolves* tearing you apart. The video will go viral. Your fans will be so upset seeing those supernatural beings ripping you to shreds, but they'll eat it up. The other deaths will be blamed on the weres as well, regardless of what the medical examiner's report states. Our followers will believe it's a cover-up by the cops. They're so gullible."

The wolf raises his head and meets my eyes. I see the strong intelligence and wisdom in his gaze, exactly like I've seen in Ren's.

This is definitely one of the shamans, and he understands what's being said and done. He's urging me to stop this before it goes any farther, but I have no weapon outside of my flashlight.

I need a spell. But which one? I'm a healer, not a

warrior. I'd need to touch Wagner to put a strong enough protection bubble around him, and most of my other tried-and-true magick is for curative situations only.

"How did you...drug me?" Wagner topples over onto his side. The raw meat disengages this time, his face only a few inches from the wrapper.

Jenny snatches up the torn white packaging and shoves it in her pocket. Then she picks up some of the meat and places it on him again. "It's amazing what the taste of sugar can cover. A little muscle relaxant dissolved into a syringe and stuck into the center filling. Piece of cake. Or should I say candy?"

Her snicker is chilling.

"No one is going to believe you," Wagner insists, but the fight has definitely gone out of him. He doesn't even try to move. "You can't get away...with three murders."

She takes the bucket and returns it to the mouth of the cave. Chuckling under her breath, she sprays a mist into the air. "I didn't intend to do it this way, but I know how to actually run a business. I'm not an idiot like you and Brady."

The owl hoots again; the rain falls harder.

I smell a renewed whiff of musk. She's trying to attract predators to this spot, and I fear she's about to be more successful than she realizes.

Do something!

I comb my memory for any spell that might disable her. I used to be able to freeze small things

such as animals, but I haven't practiced in years. I only did it to try and save them from harm, but feared the shock of making them immobile was too much for the tiny creatures.

Plus, it never worked on people, outside of Belle when she was an infant. Boy, did Mom lay into me about that.

"You were so busy competing against one another," she continues, "you couldn't see the golden opportunities right in front of you. After you ran him and Luther off, I knew I was going to have to save this team if we were ever going to be big enough to go international."

"I don't... I don't understand. I thought...we were friends."

She snorts and tosses the spray into the bucket. Then she scans the scene, determining if it needs anything else. "Brady and Luther kept sticking their noses into all of this, and you were too busy focusing on what they were doing instead of seeing all of the possibilities for us to become famous. Now, I have the chance to reunite the Caught on Camera fans with our PIT followers. We'll have one huge base, and I'm going to be in charge."

This gets a rise out of Wagner. He attempts to push up onto his hands and knees. "I'm sorry. You're right. Let me..."

Jenny uses a booted foot to kick him back down. "Stop moving. You're screwing up my scene."

He groans and stays put.

There's a rustling in the forest across the way, and I fear wild animals are coming to discover the source of the fresh meat and musk on the night air.

I sink my hand deeper into the wolf's scruff. Lenore has disappeared, but I know she'll come to my aid when I need her. "Help me now. We must protect this man."

The wood walker takes a step forward, and so do I, brushing aside the curtain of moss.

"Sorry to crash the party," I say, shivering. "But this game is over."

Jenny jumps, startled. I have no idea how to incapacitate her and save Wagner before the animals attack, but it's all up to me now. "Untie Wagner, right now, and let him go."

Her eyes go wide and focus on the giant wolf at my side. "What are you doing here? Is he...?"

"You attacked my grandfather, and the wolves alerted me you were about to do worse."

"You *are* a witch! I knew it."

"If you don't want me to curse you, I suggest you do as I say."

She takes a step in retreat, holding out a hand as if to stop me. "I didn't want to hurt your grandddad, and I don't want to hurt you, Ruby. This has nothing to do with you or your family. I actually like you. You need to back off and leave me alone."

I might have liked her, too. "Sorry, I can't do that."

"We could be friends. I could give your shop some air time, make you and your sisters stars. Just think

about it—witches running a soap shop while they're making potions and casting spells in the other room. People will love it!"

"I don't want to be famous, Jenny, especially not at the cost of a man's life."

"You're not seeing the big picture. It's simple justice. Wagner is a jerk. He hurt a wolf the other night, trying to get it to attack him so I could film it. What kind of human being does such a thing? He deserves to die."

Her logic was easy to follow until you turned it around on her. "You've killed two men, and for what? Fame?"

"That, and money. But again, they deserved it. They've been duping folks for years. Manipulating people and hurting innocent victims."

Does she not realize I heard her telling Wagner her plans?

"You know, maybe you're right." Changing tactics might be my best option. "Why don't we go back to Enchanted, warm up, and you can explain how this fame stuff works."

For a long minute, she studies me. I stand my ground and let her. Then she wags a finger at me. "You almost had me. Well done. I really do like you."

She turns her back on me and rushes into the cave. Now what is she doing?

I hurry to untie Wagner's hands, hoping she stays gone until I can figure out how to get him clear of here. The wolf whines and stands guard next to us.

Wagner glances at me with relief. "Thank you. Please...you have to stop her."

The wolf's low growl sends fresh goosebumps down my back. I look up to see Jenny returning, a look of fierce determination on her face.

She's carrying a large pine branch, wielding it like a baseball bat. It's stripped of needles, but covered in pointed, very sharp barbs.

Stomping toward us, she raises it. Calling on my magick, I prepare to throw my hands out and yell, "Freeze," but as I jump to my feet, I trip over Wagner's leg.

My weak spell misses and strikes the wolf. I hear a yelp before he's paralyzed.

The blow from the limb misses me, but ducking I slip on the wet ground. Falling, one hand lands on a piece of raw meat, causing me to slide off-kilter.

"Nice job on the wolf," Jenny says, raising the pine branch again. "That'll make things so much easier."

CHAPTER

TWENTY-FOUR

I roll quickly to the side, but the wood still makes contact with my shoulder.

The pain rips a cry from my lips. A new, deep-throated growl comes from the edge of the woods.

"You won't get far," Jenny tells me. "I wish I didn't have to do this, but you've left me no choice."

Wagner motions at me to duck and I do, the branch whacking the ground. Lenore screeches somewhere high in the trees.

The leader of the pack has regained his feet, but he's bleeding like me. Lenore flies down and lands on his back, her beady eyes watching Jenny's every move.

"This is going to make great TV," she says. "After I cut out a few parts.

She raises her arms. The wolf leaps in the air. Lenore flies up as he tackles Jenny and they both go down.

The second wolf steps from the trees' edge into the clearing, lowering his head and revealing his fangs.

I know him. He stalks toward me, and the hair on my arms stands at attention as our eyes meet.

Somehow Ren has escaped his cage, and come to defend us.

The first wolf bites Jenny through her pant leg. Lenore perches on her head, digging her talons in. Jenny screams.

I watch Ren, his massive paws moving quietly, but quickly, across the forest floor. Jenny gets the upper hand and smacks the attacking wolf in the muzzle. The giant beast stumbles and falls.

Lenore lands beside him as Jenny scrambles to her feet and looks to be ready to hit him again, but Lenore flaps at her face, trying to scratch it and she swings wildly.

"Don't you touch my bird!" I rush her, my injured shoulder screaming in protest as I grab the branch and she wrestles me to the ground.

Leaves and sticks tangle in my hair and clothes. Lenore stands on her, squawking. She headbutts me, causing stars to flash in front of my eyes, but as soon as she rises, her whole body flies up into the air.

Ren has attacked.

Wagner shouts, Jenny curses, and Ren barks and snaps at her. He clomps onto her ankle and she yelps. He shakes her leg as though it is a bone he's ready to snap in half.

"Get it off me!" she demands.

"He's not an *it*." I twist the limb from her hand and see the blood stains on it. With all my might, I throw it as hard as I can. Pain lances through my shoulder and down my back at the action, causing me to suck in a breath. My vision nearly blacks out and I stumble.

She scrambles, trying to get away, and then attempts to kick Ren like she did the other wolf. "He's going to kill me!"

"Just desserts," I mutter, blinking through the blackness tingeing my vision. Bracing myself on the boulder, I use it to balance.

I have to stop Ren. While Jenny may deserve to be torn apart by a wolf, Ren could never live with himself if he hurt someone. "Whoa, buddy," I say to him, holding out a hand. "You can release her now. Your job here is done."

Jenny claws at the ground, debris flying as she grapples to break free from his teeth. "Help me," she pleads at me. "Help me, please."

"Thank you." I have to reason with Ren, reminded by a red blinking light that we are on camera. I pray he'll listen. "I can handle it from here."

His eyes snap at me, the reflection of the lamps making them glow blue. His lips pull back farther and his low growl makes my stomach drop.

He has no plans to turn her loose.

She kicks out again with her free foot and catches his jaw. He makes a noise in his throat, but doesn't let go.

She strains her arm toward me, plain fear on her face. "Do something!"

Ren chomps down harder and jerks her leg, dragging her away.

"I can't let you do that," I say as I step forward to grab her bicep.

She manages to yank on my skirt, tugging me off balance. I fall beside her and she clutches at a chunk of my hair, shaking my head. The darkness threatens again.

"Let go of me, you supernatural freak," she swears at Ren. "I know what you are, and I will prove it. Release me, or I'll kill her."

So much for wanting my help, she simply wanted to use me to get her way. I jam an elbow hard into her ribcage and she gasps, letting go. "No one dies tonight," I tell her.

A gun goes off.

Lenore screeches. We all flinch and look to the south. Poppi is there, along with my sisters. The two wolves I left to guard him whine as they stand like sentries on either side of him.

It's good to see my grandfather up and moving. I was worried about a concussion, and although he's a bit pale, it seems my cape has done its job.

"Are you hurt?" Cinder carries the red cloak over an arm and holds it out to me.

"I'm okay," I reassure her and the others, ignoring the ache in my shoulder and my fuzzy vision. "Stay there, don't make any sudden moves."

Robyn appears, sees Ren with his jaws locked on Jenny, and stops in her tracks. "Ruby?"

"It's okay," I repeat. "Let me handle this."

Every set of eyes is on me and I see the trepidation and fear in them. They all want to rush to my aid, but I need them to trust me.

I switch my attention to Ren once more. "You can let go of her now. Please, for me."

He holds my gaze for a tense moment. My pulse beats rapidly as we all wait to see what he'll do.

"Justice will be done," I promise. "The threat is over."

The other wolf gains his feet. He throws back his head and howls. The ones next to Poppi join in.

The sound echoes through the forest and I see something change in Ren's eyes.

The danger is gone.

He slowly releases her leg and retreats.

Lenore swoops down and lands on Ren. Robyn and my sisters rush to me.

Leo and Finn emerge from the shadows beyond the lamp light to help Wagner with his bindings. Robyn jerks Jenny to her feet and places her under arrest.

Ren goes to the other wolves, the leader limping. While Belle and Zelle fuss over me and examine my wounds, I brush past them to see about the wolf's injuries.

Cinder brings my cape and I drape it over the massive body, hoping it will at least offer comfort.

Matilda, Uncle Odin, and Nonni step into the clearing. Nonni is crying and she throws her arms around Poppi's neck. "When you will start listening to me, old man?" she scolds. "I told you not to run off into the woods without me."

I chuckle, petting the injured animal's head before I embrace Ren.

He makes a soft noise in his throat, and nuzzles my shoulder. "Thank you," I whisper. "Let's go home."

TWENTY-FIVE

I sleep in Sunday morning, waking to find myself alone in the tower.

Ren, in wolf form, walked me home after the incident with Jenny. He had totally blown out the cage, the sides laying helter-skelter on the floor, the top hanging from a wall sconce, nearly disconnecting the poor thing from its base.

The amount of strength and power it took for him to break out of it with such force astounds me. Still, he was docile and came with me in the aftermath.

Robyn wanted a statement, but I pointed her to the video camera I'd turned on and told her if she needed more to call me later.

I took a shower to wash the forest off as Ren went to his bed in the tower. After cleaning up, I laid down next to him, no bars between us now, and placed my cape like a blanket over us. We fell into an exhausted slumber side by side.

In the morning light, Lenore accompanies me to the bathroom and seems happy. She wasn't injured, thank goodness, and I lavish her with attention. I promise her extra playtime with Korbin to let her know how grateful I am for her help last night.

Before we reach the kitchen, I hear conversation, light laughter, and the clang and bang of pots and pans. Entering, I discover we have three extra visitors for breakfast.

Ren is at the stove helping Nonni create an enormous meal for those gathered around the table. The smell of French toast, fried apples, and maple syrup greets me, along with good mornings from my family.

"You're up." Ren rushes over and gives me a hug. Lenore flies to her perch. "I didn't want to wake you. I knew you needed rest."

From the corner of my eye, I see Zelle elbow Belle and snicker. "Sleep well?" she teases.

"Yes, quite." I pretend nonchalance. "You?"

She smiles as I accept a cup of tea from Cinder. "You gave me a heart attack last night."

"Sorry." I turn to Ren. "How are you feeling?"

He touches my face. "I couldn't be better."

For a heartbeat, we simply stare at each other, the cup between us. Then he takes my free hand and gently guides me to the table. "I want to introduce you to my family."

A seated woman is dressed in a vibrant blue and green pantsuit that would give Matilda a run for her money. Layers of beaded necklaces lie on her chest,

and feather earrings adorn her ears. Her hair is dark like Ren's but shot through with silver. She offers a shy smile when he introduces her. "Ruby, this is my Aunt Violet. Aunt Violet, this is Ruby."

She's devoid of makeup but her natural beauty shines. "Our Renfroe has found an exceptional woman."

"Why, thank you. I'm thrilled he's moved here, and we've gotten to know each other."

"As are we." Her eyes twinkle when she looks at him. Her voice lowers as she says, "She's special. You better hang onto her."

He holds up our intertwined hands. "I intend to."

Lenore caws from her perch in the corner. "Watch it, wolfie."

Everyone laughs. I narrow my eyes at Zelle. "Did you teach her that?"

Zelle raises both hands in a surrender gesture. "I plead the fifth."

Ren motions to the man next to Violet. "This is Uncle Fraser, Aunt Violet's brother."

The man rises and shakes my hand. I feel a current of electricity pass through my palm.

"You," I say.

He has on jeans and a pale green shirt. The wrinkles in his skin make him appear older than I believe he is. He grins, showing straight, white teeth. "Ah, you're the brave one from last night. We thank you for what you did."

"She is brave," Ren echoes and I blush.

Do they not want my family to know they're wood walkers? "How do feel today, Fraser?"

The same glimmer as Violet's dances in his dark eyes. They look similar to Ren's. "My injuries are healed."

"I'm glad to hear that. If you need any salves or tinctures, please let me know. We have a small, but effective, assortment of medicinal products."

Ren touches my arm. "I hope you used some on yourself."

"I did, in fact." My vision is clear and my shoulder feels good as new, thanks to the cream I rubbed on it and the healing powers of my cape.

"My son, Marion," Fraser says, pointing to a young man chatting with Matilda. "He's a healer like you."

The boy grimaces. "Call me Rainhart. It's my middle name, and I prefer it." He also stands and takes my hand, as he shoots a warning glare at his father. "I'm currently learning acupuncture. I want to help Ren at the clinic, one of these days, as well as work on people."

"That's amazing," I tell him.

Ren looks excited. "I'm going to offer an entire line of alternative and holistic healing methods for the animals next year. Photon and aqua therapy, Reiki sessions, acupuncture, you name it."

"I love that idea."

As Rainhart resumes his seat, Matilda smiles knowingly at me.

On the other side of her, Poppi chats with Uncle

Odin. I see a distinctive lump on the side of Poppi's head, and I study it. "Don't eyeball me like that," he says to me. "I'm fine."

"He has a hard head," Nonni agrees from the stove.

Poppi rolls his eyes and resumes his conversation with Uncle Odin.

As Ren leads me to a chair near Zelle, he takes the tea from my hand and sets it down. "Your grand-mother is an amazing cook, too. I see it runs in the family."

I stay standing, even though he's pulled out the chair. "She is amazing at many things. When I grow up, I want to be just like her."

She glances over her shoulder and waves me off, embarrassed. "Don't be silly."

"Do you guys need some help?"

"No," she insists. "Sit."

Zelle tugs me down and I pinch her leg under the table as I respond, "Yes, ma'am."

Lenore prances around on her perch. When Ren plants a kiss on my forehead, she croaks, "Watch it."

As the others laugh again, Uncle Odin winks at me.

Soon, Nonni and Ren bring over serving plates stacked high with French toast. Bowls of fried apples and cherry compote are passed around, several syrups as well. Ren seats himself next to me and asks what I want on mine.

"I like powdered sugar."

He grabs a tiny bowl filled with it, and offers to

sprinkle it on. I'm not used to such pampering and insist on doing it myself.

"No syrup?" he queries.

"Nope."

"You're missing out." He heaps sugar on his, then follows it with syrup.

I shake my head in wonder, but realize he needs the carbs. His aunt watches us with a bemused smile.

Cinder fills us in on the latest from Robyn. "Jenny lawyered up, but with the video Ruby captured, it doesn't matter. Robyn's got her dead to rights for both murders, as well as an attempted murder charge on Wagner."

"Your cousin is quite the detective," Rainhart says. When we all look at him, his cheeks flush.

"Yes, she is," I agree. "Have you met her?"

"I've seen her around town."

Matilda and I share a look—one that asks if Robyn has a new admirer.

Zelle is working through a heap of fried apples. She uses her napkin to wipe her lips. "The PIT fans are going crazy. I checked the blog and social media pages this morning. It appears Wagner and the PIT members who are left are doing exactly what Jenny said she was going to do—they've reached out to the Caught on Camera followers and set up a tribute to the two men who were killed. Their 'In Memory Of' video has gone viral."

"Robyn won't be releasing what I got on tape,

though, right?" I ask Cinder. The last thing I want is for my identity to be revealed.

Ren pats my hand. "We're safe."

"Yes, quite, dear." Uncle Odin chases syrup around on his plate with a bite of toast. "I spoke to Robyn about that exact thing. She promised me your involvement will remain secret."

I'm relieved. I hope after the case is finished, that video gets destroyed.

Nonni cuts her food and clears her throat. "Well, how about we discuss something more uplifting this morning? We do have our famous Sherwood Family Thanksgiving next week." She glances at Ren and then his relatives. "We would love to have all of you as guests, if you're willing."

Ren looks to his aunt, uncle, and cousin.

I hold my breath. *Please say yes.*

TWENTY-SIX

Some form of silent communication passes between the two of them before Violet gives Nonni another of her shy smiles. "Only if you allow us to bring a contribution to the meal."

Poppi raises his fork in the air. "Just so we're all clear, the traditional meal is accompanied by a nature walk and ritual my wife insists on doing every year to honor the trees and animals."

The Redferns seem amused and completely comfortable with the idea.

Nonni shakes her head, exasperated, as if he's making a big deal out of nothing. "Of course we do an honoring ceremony for Mother Nature. She gives us the bounty that we have on our table." She waves her arthritic finger at the food we're consuming. "It's important we stay in balance with the trees, the animals, and the elements."

"I think it's a lovely idea," Violet states. "Our forest

has been through a lot in the past week. We should clear the negative energy from it."

"Yes, exactly." Nonni raises her chin to Poppi. "See? She gets me."

I raise my cup. "I'll drink to that."

Ren beams. "I'm not much of a cook, but I can bring the pets some treats."

Lenore hops up and down on her perch, Jayne barks, and Rumpelstiltskin chitters. They know the word 'treat.'

Nonni frowns at me. "Speaking of can't cook, Snow is making an apple pie for the dinner. I'll make the pumpkin, but we should have a backup."

Snow is not known for her baking skills, any more than Zelle is. This draws a laugh from those of us in the know. "No problem," I tell her. "How about some caramel apples and a few of my candies?"

Poppi rubs his hands together. "I love your caramel apples."

"I've been dying to make some pumpkin streusel coffee cake," Matilda tells us. "I saw a Food Network bake-off show that featured one. I'll bring that."

I stare at my plate and Nonni clears her throat. "That would be lovely," she says, ever gracious, even though we're both worried how that might turn out. "You'll be baking it here, right?"

In other words, not blowing up Nonni's kitchen.

Matilda looks put out, sensing Nonni's jab. "I'll have you know, I baked one the other day and it turned out perfect."

Nonni glances around for our confirmation. "It's true," I tell her.

"It was delicious," Ren adds around a mouthful.

"Thank you," Matilda says, beaming.

Belle and Zelle clean off the table when we're done. Uncle Odin and Poppi retire to the back porch to sit in the rocking chairs and talk. Our assorted animals look for leftovers and crumbs, and Cinder offers to help Ren sketch out an idea for expanding his clinic.

Soon, he and I are coming up with plenty of ideas, and she draws, erases, and sketches some more. His aunt and uncle are very interested in the process, and watch with great interest.

"We always wanted to open up a rescue and sanctuary on our property." Violet pats Ren's arm. "Now that we have a vet who has expertise with wildlife, I think it might be time."

Pride blooms on his face. He takes her hand and squeezes it. "I would love that."

"You know," Matilda walks past us to refill her unicorn mug, "the space next to the clinic is empty."

"That's right," I say, catching on to what I believe she's hinting at. "You could blow out the wall between the two buildings and turn it into a bigger place."

"I'd have to hire help," Ren states, considering it, "but it might be doable."

Matilda sighs and puts a hand on her hip. "I was mentioning it to Ruby."

I'm lost. "What about it?"

"It would be the perfect place for a candy shop. You'd be right next door to him."

All eyes swing to me. "But I don't want to open one."

She looks skeptical. "Is that so?"

Actually it is. "While I'd love to be next door to Ren, I'm happy to stay right here. I'm working out a plan with the bakery and Snow that will make everyone happy, but I'm not leaving the family business."

She shrugs. "Okay."

Cinder squeezes my arm, her delight palpable. "Can I just say, I'm relieved? I don't know what we'd do without you, Ruby."

SINCE ENCHANTED IS CLOSED on Sundays, it's an excellent day to recoup. Ren and I walk Nonni and Poppi home, Lenore and George flying above us. Korbin joins them, he and Lenore chat, and it seems as if she is introducing him to the parrot. Korbin seems a bit stand-offish at first, but soon all three are coasting on the breeze together.

Leaves rustle under our feet as we stroll. At the boulder, the crime scene tape has been removed. I've brought an old work boot of Cinder's and place it in the spot where the mouse had made a house in the trail shoe.

Resuming our leisurely walk, I tell Ren about my vision and the fact I believe I saw the first wood

walker. I mention the fact he looks just like him, right down to the tattoo.

"Wow, that's..."

"Crazy?" I finish for him. "I know, but it's very likely you might have been him in a previous life, or maybe you're simply tapping into his incredible magick."

"Not crazy. It's just you have such incredible gifts. To see into the past like that? I can't wrap my mind around it."

Nonni tucks her coat closer to her and Poppi puts his arm around her waist as we continue on. "My granddaughter is one of a kind," she calls back to Ren. "Like your aunt said, you better hang on to her."

Violet, Fraser, and Rainhart went home through the woods, too, but they took a more northward route. I'm slightly relieved they aren't with us to hear this discussion.

"If she'll have me," Ren says, tucking me into his side. "I know a good thing when I see it."

Once we have Nonni and Poppi safely situated at their farm, Ren takes my hand on the way home. Our fingers intertwine, and I am happier than I have been in a long time.

"I finally feel like I'm home," he says, as we wander the path slowly, enjoying the fresh air and the birdsong.

"It just feels right, doesn't it?"

He grins. "It does, and a big part of that is you and your family."

"Unless there's another threat to the forest, the animals, or your Redfern relatives, I don't think you'll shift at the full moon anymore."

He glances at me from the corner of his eye and squeezes my hand. "Probably shouldn't take any chances. Make that potion. Next full moon, I'll be in the tower with you."

I think about all of the nights to come, full moon or not, and everything I'm learning about my ancestors, as well as his. "Room and board aren't free, you know."

"Is that so?" He nods. "I do still owe you dinner, don't I?"

Zelle and Rumpelstiltskin have joined Uncle Odin on the back porch. When we get close, she raises a cup of steaming liquid and winks at me. Lenore and George swoop and dive, having fun.

"You do, but there's tasks to be done in the shop," I tell him, "and until the remodeling on your clinic begins, we have plenty of projects here. If you hang around, Cinder will put you to work."

"No howling at night, though, wolf boy," Zelle teases, eavesdropping.

"I actually find the sound comforting," Uncle Odin says. "Reminds me of the old country."

"Old country?" Ren murmurs in my ear.

I draw him aside as Lenore lands on the railing. "Long story. I'll tell you about it next full moon."

He loops around, putting us nose to nose. "Thank you for bringing me into your pack, Ruby Sherwood."

I wrap my arms around his neck, my cape draping

over both of us. "You can howl anytime in my book, Renfroe Woolsey."

He makes a soft imitation of the sound and we laugh. Then he kisses me and I know I'll never let him go.

READY FOR MORE MAGICK?

Don't miss the next exciting adventure! Sign up for Nyx's Cozy Clues Mystery Newsletter.

And check out these magical stories!

Sister Witches Of Raven Falls Mystery Series

Sister Witches of Raven Falls Special Collection

Of Potions and Portents
Of Curses and Charms
Of Stars and Spells
Of Spirits and Superstition

Confessions of a Closet Medium Cozy Mystery Series

Confessions of a Closet Medium Special Collection

Pumpkins & Poltergeists
Magic & Mistletoe
Hearts & Haunts
Vows & Vengeance
Cupcakes & Corpses
Tea Leaves & Troubled Spirits

Sister Witches of Story Cove (Formerly Once Upon a Witch) Cozy Mystery Series
Coming Fall 2022

Cinder
Belle
Snow
Ruby
Zelle

About the Author

USA Today Bestselling Author Nyx Halliwell grew up on TV shows like *Buffy the Vampire Slayer* and *Charmed*.

She loves writing stories as much as she loves baking and crafting. She believes in magick and that we each carry it inside us.

She enjoys binge-watching mystery shows with her hubby and reading all types of stories involving magic and animals.

Connect with Nyx today and see pictures of her pets, be the first to know about new books and sales, and find out when Godfrey, the talking cat, has a new blog post! Receive a FREE copy of the Whitethorne Book of Spells and Recipes by signing up for her newsletter http://eepurl.com/gwKHB9

CONNECT WITH NYX TODAY!

Website: nyxhalliwell.com

Email: nyxhalliwellauthor@gmail.com
Bookbub https://www.bookbub.com/profile/nyx-halliwell
Amazon amazon.com/author/nyxhalliwell
Facebook: https://www.facebook.com/NyxHalliwellAuthor/

Sign up for Nyx's Cozy Clues Mystery Newsletter and be the FIRST to learn about new releases, sales, behind-the-scenes trivia about the book characters, pictures of Nyx's pets, and links to insightful and often hilarious *From the Cauldron With Godfrey blog*!

DEAR MAGICAL READER

I hope you enjoyed this story! If you did, and would be so kind, would you leave a review on Goodreads, Bookbub, or your favorite book retailer? I would REALLY appreciate it!

A review lets hundreds, if not thousands, of potential readers know what you enjoyed about the book, and helps them make wise buying choices. It's the best word-of-mouth around.

The review doesn't have to be anything long! Pretend you're sharing the story with a good friend. Pick out one or more characters, scenes, or dialogue that made you smile, laugh, or warmed your heart, and tell them about it. Just a few sentences is perfect!

Blessed be,

Nyx 🤍

Lightning Source UK Ltd.
Milton Keynes UK
UKHW010650260922
409457UK00002B/377